The Sound in the Silence

A NOVEL BY
JARED HEATH

ISBN: 9780991389124
The Sound in the Silence: 3rd Edition
Paperback
Copyright © 2014
All Rights Reserved

Published by Jared Heath
Cover Art by Andreas Rocha
Interior Calligraphy by Lanae Manuele

For Preston and Sierra.

Never be outdone by your own imagination.

I'd also like to extend a special thanks to my wife, Sereen, and to my mom, my dad, my sister, and all those who believed in me when I didn't think I could do it.

TABLE OF CONTENTS

Chapter 1:
Of Tales and Rumors

You never hear someone die. You hear their pain—a prelude to their demise—but death is in the silence. That is how Kalif knew that death must be peaceful. And tonight, Kalif would bring peace to this world by taking a few more Neroos out of it.

Kalif lay with his eyes closed and his hands behind his head, breathing in the sun as it cascaded on his bare and lean torso. The only adornment on his chest was a leather strap that held his knife, sheathed behind his shoulder, from which he was never separated. His legs hung out of simple brown leather shorts that almost blended into his deep olive skin, and on his feet were short leather boots. The perfect hunting gear. Perfect for hunting Neroos. Perfect for luring women. Yes, Kalif was a hunter, and he was very skilled at obtaining his prey.

Since the age of sixteen when he had begun participating in raiding parties, Kalif would spend more and more time in this field with his sister, Loria. It was only a week ago that she last found him here. They would talk about anything except for the raids, and yet she always seemed to know what had happened. Kalif did not know if she was proud of him for it, and he didn't ask. Raids were not Kalif's only indulgences that would disappoint his sister, but they never spoke of them here. Here in the forest where every hunter was equally hunted, Kalif was at home. At peace. No matter their differences, Kalif could share this with his sister.

Loria's twisted body was found brutalized, bloodied, and broken just outside the city wall. Her body was mangled as if the wolves had found her, but not beyond recognition. But none of it sat well with Kalif—she was too close to the city wall for wolves, and there was something about her wounds that spoke of a different animal. A different hunter. Kalif was convinced that Loria's death was the work of the Neroos. He could feel his heart beating faster and his breath becoming shallow at the thought.

Not even Gala, his fiancée, could save him from the most profound grief he had ever felt. He had been too young when his mother died to understand her loss. He had been too angry when his father died to truly mourn. But he had always protected Loria. He always saw in her the goodness that he had lost, and he was convinced that through her, he could regain it all.

And he had regained so much—without Loria, he never would have been able to pull himself out of his downward spiral with narcotic plants and equally intoxicating women. He never would have been able to realize what a good woman he had in Gala. He owed everything to Loria, though she never would have taken the credit. And now she was gone. Worse than gone. Loria was unavenged. And with her, his peace died just as brutally.

But Kalif's anguish would end when the Neroos paid for their injustice. And Kalif would make them pay. Soon. Kalif drew another deep breath. Tonight would be the first time that he faced the Neroos since he lost Loria, and he itched to be clothed in the night. He yearned for vengeance. And he craved peace.

The sensation of cold metal against the skin of his neck broke his memories and his musings.

"Do not scream," said the intruder.

Without bothering to open his eyes, Kalif said, "Good to see you, too, Chism. Now go away before I decide to kill you."

"Big words for the idiot brother sunbathing in a wide open glade without a lookout or a weapon," Chism said with a grin on his face.

"Oh, I have a lookout."

"What?" Chism glanced up briefly to scan the tree line.

In that moment, Kalif had drawn his knife from the shoulder sheath behind his head and knocked Chism's sword wide. Springing to his feet, Kalif parried Chism's next stroke and, stepping in too close for Chism to effectively use his sword, punched him in the ribs. Chism gasped for breath and dropped his sword. Before the sword could hit the ground, Kalif had deftly spun his brother around, kicked out the back of his brother's knees, and brought his knife to Chism's throat. Chism knelt exactly in the place where Kalif lay only seconds before.

"Look out, Chism," Kalif mocked.

"Not bad," Chism said rather casually for a man with a knife at his throat. "But you didn't have to hit so hard."

"Sorry. Got a lot on my mind," Kalif said, replacing his knife in his shoulder sheath as he sat down next to his brother.

Chism often wore a uniform similar to Kalif's when he was on duty patrolling the forest—bare chest with brown leather shorts or similar covering with soft leather boots. As he knelt in the grass where his brother held a knife to his throat, however, he wore a simple green linen shirt with no sleeves.

Though of a similar, muscular build, the two brothers hardly resembled each other. Kalif had a sharp, slightly crooked nose with eyes as dark as the night before dawn. He usually kept his dark hair cut close to the scalp. Today, his head was completely shaved, revealing the scars that crept up his back and onto his neck like the flames that left them. Kalif wore the scars proudly.

Chism's brown, sun-lightened hair was pulled back in a short ponytail and tied with a piece of leather. His skin was as deeply olive as his brothers, but his eyes were a softer brown and his frame was broader. There was something in his demeanor that bespoke careful consideration of any situation before he acted. Chism often wondered if his younger brother's temerity was simply an effort to further define himself as distinctly "not Chism."

Chism nodded at Kalif's excuse, thinking he understood. "I saw Gala today in the city. Are you worried about the wedding?"

Kalif shook his head once. The wedding. Of course. If only it were his wedding that tangled his thoughts. But his thoughts were not of his wife-to-be. They were of another woman—his sister—lying on the grass, brutalized, dead with a silent scream still on her lips. The silence of death. Of peace. "No, not the wedding. It's..." but he could not say it. Shaking his head again, Kalif repeated, "It's not Gala."

The warm fall air turned suddenly cold between the brothers as Chism gestured to Kalif's raiding garb. "So you're going tonight," Chism said. It was not a question.

Kalif managed to be both amazed and completely unsurprised at how much Chism knew. His rank gave him access to a great deal of information otherwise hidden from the rest of the city, but how he knew the marauders' comings and goings was uncanny. Even disturbing.

"You know too much, brother."

"And you don't know enough," Chism replied quickly.

"You're not joining us—I mean, them—are you?"

"What, are you kidding? The army can turn a blind eye to you, but I'm . . . *bound to duty*," Chism finished sarcastically.

"Oh, please," Kalif stood up, too restless to sit. Too frustrated to sit by Chism. "Don't go hide behind your rank, Chism! You should be avenging our sister!"

Chism grimaced as Kalif referenced his title. It seemed to come up in every conversation ever since his promotion, and Chism couldn't decide which of the two men hated the fact of his higher rank more.

"It's not about rank. Our sister is gone, and no amount of Neroos blood will resurrect her." Chism stood and looked his brother in the eye. "I didn't save your life for this, you know."

"No, I'm sure you didn't. And since you mentioned saving my life, how is that promotion working out for you, lieutenant?"

Chism held Kalif's gaze until his brother turned away. "You know that's not fair."

"No, it's not," Kalif said. "So don't hold it over me, and it will be fair."

Chism took a slow, deep breath and closed his eyes. Keeping his temper around Kalif was always a struggle, and it was almost impossible when Kalif worked himself up like this. "What's this really about, Kalif?"

"It's about Loria! It's about keeping the Neroos in line! You found her body. You can't really believe it was a wolf. The wounds were too clean! Tell me you don't find it even a little bit suspicious."

Chism couldn't. Not with any certainty. He didn't know if he was being cynical and paranoid, but like Kalif, he was sure that the official story was anything but completely accurate. Between what he had seen and heard only a few weeks ago, and his suspicions about what was going on beneath the surface in the government, Chism wasn't certain about anything anymore.

"Kalif, what do you think you're going to accomplish by going with the marauders?"

"I am going to restore balance," Kalif said without a hint of remorse as he rubbed the scars on the back of his neck subconsciously. "A rabid dog has to have its head cut off. Besides, how different is it from raiding their supply lines and leaving them defenseless in the woods?"

Chism could only snort at his brother's justification. Harassing supply lines and stealing food was one thing. But the marauders… they were not even a recognized group in the Lima society.

"You sure this isn't about you? About you running from…the past? Because Neroos blood can't wash that away, Kalif. Trust me."

Kalif scoffed and turned his back, running a hand over his shaved head. He felt the burn scars that crept up his shoulder and neck to the base of his head. He had never grown accustomed to them. He let them remind him that justice had to be served.

"You and I have more blood on our hands—"

"We've been protecting this city. We haven't been attacking anyone. It's not the same!" Chism said.

"It is the same! There is no…*redemption*…for people like us!"

Chism shook his head. "I can't believe that."

"Who's going to make them pay, Chism?" Kalif shouted.

"You'll die, Kalif. Or worse—you'll wish you had died if you make it back. You're not a bad fighter, and I'm sure you'll ruin a family or two. And when some poor fools who happen to be Neroos are dead, then Loria will be avenged! Then Loria will rest in peace! Then you'll have your peace!" Chism paused. "You're a fool."

"So report me, lieutenant. Or stay out of my way."

As he began to leave, Kalif stopped, turned back to his brother, and locked Chism's light brown eyes with his own dark black gaze. "How can you have let her go so easily?"

It was not an accusation. It was a plea to make the hollowness go away. Chism's heart, which had been so light only a few minutes before, weighed heavily in his chest for the sudden loss of his sister only a week before and the slower but just as sure loss of his brother standing in front of him.

"I can't bring her back. And killing Neroos who had nothing to do with it won't stop you from missing her." Bending over, Chism picked up his sword. Wanting to say more to stop his brother but not knowing what, he began to leave. Then, turning back to his brother, Chism said, "Where are you going?"

"You know they'll kill me if I tell you," Kalif said quietly.

"So be it. Maybe you can tell me firsthand when you get back what someone as innocent as Loria sounds like right before she dies." And with that, Chism left.

Though Kalif was still standing, he felt that Chism had brought him to his knees. And he couldn't move.

~~~~~

Chism walked briskly past the guards into the city of Ombrar without any sign to acknowledge their salute. After he had received his promotion, he generally avoided the guarded areas. He had grown up with these soldiers—knew them when sticks were swords and orders were games. Now they saluted their lieutenant instead of raising their hands in greeting their friend.

Stupid raids, Chism thought. *Stupid Kalif.* It was another one of Kalif's headlong rushes into idiocy that ended in Chism saving his brother's life. The official story was that Chism was promoted for his bravery. For anyone else, the promotion would have been justice. But for Chism, it was one more irony in a growing litany of frustrations.

Chism recalled with satisfaction having soundly beaten his brother over the head with the pommel of his sword that day. Kalif had no memory of it. Chism was not surprised; it was a wonder that Kalif could remember his name after Chism took his frustration out on his brother's too-hard head. *Besides,* Chism told himself, *if I hadn't knocked him out cold that day, there would have been no telling what else he would have gotten himself into.*

Knocked out. Chism could knock consciousness out of his brother's head, but apparently he could not put reason in. If he could not stop his brother's madness, then Gala was the only person who could.

Gala and her family lived in the fishing district of Ombrar.

Ombrar was a city built on a town built on a village. The seaside village began to thrive when the Lima began to use the ocean as means for trading and communicating. When the Lima governor had sent the army with funds to fortify the city with a nearly impregnable wall, the city's growth crashed against the wall like the sea against a dam. And like a dam, the city filled up as new floors and buildings stacked one atop the other.

As the city swelled, so too swelled the social hierarchy. And with the ever-bloated social structure came political favors. The second stories were as much a social step above the rest as they were literally above everyone on the first floor. The street floor. And very much like their building and housing status, the second floor was built on the backs of those who lived lower than them. Beneath them. The third floor was for another class altogether. There were few third floor dwellings completed, though many had been started. The bare and naked fingers of wood and unfinished frames were a fitting reminder for anyone looking to lift themselves up and increase their status: there was nothing for them at the top.

Ombrar was one of the few Lima cities with a senate, each city acting as its own state in a confederation of Lima city-states. The vast majority of Lima cities and regions simply called their leaders what they really were—kings. But in Ombrar, things were different. The people wanted a republic where all things were equal. All voices were heard. It was a valiant effort to break the grip held by only a few over the masses. Twenty-four senators were elected. Food was reapportioned. Not all were happy, but all were fed.

Then, slowly, the Senate began to assume control over certain industries until they controlled the entire economy. Senators became more powerful. The people became more dependent. Anyone operating outside of the Senate's strict sanctions and injunctions was considered a fugitive. The High Tide District was the underground haven for free marketers before it became a cesspool.

The Senate soon passed a law that future senators would no longer be elected by the masses who were, as the Senate said, by and large ignorant of the complexities of government. Qualified prospective senators would be selected and voted on by the Senate when a senator was to be replaced. But even after six senators had either resigned or died, no successors were named. The Senate remained at 18 members, who had each been present far beyond the time that the law had dictated. But that was hardly an issue for the Senate who simply passed a new law, telling a story to the people of experience and trust. The people of Ombrar had no choice but to accept it along with the rest of their lives, so benevolently handed down from their leaders.

The city of Ombrar smelled of salt and flesh. For as long as he lived, Chism would always remember the smell. Human sweat and the sea air mingled with the smells of freshly killed livestock and rotting fish. The weather was moderate at best on a winter day; and in the early fall, the intense heat emphasized the human waste and other peculiar smells implicitly involved in city life. But nothing reeked in Chism's nose like corruption. Like the corruption he saw in his government. The government he served. The government he had served proudly. And, as his promotion showed to the entire world, the government he had served with honors.

The buildings and streets circled and intertwined with one another, making the city impossible to navigate for any intruders. The people of the city prided themselves on the ingenious design. Chism always thought their pride a fitting monument to their ignorance. The city was never designed to resist invasion; in fact, it was never designed at all. Design would have given it purpose. But this was something different. This was ludicrous. The city's layout was as aimless as a sick cow wandering the woods, and the citizens of Ombrar reflected the same lack of direction in their everyday lives.

And how many sick cows will wander the woods tonight, killing to satisfy a fantasy? Chism thought dourly of his brother and the marauders.

Chism wanted justice more than anyone—even more than Kalif, he imagined. But marauding only brought them to the same level as the Neroos, and unfortunately—perhaps fittingly—the Lima were more than happy to sink to their level.

Tonight was personal for Kalif; but for the marauders, a group not recognized by the government simply because the government refused to see them, any story about so-called justice would do. The Lima government would enforce its laws of no unsanctioned attacks against the Neroos only if a Neroos army threatened retaliation for the marauders' actions. But barring a direct assault on Ombrar, the Senate and even the citizens just turned a blind eye to the unanticipated addition of cows, crops, and slaves to Ombrar's markets—especially if the right people got the right amount of gold in their pockets as a result. Not for the first time, Chism wondered if the stench of his city had anything to do with the myriad smells.

Despite the scent and the society, Ombrar was not without its beauties. Chism's thoughts and feet brought him to Gala's home in the fishing district before he even realized that he had arrived. As he knocked on the sandwood door, Chism was sure that he was about to see the greatest beauty that Ombrar had to offer.

~~~~~

Kalif missed Gala. After all the concoctions that left him in a dream for days, after all the women and booze, and even after all the blood he had on his hands, she was still there. In his own search for stability, he had tried to push her away, testing her resolve and commitment. She was still here. He stood on the shore where they would walk together as Kalif's nimble fingers would braid a crown of wild flowers or fashion a boat out of leaves for Gala's enjoyment.

Even now, his fingers twisted a supple branch, molding it to a shape of their own while his mind was busy replaying events on this same beach from only a few days ago when Gala stood beside Kalif at Loria's funeral.

It was a brief ceremony. The beach had been lined with all of the people who had loved Loria. Had Kalif turned around, he would have thought the entire city had come to pay silent homage. He and Chism together released the small fishing boat with Loria's body into the high tide. That was six days ago. The wedding would be in one more week right here on the beach.

Kalif's fingers continued their dance.

Chism disapproved of the marauders, and he did not blame the Neroos. Not verbally, anyway. Kalif knew that his decision was rash, but he hated the fact that his brother was right. Or thought he was right. But he hated most the idea of Loria's death—her murder—going unanswered.

A sister that the Neroos had taken. A wedding that the Neroos had tainted. No sanction by the Lima government to attack.

Kalif began snapping twigs and leaves.

But Neroos himself had not played by the rules, as the legend goes. Why should the Neroos people then care about right, wrong, and justice? If the city of Ombrar would not demand Neroos blood to answer for his sister, then justice was up to him.

Kalif's fingers finished their work as they pulled apart sharply, creating a tight knot. Looking down to see what his fingers had created, Kalif saw that his hands had transformed the branch into a curved Lima dagger, much like the weapon he carried even now on his shoulder. Aiming at an imaginary Neroos, Kalif threw the makeshift model into the sea.

Walking away from the beach, his thoughts on the peace that justice would bring, Kalif grabbed his dagger from his shoulder sheath. As he made his way toward Gala's home to bid farewell, he played with the dagger, imagining all the ways that he would soon find peace with it.

CHAPTER 2:
THE SUN ON FIRE

Brego and Rayanna spent their words much like they spent every day—carefully, full of purpose, and with all the utilitarian character that came with living in the Neroos village of Gidionhi.

"I love it when the sun shines like this," Brego said to his older sister, Rayanna. He kept his dark-haired head down, staring only at the forest floor and never quite looking at Rayanna when he spoke to her. Rayanna always tried to coax his eyes upward so that she could look at the startling blue that he kept hidden there.

She turned her face toward him, smiling quizzically before she pulled another berry from the bag she was supposed to trade at the market, and popped it into her mouth. "I wasn't aware of it shining any other way."

Brego did not answer immediately. At only ten years old, he was a particularly somber child. Emotions were never to be expressed in front of his mother. These rare moments in the woods with his older sister were precious—too precious to burden with frivolous talk of feelings. Brego simply found his way around them.

"When the sun shines, it's light outside. But when it shines this way, it's like I'm light inside, too," he determined.

One corner of her mouth pulled slightly again in one of her rare smiles. Here in the forest, she could allow herself to smile a little more, and even to sing. This is where her heart was less heavy. *I enjoy our time together, too,* Rayanna thought.

She simply replied, "Yes, it is a beautiful day."

Brego made no move to show that he understood the exchange. Perhaps he had said too much already. He adjusted the heavy canvas sack half filled with firewood on his narrow shoulders and headed off in a new direction. His feet barely made a sound, even with the burden he bore. Rayanna watched his steps very carefully. Brego applied his sister's tutelage very well, especially for such a small boy carrying such a heavy load. In their village and especially in their family, all children carried a heavy load. And not all burdens were made of wood here. Rayanna had given up trying to trade her sack of berries for the canvas wood bundle in her brother's hands; the stubborn ten-year old would only say, "It is my load to carry" upon every request.

Rayanna bore a burden of her own six years ago when she came crashing into the woods, feeling the crushing weight of the previous night's events and having nowhere else to turn. The forest had become her haunt, her solace when her mother would put too much on her young shoulders. The forest is where she carried her burden, and in the forest she had learned to feel light. And now, no one knew the forest as well as Rayanna.

Rayanna's village would say that she tread as lightly as the sun on the leaves. Her village said much about her. She had once overheard the young men of the village talk about her skin as the soft gold of bare wood when the bark has been scraped off of a tree. Her dark hair was touched with the red of a gidionhi flower. If only she would smile, they said. Then she might be pretty. Even in the same simple, knee-length dress that she always wore. Pretty like she was when they were children. At seventeen, Rayanna was barely more than a child in age, but the village knew that her childhood and that of many her age ended abruptly six years ago. Six years ago tonight.

Rayanna had begun to show Brego her knowledge of the woods as they gathered berries and firewood together a few evenings each week. She felt the responsibility to pass her knowledge on. To keep it alive. Memories should never be lost. One of the first things she had taught Brego had been one of the first things she had learned herself—how to tread lightly. Brego was proving to be an adept pupil.

"Hey, let's go this way. There's something I want to show you," Rayanna called out. Then in an effort to test how good Brego's feet truly had become, she turned in the opposite direction and sped off without a sound.

After having run for more than a hundred yards, she realized that she had not heard Brego at all. Fearing that she had left the child too far behind, she turned again to find him. The woods were silent, and the two had traveled well beyond the borders of the village. She doubted he knew the way back.

"Brego!" She called out.

"Are you going to tell me where we're going?" Rayanna heard behind her—exactly where she had been headed only seconds before. Whipping around, she saw Brego with the grin reserved only for his most triumphant moments, standing well ahead of her and still clutching the firewood sack.

Rayanna paused at the question. It was a place that she had reserved for herself for many years; it was for her a place of reverence. Perhaps that was why she wanted Brego to know that it existed.

"Yes. But you have to make me a promise, Brego." Her tone was uncompromising. Brego stood patiently waiting. "This is something special to me. You have to . . . respect it."

"I will."

Rayanna walked past Brego and led him to a small hill. Upon cresting the hill, Brego first thought that the flowers covering the entire southern side of the hill looked like fire. He knew the flower well. It had a yellow ring on the fringes with a burst of bright red right in the center. Not only was the flower rare, but it was specific to that region of the mountains. When the first Neroos settled the region, they named the city after a flower that looked like the sun itself: *gidionhi*. It was a flower that symbolized victory and greatness. It was the flower born of the sun.

That was during the time of the City of Gidionhi. But the village that stood in the city's charred ruins told a different story. Rayanna's village now told the story of the sun itself weeping over the fallen city's victims. These flowers grew where those tears fell.

Evidence of a once-thriving city on the verge of rivaling even the Neroos capital Luminara still remained in the scattered ruins and complex road system that lay just beneath the surface and on the fringes of the humble village where Rayanna had grown up.

Gidionhi fell during the Riconi-Rierdan War. As the Neroos general Riconi fought Rierdan to the south, Rierdan sent his second in command with a hidden Lima army to attack Gidionhi. And they did not just take the city; they continued to murder after the killing was done. And then they left, taking nothing more from the city than their dead that had fallen there. An act of attrition. Killing simply because they could.

That was thirty years ago. The Lima and Neroos had signed a treaty granting peace, safe passage, and the trade of more land. There was no danger in going back, and the Neroos were nothing if not resilient. A small contingent of soldiers was sent as a precautionary measure and to provide more bodies to populate the area. And so they tore down most of the old ruins and made place for their village.

The peace lasted until this very night six years ago. The Lima had come again, and her people were woefully unprepared. The raid on their village did not merely disrupt the peace between the nations;

after the loss of Rayanna and Brego's father and two older brothers, Endar and Helam, Rayanna had wondered if she would ever know peace again. Their father had always supplied their mother with rare and fresh gidionhi. Seeing it brought back memories of peace for Rayanna, dancing across her thoughts like shadows on the ground. The flowers reminded her and her brother of home—and what home should have been.

Rayanna began gathering flowers, carefully choosing which flowers were ready, and tying them together with a long stem into a bouquet. Standing from her ritual, she looked at Brego who stood motionless where he first saw the flowers.

"Why did you show me this?" Brego asked evenly. Carefully. Like one who knew well that he tread too close to a cliff.

Rayanna did not have an answer, except that she felt that someone else should know of this place.

"I . . . I trust you. That's why."

"Thank you." They stood there, Brego at the top of the hill and Rayanna in a field of gidionhi, staring at each other and wondering what the other intended. "I have to get more firewood. Mom needs it."

Brego's feet made a little more noise than usual on the way back.

~~~~~

Brego must have forgotten about gathering more wood as he walked directly to the village. The two walked a few paces apart, like two strangers who happened to be travelling in the same direction.

Rayanna worried that their walks in the forest would forever be tainted now that he knew about the flowers. Brego had always refused to talk about his father; Rayanna thought that it was because he did not want to talk about his feelings. She did not realize that her brother went to great effort to forget their father, the man who died to save their lives.

16

As they wandered the long and increasingly lonely path back to the village, she wondered if forgetting her father could possibly make the pain disappear. But if the pain were all she had left of him, then that is what she would embrace. To forget him, Rayanna decided, was worse than losing him. It would make his life not just short, but meaningless. Quiet tears rose to her eyes as they often did when she allowed her thoughts to dwell on her father. She refused to wipe them away.

The flowers had been one of their unique trades in the market, which was typically full of the rare gems mined from the old quarry and that kept the Neroos clinging to an otherwise dangerous place to live. But Rayanna would watch in wonder as the people in the market seemed as interested in her family's bouquets of gidionhi flowers as they were in the blue, green, and pink stones fashioned into jewelry. None in the village knew about the hill, but her father always managed to carry a few home on early fall evenings such as this.

"We could always use a little more light in our lives," he would say with a wink. Her father's name—Solay—was derived from an old Neroos word that meant "the sun."

"So why don't you sell the flowers more?" Rayanna had asked as a child when her father revealed to her the small patch that grew here, deep in the forest.

"Because money isn't good enough for some things in this world," her father had replied in his gentle way that always seemed to have so much importance. Looking back, Rayanna often wondered if other people had found her father's voice as captivating as she did, or if she were now only romanticizing her memories.

Rayanna kept a vigilant watch over the flowers now that her father could not. These flowers only grew three months out of the year. She imagined every time she came over the hill that she would find him there, waiting. But he was never there. Memories were all she had left to hold on to. Even the bad ones. For all the years of memories she carried of her father, she could always see his body, torn and bloodied from battle, as she prepared him for burial. The last thing she had done was place a small gidionhi flower between the cold, stiff folds of his once-warm hands.

Rayanna dreamt of the battle almost every night. It terrified her, but she felt the desperate need to hold on to even those last memories—the last moments of when life was good.

The watcher's horn was blowing. Her dreams always began with the horn. At eleven years old, Rayanna had only heard their outpost village's horn during village meetings and while her father drilled with the other men in town in case of an attack. In case of an attack on a safe village, they said. Their village was part of an effort to expand the Neroos territory—free land to all who signed up. Young and enterprising families, or families looking for a new start, could find their place here. In the mountains where it was peaceful. The kind of peace that required a small army.

When the watcher's horn sounded through the night, the stories of peace were over.

"Aria!" Her father called to her mother. "It's time. We must stick to the plan. I will find you when this is over."

"No, Solay, please," her mother pleaded. "Please don't. I need you. Come, protect us!"

"I am protecting you. We will meet here again at dawn." Rayanna watched her father gently touch her mother's face. Then, speaking to his two eldest sons, Solay said, "There is no time. We must all go, quickly!" Armed with bows, arrows, and scimitars, the three stole out into the night.

Rayanna watched her mother with a curiosity altogether detached from the night's events.

"He's gone. He's gone. My Solay is gone," Aria worried and muttered. Shuddering with sobs and trying desperately to maintain an idea, a thought, a piece of sanity, Aria busied herself with stowing clothes, dried meat, anything into a shirt that she tied together into a sack.

"Rayanna, help me with the twins." Her voice became sharp and distinct as if delivering the order brought her back. "We must move now."

Hushed by the events she could not understand, Rayanna picked up four-year-old Karrh while her mother helped Brego. Even at eleven years old, Rayanna was beginning to have difficulty carrying either of her young brother's already-strong bodies on her slight frame. But tonight was no night for complaining.

The houses were afforded a small garden with an additional yard for pigs, goats, chickens, or other useful animals while the crops and farms were located on the fringes, circling the entire village and some of the still-standing rubble from the old city. The watcher, who stood on a tower erected in the center of the city, had a clear view of everything for miles in either direction.

Rayanna followed her mother out the back of their home on their predetermined course. Go around the garden, careful not to leave footprints in the soft earth. Pause. Check. Clear. Move. Dash to the next home. Find the ruins in Old City that her mother and father had agreed on. Hide in it until dawn.

The south side of Gidionhi was ablaze with torches, screams, and blood. Aria sat against the wall of the old ruin, clutching Brego as she tried to hide her fear from the children.

Then the sound of footsteps. No. The measured sound of concerted running. Marching. A second group of Lima marauders had come to flank the tiny village. Rayanna watched as her mother craned her neck above the half-broken wall to peer into the darkness. Aria could just see the top of the watchtower as she looked to see when the watcher would sound the horn again, alerting the town of the secondary attack. But no warning came. Aria could see the watcher slumped over on his platform and imagined the arrows protruding from his body. There would be no warning. Even with the soldiers stationed in Gidionhi, the small village militia—her husband, sons, and the rest of the inexperienced, barely trained group of farmers—would be trapped between the two Lima groups and massacred.

Aria's breathing became heavy, and her panic grew more evident with every passing second. As soon as the marching had passed by, Aria turned to Rayanna and said, "Watch your brothers. I am going to look for your father."

"What are you going to do for them?"

"There are injured men, and they need bandages. And they don't know about this second group. Stay here. I will be back."

"But papa is coming back! He will come to protect us. What if you miss him?" Rayanna looked past her mother at the blazing buildings, soaking in the image and the sounds of screams with childhood fascination. She knew even then that the memory was burning itself into her mind.

"I will find him. Be still." And with that, she left.

"Rayanna, what do we do?" Karrh asked.

"We wait," she said breathlessly. "Papa will be here. We wait."

"I am so tired."

"Sleep here. You are safe."

Believing his sister, the young boy turned and promptly slept, undisturbed in his confidence that the world was exactly as his sister said.

Turning her attention to her mother, the young Rayanna watched as she dodged from house to house, moving closer to the fighting. As she came to the corner of the street, four marauders turned the corner and ran right into her.

"A lonely place for a lady like you," Rayanna heard one say as he leered at Aria. Their Lima dialect was foreign and their manner crude as they formed a semi-circle, blocking her exits. Aria turned to run. They grabbed her and forced her to the ground. And that was when it started.

"No!" Aria screamed from the depth of her soul as the men beat, tore, exposed, and hurt her repeatedly. They laughed.

"Papa will come. Papa will come. Papa will come. Papa..." Rayanna whispered. But he still had not. And as her mother's anguished screams mixed with the horror of the battle behind her, Rayanna knew that he never would.

"Why?" Aria sobbed as she was repeatedly attacked. "Why!"

Six years later as Rayanna thought once again about that night, she wondered if her mother's question, torn from her heart in anguish, had been the same question she had asked every day ever since. Why me? Why now? Why here? Why did we deserve this? Why must we suffer like this? But there was no answer, Rayanna decided. After an hour of repeated brutality that left her mother motionless in the mud and filth, there couldn't be an answer. Animals will always be animals, she told herself, and that was the simple truth.

She had stared at her mother's form lying where they had left her. She watched vigilantly for a breath from the beaten and exposed body. Somehow, Rayanna felt half of a hope that there was no more breath to draw. Not after that. And when her mother stirred and moaned, Rayanna prayed that the Lima would not find her, would not repeat their atrocities on her mother's broken body.

The night grew deeper, the screams from the village grew louder, and her mother had not moved. She watched all night. Helpless. With her father and her brothers nowhere to be seen, Rayanna knew that she must wait for dawn. Again, Rayanna prayed that her mother had died.

Dawn rescued her from the nightmare every morning from that night on. But when the nightmare was over, reality would begin.

Rayanna forced herself to remember every detail today. She had to remember. No one should forget.

She had rushed her brothers down a different path back to their home that morning. Though ransacked, the home was still intact. She left her brothers there with a solemn charge not to move, and she hurried back to her mother's side. The streets were strewn with the dead and the dying, the raped and the widowed.

Rayanna could not see her mother's chest rise and fall with breath, but her pulse still beat. Rayanna knew that she should have felt relieved, but even at eleven years old, all she could feel was regret. Regret that she had not been orphaned. Regret that her mother would live after her entire life had been ripped away from her. Even now, six years later, Rayanna still wondered if death would have been the kinder outcome.

Rayanna had dressed and buried the bodies of her father and two older brothers while her mother recovered from the brutality and violation. Help was not forthcoming from the community as almost every family had lost their home, their father, their brothers, their mother and sisters. Rayanna knew then that her mother's body might recover, but her mind was a different matter. That had not made the six years since then easier.

And so she sought solace. The woods had become her refuge, her place away from the gray ash and sorrow that settled over her home, away from the gray eyes and empty voice that had overcome her mother. They were the last place her father and brothers had lived, and they were the place where her family had died.

The seventeen-year-old Rayanna welcomed the memories and allowed the pain as she came to the mass grave that had been dug so long ago. A lifetime ago. Today, she remembered her father and her brothers as she chose to remember them. Not dismembered and disfigured as they were when she last saw them, but beautiful and full of life as she last knew them. *I could never have asked God for a better family*, Rayanna thought. *So why would God ask us to be without them all these years?*

She did not expect an answer. Just as with her mother's anguished plea for answers, for reasons for her suffering, Rayanna did not know if her own questions had any answer. She laid the gidionhi on the grave where her father and brothers' names were inscribed with one hundred and sixty-two other names.

Rayanna turned and walked back to the house. Her mother and siblings would be needing her. Again.

CHAPTER 3:
WHISPERS IN THE SHADOWS

"Chism! I didn't expect to see you back," Gala said as she swiftly planted a kiss on each cheek. "Where's Kalif?"

"I didn't give him the message." Chism stood rooted to the spot where Gala had greeted him, unwilling to tell her about his conversation in the forest with her fiancé and yet knowing that was exactly what she needed to hear. If only her eyes didn't sparkle so much. That would make this easier.

At eight years her senior, Chism intentionally held any emotion or love for Gala to something fraternal, sometimes almost paternal. She, like many Lima, had dark hair. But somehow her hair shimmered with the light to reflect her mood—intensely deep blue as the early morning sky or the angry purple and black of storm clouds and lightning.

"But you saw him," her mother said from her seat where she sat repairing a net. Gala raised one eyebrow at Chism, sensing his reticence, before moving across the room to continue with her nets.

The Sound in the Silence

The district cared well for Gala, her mother, and her family, and they in turn cared well for the district. Since her father died, Gala and her mother had no one to bring in the fish, the main industry of the area. But every net that needed to be repaired and every injury that needed care came immediately to their home, no matter the time of day or night. It was said that when Gala's mother fixed a net, the net was ten times stronger than before. And the men were almost too willing to get an injury so that they could have a reason to visit the inestimably beautiful Gala. In return for their services, the district always bestowed a basket of fresh fish on the family with more to trade at market for other wares. The situation had grown beyond transactions into relationships.

Chism stood awkwardly amidst the nets and the waiting women in the second-floor apartment with its wooden beams and soft yellow cement floors, walls, and ceilings. Buildings were easily identified in each district as each was built at different times and for different purposes. As buildings approached the city wall, they bore signs of haste, as if erected to make certain that they were stable enough and covered enough to do their job, but for nothing more. Such was not the case here in the fishing district where the buildings' exposed wooden frames and patchwork of new and old cement, continually faded by the salt air and bright sun, bespoke another time, perhaps hundreds of years long since forgotten. These buildings required respect, and so did the fishers who inhabited them.

Though Chism was an officer in the city's army—a position that generally placed him above the rest of the citizens, and a fact that Chism resented—he was still in an old home where an old woman presided. Age in the Lima was always revered, and Chism knew that if he were to deliver his message and counsel with Gala, he would have to tread carefully.

"*Mamilla*," Chism used the Lima word for "nanny" to denote admiration and respect. "I would like to speak with Gala alone."

"That was neither a request nor a question, lieutenant," came the reproachful response. Chism carefully subdued his irritation at her reference to his rank. It was an emotion to which he was becoming rapidly accustomed, and a title he wished away every time he heard it. But his response was the same.

"No, *mamilla*. It wasn't. I am sorry."

"Am I to assume that this is state business, then?"

Gala glanced quickly from one to the other as Chism shifted his weight. Ranking officers in the military were never questioned or disobeyed by citizens; but Gala's mother was no ordinary citizen, and Chism would not impose his rank. She could read him perfectly.

"Ah. And Kalif is involved, of course." If her demeanor had become cold at Chism's request, then it nearly froze Chism's heart at the mention of his brother's name.

"I bring peace, *mamilla*," Chism softly spoke the typical Lima expression.

Gala's mother sighed. "Not yet, Chism, but I know you hope to. And I pray the gods that you eventually do. Excuse me."

Gala's mother stepped from the room, and Chism could not help but smile at the irony. Here sat a woman in sun-bleached cloth, repairing nets who shuffled more than she walked as she moved, and yet she had a presence born of self-respect that bespoke something greater than fishing nets and cloth.

Gala motioned for Chism to sit next to her as she smiled at her mother's impertinence. Chism sat, rubbed his hands together, and stood again.

"She doesn't hate you." Gala said as she went back to work, waiting for him to get to the point.

Oh, if only my greatest concern, he thought, *were whether or not an old woman dislikes me*. Still, it was an easier conversation than what he had come to discuss. "Of course she doesn't hate me," he said as he idly played with a fishing net hanging from the rafters. "But my brother—your fiancé, I might add—my *rank*," he said disdainfully, "and everything that I represent…that, she hates. Everything around me, but not me. I couldn't take it personally, because there's simply not enough left of me for her to hate."

"And is that all you are? A brother you find too headstrong and a military you yourself despise? I would not blame your troubles on an old widower, Chism." She went back to work cleaning her first aid tools.

"And a brother that I myself raised who is now intent on joining the marauders tonight? Who would you blame that on?" It was out before he could check his words, but her reaction was hardly what he had anticipated.

"Of course he's going. I'm only surprised that you're not."

"What are you talking about?"

Her tools sounded sharply as she brought them down on the table in the first sign of her emotions. "Your *pahpon* died six years ago. Your *mamerra* five years before that. My three cousins. Your sister last week. And countless others, Chism. Who doesn't want to see them answered for? Who doesn't want to see the Neroos pay?"

It was true, Chism told himself, that the Neroos had always taken what was never theirs. They had taken his mother when he was only nine years old. They took his father six years ago. They took Loria, or so the rumors said. Innocent Loria. But there were so many questions unanswered. Too many questions that pulled at the back of Chism's mind.

When his father died, the government had sent a militia to a village called Gidionhi when the senators said that the Neroos were taking Lima land. Chism's father had been killed in an attack designed to warn the Neroos of coming too close to their borders. It was to serve his people, his father had told him six years ago. The city would never let him forget how long it had been, because the fishing district still talked about the fish famine that just happened to take place six years ago. The timing of the famine with the raid that brought in herds of cattle and sheep had always been too perfect for Chism's taste.

How many sheep and cattle found their way into the butchers' district that year to make up for the lack of fish? Chism had always wondered. And always the question—*did my father die simply for a lack of fish?*

When his mother died, the government told the city that the Neroos had murdered Lima in the caravan that his mother travelled in. The caravan also happened to be laden with gold in an exchange between a city to the north and a city to the south. His mother traveled from the north after visiting her sister when they were attacked. The Neroos stole the gold, the government said, and the Lima had no reason to believe otherwise. Chism was relatively new to the army at the time, but a few loose-lipped and drunk soldiers once talked of a treasure that had been brought into the city by night close to the time of that attack.

And animals attacked his sister, the government says. But Chism was there. He saw the wounds, and he knew well how a knife slits a throat. It was either Neroos…or the Lima. *Does it matter?* Chism had often asked himself. *Lima or Neroos, they were still animals. And is it not the nature of animals to attack?* Chism had no one left to blame.

In every instance and at every loss, his military mind saw engagements and casualties, lessons that he learned from the same military he despised. His head began to spin as if it would not stop.

"I'm not interested in making them pay." Chism said as more of an extension to his thoughts than in response to Gala. "I've lost everyone. Now I'm losing Kalif. You have to make him see. Say what you will about the Neroos, but admit to yourself that they are fighters. And Kalif stands to make himself the next casualty. I won't stand by and watch him walk into death."

"You speak as if he is already dead."

"If not now, then when?" Chism shouted. "You speak of justice! Was it justice that took my family away from me? Is it peace that I feel when I patrol the woods far beyond our city and kill a Neroos in the name of protecting the Lima? If that is what the gods have for me, then I must find a way to escape them."

Gala stood and gently held his face in her hands. Her hand was warm. "We want peace, Chism. Is that not worth fighting for?"

Chism grabbed her hands and brought them down into his. He stood there looking into her eyes, searching for some sign of hesitation. "Is death the only way to peace?" He whispered. Her eyes sparkled back but promised nothing as they stood there, measuring each other.

The sound of a soft knock and the creaking of a leather belt in the doorway broke Chism and Gala's concentration.

"I told you once today that I would kill you, Chism," Kalif said in a voice that was even and steady, like a tiger approaching its prey. "Don't make me say it again. Now step away from my fiancée."

Chism seemed to wake from a dream as he dropped Gala's hand and stepped away from her.

"Kalif, I—"

"What? Please, insult me with an explanation."

Without a word, Chism pushed passed his brother and quickly descended the stairs. He did not pause as he passed Gala's mother to say goodbye before he disappeared into the late afternoon.

~~~~~

The fact that Chism felt like a fool could not concern him less at the moment. Rebuffed by the woman he thought he could trust and threatened by his brother, Chism could only think of his next move. His first two attempts had been unsuccessful. If a head-on assault on Kalif's senses could not work and a flanking move through Gala proved unsuccessful, then he had only one play left:

Chism would attack from behind.

He could not fail again. Not if he wanted to keep what was left of his family. A formal appeal to the government concerning the marauders' next move would only be supposedly lost, forgotten, or worse—Chism expected he would be reprimanded for bringing the marauder's plans to the government's attention. Soldiers were the only group that Chism could trust to intentionally undermine the marauder's boundless latitude, and there was only one place to find them on a late summer evening. And now, thanks in large part to Kalif, Chism happened to outrank a significant portion of them.

Chism could not help but smile at the irony as he made his way to a specific alehouse.

Though nearly any member of the military would happily spoil any plans that the marauders had, Chism had no intention to order a platoon to go after his brother. His rank would only get him the supplies he needed. But even his rank would not get him what he needed most. He needed someone willing to do more than set up traps or slow down a group of marauders. He needed someone who could speak the Neroos dialect flawlessly. And he needed someone on whom he could trust to keep his mouth shut about what Chism planned to do.

It was time to find Rierdan.

~~~~~

Gala and Kalif stood at opposite ends of the small upper apartment, Kalif still in the doorway and Gala next to the netting. They could hear Gala's mother busying herself downstairs as fishermen came and went for their nets, sweeping the floor, straightening random items, and generally avoiding the man who was in her home.

"Oh, just stop it, Kalif." Gala was perhaps the only person who could give Kalif a command. She could speak so plainly. Kalif felt that when she spoke, it was the honest truth. Not like when Chism spoke, who was so full of knowing that he was right. Gala simply spoke the truth, as Kalif saw it, and that was enough for him.

"Stop what?"

"Stop being obstinate, and come here. I haven't seen you all day."

Kalif softened immediately and stepped toward her, pulling her in and kissing the top of her head. "I cannot figure out why you love me."

"Mmm," she said as she rested her head on his chest. "You know why I love you."

"Because I'm such a rascal?"

Gala felt suddenly melancholy. "Because of the man I know you can be. I see him in there from time to time. Most of the time you're hot-headed and conceited and—"

"You're making me blush," Kalif interjected with his typical sarcasm.

"But you can see past my faults…and my heritage," Gala said, still somewhat ashamed of her bloodline. "You were there for me when no one else was."

"As were you," Kalif reminded her.

The two went quiet for a moment, considering the long road that had brought them here. Most people—Gala's mother, especially— could not see why Gala had chosen to put her trust in Kalif. His reputation was an embarrassment to Gala's mother and to Chism. But Gala and Kalif had found each other when they needed each other most.

They started spending time together when Kalif came to her to get sewn up. Cuts on his arms and back were not uncommon. He always told her that the wounds were from bar fights, but she knew he hadn't been drinking enough for that. There was something else about this man that she did not know, but wanted to protect him from. Gala helped pull Kalif out of his downward spiral, and he protected Gala with surprising loyalty in return.

"Can you believe that brother of mine?"

"Yes." It was the truth.

"Which part did you believe, then?"

"The part about you dying. I know that you want justice, *amoni*," she said, using the word for love and friend. "But even a panther knows when it is being hunted, and the Neroos know that we are going to repay them for what they have done this time. They must know."

The two sat down and stared into the cold hearth for some time. "Chism mentioned that he saw you at the market today. Did he try to kiss you then, too?"

Gala rolled her eyes. Kalif resented his brother for many things, but he did not need to add infidelity to the list. "Why do you tell yourself such stories? He has taken care of both of us for quite some time. Besides, is that why you came here? Because your brother told you to come?"

"He never told me to come. I came on my own to say goodbye."

Gala sat up straight, breaking away from Kalif's arms. "'Goodbye' or 'adieu'? I swear, Kalif, if you die, then I won't even cry for you. You are trying to be a hero, and no one asked you to be."

"So he turned you?" Kalif said. "He told you stop me, didn't he!"

"Oh Kalif, shut up for one second! It's not about Chism, and it's not about the Neroos! I told him that he should be going. I told him I'm not going to stop you from bringing justice to our families, but Kalif, I'm so afraid of losing you!"

Kalif could feel the anger welling inside of him. Again. He was becoming exhausted of the sentiment, and yet he was addicted to it. "Loria is dead, and so are my father and mother. How can I let this go, Gala?"

"It's not about Loria. It's not about your father or anyone else's father, Kalif, and you know it! That's not really why you're going, and you know it. That is what scares me," Gala finished.

"So why am I going? Huh? Tell me."

Gala shook her head slightly. She could tell Kalif didn't know if her head-wagging was out of disappointment or ignorance. She didn't know, either.

"I thought you were on my side!" Kalif said to break the silence.

"I am on your side. And I need you by my side. Here. To protect me."

"I am protecting you! That is why I have to go."

Gala turned her dark eyes on Kalif with all the accusatory anger that her feelings of dejection could muster. "Then go." And with that, she turned her back.

He had seen this treatment from her before. That is why he did not even try to turn her around. "Goodbye, *amona*," he said to her. And he left.

"Goodbye," she whispered after she heard his footsteps fade on the last few stairs.

She still had not delivered the message. The wedding, according to Lima custom, was to be performed as the sun broke over the mountains to the east. Not only did the sun dispel the darkness that came from their enemies to the east, but it signaled the beginning of all things. The customary pink flower that grew on the beaches adorned every Lima wedding ceremony. Its five petals overlapped each other around a beautiful green center. To the Lima, it represented five stages of life that carefully overlap one another, all surrounding the green of vitality that would ever adorn a marriage. It was a beautiful symbol, but Gala wanted to pay tribute to their fallen family and symbolize their eventual victory over their enemies.

Gala's message was that she wanted to find a flower born of the sun, a symbol of victory, just as their marriage would be at the dawn of a new day. She wanted to find the rare gidionhi flower.

~~~~~

As Chism walked into the alehouse, no one saluted him. Some had decided that when they were off duty, their rank—and anyone else's—might as well not exist. Others were far too busy with their mugs made of the milky white glass from the shore that surrounded them.

But as these soldiers drenched what was left of the day in booze, the quality of the glass made little difference to the men intent on finding oblivion at the bottom of their mugs. Chism was looking for one soldier known to frequent the tavern. Though there were many soldiers who found their way to this tavern at one point or another, none were known so well for it like Rierdan. Rierdan was peculiar, because he was a soldier who spent his time in a tavern but never, in anyone's recollection, brought a mug of ale to his lips.

Chism moved slowly to Rierdan's sitting place, wading through the raised mugs, friendly handshakes, and salutations. Though Chism was hardly one for ale himself, he frequented the tavern because, for the Lima, that is where a man left rank at the door.

"Rierdan, I need your help," Chism said with no preamble when he finally reached the table.

Though not the general of the previous war bearing the same name, Rierdan somehow commanded the same respect that one would give to someone in high command. Even in this tavern. When addressing him, Chism always spoke directly. To the point. It was an efficient method to communicate, and Rierdan demanded efficiency. Especially when you needed something from him.

"So they say," Rierdan replied casually and softly. "Me, I would have just killed him myself if I were you."

"Who?"

"You're going to have to be a bit brighter than that if you want to enlist my help, Lieutenant." Rierdan chuckled.

Chism pulled a chair back and sat down next to him. Though most of these soldiers would gladly follow Chism on a mission to sabotage the marauders, Chism preferred to keep this conversation confidential.

"Trust me, I have thought about how much easier life would be if I let him get caught by some Neroos," Chism said, speaking sardonically of Kalif. "That's why I need your help."

"Sounds like the Neroos are going to take care of that problem for you if he goes on this little scavenger hunt. What do I have to do with it?"

As Chism looked at him, he wondered how Rierdan had kept his age such a mystery. Rierdan was well known to hate the marauders, and yet he resembled them more than anyone in the tavern. With no real rank in the city military, Rierdan's role was anyone's guess. But he was untouchable. Unfathomable. A senator died of natural causes one week ago—because, naturally, a gaping dagger wound to the heart causes a man to die. It was one of the few nights that Rierdan was not at his customary table. None were willing to ask questions for fear of finding a natural death of their own.

Chism only knew of the death because of his connection to the military. To the rest of the world, the senator was away on official business. He wondered how long the officials would wait before announcing the senator's sudden and unexpected death en route, attributed undoubtedly to the Neroos—like that of Chism's mother and so many others. Not for the first time, Chism questioned the official story of Neroos having attacked his sister.

Chism studied the deep creases at Rierdan's mouth and eyes but still saw something incredibly youthful in his unshaven and stubbled face. Whatever may or may not lie behind those brown eyes of Rierdan's was of little importance to Chism so long as he could have a second hand that he could trust. Chism needed something more than just a hired sword—he needed to trust that his companion's hate of the marauders was at least as equal to Kalif's anger at the Neroos. Chism picked his words just like he picked his allies: carefully.

"I'm not just trying to stop my brother, but he has brought something to my attention—why should the marauders have all the fun while we sit back?"

Rierdan sneered at Chism. "You should know better than that, Chism. If I wanted to slaughter, I'd be in the butchers' district."

"I'm not talking about the Neroos. The marauders have been a thorn in our side long enough, and the senators look the other way. So as long as their attention is diverted from the marauders, why not be a thorn in their side? Show them that laws…and justice… aren't bent just for them."

"So we make sure that the Neroos are ready when the marauders get there," Rierdan said, guessing the rest of Chism's plan. "Not bad, lieutenant."

"About my being a lieutenant. Title and rank may not matter to a man like you, Rierdan, but it can get us where we want to go faster and with fewer questions."

Rierdan sat back for a moment with the hint of a smile playing at his lips. "I'm not saying I'm in. But I want to hear more."

"We have to leave now if we're going to do this."

"You can explain on the way."

Chism was not so caught up in his thoughts to ignore the change in atmosphere in the alehouse. After years of patrolling the woods for predators and Neroos spies, Chism was acutely attuned to his surroundings. "A silent bird is a predator heard," he always said to his platoon. In this tavern, the bird-like chatter of the men had gone silent. With Rierdan close behind him, Chism knew exactly where the predator walked.

The only time Rierdan looked at a man's back, they say, is when he is about to put a knife in it.

CHAPTER 4:
BORN OF THE SUN

"You haven't asked," Hakoni said to Rayanna as they wandered the market square together, Rayanna carrying a basket of eggs to bring home and her bag of berries to trade. Hakoni carried a heavy bag filled with fruit from an orchard he knew of in the forest. "You've never asked, have you?"

Hakoni was a year younger than Rayanna, but even at sixteen, his shoulders were broad and his stance was stooped from intense labor in the quarry. He and his oldest brother began working in the quarry at only ten years old when his father was unable to work for a year after the raid. His father had sustained a deep wound to the leg and hours of bleeding until help came. The village's medicine man told Hakoni's father that he had to take the leg to save his life. The medicine man didn't say what else Hakoni's father would lose with his leg—like his oldest son in a quarry accident six months later.

And yet Hakoni had the resilience of a stalk of grass, bending in the wind but always springing back to greet the sun. His soft brown eyes were always happy, even if his muscled shoulders were stooped from the crushing weight of carrying both stone and his family's burdens. Rayanna often caught herself focusing on his wavy brown hair that came past his jaw and halfway down his neck, fighting a desire to cut it short like the rest of the men in the village, but also wanting to run her fingers through it.

"Why would I ask a question when I know the answer? There's no way she'd come, Hak," Rayanna responded as they approached the flour merchant.

"How much?" The merchant, a slight man covered in the dust of his ware, asked.

"Four measures?" Rayanna said, placing a sack of red berries on the balance.

The merchant selected weights and placed them carefully on the counterbalance. He shook his head, a small cloud of flour descending as he moved. "Two and a half, Rayanna. It's a small bag."

"Three, and I'll bake you a *churasca*," she bartered.

With a small nod and a smile, the man replaced the weights and began to prepare a bag of flour.

"Besides, she actually gets up to dress herself lately," Rayanna said quietly to Hakoni as the merchant finished with her flour. "Do you have any idea what the memories would do to her?"

Hakoni waited until they departed with Rayanna's flour before responding. "Well maybe you don't know your mother like you think you do. She's stronger than you give her credit—or respect—for."

Rayanna whipped around and glared at her friend. "What do you know—!"

"Hey, calm down," Hakoni cut her off. "You're not the only one who lost someone, remember. You are strong. You get strength from coming to the grave, from hunting out the *gidionhi* from wherever you get it. Maybe that would help your mom. Just ask her to come to the grave with you."

"You don't know what it's like. What they did to her. What she remembers every day," Rayanna said quietly. Respectfully. "Your mom died when they...when they attacked her. And I have wished that my mom had died, too. For her own sake."

Hakoni knew that Rayanna meant well by it. He also knew that Rayanna didn't know what she was talking about. Couldn't know what she was talking about. Even when life was at its worst, Hakoni had decided, death was the cause of grief—not a way to relieve it.

"Bad things happen, sunshine," Hakoni said with a smile. He would often tease Rayanna for being so serious. Her father's name, Solay, was an ancient form of the word for the sun, and Rayanna had been aptly named as the offspring of the sun. It was why the gidionhi flower was so special to her family.

Hakoni loved to remind her to brighten up. If any other boy dared call her "sunshine," she would have broken his nose. Even with Hakoni, she pretended to hate it.

"How do you know bad things won't happen again?" Rayanna said. "We have to be prepared."

"I am prepared," Hakoni said with his incorrigible smile. "I can be happy every other day when bad things aren't happening. C'mon, sunshine, sometimes you're not happy unless you're sad. Or mad."

With her one free hand, Rayanna swung at Hakoni's face playfully. Hakoni easily grabbed her wrist and, in a single motion, dropped his bag of fruit and grabbed a flower from inside his shirt. Placing the flower in her hand, he let go of her wrist. It would have been awkward for Rayanna, but Hakoni had a way of making everything seem so normal.

"I still need to get rid of this fruit and get some meat," Hakoni said, changing topics. "You want to stick around?"

"I have to get back. Lots to do at the house, you know," Rayanna said, smiling slightly as she played with the flower in her hand.

"Ok. I'll see you around, then."

Trying to hide the smile spreading across her face, Rayanna simply nodded and headed toward the north end of the village.

As she approached her small home with weather-stained curtains in the windows, Rayanna made sure to knock as she entered. She had made the mistake of surprising her mother several years ago, and the mistake was not to be repeated.

Rayanna remembered with wry fondness the incident. They were hungry. Several months after the village had been attacked, their mother had forgotten about food again. Rayanna and her two younger brothers had grown accustomed to skipping meals while their mother sat in a corner, staring into the past.

This time it had been almost three days, and Rayanna ran to the woods, crying out for her father. Running blindly with tears streaming down her face, she ran straight into a brier bush. Extracting herself angrily with no thought or care for the cuts she inflicted, she fell to the ground covered in what appeared to be blood. Knowing she had not received so many injuries as her stained skin suggested, she licked the dark liquid on her arms. It was juice. Sweet juice from the berry bush she found herself tangled in. Then, staining her face in red juice as she wiped away the tears, Rayanna ripped off the lower portion of her shirt and began to gather the red berries.

Rayanna walked into the house that day clutching her prize, completely unaware that her body looked as shredded as her clothing, a red-stained macabre appearance. "Look!" a seemingly bloodied Rayanna cried out, standing in her shredded clothing and holding aloft the red, bulging bundle.

Aria looked. And it took her three hours to wake up after she fainted. Aria had not eaten a red berry since, and Rayanna thereafter made sure to trade them all at the market before her mother saw them.

"Hello, mama!" Rayanna announced as she pushed open the door, smiling despite herself at the memory and at her encounter with Hakoni. She deposited her trades from the market on the soot-covered table and looked around the small space. The walls had changed from their former soft brown cement to an oily ash color long ago, and now they were becoming blacker every day. The change was gradual, imperceptible to anyone else, but all too apparent to Rayanna.

"How has your morning been?" Aria asked from her chair in the corner.

"Oh, fine. I saw Hakoni at the market. He gave me a flower," Rayanna said, believing that her mother would take it as a lie. "What have you been up to today?"

"I swept, and I'm going to make *falhanna*," Aria said with a perk in her voice that Rayanna missed entirely. *Falhanna* had been Solay's favorite dessert. Rayanna dismissed it again as part of the stories the two had been telling for years. Part of the crystal palace they had constructed to hide reality. Don't talk about life as it is. Talk about life as it should be. For some time, Rayanna had been mixing truth and would-be-truths, telling herself that it was all the same to her despondent mother. All the stories had begun to swirl and blend, like a pallet of color mixing until it became a brown and gray mess. A brown and gray mess like this house. Like this village.

Rayanna felt no need to look in the corner where the broom sat exactly as she had left it two days ago, just as Aria had no need to meet a boy who may as well not exist.

"I spoke to Brego, Rayanna," Aria started tentatively.

The crystal palace the mother and daughter carefully constructed each day—the palace where boys noticed Rayanna and Aria baked and had a husband—came crashing down as reality set into Aria's voice. That gray voice.

"Oh? And did he speak back, I wonder?" Rayanna said.

"Don't be sarcastic, Rayanna," Aria said with motherly reproach. "He said you showed him where the gidionhi grow."

"Someone needs to remember these things, mom. Even if you won't." She said it before she realized it.

"I'm not trying to scold you, my dear."

I'd never accuse you *of trying to do anything,* Rayanna thought. There was a time when she would try to halt the thoughts. When she would forgive. But Rayanna felt the same way that her mother looked—gray. Burdened. And try as she might to let go of her anger and forgive her mother, it was more difficult with every passing year.

Rayanna felt like a young bird she had once found in the forest. It had landed on a branch too thin to hold its weight. The branch snapped and the bird fell, terrified, to the ground, clutching the fragile twig that was supposed to have supported and protected the bird. It could have let go and flown away or softened the fall, but it was too shocked, too scared to let go. It died when its head struck a rock below, the branch still clutched in its dead feet.

"Then what are you *trying* to do, mother?" *Do not lose control, Rayanna. You are strong. Be strong.*

"Brego is not ready for those memories, *amora*," she said, using the Neroos term for affection.

Rayanna's eyes quickly began to well. She turned away from her mother. *Amora.* Why would she call her that? Rayanna almost believed it was a genuine sign of affection. But she couldn't. No. They were still in their crystal palace. And this was not reality. This was not reality. *I am not her amora.* And like the little bird in the forest, Rayanna would not let go of her grief.

Rayanna's tears subsided almost as quickly as they had risen to her face.

"Very well," she said, turning back to her mother. "I'll remember not to let him walk so far if he is not ready to be away that long."

Aria stood up and moved toward Rayanna, moving her hands up to gently touch her daughter's face.

"I'm not ready," Rayanna said before she realized it.

Aria froze.

"For dinner. I'm not ready for dinner, and I need to clean the pot," she tried to finish.

Aria simply nodded. "What would you like me to do to help? I'm very hungry." Aria's family never discussed feelings. They just found ways around them.

Rayanna shook her head and busied herself with arranging the wares from the market. "The food will be ready soon. But I forgot the water. I will be back soon."

Karrh was out getting water, and Rayanna left without the pot. But Aria knew that was not what Rayanna meant.

~~~~~

Peace, Rayanna thought wryly. *If it was peace that Neroos himself wanted all those years ago, then he should have just killed his brother Lima.*

Rayanna silently berated her ancestor as she wandered the village, gathering her senses. Nearly five hundred years ago, as the legend says, a young man named Neroos left his home with his wife and several families in search of a far off land. They were tired of the wars and the bloodshed in their homeland and sought safety. Security. Harmony. It was the Age of Miracles when the Ancestors came from far away beyond the sea, traversing enormous distances to find peace. It was said that God had walked with the Ancestors on their journey, in the days before God turned away from his children. Before God closed his eyes. And so they journeyed here.

In that sense, Rayanna had much in common with her ancestor—if the stories were true. She came with her parents here, away from Riomna, the bustling city where a person could not hear their own thoughts. Her family wanted to be free. They wanted to be away from the noise. They wanted peace, according to her father. *My father who died in a battle,* she thought ironically.

No one knew how it was the Ancestors were supposed to have arrived. Some versions of the history said that they walked great distances and endured many trials to come to this land. The Lima people said that they came across by the sea. Of course. For the Lima, there was no life without the sea.

Neroos was named king when the people settled in the land now possessed by the Lima. The first city is now known as Tenebrar, the Lima capital. And just as her family had discovered for themselves, their peace could not last. The Ancestors settled in the valleys by the sea. And there they built. Children quickly became adults. Rules turned into laws. Elders made themselves into statesmen. And they elected Neroos as king.

Neroos was a powerful warrior with a kind heart, fighting to defend his family and his nation, but never to make or overcome enemies, they said. He was a benevolent king. He was also a younger brother.

Lima was a cunning man, and though the people had chosen his younger brother Neroos to be king, he wanted the throne for himself. In the dark of the night, he stole into his brother's house to kill him and claim the nation as his own, as Rayanna had learned. But Neroos was too powerful for Lima; after disarming his brother, he called in the guards and, instead of killing Lima, he only arrested his brother.

Neroos banished Lima to keep the peace they had sought for so long. Jealous of his brother's power and ashamed by his banishment, Lima returned and incited a rebellion. Rather than fight their own brothers and loved ones, Neroos and his followers fled into the mountains. They had been there ever since.

For centuries thereafter, land had traded hands, the Neroos defending their lands at times and at others seeking to reclaim what was rightfully theirs.

From the time of Lima's Rebellion, the Neroos had known no peace.

Perhaps she was foolish—childish, even—to simply expect to have peace. Looking back at her house full of coldness and soot, she could not help but scorn herself and her parents. If Neroos himself could not find what he sought by fleeing to the mountains, then why should they?

The blue evening light and first stars began to appear in the east as the sun began to dip below the mountains that stood between them and the Lima. It was yet early evening, but the mountains often obscured the light of day earlier than down by the sea. Some days, Rayanna felt that the mountains made her more grateful for the light when she had it. *I love it when the sun shines like this,* Brego had said today. *How much I need the sun right now!* Rayanna thought. Rayanna, the girl who tread as lightly as a ray of the sun. Tonight, the absence of the sun and the dark of the mountains was only one more reason to disdain her circumstances. *How many more things that I love are going to be taken away from me?* She asked herself. Again, there was no answer.

Though her head was spinning, she had no time for the woods tonight. Her family needed to eat, and she would light the fire.

~~~~~

Rayanna walked into her home quickly and with purpose. Brego and Karrh had returned. Two pails of water sat to one side of the fireplace, mirrored on the other side by the stack of wood that Brego had collected with her in the forest. They were exactly as Rayanna expected them to be. But nothing else was.

The boys and her mother were not in their customary places and the scent in the air was not the customary scent. Suddenly Rayanna's purpose and façade melted as she began to gather the scene playing out before her. Aria stood over the pot as it hung on its hook, clearly preparing its contents to be placed over the fire. Brego and Karrh carefully measured out flour and water with salt and sugar, two commodities that Rayanna knew nothing of. And she knew everything that happened in this house.

"Mother…" Rayanna was at a loss for words.

Aria simply smiled back. "I knew that you weren't ready for dinner tonight. I was trying to tell you earlier today that I am. I am, Rayanna."

Rayanna gestured toward the two boys who were now kneading the dough they had extracted from a wooden bowl. She did not even know how to ask the question.

"I had sent the boys to our neighbors before you came home earlier," Aria explained. "They went to ask for a few extra ingredients."

"For what?"

"*Falhanna.*" Her father's favorite dessert.

"But…why?"

Aria held Rayanna's gaze for a moment or two. Slowly, Aria raised her hands to Rayanna's face and gently touched her daughter's cheeks. "The dead must not be forgotten. Brego wasn't ready, because I was not ready. But they deserve more, *amora.*"

No crystal palace. No lies. *Amora.* Reality.

And yet the reality still burned. *They deserve more? They deserve more?* Rayanna fumed. *And what did I do to deserve this all these years?*

"You…I…!" Rayanna began pacing the room. "For years…! I…and they…we…but you! And now? Why not…?"

"Rayanna, please, calm down," Aria said as gently as she could.

"No!" Rayanna managed to shout. "When have I…why should they…how *could* you..?"

"Please, just talk to me, *amora.*"

The floodgates burst at the third mention of that word. "I have done *everything* for this family! When I was a girl, it was *me* that held *you* as you cried! *I* comforted *you!* Do you have any idea how much I have needed you all along? And you change one night, for what? For what! A boy who's as scared as the rest of us but has not *seen* what I have seen!"

"Of course it was for you!" Aria tried to soothe Rayanna, but her daughter was inconsolable.

"You forgot us!" Rayanna continued to shout as she sobbed. "You left us to die! Do you have any idea? Do you have any idea that I prayed that you would not be able to get up from that mud?" The memories welled into her eyes as the frustration began to flow freely from her mouth. "Do you know how I wondered and asked if it would have been better for you to stop breathing? To stay where the Lima had left you? You have been dead for so long! Why did you not die?" Rayanna's sobs became an uncontrollable hysteria. "Why were you too strong to die, but not strong enough to live?"

Rayanna sank to the floor, unwilling to let her mother catch her. As she leaned her back against the table, her shoulders shaking with sobs, her fingers noticed the floor. The swept floor. Rayanna could have almost laughed that now, at this moment, she noticed that her mother really had swept. Just as she had said. How many other things had been the truth? For how long had it been Rayanna living the lie while her mother waited for her to wake up? Where the stories ended and reality began was a line that Rayanna could no longer discern.

"I had a choice to make, Rayanna," Aria sobbed with her daughter, kneeling beside her on the floor. "And when I finally had the strength to make that choice—the choice to be stronger than my circumstances—then I was able to get over my fear and my grief. I had forgotten who I was. And you reminded me how much I am worth."

The two sat on the floor with foreheads pressed together and arms wrapped around each other. After a few moments, Aria turned to the wide-eyed boys sitting at the table and said, "Brego, Karrh, help me get your sister to the bed."

The only bed in the one-room house sat against the west wall, as if Aria had placed it as far away from the morning as she could get it and as close to sunset as she could be. At least, that was how Rayanna had imagined it. And when the night would become as unbearable as the day for Aria, as it did so very often, Rayanna would rise from her floor mat in front of the door and lay down with her mother. When her mother's shoulders stopped shaking and her breathing came in regular, peaceful measures instead of anguished gasps, Rayanna would allow herself to cry. She didn't know why.

Brego and Karrh approached Rayanna, stopping on either side of her and staring between her and their mother. With eleven-year-old shrugs to each other, the twins bent toward Rayanna, unsure how to support their hysterical sister.

"No, Brego, don't pull on her, just gently lift her."

"I'm not Brego, Mom. I'm Karrh!"

"Well, I wasn't talking to you, then, was I?"

"Karrh, I can't lift her that way…"

"Oh, boys, please don't hit her head on the table!"

"Well, she's just being a lump, and I'm hungry!"

"Stop, stop, stop," Rayanna said as she tried to clear the tears from her eyes. "I can do it alone."

Aria motioned to the two boys to give her sister room, and they were only too happy to oblige. Rayanna pushed herself up and, when she was sure that she had steadied herself, allowed her mother to guide her to the bed. Settling herself in, she closed her eyes, wondering, hoping, and fearing all at once that this could be real.

CHAPTER 5:
WHAT LIES IN THE DARK

Kalif walked into a house in the butchers' district, thinking of everything he had endured that had brought him to this point. While many people had to play the right political cards to become inducted, Kalif's open hatred of the Neroos garnered so much attention from the marauders that they sent someone to him, promising him access to their society in exchange for his discretion.

Not that his discretion gave him any more protection from Chism. Kalif kept a careful eye out for his brother tonight, fearing that he might be leading an officer of the army straight to this place known only to the select. The elect. The loyal.

Not even the marauders knew how many other marauders there were. They were organized into houses such as this one by orders passed down from member to member. Each time an attack was to be planned, the word would go out with where to meet, when they should arrive, and where they were going. A person rarely met at the same place twice, and almost never with the same members. When members arrived at the appointed house, directions were left for everyone to read and then destroy. Instructions were always signed by the Triumvirate, as the heads of the marauders were known, and they were so secret that vendors would attempt to sell fakes for the sheer novelty of it.

No address was ever given by accident. The Speakers, as those who were sent to deliver the Message were known, received their Message from other Speakers, and no one could trace the source. Many had tried. Those who tried often ended up dead within a few hours of trying to piece the plans together. In the Message were always the same directions: a house and a time. Anyone caught trying to enter a house before or after the appointed time was to be killed. No questions asked.

Kalif arrived at the appointed place and time, half worried that he had been given false information. It was not uncommon for Lima boys to trick each other into believing they had been recruited and leave them stranded on a street corner all night, waiting for directions that would never come. *The Speaker was clear,* Kalif told himself. *There could be no deception. None.* He repeated, hoping to believe it.

Kalif examined with a hunter's eye the threshold and surroundings for signs of activity. The dirt on the threshold showed no signs of entry in some time. There were only the marks of feet coming and going on the street. The windows, which were often obscured with heavy cloth at night to trap in the heat, were altogether boarded up.

Windows in Ombrar homes, much like other facets of Ombrar life, were purely functional. They were placed high in the wall in long shallow holes—it was more important to relieve the home of the nearly unbearable heat during the day while still maintaining the warmth at night as temperatures at the seaside village plummeted. The warm seawater would normally have kept the city at a moderate temperature, but the city was prone to intense wind that blew between the mountain pass behind them and the sea ahead, making the nights surprisingly frigid.

Kalif could detect no foot traffic entering or exiting the threshold. Dust remained on the door with no sign of hands pushing it open. Kalif looked around, trying to get his bearings as he wondered if he were even in the right place. *No one had been here in months,* Kalif determined.

But as he pushed open the unlocked door at the darkened ground-level apartment, he saw at his feet an arrow drawn in fresh chalk just inside the doorway pointing straight ahead. Looking up and down the street at the butchers and buyers finishing the day's business in the bright early evening, Kalif walked in, and the door snapped shut behind him. He was plunged into total darkness.

"You will state your name, or you will die," a rich voice said as calmly as if it were commenting on the drapes.

Kalif immediately threw himself against the wall that ran perpendicular to the door, scraping his bare torso against the rough plaster as he ducked. The room was entirely devoid of light. There was not even a crack in the door afforded him a view, and his eyes had not yet adjusted from the bright evening sun to this perfect lack of light. He held his breath, listening for the man's breathing or the telltale whisper of clothing on skin.

"Very well," the voice said again, and Kalif could hear a bow being drawn from across the room. He did not know by what means the man could discern his location, but one thing was certain: Kalif was exposed.

"Kalif, son of Faloni," Kalif stated loudly and quickly.

"That's better."

A door at the opposite corner of the room opened, revealing a space of twenty feet between Kalif and a dim glow that framed the door and nothing more. He could see no sign of the archer.

Crossing the room to the door, Kalif found himself at the top of a set of stairs. He descended, and the door again snapped shut behind him.

WHAT LIES IN THE DARK

Kalif walked through the open door at the bottom of the stairs. The room was filled with silence, smoke, and men, Lima of all ages from all across the city. Peering through the haze that hung like a ghost in the air, Kalif could not recognize or even discern a single face in the room. All were obscured by cowls, shadows, and smoke. In the center of the room stood a large hourglass ringed by three candles, the only sources of light. The candles had all burned very low, each upon the point of burning out.

For a society so embedded in secrecy that he did not even know his leaders' names, Kalif was surprised that everyone was not masked. There were no uniforms. There were only robes. The entire room wore robes that seemed to be made of shadows themselves. The cloth was darker than black somehow. It was as if they had learned to clothe themselves in the night.

As Kalif stood where he had entered, ten men scattered throughout the room stood, pushed open a door, and walked through. He could discern no signal that alerted the men to leave, and he wondered how he would recognize any cue of his own.

Kalif felt someone grab his shoulder, and he spun around to see the face of the man now standing so near him. He had seen the man only once before, when he delivered the Message.

"Terran." Kalif spoke the man's name without thinking. Immediately he felt Terran's fist deal a heavy blow to the side of his head while the man's other hand caught Kalif's mouth to silence the impending outcry. Still with his mouth gripped tightly, Kalif felt Terran pull his face toward him, forcing Kalif to stare into the eyes of his Speaker.

Terran glared at Kalif while firmly clamping Kalif's mouth. Kalif nodded slowly, reassuring Terran that the message was clearly understood—one more noise from Kalif, and his body would never be found.

Apparently satisfied that Kalif would make no more mistakes, Terran removed his hand from Kalif's face and pushed a folded piece of paper sealed with black wax into Kalif's hand. Kalif stared from the paper back to Terran, waiting for a sign. Terran nodded once to the paper, looked at Kalif, and returned to his seat.

Kalif moved toward the candles for better light and noted that one candle had burned out. Bending toward the remaining two candles, Kalif began to read:

Welcome, Kalif, Our New Brother.

Your heart is full of vengeance, Kalif. The Neroos have taken everything from you. Your father and mother are dead. You were rendered an orphan. Your sister is dead only days ago, and the government will not bring her justice. They have forgotten the legend that keeps us united. But we are strong. We owe our strength to the Great Father, Lima, who dared demand justice from his usurping brother.

Long ago in the Time of Sorrow, Lima the Wise was compelled to come with his family from a city far away to establish this land. It was a sentence of death for a child to disobey his father, and Lima would not disobey. That law has continued to this day.

Lima's family told stories of a better life. They were seekers of peace. But in their journeys, the younger and unworthy brother Neroos was guilty of much deception. Neroos, who did not deserve to call himself a brother, painted Lima as a liar and a coercer.

When the people grew into a small nation, they elected a king. Half of the nation—our fathers—followed Lima, the greater and wiser brother. But Neroos drew away the other because of his great strength and much flattery. Neroos was chosen as king. And Lima was obliged to bow to his undeserving brother.

But Neroos feared Lima's wisdom and cunning. Neroos called Lima to his home and there accused Lima of attacking him. Calling the guards, Neroos wrongly imprisoned Lima and, out of fear of Lima and his many supporters, Neroos banished his brother.

Lima returned to gather his followers, and they fought in his name. The followers of Lima took the kingdom. But they knew that Neroos and his people would grow strong in the mountains. To keep peace and ensure that war would not come from the Neroos, the people of Lima were forced to continually fight the Neroos and keep them at bay.

We must not allow the Neroos to commit such injustice again! Tonight, the blood of the Neroos at Gidionhi will atone for the sins of their fathers.

Wear your robe, Kalif. You walk with us when you wear it. You will never again be without a brother.

Depart: Third watch

Position: Flanking

Placement: Southeast corner of Gidionhi

Route: Southern pass

You must return to this room before the sands run out. You will memorize these instructions, and then burn them.

Your brothers,
The Triumvirate

Kalif burned with . . . what? Indignation? Anger? Fear? He was familiar with the story of Lima and Neroos, but it was a story from his childhood. A fable. And yet, connected with the losses that he had endured, losses which were so blatantly and completely exposed, Kalif could only describe his emotions as burning.

Burn. Burn the instructions. Burn them into his mind. Burn them so as to remove all evidence that he was ever here. That would explain the haze.

Touching the folded paper to a flame, Kalif examined the hourglass. It stood two feet tall on a wooden table that bespoke a former glory but was now stained with wax and forgotten years. The glass was encased in tarnished bronze ends connected by three ornate spindles. The spindles featured a feather, a panther, and a sword, all holding the sands of time in place.

The bronze was spotted and old, but in some places the scratches showed a brilliant color beneath the years. The tarnish just needed to be pulled away. Scratched. Scrubbed. Scarred. Hurt, even. *But it would for the better,* Kalif decided as he looked at it. *Maybe that would be the only way for it to shine.* But even now, a few spots where the once brilliant bronze were quickly obscured by the smoke and flame of his letter, now all but completely gone. Kalif found himself regretting having been the one to tarnish it further.

The glass itself did not show the effects of the time that it let slip through its two bulbous parts. Kalif marveled at how smooth the surface appeared, despite how old it surely had to be. The sand within it was not the white sand of Ombrar. It was a dark sand, like that of Hunan or Kanii, cities to the south.

Chairs had been emptied by the previous group—the first watch, as far as Kalif could tell—but there was only one chair with a robe draped across it. He crossed the room and put on the robe, searching for a pocket or some sign of when the third watch would leave. Thirty chairs. Ten of them empty. The first watch had departed.

Kalif noticed the light in the room flicker and go dim. Turning, he saw the second candle had gone out, and another group of men stood to leave. The third candle was not far behind.

Kalif forced his mind to be still. He had done nothing but absorb the scenario as if he were a spectator. But tonight he would far more than a spectator or observer. Tonight was for vengeance. For justice. Kalif sat in his chair, clothed in the night, and stared as the sands of the hourglass counted down the hours until he would claim his peace.

~~~~~

WHAT LIES IN THE DARK

The last candle was flickering, its wick disappearing into a pool of wax. It was almost time.

Drawing his cape more tightly around his shoulders, Kalif did not move his eyes from the flame. He sensed something drawing near. Not just the time to leave. Not just the personal war he was about to wage on the Neroos. Something more—as if he were about to be baptized by the darkness that the failing candle would bring, and he wanted to see every moment of it as it came.

The nervous and anxious sounds of swords clanking and arrows shuffling in quivers began to fill the room as the third watch prepared to depart. There, a little flicker. A shudder in the flame. And out. The tip of the candle glowed orange until it fell into the wax, and all went black. The darkness itself moved with the third watch as the men, shrouded in cloaks and secrecy, stood and moved as one toward the door.

Kalif was one of the last to leave the room. As each man passed the door, he quietly whispered something brief, the first time Kalif had heard anyone speak that night. "Garder." "Halan." "Yurie." Names, Kalif realized. Names of all those that had been lost. Lost to the Neroos. Lost to the animals that disturbed their peace. Tonight, Kalif would have peace. "Loria," he whispered as he crossed the threshold and entered a hallway that echoed with footsteps, weapons, and memories.

After traveling a considerable distance, their hands carefully placed against the wall in the deep darkness, the band of marauders stopped suddenly at the end of the hallway, their way barred by a closed door. The men waited patiently. Expectantly. The Triumvirate was wise. They knew when the time would come.

"Remember," boomed a voice within the hallway. "Remember those whom you have lost. Remember the treachery of the dog Neroos. Remember who has caused so much suffering. You have two hours to travel, two hours to fight, and three hours to return. Gidionhi has now scratched out of *our lands* a trove of precious jewels. Keep whatever you find. But if you are late, you will have to buy back your entry, either with jewels or blood. Now, go. Avenge your families."

And with that, the door opened into the deep twilight of a fast-fading sun. After so much darkness, however, Kalif's eyes were very well adjusted, and he was ready to travel by the light of the night.

~~~~~

The horses that Chism had acquired for tonight's activities would serve them well. The bright moon would allow him and his travelling companion to move through wild country with fair enough ease without being detected.

Chism almost missed the third group as they exited the tunnel in the near dark. How Rierdan knew that Kalif would be in the third group was beyond what Chism's understanding. But Rierdan's certainty meant that Chism could do nothing but trust his companion in this, and distrust him in everything else. Even so, Chism knew that he was operating outside of the constraints that his rank afforded him, and for that, he had no choice but to accept his mysterious partner.

"There he is," Rierdan said. "fourth from the front."

Chism counted the men exiting the well-concealed tunnel. The fourth man from the front bore a familiar gait, altogether unmistakable as his brother. His only family. And, tonight, his prey.

The band of marauders began to move very rapidly toward the east. It was not simply the prospect of fouling the marauders' plans that interested Chism. He needed to keep his brother alive, and that meant that he needed to track him. Carefully.

Patience, Chism, he told himself. *Patience.*

CHAPTER 6:
PROMISES TO KEEP

The moon was bright. Almost vindictively so, as if it were intent to reveal the marauders' movements. From time to time, it would pull the clouds over its face in...what? Anticipation of the attack? Shame of Chism's deception? Neither of them, Chism decided. The gods had ceased caring a long time ago.

Chism and Rierdan carefully marked the passage of Kalif's band. Three groups of ten men had left through the tunnel. Rierdan promised Chism that the third group was the last. The marauders worked in groups of three. Always three. The tunnel, which originated within the walls of Ombrar City, ran a full two miles below the city wall and past the glades before exiting the mouth of the canyon pass. Through that pass, the marauders could access any of five Neroos cities in less than a week.

Chism only knew what every other Lima in Ombrar knew of the marauders—they were a society unto themselves that thrived on its secrecy. No one knew how many marauders there actually were. Not even the marauders knew their numbers. They received messages dictating a place and time to meet, and there they would receive the target. All were to remain entirely secret. To speak of them was death.

But Rierdan's knowledge of the marauders and their Triumvirate was not just profound. It was intimate. As intimate as was his hate. That was why Rierdan was such a valuable companion tonight. Chism had to get to his brother in the chaos, extract him from the battle, and hide him—and above all, leave evidence to make the Triumvirate think he was dead. And if Chism and Rierdan had to kill a few marauders to get to him, then so be it.

Of course, that left the question of Gala. And of Chism's own standing in the army. If Chism were to keep his brother alive, then he would have to abandon his post. Desert the army. He would have to find a way to get to Gala and bring her with them. Kalif would have to be kept far away from Ombrar. Even the surrounding cities would have connections to the marauders there. Chism began to feel hopeless as the ramifications of his plan multiplied like starfish—the more he tried to dissect them, the more they continued to grow.

The wind picked up from the east, blowing west down the canyon toward the sea. Chism and Rierdan could now safely ride their horses without any fear of the marauders hearing them.

"Why is he so important to you?" Rierdan asked.

"Does it really matter?"

"I don't like going into a fight with someone whose resolve may be questioned," Rierdan said bluntly.

Chism did not even bother to turn or deign the slight worthy of more than a mere snort. "He's family, Rierdan. I have to protect him. Even from himself."

"He does a pretty fine job of protecting himself on fringe. He's not your problem."

"I have a hard time believing that you'd rather be back in the city sleeping soundly in your bed, Rierdan. You want to tell me where this interrogation is coming from?"

"No, I don't." Rierdan retorted. "But like I said, the Neroos will take care of the problem for you. I know where my strength is. Where's yours?"

My strength? Chism thought. *You aren't the only one who has been to hell and back, Rierdan.* "I have promises to keep," he said simply.

Keep this family, Chism could hear his father's voice. *Do what you have to. Anything at all. But stay together. Promise me, Chism.* When he and his brother were starving, unable to support themselves and their sister, Chism took a post in the army. And life was good. Or good enough. There was food on the table, and they had extricated themselves from the High Tide District.

The High Tide District had an official name, but no one knew what it was. On the south side of the city, the High Tide District ran straight to the edge of the sand. If anyone needed any services—especially those that they preferred the patrols not know about—then the High Tide District was the place to find them. From opiates to women, assassins to stolen wares, the High Tide District could provide.

Even in the dead of night, Chism still fumed at how the men in the District would look at Loria any time they went outside. After they lost their father, the three orphans had nowhere to go but to the streets. Chism was able to find work unloading cargo, and he could only afford to house his brother and sister in the lowest apartments then. The work was brutal, and Chism developed incredible strength in the space of a few short months.

It had been such a difficult time. Gray, as Chism remembered it. Gray skies against a gray winter sea. Gray eyes of children longing for their parents, knowing they would never see them again. It was time for a change of scenery, so Chism took his two siblings to the market. Loria was only eight years old the day Chism took her and Kalif to get some sweet papueia fruit. As the three siblings walked back home, Chism and Kalif talked and played together. Loria had fallen behind as she looked at the wares and ate her fruit.

It was not even a cry. Only a small yelp. Chism turned to see the fruit on the ground as the only sign that Loria had been near them at all. Chism cried out and dashed down the nearest alley to see two men struggling to tame the now-gagged Loria. Chism did not pause to think as he rushed at the two men. He grabbed the first by the head and drove his knee into the man's face. The man fell to the ground and did not move. Kalif came from behind and grabbed Loria, holding her close. The second man tried to run. Chism caught him a few yards later and smashed his head against the stone wall. Then he swung the man back by the neck and hit his head against the wall again. And again. And again.

The next day, Chism enlisted in the army. A simple soldier's pay would not keep him and his two siblings away from High Tide, but different specializations brought higher pay. A typical peace soldier—little more than a street soldier who patrolled Ombrar to make citizens think twice about stealing—only earned 15 *tregara* per day. A gate and wall soldier was trained for combat but unlikely to see any, unless the army was called up for an all-out assault; a gate soldier earned only 18 *tregara* per day. Fringe soldiers received considerably more—25 *tregara* per day—and the military always had openings for fringe soldiers. Openings and funerals. Espion soldiers earned the most money at 29 *tregara* per day, but Chism did not have the language skill to fully master the Neroos dialect. He left school early to work, and his formal education had never picked up since. *Keep this family,* his father had told him. *Do what you have to.* So he did. Chism held the longest service in Ombrar military history as a fringe soldier. Every other soldier had transferred to another position or died.

Chism had laughed at the irony—what had life come to that facing death every day was the only way to stay alive? But maybe that was not as unique a situation as he used to think.

When Kalif was of age, he was only too happy to quit his education and enlist in the military like his older brother. But Kalif's motives were different, Chism remembered. Chism had a responsibility and did what was necessary. Kalif had a vendetta and needed the skills to satisfy it. Kalif decided to forego a promising career with Gala's uncle in the fishing industry—at one point, Kalif had been offered to make 40 *tregara* per day just to start—to pursue a career in the military. But it was not a career Kalif was interested in pursuing—it was the Neroos. The Neroos and his vendetta. Chism had become a corporal by that point, and requested that his brother be placed in his platoon. He could deal with Kalif's insubordinations. He could not deal with Kalif being in danger under anyone else's command.

Kalif would often decide that a traveling Neroos who came too close or even children whom Kalif deemed spies posed too much of a threat. And, like a one-man judge, jury, and executioner, Kalif had once decided to protect Ombrar from the imminent danger that four ten-year-old boys posed to the city. Chism saw his attack just in time to stop him.

Never had Chism become so violently angry. The platoon stood in wonder as the brothers swung swords at each other, parrying, attacking, counter-attacking, and eventually throwing all weapons away and throwing punches. Some of the platoon finally came to pull the two apart. As they distracted Kalif, Chism picked up his sword and brought the pommel down with incredible force on his brother's head.

"Have you learned nothing about the Neroos?" Kalif had yelled as they fought. "They will do anything! Stop at nothing! They aren't like you, Chism. They don't have these sympathies like you do. You need to wake up!"

But Chism had woken up. He had seen that day what his brother was capable of. And Chism wondered then not if, but when, he would lose his brother. And though Chism put Kalif through every grueling task he could think of for his insubordination, he knew that nothing would change.

Picking off the occasional Neroos was not enough for Kalif. The military applauded it. Chism ached over it. For every Neroos that Kalif could find and kill, there were two more waiting for his blade, as he saw it. Chism watched his brother slip away into his past as he mourned his father and mother even more with every throat he cut. Gala had provided solace for a time; but as Chism discovered only earlier tonight, she didn't temper the fire that consumed Kalif—she fueled it.

And then came the promotion. The higher pay. The post of his choice. All for his silence about what Kalif was capable of, and what he had once stopped his brother from doing. *Keep this family.* With his promotion and extra favors for his complicity, Chism chose to stay exactly where he was. On the fringe. Every day that he served on the fringe was one less day that someone else had to. *Keep this family.* Chism got the glory, and Kalif got a headache. And Kalif burned over it.

When Loria was killed—Chism knew as well as anyone that she was murdered, but he had to try to convince Kalif otherwise— Chism knew that though he would only bury one sibling, he had effectively lost both of them. He had promised his father that he would keep this family. Chism had to remind himself that his brother was not truly lost until he was dead. As long as there was breath in Kalif's body, Chism would hope for him. Protect him. Keep him. Just as he had promised.

"I always keep my promises," Chism found himself muttering aloud to his father. Rierdan supposed that Chism was speaking to him.

"I know you do, soldier. You're not like the rest of them, you know." Rierdan remarked.

"Look who's talking."

"I never tried to fit in. But you…I never thought you'd keep your mouth shut just for a little raise, lieutenant."

Chism sneered again at the title. "Like I said. I have promises to keep."

Sitting on his horse at the mouth of the canyon, watching the marauders move skillfully through the night, Chism's mind wandered again to thoughts darker than the night. Chism had not kept his promise to his father. Loria was dead. Despite everything he had done, he had failed. But he would not fail his father again. He would keep what was left of his family safe. No matter what.

Chism and Rierdan had lost track of the first two bands. They had continued east until the two men could no longer see their movement. Many of the marauders were skilled, but some were clumsy. They left traces, making it easy for Chism and Rierdan to find any evidence they would need.

After having passed Chism and Rierdan's position by a quarter mile, Kalif's group halted. By the light of the moon, Chism saw a small shudder of movement pass through the group. He imagined the hand signals that must be passing from man to man. The band turned and headed due north at nearly a dead run.

North. North to Gidionhi. Where Chism's father died. And now, Kalif was going back. Suddenly Chism understood—this was not about Loria alone. It was about avenging their father. It was about years of loneliness and solitude, all focused on the Neroos. And because Gidionhi was only a few miles away, Kalif would be there in a matter of hours.

Rierdan uttered an oath. "Chism, it's Gidionhi." For the first time, Rierdan sounded panicked.

"We have to move. Now!" And with that, the two men turned their horses, picked their way quickly to the road, and sped off recklessly through shadow and moonlight.

~~~~~

Chism and Rierdan were sure that they had out-distanced Kalif and his group, but the rest of the marauders had a significant head start. The horses were breathing heavily and a thick layer of foam was gathering on their backs from the sweat and strain of their unending run. Still, Chism and Rierdan pushed them onward through the night. The moon appeared from time to time to light the way, giving the two men greater cause to spur their horses on all the faster.

Rierdan remarked how Chism's horse had begun to lag. No matter how much Chism dug his heels into his horse, the animal simply had less to give with every stride. The opportunity was all too perfect for Rierdan—Chism was not the only one with plans tonight.

Rierdan then found his next opportunity: a pothole in the road. Feeling a twinge of guilt and pity toward the animal that bore him so well, Rierdan quickly pulled the horse to one side where it buried its foot in the cavity. With a horrendous snap and the scream of an animal whose end had come too quickly, the horse broke its kneecap and sent the splintered bone through the too-thin skin.

Rierdan braced himself as he was propelled from the horse's back, landing with a hard crunch on his side, the momentum propelling him down the road in a painful roll. He finally came to a stop and lay prone as he focused on each part of his body. He was covered in bruises, but his legs seemed to be in perfect working order. He had disentangled his feet from the stirrups before guiding the horse into the pothole so as to avoid twisting an ankle. Each breath came with great difficulty, and he supposed that he had broken more than one rib. Even with the battle that was likely to occur tonight, a few cracked ribs and a dead horse would be worth the trouble.

He picked himself up, feeling the soreness that threatened to tighten up in his body later tonight. His horse was screaming, kicking its hind legs as it lay on its one good foreleg. Rierdan knelt beside the horse's head as he heard Chism approaching through the dark.

"I'm sorry," Rierdan whispered. Then carefully placing his knife so as to avoid the spray of hot blood, he quickly drew the blade across the horse's neck. The horse twitched momentarily and settled quietly into the night.

"What happened?" Chism asked as his horse danced and turned at the sight and smell of death.

"Fouled up on a hole. Didn't see the thing in this accursed darkness." Rierdan said roughly. "Did you plan to get to Gidionhi tonight? What the devil do you think you're doing, sauntering in at a pace like that?"

"I'm not the one who just cut his ride's throat," Chism said, plainly, "though it may come to that if I push this animal any harder."

"One way or another, looks like we're riding tandem."

Chism obviously did not like it, but Rierdan noted to himself that Chism was likely more frustrated by the setback than the affront that Rierdan had thrown at him. *Odd*, Rierdan thought. *Very odd. Why should he care to get there before the Lima, so long as he gets his idiot brother?*

Rierdan would have also preferred not to slow their progress, but the sacrifice was necessary. Chism could not know his purpose. For as blunt and rough as Rierdan chose to be with his traveling companion, Rierdan somehow felt that he travelled with a good man. Rierdan had wondered more than once that night if it were the first time he ever thought such a kind thing toward a Lima. *Good man or not,* Rierdan told himself as he climbed up behind Chism, *he's still a Lima. And some things are simply for his own good.*

For the second time that day, Chism questioned the wisdom of having Rierdan placed squarely behind him. Gritting his teeth against the possibilities, Chism pressed on for another two hours before reaching Gidionhi.

"Stick to the plan," Chism said as they reached the village. "We both want to make it out of this alive."

Rierdan ignored Chism's outstretched hand to help him off of the horse. Lighting from the animal, Rierdan set off for the village as Chism rode to the northeast section of the city to await his companion.

The plan, as Chism and Rierdan had outlined it, was simple: Rierdan would raise the alarm to warn Gidionhi of the approaching army. If the Neroos militia could hold its strength against the Lima, then the marauders would likely retreat before the third wave—Kalif's wave—was sent in. In the confusion of the retreat, Rierdan and Chism would find Kalif and fake his death. Chism and Kalif would take the horses and disappear—a critical element that now would have to be altered.

But the plan involved the death of potentially hundreds of Lima. Though not a man to be overly concerned for the welfare of the Lima, Rierdan was taken aback by how simply and easily Chism had reached his conclusion to sacrifice all of those Lima for the sake of saving his brother. Rierdan had no use for Kalif, though he could not help but admire Chism's willingness to do what he felt was necessary. As one with ulterior motives himself, Rierdan could not decide how he might factor into Chism's undisclosed plans. He really did not care, either, so long as he did not become a necessary loss in the night's fray.

Rierdan's own plan was more complicated: his first objective had become to protect the Neroos from a similar attack that he had endured so many years ago. But his second objective was almost as important: he needed to capture and interrogate a marauder and extract any information he may have about Triumvirate. And he needed Chism to single out just such a prisoner—especially if that prisoner were Kalif, who seemed to have had a personal invitation to come. Someone like that could have information that Rierdan wanted, and he would stop at nothing—not even deluding Chism in his quest to save his brother—to get it. Escaping on horses would not be an option. *Chism would now have to reorganize his plan*, Rierdan thought, *and therein make a mistake. I get the only horse left, and Kalif gets a knife in the back.*

Rierdan raced to the first line of houses and began pounding on doors while Chism carefully rode off to the rendezvous point. Rierdan could not cry out to the entire village for fear of alerting the first band of marauders that was likely in the vicinity, but he could alert the first line of doors and tell them to prepare for the attack.

Though Rierdan had spent years among the Lima, his Neroos dialect was flawless, and the dark of the night hid his decidedly Lima garments. So when he came pounding on the first few doors he approached, no one questioned his origin or his purpose as he began to alert the village to the approaching army of marauders. Rierdan knew far too well that the memory of a similar night long ago had not grown cold in the years since.

The men and boys of the village and the accompanying militia were more efficient than even Rierdan had anticipated. Silent signals were relayed up and down the streets as families along the edge of the village were evacuated and the militia began forming ranks. He could see weaponry appearing readily, women and children quickly and silently beginning to move, and squadrons forming as they tried to anticipate the direction of the attack.

Rierdan had long ago stopped hoping in any sense of victory. He had stopped winning battles when he had started losing friends. Nothing else seemed to matter after that. But no cynicism or nostalgia could make him deny that this village was prepared for a fight, no matter the outcome.

Rierdan melted into the dark and returned to the area agreed upon. He had his plans. They were working. And though his heart began to stir in him, telling him to stay and fight with these villagers, it was not time to deviate. Not yet.

~~~~~

Kalif's blood boiled from the stories of injustice against the Great Father, Lima, and his descendants. He ached at the loss of his sister, his father, and his mother. And his heart beat faster for fear of dying. But he had to do this. For them. If he lived, then he could put all of this behind him. He could start again with Gala. He could let it all go, knowing that these dogs, the Neroos, would suffer as he had suffered. After tonight, the balance would be restored and the debt owed him by the Neroos would be paid. His longing for justice pulled him inexorably onward. He ached to run into the fray but needed his group leader to take them to their assigned position for battle.

His was group three. All of the houses where the marauders had met back in Ombrar had three groups, though each house varied in size. Group one from each house was charged with initiation and intimidation. Get the Neroos scared. Group two was charged with battle—take out their defenses and weaken the ranks. Group three's responsibility was purely attrition. After groups one and two broke their ranks and burned their homes, group three would break their souls. Group three would make them pay.

As far as every marauder was concerned, there were only four people that mattered in this army: the three members of the Triumvirate, and himself. He did not need to concern himself with trusting his companions. Every man standing in that forest was present for a reason, and that reason would drive him.

The run was brutal. Though Kalif was in excellent form, having trained as a fringe soldier for the most perilous circumstances, he began to ache. They were allowed only two breaks during their run. They had a matter of hours to reach Gidionhi, rest, fight, and return to Ombrar before the sun came up. It must always be before the sun came up. The light of day could never know their acts. And so they ran hard, and they ran fast.

As Kalif's platoon slowed to a halt, each man leaning against a tree or collapsing to the ground, Kalif wondered where they had come. All was dark, and their efforts at silence had long since given way to aching muscles and fatigue. Kalif wet his mouth with a brief drink from a leather flask he carried. He estimated that midnight had come, though the mountains were often darker than his coast. He stood with his fingers interlaced behind his head, always within reach of the dagger on his shoulder and with quick access to the sword on his hip. And he waited.

Far off to his right, Kalif spotted a bright orange flame flicker in the thick forest. He marked the steady pace of that flame. Pausing for a moment to the northeast of his position, the flame began to multiply into several dozen bright points in the night. Buildings made of wood and thatched roofs stood out in the dancing flames of newly lit torches. And that was when Kalif realized that they were not pausing for a break. They had arrived.

A horn within the city began to blow. The bright flames of the torches soared into the air and landed on straw and wood rooftops, instantly igniting a blaze.

It had begun.

~~~~~

"How did it go?" Chism asked in the dark.

"Those Lima are going to have a surprise on their hands."

"'Those Lima.' Not 'those marauders.' Not even 'those *puntas*,'" Chism said, using the word for gutter, a pejorative term in Lima culture. "When were you going to tell me, Rierdan, that you're Neroos?"

"Chism, I came with you. That doesn't mean I came to help you. Don't make me kill you."

"If I thought you were concerned for me or my purposes, I would not have asked you to come," Chism said. "I came to you because of your own prejudices. You know that I am no friend of the military. My loyalty to the Lima wanes every day. You would not have come if you did not know that I could kill these men."

Rierdan chuckled. "This isn't about which side you're killing, Chism. This is about some twisted sense of repentance, isn't it? You've already got blood on your hands. Do you think killing Lima will even out the balance for the Neroos you've killed?"

Chism could not decide if Rierdan was mocking his Lima sense of right and wrong. Nor could Chism decide if he disdained his own heritage or simply what his people had come to be. He finally said, "I came do what is right."

"What is right! It would have been *right* for you to stop your brother with a knife in his back a long time ago. But you appease your own sense of duty and righteousness by allowing him to live, to be here, to kill innocent people before you stop him or bring him to face his actions."

Chism cocked an eyebrow at Rierdan's mood. But he was not sour, Chism knew. He was simply indignant.

"How long have you been away from your people, Rierdan?"

"Too long," he said with a hollowness that reverberated from his heart.

"Why?"

"To find her. And then to avenge her."

Hiding out in the military. Disguising himself in plain sight. From his vantage point as a Lima mercenary, Rierdan had a panorama of Ombrar society and government. No one could hide from him when he was so well concealed. Chism could not help but smile at his Neroos companion's brilliance.

"Did you?" Chism queried. "Did you avenge her?"

"In a manner of speaking."

"And this, tonight. Is this to protect Gidionhi or to kill Lima?"

Rierdan's rare smile played out across his face. "Is this to protect your brother, or to kill Lima?"

"Perhaps it doesn't matter. We'll probably end up dead by dawn, anyway," Chism said wryly. "Dead and at peace."

"Peace. If peace were in death, we would not be so afraid of it."

"How can you be sure?"

"Because you haven't fallen on your own sword yet, my Lima companion. And if killing our enemies filled the void, then we—a Neroos and a Lima—would have killed each other by now."

"That's a nice sentiment coming from Ombrar's most famous assassin. Then how do you fill the void? How do you find peace?"

"Justice," he said with the same hollowness. Chism wondered if Rierdan truly believed that.

In the distance, pinpricks of light soared through the air. A horn began to blow. In a matter of moments, the night was ablaze.

"It has begun," Rierdan said.

"For peace," Chism said grimly.

"For justice," Rierdan replied.

The two men left the horse tethered to a tree, and crept away into the woods from the east. It was time to hunt the marauders.

CHAPTER 7:
A FIRE WILL BURN

Night. One of Kalif's few memories of his mother was her stories about night. She would tell him that night falls when the gods close their eyes to rest. But as the flames and screams of Gidionhi rose higher and higher, Kalif knew that he and the marauders no longer needed the gods to create light. They would bring light to the world when and where they pleased.

The flames danced and swirled from one house to another in the first of many macabre and brutal dances of the night. For the first time, Kalif could see into the distance, and he was astounded at the sight: no fewer than two hundred marauders stood on the outskirts of the village as another fifty men started fires and disrupted the ranks before the opposing militia could form. The trees stopped the light only a few yards in, but Kalif imagined the hordes of marauders that stood waiting for their chance.

"Take a seat, gentlemen," one man from Kalif's group said.

"There will be more than enough left for us," said another.

"When the women and children start running, we'll be here," a third spoke.

The Neroos women and children. Yes, they would pay, just as Kalif's mother had paid. Just as his sister had paid. The Neroos dogs owed him a debt. Oh, they would pay. But women and children were not why he had come.

"So that's it, then?" Kalif spoke loudly to mask the sound of his sword coming from its sheath. "The grand and marvelous Triumvirate sent us packing all the way out here to slit the throats of a few girls and steal their jewels?"

"Do not disrespect the Triumvirate!" The response was immediate and vehement. Kalif grinned at his own cleverness for so easily touching a nerve.

Kalif had spent enough time as a fringe soldier to hear danger without seeing it. A sword rasped quickly out of its sheath—a rather short sword, Kalif knew from the sound, but longer than a dagger—and he heard it humming toward him high in the air, flashing in the growing flames of the village. He quickly brought his sword up with his left hand to parry, shocking his attacker with his capacity to defend himself, even in the deep night. Even as Kalif parried with his left arm, he reached back with his right hand to draw his knife from its place on his shoulder and quickly sliced a deep gash in his attacker's raised arm where a major artery ran. He neither knew nor cared if he might have hit it.

"I didn't come here to clean up after the others. The Triumvirate promised blood, and I will have it!" Kalif retorted.

The rest of the company chose not to attack while the first man sought to bandage his arm, swearing oaths at Kalif all the while. Either the rest of the company was afraid, or they simply agreed with him, Kalif thought smugly.

"Yes," said one that had not yet spoken. "And Lima blood apparently serves as well as Neroos blood to satisfy your thirst."

Kalif squirmed slightly at the rebuke. "I will defend myself against whoever—or whatever," he spat as he spoke of the Neroos, "Stands in my way."

"Patience," the new speaker said. "The Triumvirate does not break a promise."

Kalif felt his head suddenly jerked back as a knife was pressed roughly to his throat, drawing a deep line of blood before even he could react.

"So when I swear that I will kill you if you dare cross us again, Kalif," a voice whispered in his ear, emphasizing his supposedly unknown name amongst his comrades, "I mean it."

Two swift strikes to his kidneys dropped him to the ground where the company left him to pick himself up.

The horn within the village was sharply cut off. A higher, shrill horn sounded from the tree line, and the woods exploded in an unearthly scream. The two hundred men broke rank and ran directly into the village. Kalif could see man after man fall as arrows flew from within the village. But a few arrows would not stop the marauders, he knew. Nothing could stop them with such a righteous cause spurring them onward.

The shrill sound of a Lima horn signaled the third group. Even from his knees, Kalif shared a glance with the rest of his company. It was too early. The battle was not going according to plan. With a grin of anticipation, Kalif joined his group as they left the forest and waded into the blood.

~~~~~

Rayanna woke with a sudden start. The fireplace still burned brightly, casting dancing shadows across the walls. If the fire was still bright, then the others could not have been asleep long. Rayanna felt uneasy. Tense. As if she had been having her nightmare again. But she had not even been dreaming about that night six years ago. There had been something calm in her as she slept. As if the darkness had gone away when she came to realize all that her mother had truly been doing for so long. So why this unease?

That was when she heard the horn begin calling again. Mixed with the sound of the horn was the shrill cry of a woman, followed by a hundred Lima voices screaming for blood. The peaceful silence of the night had been shattered.

And this time it wasn't a dream.

"Oh no," she groaned, slipping off the bed. As she moved, she realized that her mother had been beside her. She had slept so peacefully that she hadn't even noticed that her mother had been holding her, protecting her all night. But now the entire house was awake. The horn was cut off mid-breath.

"Oh no!" she repeated as she ran toward the door. The sounds of battle were close. Very close. She had to see.

"Rayanna!" Aria called out. Just as Rayanna threw the latch off the door, Aria grabbed her firmly by the shoulder, pulled her back in, and held her closely before Rayanna could get the door open. "Don't go there, Rayanna. Don't look. You don't need to see this," she whispered as Rayanna thrashed about, trying to get loose.

Rayanna's body quivered as her nightmare became real again just outside the front door. But this time, they could not hurt her like before. This time, her father and older brothers were already dead. She was prepared for this. She had been preparing for this every night for six years. Rayanna realized that though she trembled, she had no fear of the attack that was quickly approaching her door. Fear lived in the unknown. But there was nothing about tonight—nothing—that was not already etched in her past, leaving the callouses and scars that had come to define Rayanna. But that did not make it easy. Rayanna forced herself to breathe slowly and looked her mother directly in the eye. "What can I do to help?"

"Thank you," Aria said, holding Rayanna's shoulders for an extra moment. "We have to hide," Aria said.

"What happened to the evacuation?"

"Perhaps they couldn't get to us in time."

"If we leave, they won't find us—" Rayanna began.

"No. No, we won't leave. We're no safer out there than in here. But they have to think that there's nothing left here. Brego, Karrh," Aria addressed the two boys as they sat, wide awake, wondering how to handle this situation. "I need you to start breaking everything in this house."

The two boys looked more stunned at their mother's request than by the horn blowing, the growing sounds of violence, and the increasing light of homes that were ablaze.

Aria walked over to the woodpile, picked up a piece of wood, and threw it at her chair in its corner. The back of the chair splintered when the log struck it. "I mean it! They can't know that we're here! They have to think we have already been attacked, so move!"

Rayanna felt empowered by this new purpose. Walking to the fireplace, she grabbed the flour from the mantelpiece and threw it, leaving a blast radius on the wall and putting a layer of flour over everything.

"Good, Rayanna! They have to think this house has already been ransacked! They have to think there is nothing left here."

The two boys together picked up the rocking chair and threw it across the room. Then they walked over to the table and upended it together. Dishes flew and shattered, wooden slats in the windows splintered, and the wood from the fireplace was scattered, plunging the house into darkness.

The sounds of battle were quickly approaching.

"Brego, Karrh, help me with the bed," Aria said. Rayanna watched her in wonder. For how long had her mother really been with them, and she had no idea? For how long had her mother been reaching out to her, but she had not been ready?

Aria, Brego, and Karrh upended the bed next to the half-demolished woodpile that sat next to the fireplace. The result was a heavily shadowed and protected corner, right where the heavy back door was located.

A Fire Will Burn

"Children, I want you to hide together in that corner. If someone comes, do not make a noise. You will be safe here."

"*Mamera*," Rayanna said, speaking the word for "mother" for the first time in years. "Please…please stay safe!" *I need you*, Rayanna thought.

"I will," Aria said gravely. "I am going to do what I should have done years ago. I am going to protect you."

The battle was now well at hand, raging on all sides of them. Rayanna's blood chilled as she heard the whooping screams of Lima battle cries.

"Keep them safe, *amora*," Aria said to Rayanna. This time, Rayanna did not flinch at the word. "If the worst happens and you cannot stay here, take them out the back way and lead them to the old city where we used to hide."

For so long, Rayanna had been sure that death would have been the preferable fate compared to what her mother had experienced. But now that her mother had returned from her land of memories and shadows, Rayanna saw how much she still needed and admired her mother's strength.

"I will," Rayanna promised.

"I know you will," Aria said. The voices and yelling were right outside. "Shh! No more speaking," Aria whispered.

Then Aria stooped, picked up a knife, and crouched by the front door as men fought and died just on the other side of it. Rayanna looked quizzically at her mother, and mouthed, *Come over here!* But Aria only shook her head. Rayanna took one of their knives and sat against the back door. This time, Brego and Karrh would not sleep. They would watch to the end.

And the end seemed close. They could not see the battle. But they knew one thing: the Neroos outside their door were losing.

~~~~~

Find him. Hide him. Keep this family! The words echoed again and again as Chism and Rierdan stole quietly through the woods. Chism's considerable experience as a fringe soldier had taught him to move in this terrain, but he was not prepared for how silently, so silently, Rierdan moved. Chism thought for a moment that even Rierdan's shadow managed to make more noise than his feet.

The marauders were not so adept.

"He was in the third company," Rierdan quietly reminded Chism. "Only the first two have gone. He's still in the woods."

"How much time until he enters the fight?"

"Depends on the fight."

Wonderful, Chism thought. *I'm hunting a Lima in a horde of Lima that is constantly moving. This isn't finding a needle in a haystack—this is finding a particular piece of straw in a haystack in a windstorm!*

Chism's experience was almost entirely in guerrilla tactics. Track your prey. Assess the situation from afar. Attack when least suspected. His role as a fringe soldier had kept him away from the mass battles. When what was left of the infantry would return from a war or localized battle, the Senate would declare the might of the Lima and encourage every young man to enlist. And the young men would line up, completely unwitting of why the army can now accept such an influx. At their induction, they would finally see the surviving soldiers' dead eyes. The eyes of a man who buried his friend. His brother. His father. Not knowing how long it would be until they too saw the world through dead eyes. All for valor.

Valor and bravery. That was the official reason that Chism had merited his promotion. But everyone knew that "valor and bravery" was tantamount to doing a particular favor to someone in the government—and burying the body after the favor was done. But there was no way for Chism to clarify, to exonerate himself from the judgmental looks of his fellow soldiers or from the loathing in his own heart.

Even as he picked his way through a battlefield, Chism remembered the specific events that brought him to this point.

A Fire Will Burn

Kalif lived on the second floor of a yellow cement building. The noises of the street would have drowned out any noise from within any apartment on the ground floor, but ascending the short distance to the second floor, even with its wooden boardwalk, gave a person peace from the sound of society. A second-floor apartment was prime real estate in Ombrar, and not something that most soldiers could afford. Chism knew that Kalif could not afford it, and though he sometimes wondered what Kalif had done to "earn" such a favor from someone in the government, he knew that he never wanted to know.

"Who is it this time?" Chism heard Kalif say as he approached Kalif's door. A heavy curtain blocked the windows out. Kalif and his guest must have been together for some time, Chism reasoned, because their voices had the quality of being kept low, but the two had become comfortable in their supposed solitude and were no longer as vigilant about how loud they spoke.

"You always ask," a deep, mature voice responded. The articulation was familiar to Chism, but he could not place it. "You are good at what you do, Kalif. But there are always more soldiers. I only need you if you are willing to do your part."

It was a thinly veiled threat. Chism knew that this had to be somebody in the government. If the government did not need you, then the government would simply get rid of you.

"And I always find out," Kalif responded. "Look, either you tell me now or I see the face before I slit their throat, anyway. What difference does it make?"

"This situation is...delicate." The man chose his words carefully. "Consider it a warning arrow to someone who stands in my way."

Kalif was silent for a moment. "How many?" He asked surgically.

"Three," came the response.

"Three is a lot to handle. Sounds like the price may go up."

"How much?"

"I want my record completely gone. Not just a few infractions wiped off the bottom of the list. I want to be free. And if you think I'm sticking my neck out to get three at one time for anything less, then you're not just greedy. You're crazy."

"If it were three men, then yes, I would understand that."

"You want me to kill women?" Kalif sneered.

"No. Not women."

Chism's eyes flew wide. He knew that Kalif had committed some serious crimes, but had he gone this far? Could Kalif really attack children? *Lima* children?

"Details, Senator," Kalif said without masking his growing impatience.

Caught between being openly disrespected and knowing that he was dealing with a man who was obviously good at killing people and covering it up, the Senator had no response beyond clearing his throat. Regaining composure, he said in a voice almost too quiet for Chism to hear, "Senator Nori is standing in my way on a certain matter. I will arrange for his three children, two boys and a girl ages fifteen, twelve, and ten, to be three miles northeast of the outer wall tomorrow in the late afternoon. I would be...ah...severely disappointed if anything should happen."

After a considerable pause, Kalif said, "Three is still three. After this, I demand to be released of all charges against me. And I want something in my pocket."

"You will be well compensated," the man said, his pleasure at Kalif's compliance evident in his voice.

"Hey," Kalif called out as if the man had moved away from him. "Half now."

"You are done making demands," the senator said coldly. "Perform, and you will be...compensated."

Footsteps approached the door, and Chism darted down the boardwalk and turned the corner as it opened. The man's footsteps approached Chism, who did his best to whittle away nonchalantly at a piece of wood he kept stored in his pouch, carefully eyeing the senator. But the man was cloaked and hooded. He would not be able to identify his brother's benefactor.

Compensated. Chism kept mulling over the term. The senator's pause. His brother's apparent desperation. Compensated. Kalif had been of service to this man before. Either Kalif had become an assassin without Chism's knowledge, or Kalif was in far over his head. Assassins who knew too much had a very short lifespan. And Kalif knew too much. Too much about the senator. Not enough about staying alive.

But Kalif had made it this far. I've seen to that, Chism thought as his attention returned to the present battle. Kalif had made it to this midnight forest to attack innocent Neroos. And perhaps Chism had seen to that, as Rierdan had so aptly pointed out. Dread welled up like bile as Chism thought of all the people that Kalif would hurt, and wondered if their blood would be on his hands. He had been so focused on protecting Kalif from his own decisions that he never thought he'd have to worry about protecting everyone else from Kalif's decisions as well.

Chism and Rierdan were nearing the first group of marauders concealed in the woods as Chism broke from his reverie. Chism surveyed each face from afar, but Kalif was not to be found in the group. The battle within the city was raging, and these marauders looked nervous. The night was not going as planned.

Not here, Chism motioned to Rierdan.

Agreed. More groups to the West. Time is short, came Rierdan's abbreviated hand signals.

The third group of marauders—those charged with attrition, as Rierdan had explained—were there only to break the spirit of the already defeated Neroos. When all was lost and their homes burned to the ground with their families inside, the third group would enjoy the spoils and the dispirited Neroos who fight for the sake of dying. Unless the battle did not go well. Unless someone had forewarned the Neroos and they were prepared. Then the third group would enter battle simply to bolster the offense when the

Lima were scared and the Neroos were at their most vicious. If Chism understood the sounds coming from the nearby village, then the third group would not be enjoying any spoils of war tonight. And Chism had to find Kalif before that happened.

~~~~~

Rierdan did not want to kill Chism.

It was a strange sensation for Rierdan. He thought it was called mercy. Or empathy. Chism just wanted to protect his family, even if all that was left of his family had already left him behind. Even if Rierdan did not admire Chism's decisions, he could not help but respect them. But Rierdan told himself that either Chism grappled with the same questions about him, or Chism had already planned how to get rid of him when they were finished. Rierdan had a plan. Rierdan always had a plan. And it always ended well for Rierdan.

If tonight did not fare well for the Neroos, then Rierdan would have a Lima to present to the Triumvirate, whether it was Kalif or Chism. *Chism is hardly innocent of any of this,* Rierdan decided, quelling the rising guilt as he so nonchalantly debated Chism's fate. *Chism is still a Lima, and there is no such thing as an innocent Lima. Especially in his family.*

Rierdan continued to wrestle with his resentful respect for Chism and a growing desire to put a dagger between his ribs. But he had to wait. He had to follow the plan. He had to take Kalif's place when reporting back. He had a growing suspicion that the Triumvirate had sent Kalif here to die. Killing Kalif either here or back in Ombrar as he knelt at their feet would be a gift to the Triumvirate—a way to enter their inner circles, if he handled the situation just right. This was the opportunity he had waited for since he killed his first Lima master. Since he was a slave.

Despite Rierdan's constant reintegration into Lima society, he was always sure to leave the Neroos with a chance to balance the scales against the Lima. Someone would pay for this when it was all over. Rierdan would rather hand over one of the marauders to the Neroos as payment, but he could settle for handing over Chism, if he had to. His people would have a Lima to carry out their justice so that their dead could rest in peace. Then there was the matter of needing to lose his companion. Rierdan prayed that a skillful Neroos warrior would eventually remove the problem for him.

But Rierdan still did not want to kill him.

The Neroos were fighting well, but they were moving the line back. The third group of marauders would be sent in soon. When Kalif went into Gidionhi, the chances of finding him were incredibly slim. And those were chances Rierdan could not take.

That was when the flaming arrows began to fall.

"*Corva!*" Rierdan used a Lima oath as he swore to himself. *This makes things more difficult.*

A volley of flaming arrows came sailing into the forest mere yards in front of them, kindling the dry leaves and branches that lay strewn across the forest floor. Standing on the other side of the conflagration were ten marauders, shrouded in their black cloaks with weapons drawn.

"That's far enough!" One of the ten marauders called out to Chism and Rierdan.

"Soldier, we have orders to carry out, and you will stand aside!" Chism tried to bluff.

"We aint soldiers, cap'n," another marauder leered. "And you aint one of us." The marauders tried to form a circle around Rierdan and Chism, but the flames were beginning to spread through the fall foliage and undergrowth.

"Five for you, five for me?" Chism said casually to Rierdan.

"Forget numbers, lieutenant. We'll push on the north and get around them. They're heavy on the south, anyway."

"Go."

Rierdan drew a knife in his left hand while he attacked with the short sword in his right. The first marauder swung a sword up from his right hip and across his body, forcing Rierdan to cross his right hand and parry with the sword.

Chism followed closely behind with his standard military sword but with no shield. Shields only got in the way on the fringe. Speed was his greatest asset. As Rierdan turned his parry into a vicious kick to his attackers ribs, Chism was forced to deal a deep cut to one attacker's hand, stopping just short of dismembering the marauder, before he had to swing high to block a club swinging downward like an axe toward Rierdan's head.

The sheer weight of the blow and the angle at which he was forced to counter the club had knocked Chism off balance. He lay on his side in front of the man whose hand he had almost cut off. His opponent's feet, it seemed, were still in perfect working order as he took quick aim and kicked at Chism's head.

Chism quickly forced the tip of his sword into the ground right in front of his face as he leaned heavily on it to stand. The marauder had neither the time nor the thought to adjust the angle of his kick and buried his foot in the edge of Chism's sword. The marauder's howl was sickeningly satisfying to Chism as he heard the screams of Gidionhi's innocent echoing from the nearby village.

"Shut him up!" Rierdan said as he shoved his dagger into the club-wielding man's diaphragm. Another volley of flaming arrows rained fire on the men like a plague of Egypt. Two of the marauders were dropped to the ground as the forest continued to burn.

"*Velsk*," Chism swore as he finished off his opponent and ran through the trees, dodging the rain of fire.

"You're welcome!" Rierdan shouted as the two men sought cover, separated by flames. The two had ended up several yards away from each other.

"I didn't want to kill them all!" Chism shouted back over the noise of the battle behind them and the confusion in the woods. Rierdan made every effort to let Chism see the contempt he had displayed on his face for the man's ambiguity, especially at a time like this.

The forest was beginning to come alive with the marauders who had lay hidden there. They could no longer wait for their signal. The fire was quickly closing a line between them and the village. They could move and die, or stay still and die. The marauders who had begun attacking Chism and Rierdan had altogether abandoned their pursuit as the flames continued to grow.

The Neroos had set up a firing line to pick off the marauders as they fled the forest. Though Rierdan was Neroos, none of his kindred soldiers would recognize him in the dark and the smoke.

Chism dodged from tree to tree until he reached Rierdan.

"We have to move south and push west until we get out of this!" Rierdan said.

"There aren't any marauders left in here," Chism explained. "And there's no sign of my brother."

"So what's the next move, lieutenant?"

"We have a few options, but not dying in here is high on the priority list," Chism said drily.

Rierdan grimaced as the flames continued to approach. "I can get us out of here, but you've got to tell me right now where your loyalties lie," he shouted over the roaring flames. "Will you fight the Lima? Will you fight with the Neroos?"

With no warning or preamble, Chism punched Rierdan in the face and spat out, "I'll do what it takes. And if you question me again, I'll kill you."

"*Corva cavesa!*" Rierdan swore as he spat out blood. He could not believe that Chism had moved that quickly. His back had been turned as he and Chism took on the three marauders. He had not seen what Chism was capable of. Perhaps killing him would not be as easy as he thought.

"Sit tight, lieutenant. And keep your mouth shut. We can't afford them finding out that you're Lima. Your Neroos dialect is terrible."

With that, Rierdan drew a whistle he had strung about his neck on a long, loose rope and began to blow. The arrows in their area stopped, and four Neroos soldiers arrived to escort them out of the forest and out of the blaze.

CHAPTER 8:
BENEATH THE STARS

Night. Rayanna's mother used to say that night came when God closed his eyes to rest. But if God closed his eyes tonight, Rayanna told herself, it was so that he would not have to witness what his children could do.

Where is Hakoni? Rayanna found it odd to think about the boy at a time like this. At a time while she sat huddled next to a wood pile, holding nothing more than a knife to protect herself and her two brothers. The world was on fire, and screams of triumph, terror, and bravery once again visited these streets now too familiar with the taste of blood.

And there sat her mother by the door, holding her own knife in front of her like a candle. Her back was pressed against the wall. Her knees were bent. Her eyes were closed, but not asleep. Waiting. Waiting patiently.

A soft knock immediately behind Rayanna startled her, and she threw her knife at the door instinctively as she whipped around to grab Brego and Karrh.

Through the door came the quiet call, "Rayanna! *Mamera* Aria! Boys!"

Rayanna glanced back at Aria, who kept her guard. She nodded her head to Rayanna.

"Hakoni!" She said as she carefully opened the back door.

"Come quickly. We can get you out of here," Hakoni promised. Rayanna looked past him to see six other men keeping an eye out and awkwardly holding their weapons. "The evacuation was cut off, and I knew you didn't get out. We came to get you."

The battle had been ebbing and flowing for the past two hours. Some men were killed just outside the front door. Rayanna had no idea what blood had been in their veins. Whether Neroos or Lima, she was sure it was still just as red. After all the stories she had heard of the Lima, she had long held a suspicion that it would be any other color, anything other than what dripped out of her older brothers and out of her father as she had prepared their bodies for burial six years ago. But the screams outside were indiscernible, and she began to wonder what more they may have had in common in life now that they, together, share death.

Rayanna again looked to her mother, who had not moved.

"Go," Aria said. "Go, children, move! Time is short." The battle was coming closer.

"We'll go two at a time," Hakoni said. "We can't have a group too large."

Rayanna debated whether to go with one of her brothers. Should she go with one to protect him while her mother stayed with the other? Should her mother go first? Of all the things that Rayanna remembered from that night, she could barely remember how to escape. She could only recall the pain and the details that made the pain sharper. Rayanna began to feel very frustrated with herself, as if she had wasted all those years by remembering the pain and yet had done nothing to try to avoid it again.

"Brego and Karrh, *dy amoris*," Aria spoke as Rayanna sat in stunned deliberation. "Go with Hakoni. He will protect you."

As they left, Rayanna felt herself being pulled carefully into her mother's arms. Rayanna had the sudden sensation of feeling something—was it love?—from her mother.

"Mama, why are they…why now…just…" Rayanna sputtered.

"Sometimes there is no 'why' to our circumstances, Rayanna," Aria said with a voice full of memory. "Sometimes there is only what you choose to become as a result of whatever happens."

"I'm scared."

"I…I am here, *amora*." *I love you, Rayanna.*

"I know, mama." *I love you, too.*

Then, voices. Rayanna was able to discern some amount of the conversation as a group of Lima men rapidly approached. The sound of doors breaking open and window slats being torn apart alerted the two women of the men's steady hunt.

"*Corva cavesa!* All these *punta* Neroos gone *alles* food *cachre*!" At least, she thought it was "food" they had said. But some words in the Lima dialect meant simply to consume, no matter what the object may be. Space. Food. Money. Women. Rayanna couldn't be sure.

Rayanna and Aria hid themselves behind the bed where only a few minutes ago Rayanna had sat huddled with the two brothers. Aria had dropped her knife in the middle of the room. Feeling around in the dark on the floor, Rayanna recovered her own thrown knife. Aria took it from her and sat crouched.

Hakoni, we need you! Rayanna prayed. Her body was quivering. She couldn't stop.

"*Na* houses *videment la*," the voices were in the middle of the street, just outside the door. "We can hide in here. *Namen* Triumvirate didn't count on the *puntas* to fight back like this," another replied.

Crash. Crash. Open came the door.

"*Quello gaspirag*," one said as four men entered the house. "I'm starving, and the food is *horomar. Ya vere quileres* got here first."

As he and another began to shuffle out, the first one in said, "Stop. Something's wrong."

"Yeah, I know. No food to eat. That's bad. Let's go."

"No. The door was locked. If no one had *arribar* here, then who was fighting?"

"*Gerchres na appartoni!*" Search the apartment.

As they began to search, Rayanna and Aria tried to move toward the back door. But there was no way to open it without alerting the men who were already heading directly toward them.

"Rayanna, you need to be ready to go," Aria whispered urgently as the table was noisily moved and feet shuffled across the stone and dirt floor.

"Mama, you must come—"

"There are things worse than death, *amora*."

Rayanna stared. Speechless. Wishing she had never wished that her mother had died with her father. Wishing her mother had never had to endure a rape. But something in Aria's eyes gave Rayanna the distinct impression that her mother wasn't referring to the brutality. "Sometimes there is only what you choose to become as a result of whatever happens. Don't lose yourself, Rayanna. Don't forget who you are. Promise me!" Aria said.

The men had nowhere else to look. Nowhere besides right where they sat crouched. Time was short.

Rayanna nodded.

"Stay hidden. When the moment is right, run." And with that last command to her daughter, Aria stood up. "I am here," she said loudly, not knowing if the men would understand even as they whipped around at the sound.

Rayanna was mortified. She could not scream. Could not react. Sheer shock held her tighter than any fear could.

Aria stepped out from behind the bed as the men formed a semi circle around her. She had taken the knife with her. "There is nothing for you here." Fearless. As if the last six years had been preparing her for this moment.

Rayanna knew their attention was focused entirely on her mother. She dared peek around the toppled bed to see the scene unfolding in the dimming firelight inside, with macabre shadows of fire outside and battle approaching once more. Her mother stood blocking almost the entire view. Rayanna wanted to see the men's faces. She wanted to put a face to the horror. Something she could hate.

"Maybe not nothing, yes?" One of them said in a broken accent, grinning fiendishly at his companions and then back to her.

"No," Aria said simply. Then she cut her own throat and crumpled to the ground. Almost in unison, the men let out a yelp of surprise.

Dead bodies and blood were hardly new to these men, Rayanna knew. But as she sat frozen staring at her mother and the men, she told herself that bravery such as they had just witnessed was completely foreign to their bloodlust. Aria's bravery did not stop the men from paying their final disrespect to the woman, each grabbing her body and pulling at her clothes. Rayanna thought for an instant that they were being more clinical than devilish—as if they were searching for something. The blood began to soak the cloth and straw in the mattress that stood between Aria's sacrifice and the daughter's life she could only hope to have saved with her final act.

But the men didn't leave. They began examining the floor and searching the rafters. *We have nothing here*, Rayanna thought. *And even if we did, the most precious thing in this house is now gone.* Their search was quickly leading to the bed that hid her. Rayanna could not wait another moment for Hakoni. Her head filled with memories and half-wished wishes, and they all lay in front of her, embodied and prone, leaking out the blood that Rayanna never knew was so precious to her. Not until it was gone.

Wrenching open the door, Rayanna ran outside. Another yelp of surprise and the shuffle of the bed being cast aside alerted

Rayanna that her attackers were in close pursuit. Whatever they wanted from her mother, she knew they'd also want it from her. Rayanna fled into the night, straight for the forest as the glow of fire within it continued to expand.

She could hear four or five of them breathing hard, barking out words in a dialect that was foreign and yet not at all strange to her ears. It was a dialect that had haunted her dreams for six years.

A protruding root brought her abruptly back to the present danger she was in. Seeing the root just in time, Rayanna dodged, risking a few loud, clumsy footsteps. She knew they'd hear her. But she was still running, and the Lima marauders could not keep up. Not even the other Neroos knew the woods as well as she. Though quieter than most, she could not remain noiseless, and her breath was coming shorter and shorter. Branches and brush clawed and grabbed as she ran. Branches became hands to her frenzied mind, and thoughts of how much she and her family had endured and would yet endure wrapped themselves around her throat. Her chest constricted from her rapid flight and her descent into despair.

Her thoughts and memories halted her beneath a tree, though her every instinct screamed at her, warning of her current danger. But Rayanna's breathing was becoming more audible and ragged. With every breath came more memories, and her legs trembled. She felt she could barely move. If she were to survive tonight, hiding was her only option.

She climbed the tree, slipping once on the bark, and ascended until no eye could see her, yet not high enough for the stars to reveal her. And slowly, carefully, she began to draw silent breaths. The fear, the anxiety, and her sudden flight stole the last of her energy, and she felt her body finally go limp as she leaned against the trunk, high up in the tree's branches.

~~~~~

Kalif would always remember the first Neroos man he killed that night. His eyes were blue. Scared. Determined.

It wasn't the first time he had killed someone. It wasn't even the first time he had killed a Neroos this way—bringing his sword down on his opponent's head, forcing a high block while he shoved his dagger into the man's diaphragm and felt the hot blood rush onto his forearm. But there was something new tonight. He could feel it in the way he swung his sword and cut out throats.

The gods were gone, Kalif decided. That's what was different. Fine. What use did he have for the gods who had never been with him? Where were the gods when he lost his sister? Where were the gods to protect his mother and his father? He didn't need the gods. He didn't need his brother. Wherever the gods were tonight, Kalif hoped they stayed there. Away from him.

And even as Kalif shoved the body aside, allowing gravity to pull his dagger out of his opponent's stomach with his arm dripping crimson, those eyes were burned into Kalif's memory.

These people—these animals—took everything from me! The thought had taken hold of Kalif, and he had likewise embraced it.

Another step, another Neroos. Dodge parry slash. Thrust cut kill. Step. All around him his party were committed to the same ideas, the same stories, the same hatred.

These Neroos have families, he told himself as a moment of pity dared beset him. But he felt his resolve harden again with the thought of Loria. Loria's kindness. Loria's goodness. Loria's death. *I used to have a family. Now they're dead.* Kalif continued his work as his tears mingled with Neroos blood on his face.

Kalif's grief at the loss of his sister was matched only by his frustration with Chism. Chism's protection. Chism's words. Chism's promise. He swung his sword a little harder as if to fight off his brother's influence and disapproving glare. For years, hate was all Kalif had, and Chism had tried to take it away. But not tonight. Tonight he would have his hate, and with it he would gain his justice.

Arrows began to fall among Kalif's raiding party. Kalif grabbed a Neroos by the makeshift armor he had draped around his shoulders and yanked the surprised solider toward himself, shielding himself from the arrows. Kalif dropped him, now with three arrows in his back. Looking to his left, he saw two Lima dead from the volley. The man who had put his knife to Kalif's throat was still alive. Kalif would have to amend that before the night's end.

I will purge the world of their bloodlust. I will bring peace! I will have justice!

Parry thrust cut. Kalif was soaked in blood. A guttural scream. It came from Kalif, but it seemed to belonged to someone else. Someone without a fiancée at home, without a brother trying to stop him, without a sister who lay in her watery grave. It belonged to a new man, born of pain with hate pumping in his veins, the very embodiment of grief.

Another volley of arrows raced into the fray, killing Lima and Neroos alike. Pain in his right shoulder. An arrow had found its mark. Distract the *punta* with the sword now in his left hand until he could issue the kill with his right hand. Use the right hand as little as possible. Reach back, yank out the arrow.

The way stood clear now between Kalif and the first buildings on the edge of the village. As soon as he could get to the buildings, he would find a side street and rest. How many of his group were left? As he looked around, the haze of his anger began to subside, and emptiness filled every crevice. Four others. Five of the ten had cleared the space between the woods and the village.

Kalif took a moment to look at the bodies that lay like autumn leaves on the forest floor. But these men had not fallen so peacefully. Kalif realized that if he died tonight, it would not be over. Peace would not overcome him. And the more soldiers, men, people he killed, the more he realized that the void left by his family could not be filled with the blood of Neroos. Even now the dark night with the shadows of a fiery forest and burning village dancing across the bodies, Kalif could not tell which bodies were Neroos and which were Lima.

But they still deserved it, Kalif reminded himself. *The Neroos made the world like this. The world has been burning long before tonight.*

Life in Ombrar had never been easy, but there had been something simpler about it when his parents were alive. Kalif's father had been a mason. A strong man. A good man. When his mother had died, Kalif's father spent more time at the tavern than at work and more money on drink than on rent. Chism and Kalif both worked in the shipyards. Their work was to scrub the decks. Their pay was to eat the food that would have been thrown out after a voyage because it was rotting. Most days it was all they had.

Chism could have gotten a better job. He was old enough. Strong enough. But he wouldn't, so long as he felt he had to look after Kalif. Besides, no one would give good money to the sons of a drunk. Kalif always felt embarrassed that his brother had to babysit him. Always felt thankful that he was there. Always hated his father and his brother for settling, one way or another, in life.

Kalif had been fourteen when he received a new assignment in the shipyard that week. Scrub the deck and galley of the ship *Eln Sadique.* He didn't know what it meant. *Must be Neroos,* he decided, though he truly had no idea where the ship actually came from. *Why are the Neroos taking harbor here?*

Kalif had shouldered his bucket and rope while shrugging off the curiosity of this foreign vessel. He could still remember boarding the ship and immediately threw his bucket over the rails and pulled up harbor water. Kalif had sloshed the water onto the aged and blackened deck and fallen to his work as the sun abused his tanned and bare back.

"*Eln esclaver! Porguay ni arbecht? Arbein massev! Massev!*" Several crew members had boarded the ship, yelling and laughing. They had been sloshing their own liquid on the deck, but only because they could not see straight enough to know the horizon from the mast.

One of them had been smoking something that made Kalif gag when the wind had brought the smell to him.

Drunks, Kalif had thought savagely as he watched three of the men approach him. *Drunk and Neroos. These aren't men. They're filthy. They're animals.*

Kalif had hardly hid a sneer as he took the opportunity to glance around the ship. The deck had been worn in ways Kalif had never seen. The aging was not so general, and the black was not so uniform. It lay in spots and lines, spread across the deck carelessly. Erratically. Kalif examined the place he scrubbed more carefully. This was no aging. These were scorch marks.

A foul smelling liquid had hit Kalif's right shoulder and neck and ran down his arm. Laughing. The sailors, supposedly Neroos sailors, had been laughing. It always started with laughter. Kalif's father would also laugh at first with his reeking breath. Then the laughing would stop, and the anger would start. The pain would start. The pain and the stench that infected his house. The pain caused by the Neroos. The Neroos who killed his mother and sent his father to oblivion every time he drank. The liquid that ran down his arm smelled far more potent than anything his father had ever drank. That just meant the time was shorter until their mirth was replaced with anger.

With a low growl that grew to a battle cry, the young child had stood up and threw his brush directly at the head of the first man he could see. He did not see his heavy deck brush break the man's nose, because he was already bent over, grabbing the bucket to use it as his next weapon. But whatever he had hoped to do next was erased in an instant. A burning cigar had been forced into his right shoulder, igniting the alcohol. The man dropped his cigar onto the deck where the remaining liquid had also ignited, engulfing Kalif in flames.

Kalif ran to the rail and launched himself into the harbor, smacking the water with the flat of his back. The pain of his burns and his unceremonious landing threatened to close his eyes as he slipped into the water. But before the water filled his ears, the last sound he could hear was laughter. Always the laughter.

Kalif remembered refusing treatment for his burns. Some of them had become infected. But still he would not cover them. He would always remember and always show the world the need to be rid of the Neroos. He would not let the flames die. Now, here in Gidionhi, the world was on fire. *So,* Kalif thought, *this is what justice must look like. They deserve this. They have to deserve this. They're just animals, anyway. Bloodthirsty animals.*

Kalif advanced with a group of Lima up the street, passing a home that was almost entirely engulfed in flames. There was shrieking inside. Against his own judgment, he glanced into the window to see a woman holding an infant with a dead man sprawled in her lap. The flames rose around her as she sobbed and the baby screamed. But she would not move. She looked out the window and locked eyes with Kalif until Kalif could not look anymore.

Even as he looked away, he knew her face would join those blue eyes that still bore into his own.

~~~~~

"Where do you need reinforcements?" Rierdan asked as soon as he and Chism were pulled from the forest. His nose had stopped bleeding thanks to the piece of his shirt he had cut and used to stop the flow, but his face was still smeared with blood, sweat, and soot.

"We can't hold on much longer," the Neroos soldier replied. "There just aren't enough of us who are trained. We started evacuating before the fight started, but we couldn't get everyone out. There are still families on the southeast corner. Can you get there and protect the evacuees?"

Rierdan nodded, and Chism followed suit. The way that Chism stared intently at Rierdan's face, waiting to know how to respond, belied his utter lack of comprehension. Rierdan now had the irritation of actually liking his Lima companion, and he did not want to voluntarily forfeit Chism to the Neroos. Rierdan kept his mouth shut, and he prayed that Chism would, too.

"Where can I find the evacuee lines?" Rierdan asked.

The soldier looked at Rierdan with suspicion. *Shosk,* Rierdan swore. *I'm supposed to know all about the evacuation plan!*

"I've been bunkered in the woods for some time. I don't know if they've fallen back to the secondary plan," Rierdan tried to save himself.

"No," the soldier said with hesitation. "Still the same plan."

"Perfect," Rierdan said briskly as he and Chism turned to go. "May God be with you, my friend."

"One more thing," the soldier called out, walking toward them. "You," he addressed Chism. "I don't recognize you."

"Why?" Chism ventured, hoping that if he could keep his replies brief, then he could keep his identity a secret.

The guard looked puzzled at the strange reply. "Because I don't think you're from here. Where's your family?"

"Dead."

"Yeah? Your skin is looking a little dark to me," the guard sneered.

"It's night," Chism said with a shrug.

"His skin's no darker than mine," Rierdan said. Rierdan could feel the surprise emanating from Chism and hoped that it wasn't showing in his face. "We don't have time for this!"

"No, we don't," said the soldier as the rest of his contingency moved in to take them prisoner.

As soon as a hand gripped Rierdan's arm, he grabbed it, pulled the man off balance, and placed a dagger at his throat. Rierdan was too close to his goal, too close to getting inside the marauders, to be stopped now. "I've got to get out there, and you can't afford to lock up two fighters like us."

Chism put up his hands, signaling a halt to everyone. "I am Lima," he said in Neroos with his stilted accent. "My name is Chism. I am not well speaking your language, but I am well fighting for you.

How can I stand here with you, no show of harm, and not be friend to you?" At that, he carefully placed his sword on the ground.

A soldier came toward Chism, prepared to swing his sword at Chism's stomach. As the soldier drew his arm back, Chism stepped toward him and smashed his head into the soldier's nose. Chism grabbed the soldier's sword from his hand and blocked the swing from the next man, then drove his elbow into the second man's nose. Rierdan savagely punched his captive's kidneys, and squared off with the soldier who gave the order to take them captive.

"We broke a few noses when we could have killed," Rierdan said to the man. "You do not know what you are doing, so we have warned you. But do not try to stop us. You will die."

"We go now," Chism said in Neroos. "If you put knife to our backs, you kill last hope."

The last man standing rushed to his companions' aid, pretending not to see Chism and Rierdan walk away from the scene.

"Well done," Rierdan said in Lima as they ran from street to street, looking for the best place to begin searching again for Kalif.

"Let's just get Kalif and get outta here," Chism said as they picked their way through the buildings.

Rierdan nodded. Yes, he would get Kalif. But that was not the most difficult part. Rierdan had to find and kill Kalif to take his place with the marauders without Chism knowing. Rierdan still hoped that the Neroos would take care of that problem for him.

After a few streets, Rierdan and Chism found a band of fifteen Neroos holding back an onslaught of Lima as they cordoned off a section of street, presumably for the evacuation.

"Can you do this?" Rierdan asked as the two men gripped their swords in anticipation of helping the Neroos. The question was no longer accusatory. It was almost understanding. Almost.

"This is not justice," Chism said. Rierdan knew what he meant. And they waded in.

~~~~~

How long had he been fighting? Kalif knew the strain in his muscles and pain where the arrow had grazed his right shoulder were more than he had ever endured. But he pushed on.

Loria. Mother. Father, he repeated with every stroke. Kalif was a terrible sight—soaked in blood and covered in ash; he had become something else that his body had never before allowed him to be. H

Here and now, with tearstains and sweat cutting riverbeds through the filth on his body, Kalif had bathed himself in blood. But he could not wash away the memories. The fire would not be extinguished. And even when the Lima horn sounded in the darkest part of the night, Kalif had to be pulled out of the fray as he desperately tried to carve peace out of Neroos flesh when he knew it could never be done. He had always known it. He just didn't know how to stop.

Kalif walked back to the woods, trying to find his way through the darkness to his rendezvous point. Without other marauders, he could not gain access back into the tunnel. And they would know. If he did not report back, he would be a hunted man. He did not know how they could tell. But the one form of authority Kalif had come to respect was the Triumvirate and the promises they made. He had to report back.

The woods still had enough life left in them this early in the season to halt the burning. And the night was freezing. Kalif had not realized in the heat of the battle how very cold it had become. He would wait. Sitting down against a tree deep in the forest, he closed his eyes and wished that he still had his cloak.

Some time later, he did not know how long, he woke up to voices in the woods. Lima voices. A ticket out. Kalif stood to move over to the group some yards away when a wet drop hit his forehead. *Rain,* he thought. But the droplet did not move quickly over the grime. And it was the only one. Touching the wet spot, he felt the texture between his fingers. *Could this be blood?* He wondered. A subtle sound above him piqued his hunter's experience.

He was not alone.

CHAPTER 9:
OUT OF DARKNESS, LIGHT

It was easy to kill someone. All Chism had to do was tell himself why a man was an enemy, and he was vindicated. Exonerated. Sometimes even venerated. He had held tenaciously to stories of protection for his family, loyalty and patriotism to his people, and justice for so many grievances for so long.

But he grew tired of holding onto the same old tales, and the stories each crumbled the longer he held on to them. He could feel himself lose grip on his reasons—lose grip on his excuses—one at a time like a desperate man clinging to a cliff and watching his fingers slowly slip. First went patriotism. Then loyalty to the city guard. Then the idea that he was protecting the innocent. And with each one, the killing got harder.

Even after cutting a man's throat, Chism often found himself jealous of the man who had just given his life for something he believed in. Chism didn't know if he had taken a man's life for something he believed in as passionately as the man who lay choking on his own blood until the silence of death took him. No sword ever pierced Chism as profoundly as the knowledge that one day he would lay dying and wonder what it was all for.

Thus he stepped over an opponent who gurgled out his final breaths. Tonight the men at his feet happened to be Lima. It had been Neroos men countless times before. Perhaps it did not matter who it would be tomorrow. *Some day,* Chism told himself, *it will matter. And then I will know what is worth fighting for.*

Chism had come here to stop Kalif's revenge. Stop Kalif's misplaced sense of justice. Stop Kalif's self-destruction. No one was there to stop Chism's.

Revenge against his people. Answers for their crimes. Crimes against innocent children. Chism had followed his brother into the forest as Kalif went to carry out the senator's orders. The trap was set. And Chism stopped Kalif, knocking him out. He had hidden his brother in a ditch as he returned the children to the city. He was honored by some. Threatened by others—others who knew what Chism knew and who could hurt his family if he ever revealed why the children were in the forest.

So Chism bargained: his silence for Kalif's safety. He had allowed a conspiracy to stay in the dark to keep his promise to his father. The promotion came by default; Chism would have preferred to lay low, but pomp and circumstance had to be observed. His platoon would have been suspicious otherwise But Chism had bargained for Kalif—he never thought he would have had to bargain for Loria. Too soon after his promotion, his sister was dragged out of the city and killed. It was a warning shot. The contract would be followed to the letter, and Chism's enemies had the power to pass judgment.

An agreement made in the dark wasn't enough security for Kalif. So when the invitation came, Kalif went to the only source of protection powerful enough to keep him safe: the marauders. The stories the marauders told were compelling, and Chism knew that Kalif needed something to believe in. So did Chism—but he stopped trusting stories that the Lima told a long time ago.

And now, here in the dark, Chism exacted his revenge and spent his frustration. Justice against the Lima. Justice against their fallen society.

The horn blew. The Neroos, exhausted and broken, allowed the Lima to retreat. And now Chism was again behind enemy lines.

"Rierdan, I have to get out," Chism said quietly.

"You're not going to find your brother in this," Rierdan reminded him.

"If he's not dead, then there's still no way for me to get him back. Not after what he has done here. I have to go."

"Stay here. Rebuild. There's a better life for you than what's waiting in Ombrar."

Chism's unbelief could not have been more plainly displayed. "You may be right that there's something better, but…not here."

"As you wish. We'll go one at a time. The horse we used to come in is either dead or stolen by now. It could have been burned alive in the blaze. We'll follow the marauders' route back."

The Neroos defense had been relatively small, but the streets were littered with Lima marauders. Tonight had certainly not gone as planned. Burned homes and bodies lay like discarded bread that had been left too long with one side to the heat, one part beautiful and golden brown, and the other charred beyond recognition.

From time to time, a moan would escape a man, woman, or child. Rierdan would quickly go over to the person and say, "Are you Neroos?" If the answer was no, he slipped his sword into their heart. If the answer was yes, he would say, "I am sorry," and then slip his sword into their heart.

Chism couldn't watch. He had no stories to justify what he saw. "Rierdan!" Chism finally said. But he said nothing else. He didn't know if there was anything to say. He didn't know if there was ever anything to say but a name, an identity, a reminder of who Rierdan was to awaken in him a sense of compassion and humanity—because Chism knew that his own identity was slipping fast.

"Who will bind their wounds?" Rierdan sneered at Chism's sentimentality. "Who will find the necessary plants to grind into pastes? Who will keep them only half alive to remind them of how broken they are?"

"But they are alive! Don't they have a right to the breath they are drawing?"

Rierdan paused. "Yes. But at what cost? To fight death's ragged breath until they lose? Because they will lose, Chism. Yes, the village will care for them as best they can, and they may make it a few more months. But they'll eat winter's store of food just before they die."

Chism said as much to himself as anyone, "They haven't lost yet."

Rierdan ignored him and continued on his way. Just before they entered the forest, Rierdan grabbed a man who lay moaning on the ground by his collar. He wore the dark robe of the marauders.

"Are you Lima?" Rierdan used his Lima dialect.

The man nodded, his skin covered in sweat and blood, shining with what little light came from the smoldering fire.

"What is your name?" Rierdan pressed.

"T…Tristan…Tristan."

"Thank you," Rierdan said as he unclasped the cloak from around Tristan's neck. He raised the man to a half sitting position as he rolled the cloak under him. When all that was left of the cloak was what Tristan sat on, Chism watched as Rierdan viciously punched the man to the ground and cut his throat. Rierdan rolled the body over to retrieve the cloak. He had no hesitation. No remorse.

"Let's spread out," Rierdan suggested. "Look for another cloak. We'll want to hide you in case we run into any marauders."

As Chism began to look about, incredibly fatigued from the night's events, he did not hear Rierdan approach from behind. He only knew the brief, incredible pain in his head from the branch that Rierdan brought down on it.

Just before Chism's eyes closed, he heard Rierdan whisper, "I truly am sorry." For a brief moment, Chism wondered if Rierdan would slit his throat and allow him to join those who died knowing what they had fought for. As the darkness shrouded his mind, Chism knew that he could not blame Rierdan, whatever his plans may be. After all, it had become easy to kill, and any story that created an enemy would suffice.

Then all was dark.

~~~~~

High up in her tree, Rayanna woke from dreams of berries, *falhanna*, and her mother. She had little idea how long she had slept. The fire in the woods had not reached her here, and the village had become a smoldering shell. Her body stiff from her flight and her mind weary from her fear, Rayanna looked all around her for signs of her pursuers. The night was so deep that not even her hands were visible to her.

Hands. Their hands. Their clawing, grabbing hands. Where were the wolves, the Lima men who were chasing her? Where were her brothers? Did Hakoni get them safely out?

Her thoughts went again, as they always did, to that fire-lit street six years ago where more than branches and briers had clawed and grabbed at her mother. Her now-dead mother. Her mother's sacrifice. Was it a sacrifice, or was it an escape from torture?

What tortures could the marauders devise for her brothers? If she could slip back noiselessly, she could keep them safe, she thought deliriously. "Do it now," she told herself. "They'll never see you!"

But her limbs could not respond—sitting and sleeping in the tree had cut off the circulation to her left leg and arm, and her right foot began to throb where she had scraped the tree. She massaged her leg and arm, shaking her branches ever so slightly.

She set her hands to exploring the damage she had sustained thus far. She bled from scrapes and cuts, but everything was superficial. Bracing herself, she reached for the throbbing in her right foot.

The piece of wood protruding from her foot was about the size of her finger; she could not tell how deep it went. If she left it in, she would have no flexibility. If she took it out, she would risk infection. She knew her time was running out—though she could not yet see the gray dawn, she knew that the night would soon break.

Rayanna held her breath, listening for any movement. All was still—even the night creatures had gone silent. She tried slowly pulling the wood from her foot, but stopped for fear of gasping from the pain. Gathering the front of her shirt into a ball, she stuffed the cloth into her mouth, bit down, and yanked the wood.

She moaned into her shirt, breathing heavily through her nose. Now that it was out, she wished she had left it in. She could not risk the noise of ripping her shirt to bind her foot, and so she began to descend the tree very slowly, trying not to slip in her own blood. She paused every time she moved for fear of being detected, and began moving a second sooner than she wished with each step.

"Where are the others?" A man's voice said in a hushed tone. The dialect was Lima. Still much too dark in the woods for her to see their location, Rayanna guessed that they were roughly twenty feet away. All the more reason to stay in her tree, out of their reach. All the more reason to get down and run, out of their sight when the sun finally broke over the mountains.

A general muttering told of at least three other men. "This is the meeting point, *schunt am*?" "What did you grab?" "*Bloeden*! Who had time to grab anything?" "Where are the others?" "Probably killing the smaller boys." Rayanna bit deeper into the shirt stuffed in her mouth. She thought of her brothers. They were still so small. Did they get out?

Rayanna barely detected the man who walked beneath her tree just as she extended her foot to another branch. She didn't hear him. She couldn't really say that she had seen him. A feeling just passed through her, and she knew that she stood, bleeding and broken and aching, above something very dangerous. He stepped further away from her tree, and he spoke in sharp Lima to the group of marauders that had congregated.

"*Na guerramen!* The time is long past. We must go, *shienzai*," the dark shadow said. They spoke too quickly for Rayanna to follow perfectly.

"*Buyao*. We wait for the others," one of the men said. Rayanna still could not tell how many there were, despite the small torch in the group.

"You read *derrg kommandans*," the man said, stopping close—so close—to where Rayanna stood above. "*Ya gravem wo hackbu jiandao.*"

"Too late…"

"*Tontay el* South access in the Gimnolo Gorge…"

"Wouldn't kill us."

"*Forga apers na soirr.*"

"*Trifecahui* will protect us."

"Senate won't know we were here."

"True," the man said quietly, wiping his arm and rubbing his fingers together as he stepped toward the small group. "True." Rayanna started to descend again as the man moved toward the group. She had to leave, now, or the entire group would soon be able to find her. She knew she had only a few minutes, and with her foot in its condition, she could not get very far.

As she grabbed a branch to take another step, she glanced over as some of the men yelped in surprise. She could finally see the man who had stood under her tree as the torchlight illuminated him. She saw him just as his sword took off another man's head. The sight awoke in her a new terror that not even tonight's massacre had been able to induce, as if fate tied her to this Lima, the embodiment of every childhood fear.

Speed was all that mattered now. Rayanna dropped the last few feet to the ground as the last remaining man from the group fought the battle he never knew he would fight tonight. Rayanna gasped as her right foot came down on the ground. Pain radiated through every limb as the blood continued to flow from her wound and the stiffness in her limbs resisted her demands to run. Run. Run.

Rayanna hobbled as far as she could. She could no longer hear the clamor of weapons. Where was she? How far had she gone? Where in this terrible darkness were her brothers? Where was the man? She glanced behind her shoulder, hoping to have no sign of him. But she left a bright red trail for any hunter to follow. The darkness would be her only hope.

A fallen branch rose up to greet her. Her foot became tangled. Her head struck a rock. Rayanna fought to move while her body relaxed against her will. She must be able to run. She must be able to escape.

Then she felt someone near. He was here.

~~~~~

Kalif knew someone hid in the trees above. He couldn't see anyone. He barely heard anything. But after years on the fringe, years of hunting and being hunted, he had learned to feel a heartbeat and hear breath flowing through a nose too small to accommodate exhaustion and fear. It hardly mattered anymore if it were a human or an animal. Kalif wasn't sure he knew the difference anymore.

But the spy above his head, if it was a spy at all, was his forgiveness. When he could bring this person back to Ombrar City, he would have a story at the ready. A story about being taken. Fighting valiantly. Capturing this spy. He would be welcomed home with open arms.

And the idiots only a few feet away could ruin it all for him. If Kalif was to spin a tale of his own capture and escape in order to stay in good graces with the Triumvirate, then he could have no one else there to corroborate the story—and mess up the alibi. He had to be alone when he entered the gates. But first he needed to know where the access point to the city could be found.

"Na *guerramen!*" Kalif called out, using the Lima word for warriors. "The time is long past. We must go, now."

"Forget about it. We wait for the others," one of the men said. Kalif scanned the woods beyond them. It was dark. Kalif had never seen darkness like this. Though he knew the smoke from the battle obscured the light, it seemed that even the men's torch dared not shine tonight.

"You read the instructions," Kalif said, stopping under the tree, waiting for a sign of what lay above. "It would be better for us that we not return at all."

"Too late…"

"Slip in through the south access in the Gimnolo Gorge…"

"Wouldn't kill us."

"Not after tonight."

"Triumvirate will protect us."

"Senate won't know we were here."

"True," Kalif said as he rubbed between his fingers the spot of blood that had given away the spy in the tree. Though he had been drenched in blood, this was unmistakably fresh blood.

"True." He repeated. These men could not be here to witness this spy's capture. He had to get back. Through the south access in the Gimnolo Gorge. He had to live. Had to survive. And they stood in the way.

So be it.

With his left hand, he swung his sword in a vicious backhand. The first man's head bounced off his own shoulders before both body and head fell to the ground. The torch fell next to the head, filling the area with the foul stench of burnt flesh and hair. Kalif would have been overcome with the stench had he not just waded into a city full of the same smell.

Then came the attack from the other two. Kalif knew it was coming; they had the same survival instinct that drove him, and that instinct never let shock grip them for too long. He stepped back from a high swing intended for his head. He should have been able to block it, but with his right shoulder stiff with injury, he shifted his weight to his left leg to step back. He could not react fast enough, and the sword cut a deep gash in his right leg.

Step back. Use his right foot to shift his momentum forward again. Swing from left to right, forcing both men back. Back swing to push them one more step. The man on Kalif's left tripped backwards. Kalif grinned.

The Lima warrior stabbed at Kalif. Kalif batted the sword out of the way and shoved the tip of his sword into the man's eye. He howled in pain as his companion came at Kalif. The man brought his arm across his chest for a heavy swing, and Kalif stepped in closer, closing the distance far too quickly for the other to react. Kalif brought his sword down hard, severing the man's arm a little above the wrist. He didn't even have time to cry out. Kalif put his sword into the man's diaphragm before the breath he drew could turn into the scream it was meant for.

Kalif knelt next to the man who howled and held his bloody face.

"I tried to warn you," Kalif said before he shoved his sword into the man's heart.

Kalif steadied himself on the sword still deep in the man's chest. Standing was difficult, thanks to this wretch. Kalif's eyes fluttered. The fatigue was almost too much. But the fire burned brighter. He would have his revenge. It would be personal.

He made quick work of his cloak, tying off the wound to his leg before he began to hunt.

Kalif stood beneath the tree. Nothing. The spy was gone. The rage grew within him, and he struck the tree with the side of his fist. It was bare. Curious, Kalif examined the spot with his fingertips. Yes, it had been scraped off. And there was something wet. Wet, sticky, and thick. Blood. He couldn't do this in the dark. He walked over to the dead men and picked up the torch.

Bringing the torch back to the tree, he spotted more blood on the ground. A footstep. Clearly this footstep was from a very adept spy. Kalif recognized the placement of the foot. This spy knew how to walk without drawing attention. But the spy was injured. Every eight feet or so, there was another blood spot. Only one foot was injured.

Eight feet. That's either a very tall man walking, or a very short man running. There—a leaf that bore a plain footprint. It was a very small footprint indeed. Only a small boy, maybe five to five and a half feet tall.

The line was fairly direct. With these footsteps, the spy had to be skilled at getting through the forest without being heard. But the foot placement was an instinct. It wasn't intentional. If this spy had been intentionally careful, he would have varied his pace and his direction. Both were predictable, meaning the spy was scared. More scared than he had ever been. Kalif smiled as he carefully drew a profile of his prey.

A crash and a sharp sound brought Kalif's attention up. He was close so very close. And then he saw the spy. He saw her. Her. Her.

"No!" Kalif screamed. She was not a warrior. She was not worth sacrificing. Not unless she were important. A political prisoner. But her plain dress clearly showed she was as common as the women Kalif had wasted so much time with back in Ombrar. She was not a spy and could offer no secrets. She was not a governor's daughter he could use for ransom. She would only be good for the priests' sacrifices, and they had plenty of men for sacrificing to their obscure gods.

She moaned at his feet.

"Ray…anna," she gasped.

"Shut up!" Kalif said.

"Name," she said. Kalif knew she would soon pass out. "Name. Me. Rayanna."

Kalif paused. He could not take his eyes off this creature for a moment she stared at him, stared at her death, and the one thing she could say was her name. But it didn't matter what her name was. Filth had no name.

"You think I care about your name?"

"Y...will. You will."

"You're as good as dead."

"Then k...kill me, you pig."

Kalif glared at her, this woman who was not even worth the dirt she lay on. An animal calling him an animal. How dare she? And yet he found himself admiring her courage. Even after he had taken her village and probably her family, she still kept her courage.

But there were ways around that.

"Yes, I could kill you," Kalif bent low to her ear to whisper. "But your filthy people have taken everything from me. I can kill and kill and kill your people. It doesn't make a difference. Maybe it's time to let you live. And I will take everything away from you."

She grit her teeth as tears streamed down her face. Then the fear and the fatigue and the injury to her head wrapped her in their darkness. Her last thought was of her mother. How she loved her. How she missed her. How she needed her now. Now more than ever.

CHAPTER 10:
WHAT DAYS WILL COME

Pain. Pain was the first thing Chism recognized. Pain was how Chism knew he was still alive, before he even opened his eyes. Pain in his head that seemed to press on the backs of his eyes. Pain where a branch had scraped his arm as he fell. Pain where several rocks dug themselves into his ribs, legs, and arms. He was laying on his stomach.

Chism opened his eyes slowly, as if he didn't believe he should be able to. Open. Shut. Open. Shut. The world was black. He placed his hands on the ground to push himself to a sitting position. First the right hand, and then the left. As he pushed, he found his left hand sat in a small pool of blood. His own blood.

Reirdan, Chism thought, *I will kill you for this. But thanks, anyway, for not killing me.*

He groaned himself into a sitting position, growling through the stiff joints and aching muscles. If he wasn't blind—and he wasn't sure about that in this perpetual darkness—then dawn would be here soon. He had to leave while he still had time. That meant that he had to find southwest, and he had to find a weapon.

Chism began a small inventory of his injuries. He passed his hand over the mud, blood, and dirt that stuck to his arms, shirt, and face. "Well, all present and accounted for, lieutenant," Chism joked to himself.

"Wake up!" A man's voice yelled harshly in the distance. Chism guessed it was about forty yards to the south and west.

The dialect was Neroos, but Chism had no idea what the accent was. He lacked any kind of proficiency to tell the difference between a native speaker and a foreigner. And though Chism had in fact slaughtered Lima soldiers on behalf of the Neroos, he would have a hard time convincing them with his Lima accent that the blood that covered his hands was not Neroos. If that man were Neroos, and he discovered Chism, then Chism knew that he stood little chance.

A weapon. He needed a weapon. Where was his sword? He felt the ground all around him as quickly and quietly as he could. He cursed the darkness. Whether the hilt of his sword was five inches away or five miles away, it was just as inaccessible in this darkness.

He looked behind him, hoping to see something in the low burning light of the village's ruins. Bodies. Bodies everywhere. Bodies and stench and death. But one of those bodies had what he needed.

Neroos in front. Neroos behind. He had no quarrel with them, but he had to leave before they could find a quarrel with him. He rushed to the wood line, dodging behind trees as he went, listening carefully for the sound of a patrol. Nothing greeted his ears but the constant, distant wail of broken families and broken soldiers mourning a broken society. They truly had nothing left—nothing but the sound of suffering and the silence of death.

Could Rierdan have been right? That it is better to let them die than suffer a winter together where the dying will kill off the survivors as the food is rationed and everyone starves? Chism found himself aching to cry out with them. Survival instinct, and instinct alone, tore him away from his grief as he continued his search for a weapon.

The first man had nothing. The second had a broken sword. The man next to him had a broken bow and a quiver with four arrows left. *That's something, anyway,* Chism reminded himself. He shouldered the quiver, hoping to find a sword soon.

Then, about twenty feet into the field between the forest and the village, he found it: a bow and a short sword. He was so tired, he doubted that he could last long with a sword. With a little time—and, if the gods were willing, a little light—he might be able to save his skin with a bow.

A shrill scream, a woman's scream, brought his attention not to the city, but back to the forest. Back where he had first heard the cry.

An orange light flickered in the trees. A torch. Between the man's harsh yelling and now a woman's screams, Chism knew what must be happening not too far off.

Chism hobbled as quickly as his stiff muscles would allow. *Was this how Loria met her end?* He pulled an arrow from his quiver, picking his way from tree to tree, feeling his way with his right hand as his left held the bow and a notched arrow. Then he could hear her.

She sobbed through gritted teeth until her voice crescendoed into a scream. Chism appeared as quickly as he could.

She lay on the ground, her head next to a rock. She lay on her side, and her skin was scorched in two places. But what horrified Chism the most was the man who stood covered in blood as he held a torch over his victim. He bent down to touch the flame to her skin again as her sobbing became more frantic.

Chism drew the bow and shouted in a drawn out scream from the darkest place in his heart, "KALIF!"

Kalif snapped his head up. Chism released his arrow.

~~~~~

Rayanna ached. The pain was nothing like she had ever imagined. Not that it was altogether new—she had been burned before. She had fallen out of a tree before. She had been weary many times. But this new pain between her legs and the shame of being abused burned more than any torch. She had never wished agony on any creature.

Not until now.

"KALIF!"

Ah. Kalif. Her demon. It had a name.

An arrow ripped the skin on Kalif's right shoulder. He spun on one foot, preparing to run. But he only took one step before his leg faltered. He stumbled, rose, and fell again just as an arrow burrowed deep into a tree at the same height as his head had been a moment before.

Rayanna could not see the assailant. She knew she could not keep her eyes open or her mind alert for long. She just wanted to see the end.

"Kalif!" the new man screamed again. Rayanna heard him let out a slow breath. Then the sharp sound of the string springing back. Kalif must have run. This new man was taking considerable aim. Another breath. Another snap. A distant crash.

Hands rough with callouses and yet obviously nimble carefully and clinically sought any open wounds on her body. She flinched as the man pulled back her dress to examine the blood and bruises between her legs.

Rayanna wanted to cry out as the realization dawned on her that the physical torture was over and the mental anguish set in. She knew she would dream horrible dreams about whatever other injuries this Kalif had inflicted on her.

The man fell to his knees beside Rayanna and sobbed. It was a familiar sound. Rayanna had come to these woods often and let the anguish out of her eyes and lungs many times in the past six years.

His eyes, having concluded their initial medical examination, finally looked into hers. She saw something there that was both familiar and terrifying. The last thought she had before she slipped away was how much he reminded her of the man he had just killed.

And all was dark again.

~~~~~

Maybe they will make the poor fool a slave, Rierdan thought of Chism as he trotted briskly down the road, keeping his breath controlled and his footsteps light. He knew it was impossible to reach the city before detection. When he reported as a marauder, he knew he would be severely reprimanded. He expected no less than thirty lashes from a faceless messenger from the Triumvirate.

But once he suffered their punishment and endured it well, he would be forgiven and welcomed into their society. There would not be many throats standing between him and the highest echelons. Then he would have his revenge. Then justice would be balanced.

A gray light began creeping over the mountains. Rierdan turned to see how far the morning had progressed and if he was yet out of the ashes of Gidionhi. He longed to stay and rebuild. He was almost ready to end the charade. But not yet. Not now. He was so close.

Then, voices. They were on the edge of the road, just beyond the tree line. A man's voice sounded sharply, then several more raised their voices to quiet him. Rierdan began to feign exhaustion and puffed through his mouth. Gripping his side, he feigned suffering a few more feet, and then he leaned one arm against a tree within feet of the men's location.

The creak of a bowstring was not what Rierdan had thought he would hear first. *This just got a little more complicated,* Rierdan admonished himself. He continued to pant.

"Are you Neroos?" A man asked behind him in what was, frankly, a horrible Neroos dialect.

"Come on, you've got to be joking," Rierdan responded in his impeccable Lima dialect, turning around to face the arrow pointed at his chest. He placed his hands on his hips to keep his lungs expanded. "I'm covered in blood, I'm on my way southwest toward Ombrar, and I'm wearing the cloak."

"That means he knows," another one said. Rierdan counted four. He expected there was another one, maybe two. Six total. They were all nervous. Nothing was more dangerous than a nervous idiot with a weapon.

"We should take him prisoner."

"No, kill him! We can use his blood as payment."

"No! He can make us look good if we make him say what we want. I say we take him."

Deserters. Had they arrived back in Ombrar early, too early, and without the accouterments of blood and ash, they would have been killed. Now that they were late to report back, severe punishment was almost entirely inevitable. Now they had to find a way to at least come through with their lives, and Rierdan was afraid he had just become central to some half-baked plan.

"Wait…" Rierdan said, appearing to still be catching his breath as he put one hand up in front of him for everyone to see. He walked over to the archer and said, "You've got it all wrong. It's… it's like this."

With the other hand that had been resting at his hip, he drew a small blade, cut the bowstring, and gashed the man's arm. He spun around and, with the fist gripping the knife, dealt a heavy blow to the eye of the next man. A quick punch to the archer's ribs dropped him to the ground. Rierdan kicked out the knee of the man coming behind him, and deflated the next man's diaphragm with a savage upper cut. The next two men came at Rierdan with swords at the ready. Rierdan back-pedaled in the low light and easily hopped over the downed archer and the man with the brutalized knee. The two with the swords found their comrades with their feet. One fell with his hands wide, and the other fell on the edge of his sword.

"This is an opportunity," Rierdan said quietly to himself as the company moaned and the man who had fallen on his sword screamed and bled.

"I have just saved your lives," Rierdan announced. "Well, most of you," he said in between the felled man's screams.

"I'll kill you!" One yelled.

"Melek is dying!"

"There's so much blood!"

"I can hardly see!"

"Shut up!" Rierdan shouted. "We need to get back to the city to report, or they'll hunt us all down. I need back in, and you all need an alibi so they don't kill you on the spot as deserters. I can help you, and if you'll listen, then you'll get back to Ombrar and see your families again—or see the tavern again, if that's more important to you."

"Why should we trust you?"

"Because I'm not slipping a blade into every one of you right now."

The moaning subdued. The screams did not.

"Oh by the gods, will you shut up?" Rierdan did nothing to hide his impatience. "If your lung capacity is so great, then so are your chances to live."

Rierdan sat the man up, ripped open his shirt and touched the wound as the man gritted his teeth against the shock and pain. Rierdan ripped off the man's cloak and made quick work of it, cutting it into several long strips that he wrapped over the wound. He honestly thought the man could die, depending on how long it took to return. But this man's well-being was hardly on Rierdan's list of concerns today.

"You're the lucky one," Rierdan said as he wiped off his bloody hands in the man's hair. "You've got enough blood on you to look like you've been in battle."

Rierdan surveyed the rest of the group. "I cut your arm, so you can spread that around. Your eye looks very painful. Get some blood from Melek here or from your archer, and you'll be fine. You with the knee—you were taken out early in the fight, but at least you killed the dirty Neroos who did it to you—stick to that story, and you'll be fine. Frankly, I was probably too nice to the rest of you."

The light was coming quickly now. Rierdan wanted to be back soon.

"Well, get on with it then. I need you to help me get back in. I can't remember where the passage is or what the password is. In exchange, I'll make sure they know of your…bravery."

Within a surprisingly short time, tunics were torn, men were lightly cutting battle scars into their chests, and one or two shed their cloaks. Their obedience was so prompt that Rierdan could almost laugh. A sneer is the most he achieved. Laughter was a stranger to his voice these days.

If all went well, Rierdan may even be able to get in close to the upper echelons by using these men. A payment was never forgotten, and a payment of deserters would be highly valuable, indeed.

~~~~~

Gala never could sleep when there was any light outside. There was something about the morning in Ombrar that enticed Gala out into the crisp air. She felt as if she were in a dream where the air could flirt with her and the sun could kiss her good morning. She didn't want to miss it. *No matter what happens,* she would tell herself, *I'll always see another day.*

Her father used to call her his little lizard because as long as there was light to be seen, Gala would be moving. She hated the nickname, and her childhood indignation had only encouraged her father's teasing.

"No girl wants to be a lizard!" she would say defiantly.

"Oh, you're not just any lizard," her father would say. "You're my Gala-lizard, and I love you!"

WHAT DAYS WILL COME

It had been a long time since she had thought of her father. Sitting up in her bed, she stared at the light creeping across the gray sky and thought of Kalif and what her father would have thought of him. *I hope you're proud of him, papi,* she thought as her mind dwelt on Kalif. *He has seen too much of life, but there is goodness in him.*

Gala was proud of her fiancé as she thought of the justice he was restoring tonight. Proud, and anxious. The Neroos had caused pain, so much pain, for her and her family and her fiancé. She was not sad to see them pay, but she needed to have Kalif's heart and mind. She needed this vendetta to end. Gala wanted more than anything to have a husband who would always be with her. Her father was a good man. So was Kalif's father. Now they were both gone.

Shaking her head to clear the gloom, she wrapped herself in her blanket and stood by the window to greet the morning. Autumn's chill was stretching its long fingers through the air today. She could smell the fresh air mixed with the spice of cold. And something else. Smoke. Smoke like she would smell when winter burned in every fireplace in the city, but not what she would expect on a bright morning like this.

She leaned out the window and looked toward the harbor. No smoke rose from the homes that she could see. Looking east toward the forest, a plume of smoke toward the north caught her eye. It was close. And large.

So, Gala thought. *Gidionhi has atoned for the Neroos' sins tonight.*

Gala turned away from the window suddenly and busied herself with simple preparations for the day. It was time to get to the market for the fresh fruits and meat. She had to keep her hands and feet occupied so that her mind would not have time to wander and wonder if Kalif was back yet. Or if he was coming back at all.

Gala walked quietly through the house. Her mother slept in front of the hearth every night. She said it was because of the cold, which was true. But it was only half of the truth. She missed the warmth of her husband, and embers from yesterday's cooking fire were better than an empty bed. Gala stole away as softly as she could, with her feet making the familiar scraping sound of skin and dust against the cold cement.

Most of the buildings in Ombrar were built of a clay-and-cement mixture. The Lima had more than enough trees to account for all of their buildings, but traditions stood the test of time and distance as the Lima people moved and expanded throughout the land. The Lima would always build with stone and cement. Besides, the Neroos built primarily with woo, and no respectable Lima would follow in their tracks.

Walking down Ombrar's twisted streets between the cool brown, greys, and yellows of Lima buildings, Gala found her way to the market.

"Good morning, Rastafe," Gala greeted the owner of the flour stand, as was her custom. Rastafe had every type of flour Gala could want, and a few types of flour that she would have no idea what to do with. With water on one side and mountains on another, the people in Ombrar had to get creative with their grains. The sea was more plentiful than the mountains, with ships delivering goods and wares from all parts of the continent, but those came at a premium.

"Wheat flour today, Gala?" Rastafe ignored her salutation and got down to business, as was his custom. He knew the answer was no, but it was his solemn duty to sell the highest priced goods possible.

"Just two measures of rice flour will do."

Rastafe grumbled on about the medicinal merits, the superior cooking, and even the psychological impact of half a dozen other types of flour as he slowly and methodically measured out the ground rice.

"Three *tregara*," Rastafe gave Gala the price.

"Three *tregara*? What happened to five *berns*?"

"What do you think happened? The price went up. Just got word this morning."

Gala was perplexed. "'Just got word'? Rastafe, this is your stand. You charge what you want."

"My stand. Their market place. When their prices go up, so do mine. Now get a move on."

It was the same story at every vendor. Gala had hoped to pick up a bag of berries from the dock, but that would have to be put on hold. The price of meat had tripled, so she settled for several measures of nuts instead, and began to walk back up the street to prepare her now-meager meal.

Solvek the tuber farmer was just wheeling his barrel of potatoes and turnips and such into his stand, the stain and smell of dirt all over both food and man, when he called out to her.

"Gala! Here you are. I told them you might be here, but they've only just arrived," Solvek said reassuringly.

Gala looked puzzled. "Solvek, isn't it a little early for liquor?"

"Eh?" Solvek's face went from the slightly lined visage of a middle-aged farmer to a deeply creased visage of one who was very old, very confused, or very indignant. "Look, I'm just saying your guests arrived! They said you were expecting them, I assumed it was for the wedding, and since your mother was probably still asleep I told them to just go in."

Gala was too busy trying to work out in her mind what had just happened to thank Solvek. There were no wedding guests. No relatives. Who would be looking for her at this time of day?

Her stomach seized. She clutched her bag of food like a weapon and began to sprint, her sandaled feet slapping painfully on the stone and dirt streets. Turn. Turn. Twist. Dodge. Run. Run. Run. And then she was there.

The door was closed. Gala paused outside of her home and tried desperately to catch her breath. Everything was fine. *Solvek, you sloppy, smelly dog,* Gala cursed him. *By* porja, *I'm going to blame the blister on my foot on your stupid name.*

She knew that the pounding in her heart wasn't his fault. Gala simply lived in a world where every event was to be endured, and every surprise was a tragedy—even something as simple as confusing passersby for houseguests. Still, it felt good to swear at someone other than herself or the gods.

Pushing open the door, lost in her own musings on the injustices of the world, she checked the contents of her bag as she made her way up the stairs.

"Mother! You wouldn't believe the prices at the market today," she called out as she absent-mindedly pushed open the door. "The meat was almost triple…"

Gala froze instantly. The table was split in half, and the chairs demolished. And the wall was smeared with something deep red. Her mother was not here, she knew. Because that deep red on the wall had to be her mother's blood. And with her mother's blood was written one word:

"KALIF."

Chapter 11:
Who Is My Enemy

Leave her.

She'll die.

You'll die if they find you.

I'll take her with me.

They'll sacrifice her at the temple.

Not if I order them to stand down.

The Triumvirate wants your family dead. Why would anyone obey your orders?

I'm no marauder.

But you kill like one.

Then why does it matter? We're both dead in a week one way or another.

You could run.

Where to? I can never escape you, father.

The tears streamed down Chism's face. She looked so peaceful, this young Neroos who walked hand in hand with death. She was the enemy. Or she was supposed to be. But with a face so young, he could not imagine any fault of her own that could mar her innocence. This was not justice. This was not peace.

Not too far away lay the body of the brother he had come to protect and save. And in his mind played out his father's admonition to keep his family safe. Chism had failed. Kalif was in his grasp, and rather than saving his brother, Chism had shot him. And now he knelt in front of his brother's victim, his head pounding from the wound Rierdan had dealt to the back of his head, and all he could think of was how to save her.

He had to leave. Now. There would be no hope to get himself and this girl out if either were to survive, and in only a few minutes, the body of his brother would be visible from this distance. The thought of seeing Kalif lying where he had shot him was perhaps the last thing he needed to motivate his body to lift the girl and carry her.

I promised. I promised him. I made a promise.

Chism picked his way quickly through the woods with no thought of the noise he made.

"This is the only way," he muttered. "I must keep this family. There is still a way. This is the only way."

~~~~~

Rayanna knew she had been lifted and carried. Reality and dreams blended together, making the most obscure details stand out while the important facts about her condition faded away. She knew she had been lifted up, but rather than being thrown over a shoulder and hauled away, she distinctly recalled being cradled and listening to labored breathing. But the breathing became shorter. The steps became heavier. And soon, she lay facedown, breathing in the soft moldy smell of dirt with the weight of another person draped over her legs.

What does it matter? Rayanna wondered as she wandered in and out of reality. *They have taken everything from me. Everything!*

WHO IS MY ENEMY

Kalif. The name was burned into her mind as indelibly as the aching scorch marks were burned on her arms and legs. Kalif, the Lima responsible for her mother's sacrifice that bought her time to escape. Kalif, the Lima who destroyed her city. Kalif, the Lima who took everything from her and turned her darkest nightmare of violence and rape and loss into her new reality.

Here at the bottom of her pit of despair, Rayanna was surprised that she had no more fear. Nothing more could be taken from her. All she had left was grief. There was only to breathe until her last breath, and she found her grief turning into anger—anger towards her God for forcing her to continue to live.

But there was one that she had hoped would live—Kalif. She wanted him to live long enough to see everything taken away from him. And when he screamed to his gods, pleading with them to end his insufferable life, she wanted to be there to whisper softly in his ear, "No."

With her cheek against the ground, she felt the rumble of horse hooves approaching before she heard them. Hands pressed against her neck in search of a pulse, then rolled the weight off of her legs. She tried to speak, but words were so difficult to grasp. She felt her grip on reality fading quickly.

"What was that?" A voice said.

"What did she say?" Another asked.

Then she mumbled again. "*Youa.*" Water. The Neroos word for water.

"Don't kill them," the first voice said. "Not yet. He's a traitor, and she's Neroos. We'll go straight to the temple and offer a sacrifice. Then we'll demand protection from the priests."

Rayanna understood very little of the exchange. But she knew that Lima temples were at the heart of the Lima city, and that's where she must now be headed. She began to wonder if there really were more to lose. Fear gripped her as dreams and nightmares gathered like black clouds on the edge of her consciousness. Then the dark clouds rolled in on her mind, and all was silent.

~~~~~

"Spread out! Keep the Lima alive when you find them."

Hakoni obeyed his group leader and began to fan out, moving intentionally toward Rayanna's favorite haunts. He had done everything he could to get placed in the right group heading in the right direction. He had never been into the woods with Rayanna, but he had seen her come in and out in this area more often than any other.

"The battle came in further than I thought," Hakoni said to Garrick. Garrick was one of the soldiers sent from the capital. Though the soldiers had become a significant part of the village, Hakoni and many others couldn't decide whether to begrudge the soldiers for not protecting more of them, or begrudge the capital for not sending more soldiers.

A line of men from the village stretched out over a hundred yards, checking pulses and checking identities. Every few minutes, someone would call out, and the nearest man would come over and help drag the half-breathing bodies back to the village. They'd come back later to remove the corpses.

Hakoni's arm ached from the deep wound that ran from the top of his wrist to his elbow. He could see the gash on the top of his arm, and it reminded him of the men he had killed and the people he could not protect.

Aria, Rayanna's mother, had been found just as the day was breaking. They searched the village for survivors and stragglers. Hakoni wasn't the first to Aria's home; he had heard Nathan, the block's militia leader, give the report woodenly to the attending officer. Each loss was a loss to the entire village. They all knew each other, and everything was personal.

"Should have been me," Hakoni muttered to himself.

"What?" Garrick asked.

"Nothing," Hakoni said abruptly, and continued to move further away. Hakoni didn't even know what he meant when he said it should have been him. Should have been him who had found Aria? Or should have been him who had died? Did he wish he had died instead of them? Did he feel guilt for having survived?

Had he stayed, had he protected the family he had come to care about so much, they could have lived. Aria could have lived. Rayanna would not be lost. And Karrh might not have bled out his little life from his severed arm. Hakoni had to believe it—whether it was true or not.

No. It should have been me who found them, Hakoni forced himself to think. *They weren't the only people who died last night. There were many that we saved. But so many who were lost. And for what?*

Hakoni turned over another body. The man groaned. He looked around quickly to see if Garrick or the others had heard. But they were now at least thirty feet apart from each other.

"*Ti ne namen sher quessol?*" Hakoni used the Lima dialect to ask the wounded man his name.

"*Ji...ji sher Yarlem,*" the man responded.

"Too bad for you, Yarlem," Hakoni said in Neroos. Then he stepped on the man's throat as he slowly, carefully checked the body next to Yarlem for a pulse. Yarlem let out a soft cough and tried to gasp for breath. It only last a few seconds before he went still.

"Hakoni!" Garrick hissed.

Hakoni jerked around suddenly, stepping back from the man who lay prone beneath his heel.

"What do you think you're doing?" Garrick whispered as he came closer.

Hakoni's breath quickened as the blood flowed to his face. "I'm fighting a war. What are you doing?"

Garrick stood frozen as he stared at Hakoni. "I had thought better of you."

"Better doesn't have to mean stupid. We've lost...so many... and for what? Huh? This wasn't about land. This wasn't about...

about…food or defense or anything! Now you want to give them our winter rations? Just, what, *give them* the food that would have been on the table of the families they came to kill?"

"He's not fighting back."

"We weren't fighting *at all!*" Hakoni shouted the last two words, his voice and his heart breaking with grief. Every man in the woods, it seemed, paused at the abrupt outburst. The forest and the village had become a sanctuary, and a profound reverence had settled on the whole area. Shouting and any other extraneous noises were highly scrutinized.

Hakoni couldn't take those eyes anymore. Garrick's eyes were as brown as any other Neroos, with his features similarly nondescript. Suntanned skin that was darker than some, lighter than others. Black hair pulled back and tied off with a small strap of leather. It wasn't the color of his eyes that bore so deeply into Hakoni's. It was something about his entire face that could so plainly understand Hakoni's grief, fear, anger, and hate. Hakoni saw it all played out in the high cheekbones and the pursed lips and the eyes with their characteristic downward slant. Hakoni saw in Garrick's eyes something lacking in his own. Peace? Acceptance? Hakoni didn't know, though he was desperate for whatever it was. He would kill a now-harmless Lima to get it. He would kill to get it. And that's why he couldn't look into Garrick's face.

As Garrick knelt next to Yarlem and the other man to check their pulses, Hakoni began walking away.

"Hakoni."

He stopped.

"You'll never be rid of them by becoming one of them."

Hakoni didn't acknowledge Garrick. He just kept moving. He had to keep moving. Had to get away from that spot. Garrick didn't call anyone over to help, so Hakoni had been successful. And he had no idea how he should feel about what he had just done.

As he passed a tree, he found a man face down with an arrow protruding from his left leg and another arrow stuck in a sturdy leather sheath for a shoulder knife that sat between his shoulders. The knife was gone, and the arrow had barely pierced the sheath through to the other side, leaving only a minor flesh wound in his back. As Hakoni rolled the man over, he saw a brutal gash on his forehead above his left eye, and the rock on the ground that put it there.

There was a pulse.

Hakoni hated him. He hated him for the life coursing through his veins when the life from so many other veins stained his skin from head to toe. From the burn scars Hakoni could detect on the right side of his body to the stubble growing out of his just-shaved scalp, Hakoni wanted nothing more than to afflict every part of this man with every sort of torture his grief could devise.

But Yarlem lay dead not fifty feet away, yet the void in Hakoni's village, in the house with the girl whose skin was as gold as honey, was not any smaller.

"Help," Hakoni said quietly. "Help. Help me." Then, willing himself to speak out louder, he said, "Help!"

Garrick was there. He didn't smile. Didn't nod. But in the moment Garrick glanced at Hakoni, that look was still there. Hakoni couldn't help it; his jealousy twisted his view of Garrick, and resentment began to set in like infection in a fresh wound. Looking down at the bloodied face of this Lima that Garrick helped him carry, Hakoni told himself that this war would never be over so long as there was Lima blood left in the village.

~~~~~

Gala heard someone knocking, but the sound was not coming from the door to her flat. It came from her room. She stood stoically as tears made silent trails down her cheeks, under her chin, and continued to crawl until they pooled near her collarbone.

"Are you going to kill me?" She said as clearly as she could.

"You know where he is," a sandpapery voice responded. Gala had no recollection of ever hearing that voice before. Was it male or female? Was that accent even from Ombrar? So many questions. And now she cared nothing to find out.

"Why did you take my mother? She did nothing!"

"Kalif. You know where he is," the voice repeated.

"Only by the smoke. I know nothing of any of this!"

"Liar! You know he was supposed to be back before dawn. You know he has a debt to pay. We demand payment."

Gala had no energy to barter. No strength to keep talking. "You killed her, you *batarkre*. You killed your last bargaining chip. Whatever you wanted from me, you're not getting it now."

"Oh she's not dead yet. But she was bleeding quite a lot last I saw her. Poor thing. She got her blood everywhere…all over the wall, too." If a voice could sneer, this voice was accomplishing the feat with aplomb. She wanted to walk out, to call the voice a liar, to refuse to be a puppet. But if her mother truly was still alive, then she had a duty.

"You're wasting my time," Gala said in acquiescence.

"We want Kalif. Before your mother bleeds out. You have a few hours, at best."

"What if he's dead? I don't know anything! I didn't even know where he went until I saw the smoke this morning, I swear. What if he's hiding somewhere?"

"Then find him."

Gala walked calmly, steadily, out of her apartment and down the street. If she were to be a puppet on a string or a dog on a leash, she would show them that she was not to be controlled. She would comply, yes, for the sake of her mother. But she would not be controlled.

She needed a hunter. Kalif didn't have many friends; not many that would stick a neck out for him, anyway. But she knew the one person she could trust was Chism.

When she had turned a few corners away from her flat, she bolted.

~~~~~

Rierdan was too proud to kneel in front of any man. No king was lofty enough, no senator powerful enough, and no man special enough to deserve that kind of respect.

But when he and his small band of deserters were brought to a dark room where faces were barely visible and entirely unrecognizable, several swift jabs to the kidney were more than enough to bring proud Rierdan to his knees. Rough ropes dug into his wrists as he tried to stop himself from falling over. Rierdan made a mental note to cut off the hands of whichever man had tied his wrists behind his back.

"We told you not to be late," said a voice in the dark.

The men he was with whimpered. The rasping sound of steel against scabbards escalated their whimpering into sobs. Rierdan hoped his captors would kill at least a few of them. Cutting their throats would be best. Then they wouldn't be able to make so much noise.

Rierdan listened to the sounds bouncing off the walls and ceiling. He counted at least six weapons being drawn. There was little reason for any one man to draw two weapons when their opponents were tied up. He imagined a room twenty feet wide and maybe as much as thirty feet across, if not larger. The light in the room emanated from two candles placed on the floor at the entrance to the room, making the prisoners visible to their captors while obscuring everything else for the prisoners.

Rierdan couldn't see the ceiling—with the dark cowl they had forced over his head, he was struggling to see anything. He'd estimated the ceiling to be much higher than the usual Ombrar house. Judging from the extensive walk and trying to keep his bearings after having been taken prisoner inside the tunnel, he assumed he was somewhere near the heart of the city. A government building, perhaps?

"Now you must be punished," the voice said, having waited for a dramatic pause before hissing out his threat. The sobbing grew louder still.

"Punish me as you will, sir," Rierdan said loudly through the cowl. "I served you last night for a just cause, and I will serve again. Surely those dogs in Gidionhi will have suffered a far greater punishment than I will."

"Bold words. Do you not cower like your comrades?"

Rierdan stood, slowly. "These are not my comrades, sir. These are my tribute. A band of deserters I captured and lured back to the city."

"You dog! I'll kill you for this, Tristan!" One of the men screamed.

"I doubt that," Rierdan said quickly.

"Deserters, are they?" The voice spoke. "Leave him. Take them down."

The men were roughly, and loudly, removed as Rierdan stood silently with his hands still tied and head hooded. A heavy door shut, and the cowl was yanked from his head. Rierdan's eyes had little to adjust to as the room was almost as dark as was the hood. He could see now from the light that the room was an oval rather than a rectangle, and the ceiling was high enough to be obscured in the darkness.

"So…Tristan," the voice spoke.

The edge of a knife bit into his throat. This was not a calloused warning, Rierdan knew.

"I hate being lied to, Tristan, so as long as you speak the truth, you get to keep the blood in your head."

"Until when? You can bleed me of information just like you can bleed me of blood. Either way, I end up dead."

"Then start talking," came a curt reply.

"You know who I am—and I never lied to you about that. Just them. So either gut me now or get this knife out of my throat."

"What does the assassin Rierdan want with the Triumvirate?"

Rierdan didn't answer. The tension in the room built. Finally he said, "I gave you my terms."

The man removed his knife from Rierdan's throat.

"I want the same thing anyone else wants—power that only the Triumvirate can provide. But I'm not one of those idiots," Rierdan nodded toward the door where the deserters had disappeared. "I'm not interested in signing up for the front lines. And in return, I have a particular set of skills that the Triumvirate needs at its disposal."

"Why do you think we need your skills?"

"Because you've used them before…senator."

"Kill him." The voice whispered.

As the men were walking toward Rierdan, he spoke quickly, "Kalif didn't come back. And if you want the rest of the information, you'd better think twice."

"Stop!"

"That's better," Rierdan said without a hint of trouble in his voice. "Do you intend to keep the newest member of your circle with his hands tied behind his back, or should I kill your men without that added help?"

Rierdan could just imagine this man's aged face curled into a look of utter contempt that brought the wrinkles from his bald head into a cluster of lines, secrets, worries, and power.

The senator spoke slowly. "Untie him."

The guards looked at each other in fear.

~~~~~

Mossad the gate guard had received orders late last night. Anyone coming in the gates in the early hours who looked like they had been through *hadieres*, the orders said, were to be arrested without question. Find out what they had been up to, and then deliver them to some new corporal or colonel that Mossad had never heard of at a house he had never seen.

The orders had his leader's signature on it. But that didn't mean that Mossad liked it. Or that he thought the orders really came from his leader.

To hadieres *with these orders,* Mossad thought. *I'm not a marauder puppet.*

But the sack of five hundred *tregara* waiting for him at his post this morning with a simple note—"Your orders stand"—was quite motivating. And terrifying. He needed the money. Who didn't? But this sum was never given without payment in return. These people would have their payment, either from Mossad or from the ones he cared about.

"Easy there," said Mossad as he put his hand up to stop the two men on a horse. One rode behind the other, while their second horse carried two bodies draped over its back. "You boys don't look so great. Been anywhere close by last night?"

Mossad motioned to the two other guards at the gate to make sure the men didn't go anywhere while he walked around to inspect the men and the bodies they had brought with them.

"We were traveling back from the areas around Limhah to the north," one explained. "Good hunting."

"You're a mess. Something tells me you were hunting something other than deer to the north," Mossad said.

"We got caught up in the smoke on the way back. We were attacked. This one," the man in front said as he gestured to the man who lay across packhorse, "put up quite the fight. We caught him trying to run off with this Neroos girl. We knew them for the spies they were and brought them back. He killed two of our group before we were able to knock him out."

Mossad ran his hands through the girl's hair. "Are you sure she's Neroos?"

"The only word that came out of her mouth was in Neroos."

"And him?" Mossad grabbed the man's hair and yanked his head back.

"Who knows? The idiot tried to tell me he was lieutenant of the city guard."

Mossad scrutinized the bruised, bloody, and swollen face. "*Corva!* It's him! It's Lieutenant Chism!" Mossad muttered under his breath and backed up involuntarily.

"Off your horse! Now!" One of the other guards demanded.

The two men looked stunned. "We're taking the prisoners to the temple! We're making a sacrifice to the—"

Mossad spun around and strode to the two who sat too stunned to move. "Get off!" He declared, and unceremoniously yanked the two down. The horse didn't move.

Mossad kicked dirt in their faces as they lay prone on the ground. "That's not a citizen's horse, you imbeciles. That horse is prepared for battle, which means you are prepared for battle." Mossad turned to shout at the other two guards. "Bind them. Take them to this… colonel someone or another."

"Colonel Ablom, sir?" One of the guards offered.

"The blazes with his name! Just get these two out of my sight!" Mossad half screamed at the guards. Mossad ignored the sound of the scuffling as the two were beaten, had their hands bound, and shuffled off. Mossad placed his hands on the saddle and stared at the ground, gritting his teeth and swearing. Passing these two idiots to the marauders was one thing, but Lieutenant Chism…. Mossad knew that there had to be a better story than what met the eye.

Being in the city guard of Ombrar did not always give Mossad the pleasure of meeting good men. He could think of a dozen men in his platoon that were openly involved in something shady and secretly involved in something worse. But not the lieutenant. No one had a cleaner nose than him. So what was he doing in Gidionhi last night, why was this Neroos girl with him, and what was going to happen to him now?

"What's the point of being a good man if this is how it ends, Lieutenant?" Mossad asked the still-unconscious Chism.

"Seezoram!" Mossad called over to the other guard. "Find Zerin. Send him out to take your post. I want you to take these two to the barracks and lock them down."

Seezoram stood where his feet were planted.

"I gave an order!" Mossad said as he walked over to face down the young recruit.

"Sir, no matter his rank, this man disobeyed orders. He's…he's a marauder. And her! She deserves—"

He didn't finish what he had to say. It was too difficult to speak after Mossad landed a fist squarely between his eyes and broke his nose.

Mossad reached down and grabbed him by the shirt. "Find Zerin. You're relieved. Prisoners. Barracks. Now."

Seezoram brought himself to his shaky feet, picked up his shield, and tried to navigate himself over to the horse.

"One more thing," Mossad said.

Seezoram stopped in his tracks, thankful for a reason to stop moving and get his bearing.

"Leave your weapons with me."

Seezoram groaned as he removed his sword belt and dropped his shield.

"Move."

Seezoram grabbed the horse's reigns and walked through the gate.

As Seezoram disappeared, Mossad muttered, "*Porja*, Chism. By *porja*, what have you done?"

~~~~~

"Zerin," Seezoram managed to call out when he got to the barracks. "You've been called to the gate. Grab a shield and report to Mossad."

138

Zerin stood smartly and began to gather his affects. "Where are you off to, soldier?"

Seezoram rolled his eyes at Zerin's characteristic pomp. No one on the city guard called each other "soldier." No one but Zerin, of course. "It's Seezoram, like I told you a hundred times. Just get your *geffes* over to the gate."

"Nice shiner," Zerin jibed. "Mossad give that to you?"

"Yeah, he did, and he gave me orders, too. Now move."

Zerin grabbed a shield and helmet and walked out the door behind Seezoram. Another guard held the horse for Seezoram, and Zerin could see two bodies, a man and a woman, draped over it. The man began to groan.

"Who're they?" Zerin asked.

"Traitors." Seezoram said as he walked away with the horse in tow.

Zerin paused to watch him go, noting where his path would likely take him, and then turned and reported to Mossad.

"Glad to see you finally decided to show up," Mossad said when Zerin arrived several minutes later.

"Seezoram decided to get smart with me. He thought it'd be better to just roll his eyes than to tell me what I needed to know."

At that moment, the second guard returned from transporting the two prisoners to Colonel Ablom's headquarters. Mossad could see blood on the backs of the guard's legs.

Mossad shook his head to clear the thoughts of what they had done to the prisoners that would splash blood in that manner, and refocused on Zerin. "Did he get the prisoners to the barracks?"

"Yes," Zerin said. "For a minute. But then they left. I gotta say, sir, I didn't figure you'd ever send someone to the temple. Even for a Neroos, that's really something awful. I can't imagine even those *batarkres* deserve what those priests do."

Mossad's face turned white. If Seezoram had taken Chism and the girl to the temple, their fate was out of Mossad's hands. The priests at the temple regularly hosted an open-air sacrifice so that the people could see justice in action. Justice against the Neroos and anyone caught helping them. And if Chism and the girl were taken to temple, then whoever gave Mossad the orders would know that he had disobeyed them.

"*Corva*," Mossad swore, and ran into the city without another word.

Chapter 12:
From the Flames

"It's hard to be impressed, Mr. Rierdan," the senator said, "when I already knew what you were capable of."

"That wasn't about impressing anyone," Rierdan said as he sawed through the last of the ropes binding his wrists and stepped over the two guards who lay impaled at his feet. "I just hate the feel of a knife against my throat. And I don't accept threats."

"Never fear," the senator rasped in reply. "I only give promises."

"Then promise me what I have earned: a place in your council."

The senator smiled slightly in the dark. "You have proven that you are an agent of chaos. You can kill and disappear in such a way that not even the shadows knew you were there. But I need someone who can be an agent of justice! I need someone who believes in our cause. Do you believe in our cause, assassin?"

Rierdan's eyes narrowed involuntarily. "I am an agent of justice. You will know it soon enough."

"No. You are an agent of chaos," the senator whispered. "A dangerous foe to have—a dangerous foe, but a powerful ally! You and I have this in common." He paused, and Rierdan felt the senator's eyes assessing him with inscrutable judgment. Finally, the senator whispered again, "Come. There is much to learn."

Rierdan wanted to smile. He was close to his goal. So close! But somehow the victory had gone out of it. And he felt nothing.

~~~~~

Gala shivered as she sat hunkered down in the doorframe to Chism's apartment as people on the street passed carelessly, so carelessly in front of her. The thoughts of today's events chilled her. The blood smeared across the wall of her home. Her mother beaten and bleeding somewhere. The possibility that she may never see her mother again. Going to the market and worrying about the price of meat now seemed so far away, as if it were part of another life. Gala had nowhere to run but straight to Chism, and he wasn't here.

The morning was quickly warming up, but the fear in Gala's heart seized her like cold steel shackles binding her to a phantom that cackled at her from the shadows of her own home. She hadn't even had the courage to face him. Now she was running about to do the voice's bidding. Though her wrists were unfettered, she felt like a slave. A slave to the voice. A slave to her own cowardice. Gala hated herself for it.

"Make way!" A man cried. The sound of horse hooves clattered against the stony ground and reverberated down the narrow, packed street. Rather than stepping out of the way, passersby paused in their tracks to look toward the noise. The entire city was abuzz with speculation on what had happened the night before. No official message had been announced yet, and the rumors swarmed like locusts, feeding on any piece of fact, gossip, or hearsay they could find.

The voice cried louder, "To the temple! Make way to the temple!"

At the mention of the temple, the people immediately stepped aside, and the man came through as quickly as he could with a horse in tow. On its back lay two bodies. A man and a woman. The man had thick brown hair, and his shoulders were broad. Gala knew that man. He was her only hope to save her mother's life. And he was unconscious on the back of a horse, on his way to be sacrificed.

Gala immediately stood and ran after the horse. She was not the only one. What had been a hapless crowd of meandering people became a throng of Lima anxious to witness the latest evidence of their nation's greatness.

By the time Gala reached the temple, she had to struggle to push her way through to come closer to the altar. Two burly priests with naked torsos and a red cloth wrapped around their waists as their only covering pulled the two off the horses. They then carried Chism and the girl next to him up the short steps laid them on the dais.

The temple of *Na Shuhn Mun,* the many gods, was mostly an outdoor structure that consumed a large portion of real estate in the burgeoning city. The streets and buildings themselves seemed to give the temple a wide berth, though whether it was out of deference or abhorrence, Gala never could decide. She made a point of staying away from this place. Too many memories haunted her.

Gala shuddered yet again as she passed through the slave market, which stood adjacent to the temple, and remembered a day burned in her memory when she last dared approach the slave market. She had only been a child when a slave seized her by the arm and pulled her face to his. "*I bleed red!*" The man had cried. "*I bleed red!*"

The temple was right next to the slave market, and it served as a reminder that these outsiders, stolen from Neroos villages and lands beyond the seas, were an ever-present threat. It was the Lima duty to protect the city from these people. The sacrifices that these few made would save thousands, the priests would always declare. These sacrifices would keep the city safe.

The altar of the temple was a platform of once-gray stone that rose several feet from the ground and spanned fifty feet across. Twenty tall posts, each adorned with wooden posts and shackles, lined the outer rim of the platform. In the center of it stood a smaller altar of stone four feet wide, four feet high, and seven feet long. The gray stone of the altar and the platform had been awash in blood and flames on countless occasions, staining it permanently black. No effort had ever been made to clean the stone.

Walking to the temple on any given day, a Lima would usually find two or three bodies with hands shackled and raised above their heads, the balls of their feet barely touching the ground. Their skin, when not burned black, ranged in color from soft whites to beautiful browns and deep ebonies. As a girl, Gala had often found herself wishing she could hear their native languages. It had once been music to her ears.

The priests shoved a pot overflowing with smoke in Chism's face and in the face of the girl that accompanied him. Gala was snapped back to the here-and-now as Chism and his companion were both shackled to the posts where the priests could question them in front of the gathering crowd.

As the priest stepped toward Chism and the girl, Gala could see the astonishment written across the priest's face. This was a ritual he performed every day, and the temple yard's only occupants were slave traders coming to and from the slave market, ignoring his braying as they passed. But today, with the plume of smoke in the northwest and this dramatic presentation of sacrifices, the priest stood before the largest crowd he had ever seen. And he was not about to let his moment of fame pass him by.

~~~~~

FROM THE FLAMES

Mossad was astounded by the masses that had gathered at the temple as he raced up to the edge of the crowd. There, tied to a pole, was his lieutenant. So where was that piece of dirt, Seezoram?

"My children!" The priest bellowed out to the crowd. The priests of *Nah Shuhn Mun* always referred to the people as their children, presuming to take on themselves the name of Lima himself as their endowed right. "We congregate today to make a sacrifice to our gods for sparing us yet again...*from them!*" He said, pointing dramatically to Chism and his companion.

"Oh, *porja,*" Mossad swore and began pushing through the crowd. If his family got hurt for this, he would make sure that Seezoram paid for his disobedience.

Then he saw Seezoram, standing shadowed between two buildings toward the back of the crowd, holding the reigns to what he must have thought was his new horse. Mossad's blood ran cold, and he began to devise a plan. He had no idea how well it would work, but it was worth a try. It was worth the revenge.

He spun around, darted behind the buildings, and began to come up on Seezoram from the rear.

"Speak for yourselves before the gods consume your miserable existences!" The priest said with as much flare as he could muster. Had Mossad had the time or interest to stop and listen, he might have doubled over laughing at the spectacle. Many in the crowd already snickered at the priest's pomp.

Requiring the detainees to speak for themselves was a formality, because those being sacrificed either had a rudimentary understanding of the Lima language at best, or no understanding at all. It was then the priest's obligation to interpret whatever wailing, screaming, or speaking the accused would say. When the priests had the opportunity to interpret, the slaves and prisoners always confessed plans to destroy the Lima way of life, along with a litany of sins for which they begged the gods to punish them.

The Sound in the Silence

Just as the priest was about to interpret the two prisoners' silence into a lengthy confession, something happened that neither the priest nor many in the crowd expected: Chism spoke.

~~~~~

Gala stood on the west side of the crowd, as far away from the slave market as she could. Fear for her mother's life and her need for Chism were the only things that could compel her to come over here. Just as the priest began to expand his lungs in preparation for a speech about wrongs, misdeeds, and sins of the vilest nature against the Lima nation, Chism began to speak.

"I am...I am Chism," he said, somewhat breathlessly. "I am Lieutenant Chism of the city guard," he repeated. "I report to Captain Forya. I have served the Lima of Ombrar all my life, and it was in their service that I was taken captive."

The priest looked stunned. Gala could see the wheels spinning in his head, trying to recuperate his theatrics so as to continue with the execution. Chism continued.

"I saw from my post that a band of Neroos might be gathering to attack our beautiful city. I set out to gather intelligence on their position, their numbers, and their timing. I tracked their spies back to Gidionhi where another contingent of, umm, brave Lima warriors were already defending our ...uh...beautiful city," he said awkwardly.

Gala's mouth hung wide. She had never heard Chism try to speak so eloquently and so horribly, let alone be so complimentary of Lima society.

"Then why," the priest said, entering into what he supposed was a clever cross-examination, "were you traveling with...*this*?" he said, spitting on Rayanna who was too disoriented to notice the slight.

"She..." Chism faltered. "She was my prisoner. Before we were ambushed."

Even from the distance that she stood, Gala could see plainly written on Chism's face the pieces of some elaborate puzzle fall into place.

"And she is *met etonalle*," he said loudly. *Met etonalle*, one of several Lima words for "mine." But it was hardly just a matter of possession; it meant that he had taken herself to him and had made her his wife.

Gala's eyes flew open. She knew that Chism was incapable of such a thing as rape; she seriously doubted he had any experience whatsoever with women. But if that Neroos girl were not pregnant and showing in the next few months, then Chism would have quite another problem on his hands. Unless he didn't need more than a few months to accomplish whatever he had planned.

"*Met etonalle?*" The priest repeated incredulously. "You have taken a child of the Great Enemy to yourself? You shall both burn for this!"

The crowd had been listening with bated breath and some began to cheer, having been taken in somewhat by the priest's enthusiasm.

"No! It is only right that the Neroos be made to bear the burden of Lima's children! And now this Neroos bears the burden of my child. Is it not what the gods want? This is my sacrifice to make, and I make it in the name of Lima and of *Nah Shuhn Mun*." Chism said. The crowd began to mutter amongst itself, dazed at this bizarre turn of events.

"How is it you were brought here, tied, and led by a Lima?" the priest asked, sure that he had caught Chism this time.

Chism's mouth opened and shut. "I…well we…it was very…."

Then a scream drew every eye to the back of a crowd.

"It was him!" said a soldier, who was pushing another man, screaming, in front of him. The crowd parted as the two made their way to the platform, and the first man, a soldier, threw his prisoner onto the platform. "I am Mossad. This man, Seezoram, is a traitor to our people! He knowingly tried to sacrifice our lieutenant, because he is loyal to the Neroos!"

Seezoram bled profusely from a hole in his side, and Mossad held a dripping knife in his hand. Gala had to look away as she realized that Mossad had stabbed the man and used the knife to push him forward to the stage.

The priest smiled at Seezoram's pleas and accusations. He would have his sacrifice after all. "Release them!" he cried, pointing to Chism and the Neroos girl. Then with a dramatic wave of his arm, he pointed at Seezoram and cried out, "Bind him to the altar!"

Gala watched as Mossad quickly grabbed Chism and the girl and rushed off the platform. She raced toward them, desperate to get to Chism. She had to get to him. She had to save her mother. It had already been almost two hours since she found the blood smeared on the wall and received her orders.

All the while, she could hear Seezoram's shrieking as they tied his hands and wrists to each corner of the altar. The priests never did gag their victims. It was justice, they would say. It was the sound of the suffering that the Lima would now no longer have to endure. Some in the crowd stayed and cheered while the rest began to quickly disperse. They had come for the news, not for the pain.

"Chism!" Gala cried out above the crowd as she pushed and shoved her way toward him. "Chism, please! Help me!" The crowd seemed eager to leave this place as Seezoram's last breaths wailed in their ears. *He will be at peace soon enough*, Gala thought.

Chism was holding the Neroos girl as tightly as he could, presumably to protect her. But Gala could tell that his grasp on the girl was more out of desperation than protection. She was a lifeline, a drifting piece of wood for Chism to hold onto as he sunk further and further into his fears. With one arm around her shoulder and the other arm using Mossad as support, he could only turn his neck this way and that to find the voice as Chism led them both away as quickly as he could.

"Gala!" He yelled.

Finally reaching the trio, whose movements were restricted even more than her own, Gala began to explain everything and nothing:

"Chism! It's my mother. They have her, and she's dead, or she might be dead. They attacked her while I was out this morning. I saw the smoke, Chism. I saw the smoke, and I knew where Kalif and the others must have gone, but they want him, and I don't know where he is. Oh, please help, Chism, they'll let her die if I don't bring them news of Kalif!"

Mossad continued to push them along. "Get out of here, lady! There's something bigger going on here than you right now."

"No," Chism said, panting for breath as his head reeled and his stomach ached for food and water. "Mossad, she needs us."

"Then drop the Neroos," Mossad said as he scanned the crowd for anyone following. "I came to save your skin, Lieutenant, not hers. You can't save everyone."

Chism's head was splitting. Rest. He just needed rest. "I'll take the girl. We'll disappear into the High Tide District. Go with Gala to help her mother, then find me afterward."

"Chism!" Gala shrieked, her anxiety building to hysteria. "Where's Kalif? Where is he? They'll kill my mother if I don't tell them!"

Chism didn't have to ask who had her mother. "He's dead."

She froze. Chism could see the grief in her eyes colliding with the shameful feeling that perhaps Kalif had deserved his fate. One emotion touched the other like fire touching sulphur, and the reaction was almost more than she could bear. "Are you sure?"

"Yes," Chism said. "I...I saw it."

This would not be the end of that explanation, Gala decided. But for now, it would have to suffice. Her face relaxed as she lost her hope, her will, and her grasp on her reality. She turned and began walking briskly.

"Mossad, go with her. Please."

He stared at Chism for a moment, then turned to go.

"And Mossad!"

He paused, turning his head slightly.

"Thank you. For everything. I know you've put yourself in danger today."

Mossad only nodded, and trotted after Gala's quickly departing figure.

Chism looked around the street. Everywhere he turned his head, the people suddenly began busying themselves, trying not to be caught in their wide-eyed observation of these two. But Chism was less concerned about those in the crowd who turned away; he wanted to know who wouldn't turn. He counted three—two glanced away for a moment without turning their frame; another kept vigilant eye contact.

"Can you understand me?" Chism said in a Lima dialect to his Neroos companion.

She squinted her eyes briefly, then gave a curt nod.

"Can you walk?" Chism asked.

Again, she nodded.

"Good. We're going to have to move fast. We don't want to be seen anymore."

Chism kept a firm grip on her and began to move. Out of the corner of his eye, he saw two move after him; the third stayed where he was.

Corva cavesa, Chism swore to himself as they moved swiftly along while trying not to call attention to themselves.

Out of the corner of his eye, Chism discovered a narrow alley that backed itself into another building: a dead end. He immediately steered his Neroos companion toward it.

"We need to hide in there. Now," Chism said.

The girl stiffened and began to back pedal. "There is not escape there!" she said in halting Lima.

"I like my odds better when I take them on one at a time," Chism said grimly.

The alley was strewn with refuse from the street—old wooden crates piled high, pieces of wood, scraps of cloth, and feces of stray animals.

"You like this?" She said with an arched eyebrow.

"To be honest, I don't like any of it," Chism said as he began pulling crates apart. He yanked hard on a long wooden box. Rusted swords and daggers fell out. "But I won't say no to a little help," he muttered.

"Rayanna."

"What?"

"My name. I am called Rayanna."

"I'm Chism. And I'm sorry for all of this. How about you hide behind those crates and pray to whatever gods you believe in that we live through the next fifteen minutes, OK?"

"Not good plan," Rayanna said. "But I do what you say."

Chism couldn't help but smile. He bent over to see what treasures had just landed at his feet when an arrow cut a shallow, bright red line across his back. He snapped his head around to see the man at the mouth of the alley notch another arrow and draw his bow for a second shot.

CHAPTER 13:
WHAT CHAINS MAY BIND

Kalif opened his eyes. Slowly. His hands ached. He sat against a stone wall, and cold metal brushed against his shoulders and clanged against the wall above his head. The room where he found himself reeked of manure and hay, and the clattering sounds of chains filled the long makeshift prisoner barracks. His wrists were shackled and left hanging six inches below his shoulders. His wrists were bent in such a way that the circulation was cut off to his hands, and the swelling ached in every finger. The cuffs were linked to a chain that looped through a peg above his head.

He was an unmitigated prisoner of war. That much was easy to understand. What Kalif could not understand was why he was in this stone-floor-and-wall stable that had been so hastily and poorly mucked out. By all accounts, he should be facedown in a mass grave.

If only you could see me now, Gala. Is this the man you saw in me? Kalif yearned for her company, yet he simultaneously rejected the idea. *She can't see me like this. Not after what I've done. Not after how I've disappointed her.*

Kalif felt a surge of emotions, loathing toward himself not being the least among them. But for the first time in a long time, he couldn't understand where his ire came from. Was it anger for not triumphing over more Neroos, or anger at the Neroos' triumph over him? Disappointment that he wasn't dead, or disappointment that he hadn't succeeded? Shame for being caught, or shame for what he'd been caught doing?

He shook his head and tried to focus. No time for emotion. He needed a plan, and he needed to execute it. Discover their motive. Learn their schedules. Assess their weaknesses. Exploit them. And stick a knife in the gut of that *punta* that chained him up like this.

It was a reactionary plan. It was the same as every other plan he had devised to escape the consequences of his actions: exploit a weakness, take revenge, and never answer for what he had done. But the thrill of the hunt and of the escape was gone. Even with his arms dangling and aching and Neroos right in front of him to blame for it, he couldn't savor the thought of killing yet another man.

Stop it, Kalif reminded himself. *No more sentiment. Just do what needs to be done. Lose yourself in a plan.*

Lima soldiers lined both walls of the dirty stables that measured fifty feet long by ten feet wide. Each had two feet between himself and the next man. There were only twenty Lima soldiers in here. Five guards stood in view on the other side of the short stone wall. One well-armed soldier to four unarmed Lima prisoners. The odds were not in Kalif's favor.

Kalif had to hand it to the Neroos—they had suspended the hands of all the Lima in an incredibly short amount of time. But it wasn't just the timing that he found impressive; it was the strategy behind it. With their hands suspended, the prisoners would find it impossible to get too clever or cause trouble. Each arm would have to be lowered so that the other could be below the heart and get blood flow. Their movements were extremely limited. And by spacing each man far enough apart, they could not help each other, and all communication between the men was loud enough to be obvious to the Neroos guards. The Lima were completely at the mercy of their captors.

"Hey," Kalif said in as low a voice as he could, trying to get the attention of the man next to him while keeping his eye on the guard only fifteen feet away. "Hey, *convren*," he said a little louder, using the Lima word for companion. The Lima prisoner still didn't turn to look. Kalif stole a glance to his left to see if the man there had heard. Kalif's neighbor moaned with his eyes closed. A heavy sweat was breaking out on his brow, and a deep red bandage encircled his ribcage. His breathing was ragged.

Kalif pursed his lips and, after glancing quickly at the soldiers, turned to the man on his right. "*Convren*, can you hear me?"

"Yes. I hear you," the man said evenly, as if he were back in Ombrar in the market or on a small fishing boat.

The man's voice unnerved Kalif more than the guards, the chains, or the situation he was in. But Kalif needed information. "How often do the guards change?"

"I haven't seen them change," came the even reply.

Kalif looked at the guards to see if any were trying to listen nonchalantly. One guard, a shorter man with broad shoulders and short brown hair, leaned against the wall with his back to Kalif. The guard gave no indication of listening to their conversation, but he knew that every move he made and every word he spoke while in this place was a risk. There were always ears listening.

Kalif was careful to shift his hands, causing the chains to clatter above while he spoke so that he could hide his voice in the din. "What do they plan for us?"

The man only shook his head, staring straight ahead the entire time.

Just then, three guards opened a gate and came down the line, stopping in front of the man to the left of Kalif. Two guards stood on either side of the Lima. The guard who stood next to Kalif was the same broad-shouldered young man Kalif suspected of eavesdropping only moments before. He looked down at Kalif with a fire in his eyes that Kalif had once known so well.

The guard blocked Kalif's view. All he could see was the third man kneeling close to the Lima with the blood-soaked bandages. A horrific scream reverberated off the stones in what Kalif could only assume was pure torture.

"Stop it!" Kalif yelled. "Stop it! Can't you see he's hurt? Leave him alone!" The sudden sense of injustice overwhelmed Kalif and surprised him so much that he barely registered the guard's backhand across his face.

"You stay silent!" the guard yelled at Kalif in accented Lima.

"It's all right, Hakoni," the third man said in Neroos to the soldier who stood glowering over Kalif. Kalif had not expected to hear so calm a tone from a man he had suspected of torturing a wounded soldier. "This one's got to go. Let's get him to the infirmary. Make sure the bandages get changed."

Hakoni stood for a moment longer staring at Kalif, his hands quivering. Kalif knew the feeling well. And he knew just how to touch that nerve to send a person over the edge. He looked up at Hakoni, and smiled in defiance as he spoke in Neroos: "I think your master just gave you an order. Little doggy."

Hakoni's reaction was immediate. Even as Kalif waited for the blows to rain down on him, he grinned. *So easy to manipulate,* Kalif thought.

"Hey!" The third soldier who had given the order quickly pulled Hakoni away from Kalif as Kalif laughed at Hakoni's struggling. "Get to it. Now."

Hakoni shrugged off the encounter and, accepting the keys to the Lima's cuffs from his superior, unlocked the wounded Lima soldier. He supported him under one arm with the other soldier opposite him.

The soldier who appeared to be in charge stood in front of Kalif and watched the two men leave with their charge. Then he kneeled in front of Kalif.

Kalif said, "At least the little doggy knows how to take orders—"

The soldier swiftly punched Kalif in the throat with his fingers curled to the second knuckles, paralyzing Kalif's windpipe for a moment.

"Now, you listen to me," the soldier said calmly as Kalif struggled and gasped for air. "My name is Garrick. Yes, I run a few things around here, including Hakoni. And more importantly, including you. There are a lot of people here who want you dead, so don't push your luck. Little doggy."

Kalif coughed, choked, and gasped for air until Garrick reached forward and massaged his neck to help the blood flow again. Kalif began breathing heavily but normally.

"Now let me check those bandages," Garrick said.

Kalif recoiled instinctively from Garrick, but Garrick grabbed his right arm and pulled his shoulder around. "Too bad you have to be in these chains. It's not helping the stitches at all. How's your leg?"

"Are you done?" Kalif said irritably.

"Yeah, for now," Garrick said. "But we'll need to take a look at those soon. We need to get you outside as soon as we can, and you're in better shape than anyone here."

"Outside for what?"

"Work," Garrick said simply. "Rest up, *escarren*," he said, using the Neroos word for "slave." "You're going to need it."

~~~~~

Rayanna was too stunned to react as the arrow hissed in front of her and shattered against the opposite wall. The burns on her arms ached and stretched. It hurt to stand after the rape. Lack of food or real rest left her body quivering. She hardly registered the second arrow as it, too, zipped by, and the abbreviated cry of pain cut short by a snapped neck sounded as inconsequential as the wind in the trees or the water of a nearby stream. There was only survival. Taking the next breath.

Tools of survival lay strewn at her feet. That much she knew. Swords. Knives. Rusty, but solid. She had one in her hand, and she held it at her side. She didn't even remember having picked it up, and she didn't know how to use it. But she would use it—that much was certain.

Despair welled up through the pain and the terror. Like a drop of sweat running down her face, the despair grabbed her aches and pains and fear until it built into an unstoppable river that fell down, down, down. Her heart pounded in her chest, and she imagined the bite of a knife sinking into it. *Would it hurt? No. Nothing hurts more than this. Nothing hurts more than losing everything,* she told herself.

Then she heard her mother's words. Some of the last words her mother would ever say. *"Don't lose yourself, Rayanna. Don't forget who you are. Promise me!"*

Tears coursed down her face as she raised her eyes heavenward, praying that her mother and father were there to meet her gaze. How she longed to be with them! But this was her moment to decide. This was the moment where her mother broke. This was how despair wreaked havoc on their lives for years. *Despair has owned me for too long*, Rayanna told herself. *I cannot give it another day.*

A thrill passed down her spine at the thought, warming her soul and calming the raging hopelessness that threatened to drown her. Her flesh raised in goosebumps, and she wanted to believe that her parents stood there with her.

"Corva!" A voice broke her reverie. It was the man who brought her here. Chism. He had said his name was Chism when they were tied to posts on that dais. That horrible dais. She had a hard time following everything that had been said, but she knew one thing: she was captive in a Lima city, and this man was Lima. The thrill she had felt was quickly replaced with a chill as her mind focused

on on her captors. If she were to die today, it would not be at her own hand. But it wouldn't be for lack of a fight on her part, either.

She watched Chism drag the bowman to the end of the alley, panting heavily. Rayanna could see the fatigue written in the bloodstained crevices of his face. Chism was obviously very strong, and clearly very weakened by the atrocities he must have committed last night. No, this was not the man who had hurt her, but Rayanna had little doubt that others had been raped. Nor did she doubt that if this man who called himself Chism hadn't committed the crime, it was only for lack of opportunity.

"Ok, we need go," Chism spoke to her in a broken Neroos dialect as he came near her to hide behind the crates while he made sure that no one was looking down the alley way.

Rayanna flinched around and swung the knife at Chism. Her reaction to his presence was visceral, unplanned, and motivated by self-preservation. Chism jumped back, but not quickly enough. The knife sliced a deep wound above his right eye, biting into his nose, and finishing with a line less severe on his lower left jaw.

Rayanna grasped the knife and bent low, bending her legs to prepare for the counter attack.

But none came. Chism tried to hold the wound above his right eye closed with his right hand and, squinting through the pain from his left eye, he raised his left hand and spoke slowly.

"I no hurt you."

"Then why did you bring me here?" Rayanna cried out.

"You die. At Gidionhi. Here, you have doctor. Care. Food."

"Why do you care?" She shouted.

Chism paused, his mouth opening and closing, searching for the words.

"Oh, just speak your dirty dialect," Rayanna spat out.

Chism glared at her momentarily, then said, "Because I have promises to keep. You need help. I have to *expianore* for what he did to you."

"*Expianore?*" Rayanna asked.

Chism sought a simpler way to explain what she obviously did not understand. "I need to make it right. I need to pay for it. I will pay with my blood, if I have to."

Rayanna's head was spinning. This man—this Lima whom she had maimed—had wanted to help her? And he still wanted to her help her, even as he clutched the wound she left on his face? "Why?" She asked.

What part of Chism's face that was not covered in blood darkened. "Because he was my brother."

"Who? Who was your brother? You're not making sense!"

Chism pointed at Rayanna's wounds one by one. "He was my brother. I must...*expianore*."

Rayanna dropped the knife and brought her hand to her mouth, recoiling from him until she had nowhere to go. Her back was to the wall and the crates.

Speaking again in what Neroos he knew, Chism said, "We go. Now. Not live more if stay. Not live more if no together. Please. I help. I help."

Rayanna nodded slowly with tears streaming down her face.

Chism nodded in return and removed what was left of his tattered and stained shirt. He spun the shirt around to the backside. It was covered in sweat, dirt, and blood, but it was a far better alternative to the bloodstains of so many other men that covered the front of his tattered tunic.

Rayanna watched as he ripped the back of the tunic off and then tore that into three strips. The first he used to mop up his face, inhaling sharply as the salty sweat and dirt mingled with the wound. Then, after soaking the first strip, he wrapped the second strand diagonally to cover the nose and eye wound, and then wrapped the third strip around his jaw.

The bandaging was rudimentary at best, and the strips were soaked with blood within minutes. Rayanna felt a twinge of guilt for having harmed this Lima who already defied everything she had supposed about him.

"Come. We move." Chism said and walked past her. He seemed to have little interest in supporting her now as he had before, and Rayanna could hardly blame him. Then he paused, sighed, and turned to her with his arm outstretched. "Much to explain. But now, you stay beside me. Good?"

Rayanna nodded slowly and walked toward him. For better or worse, her fate was in this man's hands.

Peering cautiously out of the alley, Chism grabbed her hand and quickly led her into the city, weaving through alleys, between buildings, and constantly peering over his shoulder. The more ground they covered, the more Rayanna understood that they were moving toward a dangerous part of the city. Eyes followed them everywhere they went. The thought of hiding where everyone had secrets to keep came as some small comfort to her.

She kept her feet light and her eyes always on this strange guide, praying that they would find safety. Yet something in the back of her mind whispered that safety was only an illusion.

~~~~~

Mossad and Gala cautiously pushed open the door at the top of the stairs.

Gala's mother sat in a chair with her back turned to the door. Her head slumped forward onto her chest. The dark blue dress she always wore was torn and frayed on the left shoulder. The cloth itself was covered in dirt, and the skin beneath it bore the signs of a road rash that was concentrated on one place. She had obviously been dragged after she had been knocked unconscious.

Mossad could see the warning signs of an old woman who had been beaten and placed right where anyone walking in would run to her. Gala could only see her mother, waiting for her daughter to rescue her.

"Mama!" Gala cried out. Her mother didn't respond.

"You're late," said a voice hidden within the apartment.

160

"Kalif is dead!" Mossad shouted. "He's rotting in the woods outside Gidionhi! Are you satisfied? Let this woman go!"

"You're very late," the voice repeated without emotion. It wasn't a mocking tone, but it had no remorse, either. It was so detached that, had they been able to pause to consider it, Mossad and Gala would have thought it had no body. No heart. No soul. It was just a voice, as if carried on a wind.

Gala was frozen by the situation, wanting desperately to run to her mother but afraid to endanger her any further. Mossad could stand this situation no longer. He strode into the room and grabbed the woman's shoulder.

"Don't!" the voice warned sharply.

Mossad's eyes widened as he felt the woman's body slump lifelessly under the weight of his hand. "You *batarkres*! How could you? She was innocent! She had nothing to do with—"

Gala didn't see the archer. But she heard the twang and saw the arrow protruding through the back of Mossad's neck in the same instant. She was flying down the stairs and out into the street even as she heard the creak of a bow being drawn again.

As Gala ran, she gasped for air, sobbing uncontrollably, and flying through the crowd. She raised her arms in front of her to feel, push, and warn anyone in her way of her frenzied escape. Hysteria had set in, and she had neither thought nor care for her well being. She ran into a table with wares set out on it. The pain in her thigh did nothing to slow her down, and she was gone before the cries of the merchant could reach her ears. She stepped on garbage, wood, pottery, and felt nothing on her sandled feet.

She was gone. Her mother was gone. The only person she had left in this world was dead and had been long before she had arrived. Had she suffered, hoping and waiting for her daughter to save her? Had she failed her mother? Or had they killed her mother outright and turned Gala into a puppet? And then they dragged Mossad into it. She dragged Mossad into it. She had no idea who he was. No idea what sins stained his past, if any. But for her part, she counted him as a good man. And now he was gone.

Gala turned down an alley that reeked of feces and rot, planted her back against the wall, and tried to breathe. But her breaths were coming faster, and her lungs could hardly fill before she exhaled again. And again. And again. Wide eyed and with her heart racing, Gala slowly slipped down the wall until she could feel the moisture on her legs through her simple garments, and the world began to turn black.

No, Gala said to herself. *Breathe! Breathe now! Take control!* As the tunnel vision began to close in, she closed her eyes and forced herself to breathe in. Hold the breath. Breathe out. Slowly. In. Hold. The terror would stab her in the heart again, and for a moment she'd lose control. Then she would wrestle it back, and force herself to breathe. She drew her knees to her chest, and continued to breathe deeply.

Her body was trembling. Fine. Let it. She would breathe now and stop trembling later.

She wiped her forehead with the back of her hand, and then wiped the sweat from under her eyes with the heel of her palm. Opening her eyes, she noticed that her hand was smeared with something crimson. *What did I do to myself when I was running?* Gala could feel a cramp developing in her thigh where she had hit the edge of the table, but even her feet hadn't suffered any cuts thanks to her sandals. So how had she drawn blood on her face?

Then she remembered: she had been close, so very close to Mossad. When that arrow pierced his throat and came through the back of his neck, his blood must have sprayed her in the face.

Gala's stomach heaved at the realization. She barely had time to turn her head away from her knees before food, liquid, and bile forced itself up and out of her mouth. She heaved again, and again, until she cried out in pain and sank back against the wall, mentally begging the contractions in her stomach to yield. *The blood of a good man,* she thought. *The blood of a good man, and it's all over my hands.*

The terror was coming back. Gala was becoming more concerned about her sanity than about her own life, though both were in serious jeopardy. She had to form a plan. Had to make a choice. Had to move.

Chism. Chism had told her to meet him in the High Tide District. She had no idea how she'd find him once she got there. But that was a good thing. It was a challenge. Something concrete for her mind to focus on and work out.

Kaulana. The doctor. She knew a doctor here in High Tide. She would get supplies from him on occasion, because he could get them cheaper. Chism and that wench he brought back from Gidionhi would need attention, and they'd either go to Kaulana or someone he knew. Gala was beginning to see a small ray of hope, even as she contemplated hiding out in the High Tide District.

But her face was now painted in blood. Ombrar had its rough areas, but nowhere could she walk around with her face smeared with someone else's blood—especially not without attracting far more attention than she could possibly afford. She needed to be clean. *But where could I get water in this disgusting alley?*

A small stream ran down the center of the alley where the sloped ground fed into the gutter. Gala bit her lower lip as she considered her next move, and made a choice.

She tried to rip the hem of her dress to get some cloth, but she had no way to tear the fabric. Looking around, she found some broken pottery several feet away. Standing slowly, carefully, she moved over to the broken shards and used them to cut a patch of fabric the size of her palm from the left side of her knee-length dress.

Can I wash this off? Gala wondered. She realized that Mossad was dead—was *dead*—because she hadn't stopped Kalif. *Or could I have stopped him?* She wanted an answer—wanted it and feared it. If she couldn't have stopped him, then her hands were clean. But if she could have stopped him, then Mossad's blood would not have soaked her face. No, perhaps she didn't want an answer. But she needed one all the same.

Will I ever be free of the consequences? Her breath was short as she stared at the muddy water. The water she would try to clean herself with. Not pausing to recognize the irony, she stooped to the gutter, took a few more deep breaths, and dipped the square of cloth in.

~~~~~

The corridor was dark. Light only came from the two ends of the hallway where stairs led down the side of the building. But the sun never shone directly in, giving the entire space a perpetually gloomy look. It was perfect for the tenants here. This was the High Tide District, and the less light that intruded on the goings on here, the better.

"Who was that boy?" Rayanna asked.

Chism turned quickly and chopped his hand sharply through the air, motioning for silence. Chism looked up and down the hallway to ensure that none of the other tenants were about. It wasn't the noise that worried him. It was her accent. Besides, this particular row of houses in the High Tide District was the last place Chism wanted to be overheard.

As he and Rayanna quickly made their way to this building, Chism had contacted an errand boy on the street. "Remind the good doctor of the favor he owes his friend from that cold night," Chism had said briefly, and then moved on as quickly as he had come. He knew Rayanna understood nothing of it, even if she had heard every word. For all the effort Chism had put into improving his life, he always knew the contacts he had in the High Tide District from his previous life coupled with his authority as a member of the city guard would weigh in his favor. He hoped that today, those contacts would not forget the help he had rendered them so long ago.

Chism stopped at the third door of five and put his finger to his lips to emphasize the need for Rayanna to remain silent. Then he stooped down to the patched cement at the base of the doorframe and, with one hand holding his bandaged face and the other holding the heel of a knife to the wall patch, he started pounding.

"What are you doing?" Rayanna said in Lima.

"Key," Chism grunted.

A chunk of the wall as big as an apple broke off. Chism grabbed the broken rock, held it close to his unbandaged eye, and threw it with incredible force against the opposite wall. Rock pieces flew in all directions, and Chism listened carefully. Down the hall to the left came the soft sound of a small piece of metal landing on the yellow-and-gray cement.

"Help me," Chism said through labored breath.

Rayanna had little understanding of what exactly she was supposed to help him with, but she followed him down the hall.

"What are we...?"

"Key," Chism grunted again.

Then Rayanna kicked a small chunk of rock, and the sound of metal skittering across the floor brought their attention to it. Chism walked over to it and ground it against the floor. In one motion, Chism bent over, picked up the key, and put it in his mouth. It was more than just a key; if Chism hadn't had it customized himself, he probably never would have recognized it for what it was.

The key was perfectly oblong, rounded like a raindrop and tapered on the edges. The edges were lined with measured, detailed teeth. A small ring was attached to a rod that went straight down the center. The whole contraption was only two inches long. Chism took the key out of his mouth as soon as he was confident that he had removed all dust and cement.

Had he used any other cement, the task would have been impossible; but this mixture was made to dissolve with water. He had carefully encased the key in this mixture and then covered it with cement when he prepared this apartment as a safe room in case the worst happened. *In case* this *happened,* Chism thought as his mind raced in a fevered sprint from one idea to another. *In case my brother should go on a killing spree, and I should have to rescue a girl who would try to kill me at the first chance she would get. How could anyone prepare for this?* And yet, Chism did. It was either a comedy or a tragedy that he had sensed that things would come to this.

Chism pushed on either side of the key, offering a silent prayer of thanks to any gods who may be listening that the two slides opened quickly. Grabbing the rod that protruded from the center, he inserted his key into a lock in the upper right corner of the door; another lock in the center of the door; and then he removed a panel of wood to reveal a final lock in the center of the door about a foot from the floor.

Chism stood, opened the door, and quickly shut it as soon as Rayanna had entered.

"Let me go," Rayanna whispered as soon as the door was shut. She placed her back against the wall and sank wearily to the floor. Chism watched her face, noting the shooting pain that wracked her body from the many severe injuries she had sustained.

Chism closed his unbandaged eye, and shook his head slowly. So slowly. "I can't just let you go. They'll kill you and me both at the gate day or night if we're caught. And we will get caught, I can promise you that."

"Does it matter?"

"You're innocent. Of course it matters."

"I'm not innocent," Rayanna said with a curled lip and a look as dark as the burn wounds on her arms. "Who is innocent anymore?"

Chism didn't know what to say. But the pain in his face from Rayanna's attack was beginning to pound. Blood leaked from his wounds and cascaded down his face and neck.

"We just need my brother," Chism said more to himself than to Rayanna. He could not conceal the disappointment and disgust in his voice when he spoke of Kalif. "He would know a hidden passage out of this city."

"I would have killed him. Your brother. I wanted to watch him die slowly."

Chism sat heavily in one of the two chairs in the room. "Believe me, I understand. What he did to you…"

"I would have killed him, anyway. I would not have helped him. Not like you helped me."

"You can't know that."

"Did he really die?"

Pause. "Yes."

"Did you kill him?"

Silence.

"Why are you helping me?"

"Because I have to…" To what? To believe in something? To atone for Kalif's sins? To keep his family, a burden that never should have been his—a burden placed on him long before he met Rayanna? "Because I have to," he finished.

The doorknob rattled conspicuously, as if the person on the other side did not want to alert Rayanna and Chism. Chism rose quietly, quickly placed his shoulder against the door, and pulled his knife out.

A voice whispered softly through the door. "Only a dead man would knock on this door unwarranted," came a cryptic message.

"How can a dead man knock?" Chism said just as softly.

"Because he is good as dead as soon as he shows his face."

Chism could see the utter consternation in Rayanna's face. He would have grinned at her confusion and at the absurdity of his coded parlance, but his face and his battle wounds ached deeply. He pulled open the door and allowed the man in.

"Next time you should try to keep your face in one piece," the Lima said with no preamble. He carried with him a rolled up piece of canvas to which he had tied a rope and slung over his shoulder. The bag was half the length of his torso, and it fit securely between his shoulder blades.

"She needs help," Chism said as he sank deeper into his rickety wooden chair.

The man looked over to see the bewilderment in Rayanna's eyes. He looked back at Chism and said, "I don't—"

"Yes, you do," Chism cut him off before he could refuse service to a Neroos. "Because you owe me. And if I have to seek service elsewhere..."

The Lima had a look on his face that Rayanna would have expected to see on an adolescent's face who didn't want to muck out a stable. But he didn't argue. "You're both in bad shape. But if I don't put your face back together, you're going to have bigger problems than just bringing her kind to this place."

Chism shook his head weakly. Rayanna spoke up. "I'll be fine. Please."

The man had already unslung his parcel and unrolled the canvas on the floor. Glass vials and metal instruments were tucked neatly into pouches that lined the bag. He grabbed two items and went quickly to work in the fireplace on one end of the room. He kept the flames impossibly small, and smoke was absolutely imperceptible. He then rolled out a piece of cloth on the ground about the size of a bed next to Chism's chair. After tying a cloth over his nose and mouth, he dabbed another rag with a solution. Chism had nearly stopped responding by this point.

"I'll begin," the man said through the cloth draped across his nose and mouth.

"Kaulana," Chism said suddenly. Urgently. "Take care of her. He hurt her. She is innocent."

With tightened lips, Kaulana nodded. Chism slumped back into his chair and breathed deeply from the rag that Kaulana held to his mouth. Kaulana placed the rag on the other side of the room, dropped his own breathing cloth, and lowered Chism from the chair to the mat he had just placed on the floor.

"You need rest," Kaulana said without looking at Rayanna. Had she not known without a doubt that she was the only other conscious person in the room, she never would have thought Kaulana were addressing her. He began rolling out another mat.

Images of the night sky seen from a forest floor stirred within Rayanna a deep fear. She began trembling and tried to stand. But her legs had become incredibly stiff. The fear seemed to pound in her head right on the spot where she had struck a rock. And the pain below her stomach seemed amplified by the memory of the last time a Lima had found her lying down.

"I won't hurt you. I swear it."

She couldn't believe him. She wouldn't believe him. She didn't know why she had volunteered to be treated after Chism. Why she had cared for him in that instant. But Chism was just the same as the others. And so was this doctor. Neither of these men could be trusted. No one could.

Her head was spinning. And before she could go anywhere, a rag with a musty sweet smell was forced over her nose and mouth. Then everything stopped.

CHAPTER 14:
AFTER THE END

They're dirty, Hakoni told himself as he threw yet another rock and stood idly at his guard duty. *And I'm nothing like them.* He spotted Kalif—no, he spotted the one they called Kalif, Hakoni corrected himself. *Don't give it a name. Don't give it the honor of being a person. He's... it's an animal.* As he watched Kalif's movements, Hakoni tried to find out once again why he hated this Lima, this piece of dirt, more than any of them.

A little more than a month had passed since Hakoni had found him facedown and coated in blood on that forest floor. And now Hakoni was given the charge to guard Kalif and three other men in the quarry. The soldier handing out the assignments had cited Hakoni's experience in the quarry as the reason he was put there. That may have been true. But why he had been assigned to Kalif could only be for one reason: Garrick said so.

"You've got to be kidding me," Hakoni had said to Garrick after he had received his orders. The entire village was run by the military at this point, and orders had to be followed.

"And you've got to grow up," Garrick responded even as he pounded a support into place with a mallet. Hakoni couldn't help but admire that Garrick handled the administrative duties in the village and yet would not excuse himself from the day-to-day requirements of rebuilding. It made Hakoni feel guilty to approach Garrick to complain about his assignment while Garrick worked. Hakoni always felt guilty when he was around Garrick. Guilty and naked. Bare. Exposed. Hakoni had not forgotten that day in the woods when Garrick caught him stomping the life out of a Lima soldier. And now, considering his new assignment, he knew Garrick hadn't forgotten, either.

"Just tell me why. What is this about? Are you supposed to be *changing* me or something?"

"Everyone's supposed to change, Hakoni," Garrick said as if he were saying it for the hundredth time that day. Then he turned his brown eyes on Hakoni and said with no preamble, "What was his name?"

Hakoni stonewalled again. He knew Garrick was asking about the soldier in the woods. The soldier who had whispered his name to Hakoni before Hakoni put his foot on his throat and watched his eyes bulge out as he suffocated, trying to breathe through a crushed and closed windpipe. His name was Yarlem. Yarlem had a name, and Hakoni couldn't change the fact, nor could he forget it. But he wasn't going to tell Garrick. Yarlem's name would belong only to Hakoni.

"I told you he was already dead."

"Yeah. I know what you told me. Now get out of here and go to your duties."

That was the last time Hakoni had spoken to Garrick. Hakoni didn't know the man, though he felt almost inextricably tied to him. Garrick appeared everywhere, always with that look in his eyes. That look that Hakoni had lost and couldn't find. He could remember Rayanna's smile break through her stern exterior just before she would stare at the dirt and pull a strand of hair behind her ear. Just thinking about her began to fill the hole in his heart. Then he would remember Rayanna's mother. He remembered Brego, her only living brother who now stayed in the structure they had built for the orphaned. Brego was constantly in trouble. The village would have pitied him if they had the time for it. And there was no trace of Rayanna. Then whatever had begun filling Hakoni's heart by remembering his beautiful friend left as quickly as it had come. But Hakoni knew that Garrick hadn't lost that hope, and Hakoni envied him for it. And for whatever inexplicable reason, he blamed Kalif for his loss.

And there Kalif stood, thirty feet away from Hakoni's position. Guards stood at regular intervals so that the Lima prisoners would have no hidden stores of tools or side projects performed beyond the guards' gaze. Though a working prisoner was the easiest kind to guard, a prisoner armed with a pickaxe or hammer is also one of the hardest to kill. And the Neroos would take no more chances.

This was one of three working crews. A second crew kept busy by cutting and hauling timber, and the third crew built and repaired all of the buildings. The Neroos had captured seventy-two prisoners a little over a month ago. Eight died from their wounds. Sixteen more were killed for rebellion.

Besides the thirteen Neroos soldiers from the garrison who survived, there were only thirty-three capable men left in the village—thirty-three, if sixty-two-year old men who suffered from partial blindness and poor health were considered capable, and if sixteen-year-old boys were considered men.

From his vantage point, Hakoni kept a handful of rocks, throwing them idly at imaginary targets. He could hear virtually nothing of individual conversations in the quarry, but he watched hawkishly for any patterns among the prisoners, especially where

Kalif was concerned. He didn't trust him. And he needed a reason to pull the string on his bow and release an arrow.

Hakoni threw another rock, this time right at the feet of the guard positioned to his left. The guard's name was Erron. Erron casually walked over and picked it up. That was the signal. Hakoni walked casually toward him, who also drifted toward Hakoni's position. Without looking at each other, the two began to talk.

"You're being paranoid, Hak. He's not up to anything."

"Are you sure you're looking at the right one? That one there, with the scar on his right shoulder—"

"Hak, they all have scars on their arms and shoulders!"

"I need information, Erron."

"There's nothing to say. They're guarded too well and they're too tired. We're all tired, Hak."

"You just wait. I know there's something going on. You better be ready when it all goes down."

"Yeah," came the same dry response. "I'll do that."

Hakoni fumed and walked back to his position where he took up his rock throwing again. After a few throws, he threw one to the feet of the guard to his right. The guard noticed it land and kicked it away with a shake of his head and a sneer on his face that he made sure Hakoni would see.

"Fine," Hakoni said quietly to himself. "Then you're all dead."

Had Hakoni stepped back, he might have realized that no one else had a fire still burning within them. They missed their families. They had seen so much violence and bloodshed. They had carried maimed bodies of beautiful children to a mass grave that lay just a few hundred feet away from the quarry. They didn't have the energy for hate anymore. All they had was survival. And Hakoni wouldn't have blamed them for their inaction.

But Hakoni couldn't step back. Nor could he ignore the sinking feeling of anticipation. He was convinced that this Lima, this man they called Kalif, had one more fight left. And Hakoni itched for it to be with him.

~~~~~

Kalif could feel the eyes on him. He was a prisoner. Of course he was being watched. But not like this. The guards were watching him, but that guard was hunting him.

"Is he still looking?"

"He's always looking, Zoram," Kalif responded between swings with a pickaxe.

Kalif's right shoulder continually ached, and he was tired. So tired. He worked hard, even with zeal, every day in the quarry. A part of him whispered that it would be to his advantage to gain the guards' favor through hard work. Of course Hakoni, his hunter, would never favor him. But his motives for work were far less calculated than that. He worked to weary his body so that he could sleep without dreams.

In his dreams, he was hunting in the woods, and he would find Loria's maimed body. She would stand and look at him, saying, "You did this to me." Then she would change, becoming the girl he had tracked and raped. She gave birth to a baby, but the child was immediately thrown into a pit of children. Beautiful children. Innocent children. And then Kalif was standing in the mass grave he was forced to dig for the Neroos, surrounded by the burned and hacked and bloodied bodies of the people of the village. Then every man, woman, and child in the grave would turn slowly to look at him and say, "Is this justice?"

Kalif shivered as the dreams overwhelmed him, even now as he stood in the quarry with his pickaxe. He tried to pass it off as the cool air chilling his sweat-drenched body. But he knew better. He knew better. And he couldn't escape. He swung his pickaxe harder.

"Do you or don't you want in?" Zoram asked, shaking him from his reverie.

Kalif put down his pickaxe and leaned his back against the wall. He could feel the sweat running in rivulets down his back and hanging from his eyebrows and nose, even though the crisp air of fall was penetrating deeper into his lungs with every new day.

What more trouble do you want to get into? Said a voice in Kalif's head that sounded an awful lot like his brother Chism.

And what's this, if not trouble? Kalif rebutted in his own mind as he hefted again the axe and felt the iron around his ankle bite into the skin and bone. His captivity spoke louder than his reason: *Always have an exit plan,* he told himself.

"I…yeah, of course. Whatever it takes to be free of all this," he heard himself say. *Loria didn't have an exit plan. And* she *didn't have an exit plan,* he thought of his sister and the girl he had hurt in the woods.

"First you have to lose your shadow," Zoram said, referring to Kalif's guard, Hakoni.

"Well I can't kill him. He's not exactly lost in the crowd up there, if you know what I mean."

Zoram grinned, not at Kalif's wit, but at the thought of injuring a Neroos. "Lose him. Do whatever it takes. Or I will."

Kalif nodded. Zoram took it as consent and turned away.

A horn blew, signaling the time to return to the stables. Three soldiers descended from the rim to collect tools. Each Lima was supposed to walk as close to the center of the pit as his chain would permit, drop his tool, and walk back to the wall. Any man suspected of concealing a tool was instantly shot. There were no courts. No search. One odd look garnered an arrow in the stomach or chest. Three men had been shot the first day. Two more the week after that. Only one had actually been holding a weapon. There had not been any more problems since that time.

One soldier bent to unlock each prisoner and lock him again to a long central chain that measured twenty feet long. Each link in the chain weighed twenty pounds, and there were two links per prisoner. Zoram was chained next to Kalif and immediately picked up his night diatribe against the Neroos. Kalif mildly considered concealing a weapon at day's end so that either he could bury it in Zoram's chest or so that he could get himself shot instead of listening to the same oaths and curses every night. *Listening to him is the real torture in here.* Kalif almost grinned at the thought.

Drums began to beat, signaling the beginning of the mile-and-a-half march.

~~~~~

Of the six counselors standing in the room, Rierdan stood nearest the door. He barely had to think of the next move he would make. It was instinctual. Like retracting your hand from fire or putting food in your belly when it feels hunger. Rierdan knew that the door would be the most defensible position. No guards stood outside, and he could create a bottleneck and dispatch each man one at a time as they approached through the corridor.

But today was not a day for attacking. Not yet. Though he yearned to cut out the hearts of each of the two men and one woman sitting at the council table and mete out justice, he would have to wait. He would have to know that when they died, they were the last of those responsible for the death of those he loved.

So for now, he served them.

The room was lined with six men, two counselors to each member of the Triumvirate. To become a counselor, one had to be both intelligent and brawny. Rierdan was the smallest of the six, but he was hardly impressed by the bulging muscles or sharp minds of the other five. His ruthlessness and their uncertainty of his reputation gave him the advantage. A predator didn't need to be stronger or even more agile than his prey. He just needed to be in the right place, at the right time.

"Rierdan," the Master said in his sibilant, raspy voice. In another life, it may have sounded like a kindly grandfather to Rierdan. Rierdan didn't detect a hollowness to the man's voice; nothing indicated the cavity in his heart where his soul once resided. Nothing lacked; and that's why Rierdan felt that the Master's evil was so palpable. It was full of thought and consideration. This wasn't a man who killed because it was his nature, as one might think of a hawk or a jaguar. He ruled simply because he knew he could. No one would stop him. "Rierdan, what do you think?"

Rierdan felt the tension emanating from Criton, the Master's other counselor. Something about the way his arms bulged and his nostrils flared at the Master's continued deference to Rierdan's opinion made Rierdan smile. Rierdan was the second in seniority, having killed the other counselor on the day that Rierdan was inducted into the Master's inner circle. But despite Criton's seniority, the Master trusted Rierdan more than him. That gave Criton more than enough reason to want to watch Rierdan die a slow, agonizing death. But Rierdan knew there was more than simple jealousy there. Criton seemed to know Rierdan was more than what he seemed, and that made him an even greater threat. But Rierdan considered Criton's hate and distrust to be a weakness, and Criton displayed it so willingly.

"I think your best option, Master, is to wait," Rierdan replied.

Criton snorted.

"So vocal, Criton?" The Master said.

"Rierdan is as careful as a woman over a suckling child," Criton said plainly. "There are three cities within our reach, and each has a significant store of cattle, horses, and even precious gems."

"Yes, and Gidionhi had—and still has—plenty of iron ore and gold," Rierdan cut into Criton's argument. "That's the short game. And the Neroos have obviously discovered your short game, Criton."

"Master, don't listen to this—"

"You forget your place." The Master said abruptly and turned a sharp eye to him. Criton neither lowered his head nor expressed any emotion. Rierdan was surprised at his temerity. Such rash actions in here would surely be met with a swift execution. Rierdan admired his ability to regain composure, but it was plain that Criton was getting desperate. He was overreaching. Rierdan had him in his palm.

The Master turned back to Rierdan. "Criton makes a strong point, and you only have one counter argument. I want reasons, not bickering."

"It's not just the Senate's pockets that are lighter as a result of Gidionhi," Rierdan said. "All of Ombrar knows of the attack and its failure. News has reached far beyond our borders, and the marauders appear weak. The best course of action is to build our numbers, pay off the right people, and attack at the heart of the Neroos nation. We need a decisive win, not a few pathetic raids. That takes time and careful planning."

The Master did not give any response, verbally or otherwise. "Criton?"

"You know where my heart stands, Master. I defer to your wisdom."

The Master turned back to the table. "Teacher?"

"How long?" Came a man's voice, though his face was concealed by shadows in a deep cowl.

"I estimate another six to seven months." Rierdan said.

"Judge?" The Master addressed the third member.

A woman's hand and upper arm appeared through the deep sleeves on her robe. She did not speak. She only gestured with her hands in a language Rierdan did not understand. "How many men?" One of her counselors interpreted.

Rierdan paused. This would be the largest sticking point. But his plan had to work. He only had one shot. "Every marauder in the city. Plus half of the city guard."

"An attack of that magnitude will plunge us into an all-out war."

"Yes," Rierdan said. "And that's where we increase our power. Not just with military might, but with economics. I propose that the Triumvirate begin increasing its holdings in textiles and ore."

"To achieve what?" Criton asked out of turn.

"There are two things every soldier needs—a blade, and bandages," Rierdan said. "That's how you play the long game."

And that was only the start. As he was the mastermind of this plan, Rierdan would have to be the one to see to the details. Travel the countryside. Make certain acquisitions. And most importantly, be gone for weeks at a time. He had to have the freedom to roam. Because starting a war was exactly what he wanted, and the Triumvirate must always believe that they would benefit from his actions. Right up until the moment that he cut off their heads.

CHAPTER 15:
CHOICES MUST BE MADE

Rayanna was now four weeks late. Two weeks after the raid on Gidionhi, Rayanna knew that it was time to prepare extra padding and keep a wash bucket in her corner of the room. It was a ritual she had performed every month for the past three years. But this month, the bleeding didn't start on time. Then it was a week late. Then two. After three weeks, the nausea set in from the sheer realization that there would be no menstruation. And that could mean only one thing.

Gala didn't say anything. But Rayanna noticed her eying the strips of cloth Rayanna had prepared for herself. That had still been when Rayanna was only one week late, and she had refused to pass them over to Gala. It wasn't jealousy. It wasn't spite. Rayanna just needed to hold onto one last thing that was hers, the one thing her body could control and that no one could take away. The strips of cloth were a symbol that her body had still belonged to her. But even that, apparently, had been taken away.

Choices Must Be Made

Now Rayanna sat on her floor mat, staring at the strips of cloth she had laid on Gala's mat in the opposite corner. She had waited for Gala to go out before she passed them over. Rayanna had knelt solemnly and laid the strips of fabric, one at a time, on Gala's mat. Then she stood and calmly walked over to her corner, pulled her knees to her chest, and bid farewell with silent tears flowing down her face. That had been two hours ago.

Rayanna decided that she hated yellow. She never had before, but the ten-foot by twenty-foot apartment was nothing but a box made out of yellow-brown cement, and the sight of it made her stomach turn. But then, her stomach was turning much more frequently lately, and now she knew—no, now she accepted—why.

The door sat in the middle of the twenty-foot wall. When Rayanna stood in the doorway, the fireplace was on the ten-foot wall to the right. Her sleeping area was in the corner to the right of the fireplace. Rayanna had heard Gala whispering in rapid Lima to Chism behind the curtain that lead to his small room one day. She was upset. He was conciliatory. The next day, Gala had stood with her arms crossed while Chism brought out a thin mattress full of straw and placed it in Rayanna's corner. Rayanna wouldn't sleep on it for a week, until finally the pressure of sleeping on a concrete floor was too much, even for a girl who was used to sleeping on dirt floors and piles of leaves. Besides, if Gala had seemed upset about Rayanna having it, then maybe she *should* use it if only to spite Gala.

A small woodpile sat to the left of the fireplace, and Gala slept on the opposite wall between the woodpile and the shelves that stored their meager supply of food. Just beyond the shelves was a small closet with a bucket sitting in the middle of the floor to serve as a latrine, and nothing but a curtain for privacy. That bucket was emptied (*not often enough*, Rayanna always thought) out the small window that sat six feet above the floor. Thanks to Rayanna's petite stature, she had to stand on the only chair in the apartment in order to reach the window and dump out the bucket's contents. Chism's small room was on the other side of the wall from the closet.

Gala walked in, carrying a small sack. Chism would be back later, Rayanna knew, with more food. Here in the High Tide District, nothing could look ordinary. Everything had to be varied—from the vendors who sold you the food to the days you chose to pick it up. The route back to your apartment had to be different every time, and most people had multiple apartments. Living in the High Tide District was like being a deer in the woods: the cover of your surroundings was your only protection, but even then, standing still for too long would get you shot. Chism had done a fine job of providing a certain amount of anonymity and helping Gala move about on her own, but Rayanna could see thatGala still felt exposed. Both women were new to this world, and they felt like eyes were always on them.

Gala glanced at her floor mat and noticed the clean strips that Rayanna had been holding onto like a lifeline. Rayanna watched one eyebrow arch as Gala paused for a moment. *Yes, I have cut my lifeline,* Rayanna thought. *Now am I lost?*

"It's not that bad here. For a Neroos girl, I mean," Gala said in Neroos without looking at Rayanna.

Rayanna knew there must be pity behind those words. But why pity? *What does she really want?* Rayanna's eyes narrowed in suspicion.

"And what—" Rayanna's voice cracked as she spoke for the first time in days or even weeks. She cleared her throat and started again, wanting the incredulity in her voice to sound loud and clear. "What do you know about life here as a Neroos girl?"

"Everything," Gala said simply.

Rayanna was stunned. "You don't mean you're a—"

"Yes."

"But…you're not as…I mean your skin isn't…."

"What? Not as light as yours?" Then Gala crossed the room and placed her arm next to Rayanna's. The skin tone was slightly different, but the difference was subtle at best.

Rayanna didn't know what to say as reality clashed harshly with the stories she had been told. The Neroos were lighter. The Lima were darker. That was simply the way it was. Wasn't it? And yet she had noticed how fair Chism appeared—or was it how dark she really was?

"I've just always been told…"

"We all have. Do you have any idea how much our people have mixed with theirs—I mean, with yours?" The discordant identities were difficult for Gala to process as she acknowledged the heritage she had been trying to shun for so long.

Rayanna's face fell, and a cold fury boiled quickly to illuminate her eyes with hate. "What do you think?"

Gala closed her eyes and turned away, embarrassed at how carelessly the words crossed her lips. She opened her mouth to try to apologize, take it back, make it go away. But it would never go away. It grew within Rayanna's body right now, and nothing Gala could say would make it go away.

Rayanna could see the turmoil in the woman. She realized how little she knew of these people that she was supposed to hate. But these two wouldn't hate her in return. She was still alive and had not been mistreated, which was far more than she ever would have expected. Before Gala could regroup, Rayanna said, "It's not your fault. You didn't do this to me."

Gala froze for a moment at Rayanna's words. No, she had not been the one to attack her, but hadn't Chism asked her to stop Kalif from going to Gidionhi? Hadn't she refused to hold him back when she knew she could have? Or could she have? Kalif had always been so headstrong. So willful. But she had stopped him from intoxicating himself with the medicine man's acrid-smelling herbs and smoke. She pulled him back from the women and the alcohol. But she didn't want to hold him back from the Neroos. She told herself that they deserved it. She told him that they deserved it. And now here sat the consequences of her hate.

"I didn't stop it from happening to you, either," Gala said slowly, thinking about her mother's horrible demise, her life turned upside down, and this waif of a girl carrying the child that should have been hers.

The door rattled ever so slightly as Chism fished his key into the first lock.

"*Shosk*." Gala swore under her breath in Lima as she realized that she hadn't locked the door as soon as she came back in. She stepped back in time to avoid the door swinging in quickly, and both Rayanna and Gala saw Chism standing battle-ready in the entrance.

"Was anyone else here?" Chism said without so much as a hello. His face, once so calm in the face of danger, now had a horrible scar that ran from the top of his right eyebrow to the bottom of his left cheek. That scar would turn bright red when Chism's heart rate was elevated. Rayanna thought that it was bright red more often than not.

"Chism, I'm sorry, I—" Gala began.

He turned and shut the door, spinning the locks and resetting a heavy piece of canvas at the bottom of the door to mask any light and sound escaping the small space.

"How can I keep you safe if you won't protect yourselves?" Chism said harshly but quietly.

"Protect us?" Gala said with a laugh. "Chism, we haven't seen you for three days."

"It's bad," Chism said. "Looks like there's enough of my pretty face left to recognize."

Rayanna didn't even blush at the comment, though the scar running across his face was irrefutably her doing.

"Why can't they just leave us alone," Gala groaned.

"Why can't you just take me home?" Rayanna said in reply, speaking Lima to the best of her ability. She was quickly improving from her weeks of sitting and listening intently to Chism and Gala. "Looks like your own people want me dead, and from the comments you keep making, it sounds like they're not thrilled with you, either."

Gala arched an eyebrow at Chism. For once, she agreed with the girl.

"What did you do to them, anyway?" Rayanna asked.

Chism was taken aback at her questioning. This was the most he had heard her speak in six weeks now. "Well, I…umm…I saved you. And some people aren't happy about it."

"All the more reason to let me leave."

Chism heaved a sigh. She was young, but obviously possessed a strength and wisdom beyond her years. Chism didn't know who she was or what had happened to her to bring her here, but perhaps in another life, he would have liked to know.

"We will," Chism said. "But you have to be healed. Life in your village is hard right now, and you have to heal up before we can bring you back there because…well, life is hard. It's, uh, very hard right now, and you're not healed, and you need to be—"

"Stop." Rayanna interrupted. "You're not bringing me back. Don't try to lie to me about it. You're a horrible liar."

"Yup," Gala muttered under her breath.

Chism turned to glower at her.

Gala refused to wilt under his glare. "The kid's got you pegged, Chism. You're not bringing her back until that baby's born, so you may well just say it."

Tears welled in Rayanna's eyes. "Please. Please let me be with my people."

Chism bowed his head and rubbed it with one hand.

"I would. I really would. It is dangerous to have you here, and I don't want to make a slave out of you. You're strong. You have a strength that few possess, and I respect it." Chism sighed again. "But what can you tell me about a *meurtrinarihah*?"

Rayanna was taken aback. "How do you know…?"

"My parents left the Neroos society," Gala said, "because of what they saw in a *meurtrinarihah*."

Rayanna didn't speak. She had seen a *meurtrinarihah*—a killing ceremony—only once in her village. There were two kinds: one, if a girl was pregnant and the father did not step forward, then her family had the right in some Neroos villages to exile her or to kill her. When a person was exiled from Neroos society, a mark was cut into the left forearm—three lines stacked on top of each other with an intersecting line running down the middle. No one bearing that mark could be allowed into Neroos society. Some defected to the Lima. Most wandered in the woods until they starved of hunger or were eaten by the predators there. Rayanna had heard of such *meurtrinarihahs*, but she had never witnessed one. They were technically legal but severely frowned upon. Even the families who committed a *meurtirinarihah* often exiled themselves or completely uprooted their lives to avoid the judging stares from the rest of their city or village.

The other type of *meurtrinarihah* came nine months after the first raid on Gidionhi. The Lima had raped the Neroos women, and the children that came as a result were killed. Four families had committed a *meurtrinarihah*, and the rest of the village never spoke to them again. They too left in a self-imposed exile.

Rayanna wasn't supposed to see it; her mother had covered the windows and refused to let them go outside. But Rayanna had slipped out the door to see what was happening. She could never get the image out of her mind.

"My family," Rayanna said slowly as if trying to wake up from a dream, "would not do that to an innocent child. It is vile. I won't do that."

"Perhaps not," Chism said. "But can you protect the child from the rest of the village? It will be scorned and abused by your people."

"We could adopt the child to another village—"

"And suffer the same fate there!" Chism shouted despite himself.

"And do you think it will be accepted here among the Lima? Do you think you're so much better than us? You're not!"

Chism paused as the words hit home. "I see goodness in you, Rayanna. I do. And the Lima are by no means innocent of similar atrocities. But when I learned of the *meurtrinarihahs*, I couldn't help but stand aside and hold my tongue when I learned of raids against your people. I couldn't condone the raids; but I wouldn't stop them, either."

"Then why did you help me that night?" Rayanna said.

"Because I had to believe in what you could be. And not just your people, but you." Chism gave a wry laugh and said, "I actually learned that from my brother. For a while, before he got angry and started…" Chism's voice trailed off as memories of the drugs, the women, and the assassinations came to mind. He almost stopped breathing as he thought about who his brother had been, and what he had become. "Well, he had a way of believing in people, once. Any underdog or kid getting bullied, Kalif was there to cheer him on—and knock out the teeth of anyone he deemed guilty. That man…he disappeared for a while, but I always knew he was still in there somewhere."

"And now he's gone," Gala said. Her tough demeanor broke on the last word, and she was forced to whisper it through tighten vocal cords as tears coursed down her cheeks. "And you're carrying…the child that I would have…!"

Then she turned and walked out of the apartment. Rayanna thought she heard a faint sob as she quickly closed the door. Chism turned and stared at the door long after it had shut, then walked back into the small bedroom in the back.

Rayanna was having a harder time holding onto her distrust of Chism with every passing day. She almost grinned as she thought about the day he half-apologized for not offering her the more private room; it was just too small for two people, and he couldn't ask Gala to share the same space as him where they cleaned and changed clothes. She almost laughed out loud that he would be so concerned for modesty—who was he to care about her after what his brother had done to her?

"Same blood," Rayanna muttered as she thought of Kalif and Chism, condemning Kalif as a matter of course and condemning Chism as a matter of habit. "Same Lima blood."

Rayanna sat down in her corner, contemplating the life she carried inside of her. *There's only one way out of this one,* she thought as she gently placed her hand on her lower stomach. "But I suppose you didn't ask for this either, did you?" she muttered again, this time to her womb. "What choice did either of us have?"

The yellowish gray walls of the apartment echoed her question back at her. *What am I supposed to do, mamillera?* She silently asked her mom.

"*I had a choice to make,*" she could hear the echo of her mother's words from their last conversation. "*You reminded me how much I am worth.*"

"But what am I worth?" Rayanna asked out loud as she stared blankly off into the distance, as if she could see through time itself and yet see nothing in front of her. *They have taken everything from me. I have nothing left but my breath.* She was vaguely aware of hot tears running slowly down her face.

The touch of a hand against her cheek brought her back to the present. Kneeling in front of her was Chism. She felt like she were seeing him for the first time—not just the purple and swollen scar or the imposing figure, but the man behind the kind eyes.

"You are worth more than you know," he said as he wiped a tear away from her face. "A person's worth is something they have to give up. Pride may be broken. Skills may be lost. Families…families may be torn apart. But as long as you have a breath in your body, your worth can never be taken away."

"Why do you care?" Rayanna said as she slapped his hand away. She was desperate for a real answer. Desperate for something to hang on to. "You're the brother of the man who took…*everything!*… away from me! It's the same blood in your veins that's now in mine!"

"Same blood. Different decisions." Then in a moment, as if embarrassed by his forwardness, he stood and walked to the small room on the other side of the apartment.

Decisions. What kind of an answer is that? Rayanna wanted to retort and lash out. But before the words could come to her tongue, she remembered her mother. How long had her mother escaped her self-imposed prison, and Rayanna wouldn't believe it? How many times had Rayanna wished her mother had quit breathing that night, because she thought everything had been lost? But it hadn't been lost. Her mother still had a breath. And though it took years, her mother found herself again. *Don't lose yourself,* her mother's words echoed again.

Decisions. The word germinated in her mind and began to push roots into the dark parts of her heart.

I'm still breathing, Rayanna told herself. *And I will keep breathing. I am not worthless. No one is going to give me my happiness back, so I guess I'll just have to take it.* Suddenly, she felt free. She felt more powerful than she had ever felt in her life.

Feeling the first rays of a newfound and unexpected courage, Rayanna stood resolutely and walked over to the fire pit. She stoked the coals, placing a minimal amount of wood on, and then began to rummage through the food that Chism and Gala had brought.

Chism stood at the doorway to his room looking into the small living space. "Umm…" Chism uttered. He wanted to ask what she was doing, but after what had just happened between the three of them, this was the last reaction he had expected.

"If I have to be a slave here, then so be it," Rayanna said with much less anger than normal, though she reverted to speaking Neroos. "But I refuse to eat like one."

"May…may I help?" Chism asked cautiously, choosing to speak Neroos.

"Dinner's in two hours. We'll have to wait until the wood burns down to better coals before I can cook. I need dried beef and *jumak* root. The water and salts we have here will have to suffice."

Chism stood rooted to the spot, unsure what to do about this new Rayanna and unsure what she meant by the orders she just gave.

"Go to the market. Get dried beef—" Rayanna began to explain very slowly.

"Right. On it. Now." And Chism left.

~~~~~

"Be ready when you hear the sign," Zoram said mysteriously. "Unless you're getting cold feet, eh, *merdapot?*"

Kalif rolled his eyes at Zoram's latest nickname for him. "You haven't even told me what the sign is. And how are we supposed to fight off the entire battalion with just a few pickaxes, huh?"

Zoram relayed the instructions as he had memorized them, pausing at every phrase for another swing of the axe. "You'll know the sign when you hear it." Swing. "Just pull up the stakes on these chains," swing, "take out as many guards as you can," swing, "and meet the building crew on the southwest side of the village."

"I need more info than that," Kalif said.

"You're not going to get it," Zoram replied evenly.

The two men swung their pickaxes evenly, using short sentences between strokes. Talking was technically not allowed, but the guards couldn't pick up the short discussions from their stations, and the prisoners were careful about keeping their voices just softer than the sound of a pickaxe. Luckily for the prisoners, that was not very hard to do.

Kalif had noticed Zoram carefully duck behind a larger stone in the quarry two weeks ago, trying to avoid the eyes of the guards. Just as some guards had turned away, Zoram yanked a piece of parchment from within his tunic and began reading frantically. The scrap was hastily cut with handwriting just as hastily scrawled. Zoram's eyes devoured the information within a few seconds and he shoved the paper back into his shirt.

Choices Must Be Made

"Hey!" A guard yelled from atop the rim of the quarry just as Zoram stood and picked up his pickaxe again. "Get back to work!"

"Where in the *porja* did you get parchment?" Kalif had asked, bewildered.

"There's only one place you and I aren't chained together, *merdapot*," Zoram had replied. *Merdapot* was a derogatory Lima word to call someone an idiot. It also referred directly to a latrine. Zoram had glanced again at the guards on the rim, and then he grabbed the parchment, wadded it as tightly as he could, and shoved it in his mouth.

After a brief pause to consider Zoram's double meaning, Kalif had said, "You got that from the latrine...and you just ate it?"

"No one's finding this thing on me, *merdapot*. Survival's all that matters," Zoram said with a wink as he swung again with his pickaxe. "Besides, at least I get one more mouthful around here."

That was two weeks ago. Zoram was getting his messages every couple of days, and Kalif was desperate to find out the entire plan. But Zoram wasn't talking. He just passed along only need-to-know information and ate the instructions before Kalif could steal them.

Kalif had been trying desperately to catch the mastermind at his game. Every time the quarry team was taken to the latrine, Kalif strained to see a member of the previous crew looking back at the outhouse for some sign that his messages would not be lost. But there were no telltale signs from any of the prisoners. A guard inspected the latrine after each group, and Zoram was always allowed access before Kalif. Kalif searched high and low, once even foregoing his opportunity to relieve himself to search the small hut for a hiding place. But he found nothing.

Kalif was confident that whoever it was had to be outside of his crew; the quarry crew had intelligent marauders, but they were too isolated from the rest of the village. The Neroos rarely allowed the Lima to come in contact with many other prisoners. Two could get themselves into trouble, but they would have an enormously difficult time of strategizing, organizing, or planning anything at all when the only people they could talk to are on their left and right.

But no system was perfect—and not every Neroos knew enough of the Lima dialect to understand quick sentences and fast, jargon-filled sentences. But where was the chink in the armor, the weak link in the chain, the advantage that a prisoner could exploit?

Kalif knew that the plan centered around the stakes that tethered a group of workers to their assigned area. Every three weeks, the stake had to be moved for the quarry crew, but the building crew and the lumber crew had to be readjusted on a daily basis. The quarry crew's stakes were weakest at the end of three weeks of the prisoners pulling and straining against it. The quarry crew could loosen the stakes and assemble to fight the guards before they arrived. The other two crews could remove their stakes easily enough by overwhelming the guards that stood there.

"You've got to give up control on this one, *merdapot*," Zoram said. "This isn't one of your fringe raiding parties. This is bigger than you and me."

Kalif knew Zoram meant every word of it. It's what Kalif would have done—keep the individual players ignorant so that they still depended on the leader. People are easier to manage when they don't hold all the pieces. Kalif needed more than his small piece of information before he could even think about his own escape plan. He knew trying to start a fight between the prisoners and the guards would end up with any Lima survivor strung up by the neck or slit at the throat and dumped in a ditch. The odds weren't in his favor. No, there was only one way that Kalif was going to make it, and that was going along with Zoram's plan—for now.

Going along meant that Kalif had to get Hakoni to pay attention to him—and to trust him. And the only way to do that was almost as suicidal as an all-out attack on the guards—he had to hand the information Zoram had just given him over to Hakoni.

For their evening meal, the prisoners had lined up and were scooping gruel out of wooden bowls with their hands. Kalif had stopped tasting it long ago. But since the gruel was nothing more than salt and oats boiled in water, there was really nothing to taste, anyway.

"You've been watching me," Kalif said as Hakoni passed by. Out of the corner of his eye, Kalif saw Zoram try to nonchalantly shift his position toward the conversation.

"Eat your gruel, *escarren*," Hakoni said, putting emphasis on the Neroos word for "slave."

"Oh, but I'm no *escarren*, little doggy," Kalif taunted loudly enough for Zoram to hear. "I'm just a prisoner. *Elns escarrens* are against your precious Neroos law."

"Our laws only apply to people. You're just a beast. Cattle like you are to be worked, and when there's nothing left, you're to be slaughtered and eaten."

Kalif glanced up again to see Zoram shift a little more. Zoram pulled a long, sharp stone that looked uncannily like a dagger out of his shirt and put it away just as quickly. Just quick enough for Kalif to see. Just small enough for Zoram to use on this watchdog.

"Listen to me, boy," Kalif said under his breath quickly. "We need to talk. And you need to be careful."

Hakoni whirled around and grabbed Kalif by the throat, knocking his bowl of gruel out of his hands. "Why? Huh? Tell me why!"

Kalif could have stopped Hakoni. He had seen the telltale jerk of Hakoni's knee, the sudden bunch of muscles in his arm, and the all too obvious open hand swinging around as Hakoni turned his entire body so that his right arm would be closer. Kalif knew that he could have easily slapped away the seventeen-year-old boy's hand, broken his knee cap, and crushed his esophagus long before Hakoni had reached Kalif's throat. But he didn't react. He had gotten Hakoni's attention—albeit with very little tact, because Zoram was watching. Now Kalif needed to get his trust. And breaking his kneecap was not a great way to build trust.

Just as Zoram reached into his shirt and grabbed the sharp stone, two soldiers were already there, pulling Hakoni away.

"He knows something! He knows something!" Hakoni shouted as he was wrestled away from Kalif.

"Hakoni!" Garrick yelled as he approached the group.

"Garrick! I told you. I told you he knows something, I swear it, he just said—"

"On your life, will you shut up for one second!" Garrick hissed.

Hakoni was so stunned at Garrick's abrupt reply that he couldn't have spoken if he wanted to.

"We need to get them back to the quarry. Now." Garrick said with finality.

The soldiers looked at each other, confused at the orders. They had only just come out of the quarry, and the last man had not received his bowl. Though the Neroos cared little for the prisoners, they knew something was out of the ordinary.

"We'll let them eat later. But right now we have to go," Garrick repeated as if each word weighed as much as link in the prisoner's trunk chain. "A *meurtrinarihah* is about to pass by."

The soldiers' faces went ashen even as they quickly began the march. But once the drums started, a sound could be heard in the woods as a group approached. Kalif heard several people sobbing. One woman wailed, and there was the distinct sound of a body crashing and struggling in the woods. Kalif had heard something similar when he would hunt deer. After it was wounded, the deer would still struggle to escape, though its lung or throat had been pierced. When Kalif heard the sound from the woods, the hunter in him knew that the end was near.

"HEAVE!" A soldier bellowed.

The chain heaved, and it almost took Kalif's legs out from underneath him. He was at the back of the gang, and he had failed to move his foot in time. His eyes were fixed on the events in the forest.

An old man and a young girl emerged simultaneously. He maintained a fierce grip on her upper arm as she struggled against him. Her mouth was tied in a gag, and she sobbed and cried through the binding. Her dark hair was knotted and wild, and her face was bruised and cut. Her puffy eyes stood out with dark circles rimming the redness as tears fell to the gag and soaked the cloth.

"Loria," Kalif found himself whispering.

"HEAVE!" Came the order again.

An old woman wailing in grief followed the two, and two younger boys came silently at the end of the procession. But all Kalif could see was the young girl with her dark hair. Hair so much like Loria's. By the gods, he needed his sister now. And she needed him. She needed him.

"HEAVE!" The order sounded.

"Loria!" Kalif cried out as he craned his neck to keep an eye on them. "Loria!"

Guards shouted at him to turn around, to march, to follow orders.

"HEAVE!"

Kalif quickly bent down and with the strength of a man working with stone for months, dug his heels into the ground, grabbed the chain, and yanked backwards just as the momentum carried it forward. The entire procession of twelve men stumbled and fell.

A guard rushed to Kalif to subdue him, but Kalif was too skilled, too focused to be stopped now. Kalif broke the guards nose, grabbed the knife from his belt, and jammed it into the lock. He twisted the knife back and forth. He felt the lock begin to give even before the other guards had a chance to even see what had happened.

The first guard screamed in pain as he clutched his broken nose. Two guards turned toward Kalif as he continued to twist the knife. The lock gave a little more, and he stood up to yank on it with his foot.

"LORIA!" he shouted again, and with a massive jerk of his leg, he pulled the lock out of the mutilated mechanism inside.

Just as another guard reached him, Kalif deftly tripped him and tried to run toward the procession. But another guard was there too quickly. Then another. Kalif fell to the ground on his chest with his legs pinned.

Then it happened. There was nothing Kalif could do to stop it. The man threw the girl to the ground right on top of the mass grave, drew his sword, and brought it down on her cowering figure. She didn't die. Not immediately. Kalif knew she would bleed out her life in about fifteen minutes. Her lung had been penetrated, and she could only gasp and gurgle in pain. Kalif's body went limp, and he began to sob as the man afar off dropped his sword and walked away without turning back. The older woman sank to her knees and reached out to the girl as if a wall or fence separated the two, stopping her from reaching her daughter.

"No! Please no! Loria…I'm sorry! I'm sorry!"

The guards heaved Kalif back to a sitting position. He didn't struggle any more. He breathed deeply to regain his composure, but the tears wouldn't stop. Kalif pushed his palms against his eyes, trying to push out the images of his sister, of the girl, of what he had done. But he couldn't undo the pain. He couldn't rid the guilt.

All he can see is Loria, innocent Loria, dead and lying in the woods. His mind flashed to a dark haired Neroos girl—an innocent Neroos girl, for all he knew—lying in the woods, dying from the torture at his hands. Now this girl. And the bodies of the maimed children lying only a few hundred yards away. What was justice? What was peace? Peace. It was in the silence. The silence of death. But not their deaths. Not these people's deaths. Yes, Kalif had a debt to pay, and the debt could only be paid with his life. But not to the senator who hired him to kill those children so many months ago. Not to Chism. And not from a pickaxe in the quarry. He had to fight for something now, for someone who could no longer help herself. But he had lost even the ability to fight. He stood in chains, and there was nothing he could do. The despair overtook him like black, billowing clouds, stinging his conscience with salty tears like rain and striking his heart with guilt that pierced like lightning.

Somewhere, someone was whipping Kalif's back mercilessly. He tried desperately to bring himself back to reality, to feel the pain arcing through his spine and tying into a knot in his stomach. The lash upon his back was far easier to endure than the torture he endured inside.

The chain gang moved out without Kalif. He lay on his back, his flayed flesh stinging as the grass and dirt worked its way into the wounds. A guard chained Kalif to a stake and stood nearby. The man they called Garrick stooped and checked Kalif's eyes. They dilated when Garrick peeled back Kalif's eyelids, so Garrick knew that Kalif was still conscious. Conscious, but fading fast. Hakoni and the other guards had beaten him without restraint.

"Wh…why…why?" Kalif managed to choke out, even as he struggled to maintain consciousness.

"They say it's in the name of honor," Garrick said quietly enough so that only Kalif and Hakoni could hear. His mouth was turned down as if he had a mouthful of vinegar. "Stupid Neroos honor. If your family has done something to dishonor you, then they think they have a right to set things…*right*," he finished with disgust. "And we stand by and allow it to happen simply because they claim it's their right."

Garrick shook his head as he looked down with pity on Kalif. "Sometimes I wonder if our people actually deserved what you did to us."

~~~~~

Garrick stood up and continued to stare at Kalif's face. As Kalif slipped into unconsciousness, the hard lines in his face softened slightly. Slightly, but not fully. Garrick wondered who this man was, who he truly was, and what had brought him to this place.

"Hakoni," Garrick said quietly. The chain gang had already been marched into the quarry. All was quiet as the horror of the *meurtrinarihah* darkened the mood of everyone present, and the spectacle of Kalif's reaction shocked the bystanders even more.

Hakoni approached Garrick, stopping on the other side of Kalif's prone and unconscious body. The more distance between them, the better. Hakoni could not bear Garrick's piercing, knowing eyes right now. He felt full of a hate and anger that had been fed, and that now had turned to profound sadness and darkness. He longed to escape. Escape Garrick's eyes. Escape the dark hole he seemed to be lost in. Escape all of it.

"Do you still think this man is irredeemable, Hakoni?"

Hakoni stared transfixed at absolutely nothing as his breathing quickened. He said nothing.

"He has done horrible things," Garrick continued. "We probably don't even know how bad. But he still loves someone out there." Garrick stopped looking at Kalif and stared hard at Hakoni, whose eyes were fixed on Kalif's face. "Never underestimate the good that can come from someone motivated by love."

Hakoni closed his eyes, no longer able to look at the man he hated so much, and no longer able to avoid Garrick's gaze. He bowed his head and nodded slowly.

"Get him to the barracks. Call the garrison's medic."

"Can't we just let him die?" Hakoni finally said. Garrick could hear that there was no malice in his request. It was almost mercy, but not quite. Not quite. "I mean, we're just going to work them to death, anyway, aren't we?"

"No," Garrick said with no other explanation. "Get the medic."

"He knows something, Garrick. I was right."

"Then talk to him," Garrick said in a low voice again. "And come talk to me when you're done. Leave everyone else out of this, especially Erron and Hamas."

And with that, Garrick turned, called two guards to help Hakoni with Kalif, and walked away.

CHAPTER 16:
RISE AND RISE AGAIN

This was going to be harder than Rierdan expected. Things had changed dramatically since he had last been in Neroos society.

When Rierdan walked into the judges' hall at Gideon, a Neroos city a week and a half's journey to the southeast of Gidionhi, he was greeted by smooth marble floors that reflected the multi-colored light from stained glass in tall, oval windows. Rierdan was surprised to see the glass; the Neroos were not known for glass windows, some cities shunning it because glass was so typically "Lima," and others simply not having access to the materials requisite to make it. The hall was lined with the politically elite and the politically aspiring. This is where money changed hands and deals were brokered that went unnoticed by the people who were too busy in their farms and orchards to keep up with political machinations.

Then judges, each appointed through a series of general elections by the people to lower courts and then hand-selected to the highest seats from those already in power, sat in a semi-circle dais raised several feet above the walkway. It was a basic military tactic: you master the field when you take the high ground. When judges gave audience, the speaker was to stand in the middle of the semi-circle with the judges looking down at the speaker, the light coming from above them. The speaker was then partially blinded by the sunlight or candlelight, making the judges' faces difficult to discern. The speaker was also forced to look up at the judges, giving the feeling of inferiority.

But inferiority was one emotion that few could invoke in Rierdan. Infuriation, yes. Inferiority, never. Today was no exception.

Standing in front of the panel of judges, Rierdan delivered a clear and simple proposition: attack Ombrar and eliminate the secret society that was the cause of so much Neroos death, all with minimal Neroos casualties while the Lima army and marauders were outside of the city.

The idea was invigorating. The strategy was sound. To Rierdan's highly militaristic and analytical mind, this was the best opportunity for attack that the Neroos had seen in decades. And yet he was facing more opposition than he had anticipated.

"And just where will the Lima plan to attack us?" A judge said as he leaned against a bar placed at elbow height across the entire panel.

The judges wore their customary blue robes. Each judge also had an ornate hat with the image of a panther engraved on gold, but none wore the heavy headpiece. Rierdan was taken aback by the intricacy of the ceremonial garments. He thought he remembered woodcarved images rather than gold, and robes that were dyed wool rather than silk. But he had little time to spend pondering these judges' raiment; it was time to act, and he had only a few months' time to build a force large enough for the right attack.

"Their target is Borinihah...sirs," Rierdan hesitated as he momentarily forgot the customary title for judges. How long had it been since he had been in Neroos society?

"You're sure of this?"

"Yes."

"How?"

Because I planned it, Rierdan thought with a hint of irony. But that was the last thing he should admit at this point. He had spent thirty minutes outlining an attack plan involving military support from several large cities. He had intentionally neglected to say that he lacked support from those cities and that Gideon was the first city he approached. But that didn't matter—the judges had spent the next hour interrogating him, and he was finally making some headway. Admitting that he was the mastermind behind both attacks would be, in a word, suicidal.

"Your honors," Rierdan said, hoping that his confidence would inspire within these bureaucrats the same ardor that drove him. "I have spent…many years…ingraining myself in the social structure of Lima society. I have intentionally placed myself in harm's way so that I could protect the best interests of Neroos society. So when I give you information that I have earned through hard work and at significant risk to my own life, I give it with full authority. They will attack Borinihah, it will be on the night I have specified, and Borinihah must be fortified."

Rierdan looked each man and woman in the eye in the silence that ensued. There were eleven judges in all, with each judge representing ten thousand constituents. Rierdan needed the strength of Gideon to join him so that he could convince the other cities more easily. This first win was crucial; if the Neroos cities didn't fall in line after this, then he will have signed away the lives of the people of Borinihah without their knowledge or consent.

Another judge spoke up. "How do we know that you are not Lima yourself? Perhaps you were born into Lima society and spent enough time among our people to learn our language, or you have defected to our common enemy after having spent so much time with them?"

Encouraged by his colleague, another added, "We can't allow this man to walk in here and demand our military without us knowing who he is. We'd never be appointed to the chief judges' bar next year with that hanging around our necks!"

"Here here," a few more said under their breath as they tapped the bar that supported their weight.

Rierdan was incensed. After an hour and a half's time of talking, selling, and convincing, he was fed up with these judges in robes that they had not earned, passing judgment on the one man trying to do more good for them than they had done for themselves—or for their people.

"Do you not see the opportunity?" Rierdan replied. "This isn't just another offensive. This is the marauders' greatest force they have ever amassed—and that means that you stand to break them once and for all! If you win this battle and crush their army, our region will not face another major threat from the marauders for the rest of our lives. *This* is your chance!"

"Pretty words. But we need more proof," a silver-haired judge said.

"How about a sacked and pillaged Borinihah in only a few months, with Gideon to fall weeks afterward?" Rierdan retorted.

"Don't you threaten us!" One of the judges cried out.

"Then join me!" Rierdan shouted in return. "The wheels of war are turning. They cannot be stopped. Borinihah is sitting directly in the sights of the Lima commanders and marauders, and you would lean on your precious bar and do *nothing!* I have not worked this hard and come this far to listen to political posturing!"

The judges glowered at Rierdan and looked from one to another. Rierdan knew that they were weighing his words. If what he told them were true, then it would be a decisive military victory—one that these pompous politicians knew would surely get the electorate to appoint them once again. But if what he said were false and he wanted to draw their armies out of their city, then there was more at stake than the next round of elections and appointments.

"Rierdan, I think there is a compromise," said a middle-aged man, one of the youngest of the eleven, with his left hand stroking a ring on his right hand. "We are willing to commit...a portion...of our military to protect Borinihah. But we cannot send them to war on your word alone."

A murmur of assent rippled through the judges, but the noises of dissent began to crescendo once again.

Rierdan tried to unball his fists. If some were willing to commit at least a portion of their army, then that would certainly be more than he was beginning to expect from this group.

"Three quarters," Rierdan said.

"We cannot commit..." the judge began to say.

"I don't care what your politics say you can or cannot commit! The people at Borinihah alone cannot withstand the coming onslaught. They need three quarters of your army," Rierdan demanded.

"Three men out of ten," came the reply.

"Five, and not a man less. There will be enough to protect Gideon while still supporting Borinihah. I would not ask you to sacrifice your own safety, but you cannot sacrifice the safety of the people at Borinihah."

The judges looked around the table at each other, and the whispers continued.

"We will write an edict for four out of ten," the middle-aged judge said. "We cannot leave our brothers at Borinihah alone—but we cannot trust you, either."

"Don't worry," Rierdan said. "You'll know I speak the truth soon enough. I just hope you are prepared for what is to come."

"When will we hear from you?"

"I will send a communiqué within three months. Look for my messenger, and keep your scouts abroad. The entire western region of the Neroos province will have a great deal to worry about before the next five months are through."

And with that, Rierdan approached the bar, shook the middle-aged judge's hand and turned to go. Once he had shaken the man's hand, his concerns were allayed. A handshake to a Neroos was gravely serious.

But one thing nagged at the back of his mind as he exited the marble-floored room. Their garments were so different. And their resolve was weak. Things had changed. Significantly. Could he still depend on a mere handshake, an ages-old tradition that bound any Neroos to his word, when so much was already shifting?

He tried to put it out of his mind. His first objective had to be to protect Borinihah. His second was to raise an army. If these men went back on their word, then be it on their heads.

And Rierdan promised himself that if things went wrong, he would bring it down on their heads.

~~~~~

Hakoni walked out of the town hall in a daze. The information that Garrick had just given him was stunning. He paused on his way to the stables where the prisoners were kept. *How old am I? How long has this war been going on? Is there any end to this?* The thoughts swirled through his head, looking for answers to anchor themselves to but finding none. None that Hakoni was prepared to accept, anyway.

"Hakoni, you're right," Garrick had begun. That admission alone had surprised Hakoni as much as anything up until that point. He was so accustomed to being corrected, shown why he was too rash, and told to stop being a child every time he encountered Garrick that being right was the last thing on his mind.

And after seeing Kalif's reaction to the *meurtrinarihah*, he didn't want to be right anymore. He had no idea what was right anymore. He had been perfectly happy believing the worst of all the Lima, but he knew that he had just seen the best that Kalif had to offer. And it flew in the face of all the stories he told himself day in and day out.

"There is something going on among the prisoners," Garrick continued. "And Kalif probably has something to do with it. But they can't plan anything on their own. They're too disconnected to do something in concert."

Hakoni had a hard time understanding what Garrick was trying to say. "But…they have to be able to connect somehow. They can't plan anything if they really don't have a way to get the information out."

"So you agree that there's a weakness in our system being exploited," Garrick prodded.

Hakoni paused, wondering why on earth Garrick would bring this kind of information to his attention. But the idea that there was a weakness in the Neroos guard was frightening—they were spread too thin as it was. Any weakness at all could have dire consequences.

"Sir," Hakoni said to stall and gather his thoughts. "Sir, logically I agree with you. But I can't see where we're giving anyone an opportunity to communicate or plan."

"We aren't," Garrick replied.

"I don't understand."

"Our forces are few, but I still believe we've deployed them correctly. We have just enough to get the work done and guard them properly. So if there's a weakness, then it's not in the numbers or the deployment. That leaves only one other option."

The realization broke over Hakoni's mind like a stone falling from the quarry. "But sir…do you mean…" He tried to gather his thoughts one more time. Speaking slowly, he said, "Are you saying that one of our own men is helping them?"

Garrick bowed his head, unable and unwilling to say it out loud. He just nodded his head. "That's where you come in."

"Are you switching our posts?" Hakoni asked, hoping that he would be relieved of Kalif much sooner than he expected.

Hakoni expected Garrick to switch around assignments immediately. The less a guard stayed in one place, the less opportunity he had to exploit the weaknesses and opportunities of his post. He began to explain his ideas to Garrick, but Garrick waved his hand as if swatting away the gnats.

"Hakoni, if I started moving soldiers around right now, then I'd be spreading the disease. I don't know who it is, and giving this person—or people! —the opportunity to have more contact with the prisoners will only exacerbate the problem."

Hakoni's shoulders slumped. He just wanted to leave. He still could not see Garrick's plan for him, but despair was quickly encroaching on his heart.

"What do you need me to do?"

"I need to find the mole. And that means they can't suspect I'm looking for one. You have to find a way to get Kalif to tell you what he knows. And find out what his motives are."

Hakoni's mouth dropped. Hakoni had just beaten Kalif unconscious that very afternoon, and now Garrick was asking him to gain the prisoner's confidence. "I think I'm the last person he'll confide in."

"A weakness is only a strength seen from the wrong perspective, Hakoni," Garrick admonished. "You've got to get the information from him that he seems to have without the other prisoners knowing that he's telling you anything. I need to know who this is, Hak. I have to count on you. Will you help me?"

"Why me?"

"Every Neroos in this village hates these Lima. But you're the only one with such outright animosity. But because of your age, you're not considered a threat. I'm counting on you to use that to get what we need."

Hakoni nodded. He couldn't find his voice. He was only seventeen, and he was tasked with espionage. Tasked with saving his village from a prisoner's rebellion. And time was short.

Walking back to the stables in the fading sun, Hakoni began forming a plan. And the plan would not turn out well for Kalif. Hakoni had surprisingly little satisfaction as he considered what he had to do to extract information while keeping the other prisoners from knowing what was happening. But Kalif had come to him. Kalif had offered information. *Can I trust it?* Hakoni wondered. *Can*

I trust him? How can I know if he's telling me the truth? Hakoni prayed that his plan was not a matter of self-gratification. Of revenge. He prayed that Kalif would be able to survive the plan long enough to give the valuable information they needed. He prayed that Kalif had any information at all.

It was the first time Hakoni actually prayed in a long time. Too long. And he was sure that right now, he wasn't praying for the right things.

~~~~~

Rayanna stared at a split in the cement where the wooden wall frame was visible above Chism's room, not seeing it at all as her mind wandered. She sat with her back against the wall next to the fireplace. The fire was always small, but always lit, and the concrete around it retained the warmth. With the window from the water closet constantly letting in cold air, it was all Rayanna could do to stay warm.

She was proud of the day she had replaced the thin curtain—which had a habit of blowing aside with a breeze while one was using the latrine—with her heaviest blanket.

"Are you kidding? You're how many months pregnant, it's winter, and you want to hang your heaviest blanket over the water closet? I appreciate privacy, Rayanna, but this is too far," Chism lectured, even as Rayanna pulled a chair over to loop the blanket over the bar.

"Give it one afternoon, Chism. *One* day. It'll be so much warmer in here, I won't even need a blanket," Rayanna said. "There's only one way to live through a winter in Gidionhi, and that's knowing what it takes to keep the cold away."

Gala had stayed quiet, no doubt because she had no qualms with Rayanna freezing to death, as far as Rayanna could tell. Rayanna hadn't forgotten that Gala hadn't wanted Chism to hand over his straw mattress. Admittedly, the lumps in the straw mattress weren't much better than the flat cement, but at least it was something. Rayanna would have gladly given it to Gala and tried to bury the animosity, but now that her stomach was beginning to swell, new aches and pains were assailing her night and day. She couldn't give up the lumpy mattress, even if it meant keeping the peace.

The blanket had been over the closet for several weeks now, and though it could never entirely seal the doorway, it proved that Rayanna had something to offer. She felt empowered. In the smallest ways, even here in Ombrar, she could control part of her universe. Sealing a doorway as the Neroos did. Cooking with her Neroos blend of spices. Certain things about Gala and Chism's lives were becoming more Neroos, because she was there. She had influence. She had value.

But Rayanna could not deny how much of her life was becoming highly Lima. The clothing that she now wore and the meat she now ate were things she never would have had in Gidionhi. Even her own thoughts were becoming a blend of Neroos and Lima dialects as common words began to replace the Neroos she was so accustomed to using.

The door swung open, obscuring Rayanna's view of the opposite wall and breaking her train of thought. Gala swiftly shut the door and turned to look at Rayanna. "Why wasn't this door locked?"

Rayanna opened her mouth but no words came out.

"Rayanna, you just *sit there!* Why can't you just get up and lock the door when we leave?"

It was a low blow. Rayanna worked throughout the day in the little apartment to make food and clean, and Gala knew it. "It was one time, Gala. I haven't left it unlocked in weeks. Don't start a war over it."

"It could have been one time too many."

Rayanna raised an eyebrow. "I thought you were supposed to knock before you entered."

"Well I didn't!"

"Well you wouldn't have known I hadn't done my part if you had just done your part. So which of us is really at fault here?"

Gala's hand flew up in the air as she squeaked out the start to several sentences, but never got through the first word. Rayanna grinned a little, despite the small feeling of guilt she had. She could push any of Gala's buttons, she knew. She wouldn't do it so often if Gala didn't make it so easy.

Finally finding her words, Gala said, "That's the most illogical… stupid…childish…!"

Rayanna raised her hands in defeat and said in a light voice, "You're right. I should have locked the door. But what are you so upset about? If someone came in here and, you know, killed me or something, you wouldn't be too disappointed, would you?"

Gala looked as if Rayanna had slapped her. Not answering, she carried the heavy pot she had brought in with her over to the shelves, covering it with a lid. The lid was actually a wooden box that didn't fit over the entire water pot, leaving several inches visible at the bottom. Chism brought the empty box back from the docks after Rayanna complained about getting dust in the water when she swept.

"Why would you say that?" Gala said.

"Oh, come on," Rayanna replied. "You were completely against me sleeping on this mattress. And when I hung the blanket on the door over there, you didn't say a word about how cold I might be without it. Admit it, Gala. Your life would be better without me."

Gala didn't sit down on her floor mat. She stood with her hands on her hips and stared at the floor. Rayanna hadn't seen this Gala before, and she began to feel guilty for pushing Gala too far. "I don't want to hurt you, Rayanna. I was telling Chism that it's not wise to put a straw mattress next to a fire, but he wouldn't sleep out here himself, insisting you needed the warmth of being next to the fire."

"And the blanket?"

"You're annoying, Rayanna, but you're not stupid. I was curious to see what would happen."

"You really have been concerned for me?" Rayanna said, obviously perplexed.

Gala didn't answer immediately. She finally sat down and rocked back and forth before finally speaking. "What do you know about Kalif?"

All the mirth and teasing went out of Rayanna. She narrowed her eyes, trying to discern if Gala were delivering a low blow to get back at her. Her breathing became shallow, and she instinctively touched a burn mark Kalif had left on her arm. "What does that have to do with anything?"

"Were you unconscious when he...?"

Rayanna nodded.

"So it may not have been him?" Gala said with a touch of hope left in her voice.

Rayanna shook her head slowly. "It was him."

Gala sighed deeply and sat down on her mat. Staring at a spot on the floor and seeing only memories in front of her eyes, she spoke with a hollow voice. The setting reminded Rayanna of her mother, and the hairs on her skin began to rise.

"I was a nurse," Gala began. "Kalif was...well, he was a mess. He was a fringe soldier, and he was very good at what he did."

You mean killing Neroos, Rayanna thought. But she felt that something sacred to Gala was happening, and she didn't dare break Gala's concentration.

"But he was angry. When he was younger, a group of sailors that he swore were Neroos poured something on him and lit it on fire. He has burn scars up and down his back from it. Ever since then, he has blamed the Neroos for every hurtful thing in this world.

"The Lima hate the Neroos for all the same reasons that the Neroos hate the Lima, but for Kalif it was personal. The Neroos killed his mom and dad, and his sister had just died a week before he attacked your village. Of course, he blamed the Neroos for her death."

Gala shifted her legs and wiped moisture out of one eye. "When I met him, he came to me with injuries he said were from work on the fringe, but I knew bar fight wounds when I saw them. But as I stitched up a cut on his head, we just started talking. We ended up falling asleep—him on the floor, me against the wall—and my mother..." Gala paused at the mention of her mother as tears streamed down her face. "My mother saw us and was so angry that I had fallen asleep in the same room as a man! She chased him out, but I happened to run into him at the market, then by the docks, and then in other places. We'd talk for hours every time. I could see so much goodness in him—he just needed someone to help pull it out. Over time, he became a very kind man. He loved me despite my Neroos heritage when no one else would, and I loved him despite his past.

"We were supposed to get married the week after the raid on your village. He was supposed to give up life as a soldier and become a fisherman. We'd both have the family we'd always wanted. But I knew he couldn't give it up that easy. I didn't stop him from going to Gidionhi, because he wanted justice. So did I, really. He was supposed to come back, and we were supposed to get married. I might have gotten pregnant..."

As Gala wiped her red and puffy eyes, Rayanna said slowly, "So I'm pregnant...with the child that was supposed to be yours." Tears welled up in Rayanna's eyes as she saw the anguish in the person she had taken so much pleasure in teasing. "And that's why you want me to die."

"I told you already—"

"I know what you said. But I don't blame you for feeling that way, if you do. I mean, was it really that you were concerned for me, or was that just a story?"

Gala shook her head and stared at the ceiling. "I don't know. I told myself it was because the mattress was dangerous next to the fire. I told myself it was because I was curious. But maybe down inside...maybe I was telling myself stories to justify why you should be cold and on a bare cement floor."

Rayanna nodded and wiped her own tear-stained face. "Well, thank you."

Gala shook her head. "Why?"

"That was honest. I'm glad you didn't lie to me. I can't stand it when people lie."

"Then maybe we understand each other a little better now," Gala said with a little smile. "I just don't understand how you keep yourself sane. How do...how do you get through the pain?"

"Work helps," Rayanna said, seeing Gala for the first time not as one of her captors, but as another woman enduring her own anguish. "My mother was raped when Gidionhi was attacked six years ago, and my father and brothers were killed. She lost it. I had to work to keep my brothers and myself alive. Now, I clean and cook here to keep myself busy. But that's not enough in the small hours of the night when it's just me and my thoughts. I have to remember that I'm still valuable. A smart man once told me that self-worth can't be taken away. It has to be given up. I refuse to give it up."

Just then, Chism opened the door and strode in. "How many times do I have to tell you to lock the——!"

He stopped short of finishing his sentence as he saw the two women with red, puffy eyes staring up at him. "Umm. Well. I mean, please...please lock the door."

He shut the door and quickly began busying himself with food on the shelf.

"Chism?" Gala said.

"Yeah?"

Rayanna finished, "Lock the door."

Rayanna and Gala shared a smile as Chism made excuses under his breath and locked the door.

Chapter 17:
To Pay a Debt

Rierdan felt a thrill he had not experienced in...how long? How long had he been at this? Time seemed almost irrelevant now. His senses told him the end was near. Anticipation, elation, and anxiety all swirled together, sometimes clashing violently and other times playing a perfect harmony within him. Rierdan had experienced some Lima drugs while he was maintaining his cover, and this particular feeling was akin to the high he'd received from a bizarre mix of herbs, except...purer. More complete.

Almost there, he told himself. *I'm almost done. Justice is about to be served, and my people will know some peace. I'm almost there. Almost there.*

But on the surface, he was calm and flat, as unreadable as a blank slate.

He had not experienced joy or satisfaction in so long that he could not immediately recognize them for what they were. Even now, the emotions had become more of an irritant than a natural reaction. They distracted from his goal. And Rierdan could not afford to be distracted.

Rierdan stood back in the council room behind the Master alongside his two counterparts. All eyes were on him, and the Teacher and the Judge were interrogating Rierdan on the progress of his plan. Standing behind the Master and with the taste of success almost on his tongue, Rierdan began to fantasize about grabbing the old man's chin, pulling upward, placing his right hand at the base of the Master's skull, and twisting with all the power in his lean and muscular arms. Breaking someone's neck was a very difficult feat; but the visceral elation Rierdan experienced from the loud pop brought the skill he acquired as an assassin to his mind every time he stood here. Right here. Right in arm's reach.

"...and when I speak to you," a hand came crashing down on the table, jolting Rierdan out of his reverie, "you listen!"

All eyes were on Rierdan. "Yes, Teacher. My humblest apologies."

Rierdan could think of no worse moment for him to lose focus than now. The time was drawing nearer. The plans were falling into place. Any error on his part would be...unhealthy.

"I will only repeat myself once. If I need to do so again, you will be dismissed."

"Yes, Teacher," Rierdan replied. The threat was thinly veiled. No one was "dismissed" from the proceedings in the council chamber. One either walked out of this room with the council's full confidence, or one's body was dragged out and dropped in an alley for some poor vagrant to find and pick over for anything left of value.

"Your report," the Teacher said, wasting no words.

"We have taken control of three linen and cloth facilities, and we now pay two blacksmiths and one goldsmith handsomely. We also control two quarries," Rierdan began. "The three linen and cloth facilities are in Gideon, Borinihah, and one city further into the Neroos territories, a place called Ammonihah."

"What is your strategy behind sinking the resources into Neroos holdings?"

"Quite simple, really. We own the bandages when the fighting really breaks out, and we're getting the Neroos' stockpile. The Neroos don't know that their benefactors are Lima, and they are paid well enough to do exactly what we instruct them to do. So either we sap them of their resources, or they pay a premium to bandage a Neroos in Lima cloth."

The Teacher gave a faint nod. Rierdan thought he saw a smile begin to play around the corners of the Judge's mouth.

"And the smiths and quarries?"

"All Lima. Our brothers will all need weapons, and those will also come at a price. But if we intend to win a war, we had better use weapons we can trust. The Neroos never were clever enough to use fire the way we do for our glass and steel."

A few snickers made quick rounds throughout the room. Rierdan knew he was playing his cards well. Insult the Neroos, play to a Lima's pride, and a host of critical information gets passed right by.

Rierdan had, in fact, acquired all of the holdings he had described. But he was now using Triumvirate funds to bolster Neroos war preparations in key cities, and he was finding more places to help the Neroos as he drained the Triumvirate's coffers on these "investments." The quarries were also promising, but understaffed. The smiths were new apprentices eager for a benefactor to help them start their own shop. No valuable weaponry was coming from these smiths any time soon. The very delicate part of the operation was to completely conceal the hard facts about each of these holdings until the Neroos could strike.

Huron, a counselor to the Teacher, reported on the progress of the army. He had been busy recruiting from two cities to the south. Managing so many soldiers in relative secrecy was proving difficult. Huron was in the process of training regiment, platoon, and detail leaders. There was no reason to control individual marauders when they only needed to train the leaders and delegate.

"Then there's the matter of the target," the Master spoke. "What intelligence do we have on our potential targets?"

"I have done a reconnaissance," Rierdan said. "Gideon and Borinihah are well defended. Gideon has higher walls, but they are weaker. We can break through them faster."

Criton spoke up quickly. "Borinihah has more accessible walls, and we'd have to pass it to get to Gideon. Borinihah is the more logical target."

"Yes," Rierdan admitted. "And that's why they are better defended."

"The Neroos are fighting battles with their own people away to the North," Criton countered. "Their armies are stretched thin. Borinihah is the better target, especially once we get through the gate."

Rierdan scoffed openly and then addressed the Triumvirate. "Your honors, if what Criton has said is true, then Gideon will be less easily defended. We'd have to find some way to lower the gate at Borinihah. Their walls are too well defended, and they're too thick. Only when that gate is open will we have any prayer of sacking the city."

Criton countered, "Your honors, I propose that we hide an assault team within the walls of Borinihah to breach their defenses at the start of the battle, while we all have energy. Then we open the gate and take the city. It will only take a matter of hours."

"I am disappointed," the Master said. "I would have thought you more prescient than this, Rierdan." He eyed Rierdan with suspicion. Rierdan had fought too many battles to not see all of the possibilities.

Of course, Rierdan had intended all along to goad Criton into fighting him. Rierdan knew that if too much of the plan went his way, then the Triumvirate would depend on him. And the Triumvirate was not known for its dependence on anyone or anything.

"If I may," Rierdan began cautiously, "I would like to present the case for attacking Gideon. First of all, I doubt that the Neroos would leave Borinihah without its defenses. The nation has civil troubles in the North, yes. But the last thing they need is trouble to the West. I contest that they will be better defended on the fringe; Gideon, which is further in, will perhaps have even loaned part of its army to Borinihah. Furthermore, we have never tried an assault team because of how incredibly difficult the Neroos dialect is. Do we have a handful of marauders capable of speaking Neroos? Of course. But each would have to be perfect—perfect!—in their dialect so as to remained concealed. Criton is a brave warrior, and I would hate to lose him…or other soldiers of his kind."

Criton snorted at Rierdan's feigned care for his wellbeing. Everyone in the room knew that Rierdan and Criton would like nothing better than the chance to kill the other in his sleep. But Rierdan hoped it would be enough to solidify the idea to go ahead with Borinihah.

"We will discuss the matter," the Judge said. "This meeting is closed. Counselors, you may leave."

Rierdan left the council room and took several turns through the tunnels, carefully leaving scuffs in the dust and shaking his knife in its scabbard as he went. Before long, he noticed a shift in the light behind him, alerting him to his pursuer. *Corva cavesa,* Rierdan thought with a mild oath as he thought of Criton, his likely assailant. *He's too easy to manipulate.*

Rierdan spun suddenly on his heel and stepped right into Criton. As he had expected, Criton had his own short sword drawn. By stepping directly into his path, Rierdan completely took away the man's ability to use his blade—but not his ability to use his fists. Rierdan stepped to his left, closer to the sword in Criton's right hand and allowed the awkward left hook to glance off his head and knock him over.

Rierdan behaved as if disorientation had overtaken him and waited for Criton to make his next move. Criton wouldn't kill him;

at least, Rierdan hoped he wouldn't. He was here for information, and he wouldn't spill Rierdan's blood until he had what he needed. And Rierdan was ready to fan the flames. He waited for the cold steel to touch his neck before he froze and spoke slowly. Evenly. Murderously.

"I've killed men much stronger than you for much less than this," Rierdan said. "Get that steel off my neck, or I swear you'll never see the other side of this tunnel."

Criton pressed the sword in, cutting a thin line into Rierdan's neck. "Why Gideon?"

Rierdan looked up with incredulity in his eyes, though he doubted that Criton could see the expression written on his face. The sparsely spaced torch sconces cast only as much light as was absolutely necessary. Rierdan had chosen this spot with very low light, looking for an advantage over his opponent who already had thirty pounds of muscle as an advantage over Rierdan.

"I'm going to kill you for putting your sword to my neck, and all you wanted to know is what I've already said? You're about as dim as this hallway."

"There's more. I know there's more! You aren't everything you seem to be, assassin."

"I have much better places to be—"

"Why Gideon—"

"—And much better things to do—"

"Why Gideon!"

"Because I have a brother at Borinihah!" Rierdan spat out, letting his voice fill with vehemence. "Because I hate the Neroos for tearing apart my family! He met some Neroos wench who filled his head with stories, and though I loathe her for taking him away from me, he's still my brother."

The sword withdrew from his neck as Criton laughed. "So. You are protecting the Neroos after all. And here I thought it was because you were one."

"No," Rierdan said. "You just wanted a reason to hate me, because you know the Triumvirate listens to me. And you get swept to the side." And with that taunt, Rierdan slipped quickly and quietly to the other side of the narrow tunnel.

A sword swooshed through the air and came down ringing on the stone where Rierdan had been a moment before. From his place just behind Criton, Rierdan plunged his knife into Criton's right shoulder. A cry of pain and the sound of a sword falling to the ground filled the tunnel. When Criton craned his neck back to cry out in pain, Rierdan yanked his blade out and cut a quick line across Criton's exposed throat. Then, kicking him in the small of the back, Rierdan sent his opponent flailing against the opposite wall where he fell to the ground. Rierdan knelt on the back on his neck and pressed his knife into the lower part of Criton's eye socket. Criton froze.

"I told you I've killed bigger men for less," Rierdan said evenly. "And everyone who knows about my brother has stopped breathing a long time ago. But I still need you to finish this attack against the Neroos. So I'm going to let you live, but remember: I'm letting you live. Don't attack me again, because I may revoke your privileges for breathing. Now place your palms down on the floor and push yourself up."

Criton obeyed, breathing heavily in anger. But with Rierdan's knife still pressed to his eye, he knew compliance was the only way out in one piece.

With his opponent's palms safely on the ground and his head lifted to just the right height, Rierdan couldn't resist the urge to kick him in the face. That done, he then departed swiftly and quietly, enjoying the moaning emanating from the place he had just left.

Rierdan had no brother in Borinihah. But he thought it might be just enough to push the Triumvirate over the edge to choose Borinihah themselves rather than at Rierdan's behest. It was a risky game he played, but the risk was the only way Rierdan experienced pleasure these days.

Stepping out of the tunnel, Rierdan allowed the feelings of anticipation, elation, and anxiety to wash over him again. Blinking against the light as he opened the door and walked into a courtyard of the government building, he turned and headed toward the city gate.

Then a black bag was forced over his head and two hard punches landed directly on his kidneys. Rierdan was kneeling before he ever saw the new assailants. A gag was forced into his mouth before they tied a rope around the outside of the black bag and cinched it tightly. With his arms forced behind his back, ropes rubbed his wrists raw in very little time. Someone dealt a wicked blow to Rierdan's groin before another pair of hands quickly lashed his ankles together. It was over with incredible efficiency.

So close, Rierdan thought as waves of nausea washed over him from the pain in his groin, kidneys, and head. *I was so close. And I lost focus.*

A pole slid down the length of Rierdan's spine through the spaces between his bound arms and legs, and he was suspended by his ankles and wrists. The men who carried him seemed to intentionally cause Rierdan intense pain by jostling the pole as they walked. Rierdan felt a pulling sensation in his left shoulder, warning him that it was about to dislocate. He shifted his weight carefully, trying to avoid what would inevitably happen if he were suspended much longer.

A guttural noise started in Rierdan's throat and grew to a moan as he felt his shoulder slipping. If by sheer will he could retain the use of his arms, then he would exert every ounce of considerable will he had. His wrists and ankles had already begun to bleed, and the warm blood trickled down his legs and arms.

Just when Rierdan thought he could handle no more, he was dropped on his stomach and face in the back of a wagon. The wagon shifted once, twice, three times in close succession. Three people just climbed aboard, and the wagon began to move before the last man had quite climbed on. Either the first man on the wagon was very quick to the reigns, or there was a fourth man driving it.

Another dark cover blocked out the sun. They had covered the wagon for improved mobility.

"Did you give him the stuff?" One of the men asked.

"*Shosk*," another swore.

Then a pot clanged against the wooden floorboards of the wagon. Rierdan caught the sweet, pungent smell of something burning. A special herb. With his mouth gagged, he had no choice but to breathe through his nose. He knew this herb—perhaps too well. If he could breathe through his mouth, then he would be able to resist; but without being able to empty his lungs quickly through his mouth, he would be taking a concentrated dose through the nose, and the cover over the wagon would serve to permeate everything. He estimated he would be completely disoriented, if not entirely unconscious, very soon.

He had no idea where they were taking him, but he knew he would soon find out. Right before they killed him.

~~~~~

The wind whipped off the sea and sent an icy spray across the dockworkers.

Dock work was something that Chism was familiar with, and he had slipped back into it with few questions from the foreman. The foreman knew that most if not all of these men had something to hide from the law. All he cared about was having men strong enough to unload the docks and restock the ships in the amount of time he needed. The foreman never worried about the city guard coming to High Tide to round up the criminals; half the men on his crew were wanted for murder, and the other half probably would be if anyone ever found the bodies. None of them would hesitate to dispatch of a few city guards that came poking around.

Chism's scars seemed to ache more and more as the cold set in, but he had learned to bear it. Chism had learned through hard experience to bear almost anything.

There's always something worse, son, his father would tell him. *Your job is not to worry about how much worse it could be. Your job is to figure out how to make the situation better.*

As he pulled the hood of his wax-and-canvas dock coat down over his face to the stinging sea spray out of his eyes, Chism found himself grinning sardonically. *Make the situation better?* He thought as he lifted another crate and walked aboard the fifth ship for the day. *I shot my brother and kidnapped a Neroos girl who, by no fault of her own, now bears my nephew. She lives with my brother's fiancée—ex-fiancée—and me. That's much better than what things were like only five months ago.*

But just as his father's voice always rang in his ears, he could also hear Rayanna's accented admonishment.

"You're not looking at the whole situation," Rayanna had told him only a few weeks ago. Her voice had been completely devoid of pity as she looked on Chism, who had had too much to drink and was spilling his thoughts just like he was spilling beer. "You didn't attack my village. You didn't attack me. You were handed this situation, so shut up and just smile about it!"

Somehow her words had pierced Chism's alcohol-induced fog. He went to the window, poured out his bottle, and refused to drown himself in pity—or ale—again. This plucky girl, barely more than a child, had been through hell and now bore the consequences of someone else's actions. All Chism had to carry were a few scars and the heavy weight of disappointment and disenchantment. She bore the much heavier burden of having been violated by her worst nightmare, and possibly of being repudiated by her own people. But she hadn't given up—why should he?

Chism found himself smiling ever so slightly, the skin on the left side of his face tugging where the scar ran. Chism began to descend the ramp from the deck to the pier. The ramp was made of three boards roughly thirty feet in length connected by cross pieces, which doubled as makeshift steps. Nothing on a pier ever stayed dry for longer than five minutes, and a long wooden plank quickly became slick. When the winter set in, the salt spray would freeze to riggings, masts, coats, hair, and especially ramps between the pier and the top deck. Today was a particularly blustery day with ice freezing the crates that Chism and his crew were using to stockpile the ships, but Chism's experience over the last four months and his prior experience as a young man made him almost impervious to the ice and cold.

But there was something else inside of him, getting brighter like the sky moments before dawn. Chism couldn't say for sure what it was that seemed to be changing, but he likened it to warming his hands close to the fire after days much like this one. Something inside of him was able to flex and move with an agility he hadn't known for sometime. And the possibility of something new on the horizon made him crane his neck, waiting to see what this new light could bring.

As he descended the ramp, he glanced over to the buildings and thoroughfare. Very few people were outside today. In the distance he saw a woman with dark hair wearing a coat that looked strangely familiar to him. It wasn't Gala. Gala was taller. Then Chism got a sinking feeling in his stomach—a feeling that if he were closer, that dark hair would have a slight tinge of red to it.

What is she doing out here? Chism thought angrily as he descended the plank and rushed over to her.

"Rayanna!" Chism hissed as he came closer.

She jerked around, surprised to hear someone who knew her name. Her eyes went wide and her hand swing around at Chism's shoulder height. As soon as he saw her body brace and her shoulder lower to come in for the strike, Chism immediately reached out to grab her wrist. His hand was there before she was even halfway through her swing. Chism gripped her wrist a little tighter than was absolutely necessary—but then again, she was holding a knife.

"Haven't you cut me enough?" Chism said abrasively. He pulled her down an alley and hid from the other dockworkers.

"Chism, I just had to…had…needed to get out," Rayanna said in Lima. Her accent was still evident, but hardly jarring. Chism was beginning to think that it would be difficult to take her for a Neroos by her accent, though she was obviously a foreigner. With a little more confidence in her speaking ability, she might be able to pass herself as a Lima quite well.

"What, are you and Gala arguing again?"

"No!" came a quick reply. "We're not. We're just…breathing each other's air. Besides, she's been a lot happier since apprenticing with one of the medicine women."

Chism just shook his head. "You know, sometimes I wish you'd just complain about *something*. Like being stuck in there with the same person all day every day. That's an OK thing to complain about."

Rayanna simply shook her head. "My mother was a great example to me. I learned not to let despair overcome me. Complaining about the rain doesn't make the sun come out, you know."

"Well look," Chism said as he forced himself not to get sidetracked into another long conversation with her. "The High Tide District is not a place for an afternoon stroll. The last thing any of us need is for these dockworkers to notice a beautiful lady and know where she lives."

Rayanna smiled a little, and Chism suddenly felt very self-conscious about having called her beautiful.

"Don't worry so much. I'm not speaking to anyone," Rayanna said as she tried to ease the tension. "Just you. I am…agh, what's the word? I am…*fecanne*, but I am not a slave."

Chism's eyes went wide, and a small smile began to creep across his lips. The more he tried to hide it, the more he failed. "You're… umm…you're what, exactly?"

Rayanna was completely perplexed. She repeated, "I am not a slave."

"Right," Chism said, still smiling. "But...what did you say you are?"

"*Fecanne*," Rayanna said slowly. Chism closed his eyes and buried his face in his hand, stifling a laugh. "It means that I have a baby in my belly, right?"

"No, Rayanna," Chism said. "*Feconde* means you're having a baby. *Fecanne* is a word that means...well...excrement."

"No it doesn't!" Rayanna replied indignantly. Her rosy cheeks had less to do with the cold now as she began to understand her mistake. "You've never taught me that one!"

"Yeah, well, that's because it's not a nice word."

Rayanna's eyes flared. "How am I supposed to learn this stupid dialect if you don't teach me what I need to know?" She was almost shouting as the embarrassment set in.

Chism shrugged and said, "Now you know."

"Anything else I should be aware of?" Rayanna placed her hands on her hips.

"Yeah," Chism said more seriously. "You should know you're in deep *fecanne* if anyone finds you out here."

Rayanna nodded. Chism had the distinct impression that she only nodded because she came to the same conclusion that he had rather than out of obedience. "Thank you," she said as she rose up on her toes and lightly kissed his cheek. "It's nice to know you care."

Chism watched her pick her way through the alleys and between the buildings. As she went, he found himself watching her midsection, looking at the slight bulge beginning to push at her dress. There was more at stake than just her safety now. And Chism had made a promise to keep his family. Keep them together. Keep them safe. That spunky girl carried all the family he had left.

~~~~~

Hakoni swallowed. Again. He couldn't stop swallowing, and the more he focused on not swallowing, the less successful he was.

I'm seventeen, Hakoni repeated in his mind as he stood at his post, his eyes fixed on the man who could prove the salvation or ruin of his village. *I'm just seventeen. I'm supposed to be flirting with Rayanna and cutting stone and farming for my father.*

But no matter how daunted he felt, the task still lay before him. As he thought of finally getting the chance to exact his revenge, Hakoni felt no elation. He was surprised at the turn of his stomach— or was it a change in his heart? Having worked in the quarry for the better part of his young life, he had developed broad, powerful shoulders and thick arms. Hakoni had dreamed of sinking a fist into Kalif's stomach and punching Kalif's jaw back into his skull with the muscle that hard labor had bestowed on him. And now here he was, given permission to extract information from Kalif by whatever means were available to him, and he couldn't bear it.

After seeing Kalif's reaction to the *meurtrinarihah* and his deep-seeded love for someone named Loria, Hakoni realized that this man who had taken everything away from him still had some humanity left in him. And behind the arrogance and the anger and the rage, Hakoni saw a grief that reminded him of himself. Now the lines were blurring; Hakoni could see that he had no comprehension of the road that brought this man or any of these men to this place. Though Hakoni could never excuse them for what they had done, he was feeling less and less sure of himself as judge, juror, or executioner.

Hakoni walked over to Erron, who held the keys for the shift, and said, "Let's bring him up."

"Hak, what's going on? I got the orders from Garrick, and—"

"If you got the orders from Garrick," Hakoni cut him off with a voice devoid of emotion, "then I suggest you follow them."

Erron stared at Hakoni with eyes full of bewilderment and fear.

Hakoni closed his eyes instead of looking at Erron. "Don't make this more difficult. I have a job to do. And no matter how much you may think otherwise, I wish it had fallen to someone else."

226

Erron stayed silent and simply motioned for another guard to accompany them. When that guard approached, Erron called out, "Tools down!"

His shout echoed throughout the quarry, amplifying itself naturally so that the workers heard it even above the din of their pickaxes and shovels.

~~~~~

Kalif was almost surprised that he understood the command. When the call for "tools down" rang out in the Neroos dialect through the quarry, he didn't have to process the words or translate them in his mind. It was becoming second nature to him. For months, he had refused to acknowledge their commands. All he cared about was that when one of them yelled, he dropped whatever he had in his hands—which was only ever a pickaxe or a bowl of gruel—and stood in line. Though he could always speak Neroos fairly well, his refusal to process their language had been his last act of defiance. And now that was gone.

But this time, there was a feeling of anticipation. It was a familiar feeling to Kalif these days. He had been anticipating the signal from Zoram for weeks, but he wasn't passing along as much information these days. Lots of messages of rebellion, of justice, and of how much the Neroos deserved to die. They were clever messages, and Kalif even felt the old stirring of malevolence from time to time. It was easy to look at the shackles on his wrists and ankles and blame the Neroos. It was easy to think of Loria and how she had died. But following on the heels of every thought of his sister was that girl with skin the golden color of a tree stripped of its bark, and her dark brown hair tinged with red. Tinged with the color of the sun. And the shame washed over him again.

This time the anticipation was different. It was immediate. The thrill that went down his spine and raised the hair on his arms told him that they had called "tools down" because of him. He just didn't know why.

Here he came. Hakoni the watchdog. Several years his senior and far more experienced in battle, Kalif had little to fear of this boy. But he knew that if he were cuffed and Hakoni were let off his chain, there was also no doubt in Kalif's mind that the "little doggy" could kill him with his bare hands.

Kalif stood up tall with his hands by his side and looked straight at Hakoni as he approached. Hakoni's demeanor was not what Kalif had expected. Hakoni's brow was furrowed, his manners rough, but the boy wouldn't look at him. No insults. He stood a few feet back while a guard disconnected Kalif's ankle chain from the stake. The guard then cuffed his hands and feet together with just enough chain to walk.

Kalif squinted slightly at Hakoni. The boy was shifting back and forth, and walking in short circles. Kalif had seen this before— the signs of a man struggling with himself. And when a man is his own enemy, then everyone in his path becomes a danger. And right now, Kalif stood right in his path.

Porja, Kalif swore as he saw what was coming next. Hakoni stepped forward, twisted his hips, and brought an arm bent at the elbow with incredible force into Kalif's stomach. Kalif had never felt so much strength in his life—nor had he ever had such difficulty breathing.

"Hak, you want to wait a few minutes?" One of the guards said irritably. "We still have to get him out of here, you know!"

The two guards stood Kalif on his feet. One man pushed his hand roughly into the middle of Kalif's back, forcing his diaphragm back into action and allowing his lungs to expand. "Let's go," one said and half dragged Kalif out of the quarry as he struggled to keep up and catch his breath.

After exiting the quarry, they turned toward the woods close to where the *meurtrinarihah* had been committed. *So it's the woods. Where none of the prisoners can see them kill me*, Kalif thought. *What a peculiar people, these Neroos. They don't even know how to make a proper example out of killing a slave.*

The two soldiers wrapped a chain around the back of a tree and connected either end to Kalif's wrists. Then they walked back to the quarry. Kalif stood staring at Hakoni. He didn't have enough slack in the chain to bring his hands past his own legs. Kalif didn't bother to struggle.

"You're...calm," Hakoni said.

Kalif almost rolled his eyes at the teenager's awkward moment. "I'm about to die. No need to scream about it."

"What? Oh, no. No, I'm not going to kill you," Hakoni said distractedly.

"No, I imagine Garrick wouldn't like that much, would he?"

Hakoni shot Kalif a sharp look. The first time he looked at Kalif during this bizarre encounter. "I, umm, I'm sorry. About punching you. The other prisoners couldn't know."

Kalif's perplexity was evident. "Couldn't know what?"

"That you're going to help me," Hakoni said evenly.

Kalif laughed. "How old are you, little doggy?"

"My name is—"

"Shut up. I know your name. How old are you?"

Kalif could see Hakoni felt entirely out of place. He was as captive as a person could be, and yet Hakoni obviously felt like the one who didn't want to be here.

"Old enough," Hakoni said slowly and then spoke more quickly as he gathered courage, "to see the ravages of war. Old enough to know what men like you are capable of. Old enough to learn what men like me can be capable of." Hakoni was pacing now, his hands clenching and unclenching. He was maintaining eye contact with Kalif now. "Old enough to pick up severed limbs and heads. Old enough to carry the charred corpses of mothers still holding their dead babies. Old enough to care for my own people rather than disgrace their bodies by letting *you scum* put them to rest!"

Kalif lowered his head.

"What is this? Shame from a Lima? You did this to us!" Hakoni shouted as he struck Kalif hard in the ribs. Hakoni's voice cracked as his throat tightened and his face curled into an image of grief.

Kalif cried out as the right hook caught him squarely in the left ribs. It wasn't strong enough yet to break them, but once Hakoni overcame his grief and really began to administer his punishment, Kalif wondered if the damage would be irreparable.

"That's good," Kalif wheezed out. "Avoid the head. Start with other parts of the body. Let your victim be aware of all the pain."

"YOU'RE NOT A VICTIM!" Diaphragm, spleen, left lung, right lung, jaw. Kalif was doubled over on the ground with his hands pulled behind him.

"No...I...I'm not," Kalif struggled to speak and to breathe. He had at least three cracked ribs on his right side. *Hakoni is left handed,* Kalif noted automatically as he struggled to put his feet in front of him while straining against his hands chained to the tree. "And yes, I will help you," he said as he spat out blood. A tooth felt loose, but it hadn't been completely dislodged yet. "But you have to leave me enough teeth to speak, OK?"

Hakoni looked at Kalif suspiciously. "Just like that? I beat you and you're ready to comply?"

"No. I...I was ready...to help you...before I came out of... of...that quarry."

"What is this, then? Repentance?"

Kalif arched an eyebrow on his pain-ridden face. "You think I can be forgiven of any of this?"

Hakoni thought before he replied. "I'm supposed to. But for you, I might have to make an exception."

Kalif chuckled briefly before the pain in his right rib stabbed him sharply. "So how is it that I can be of service to the little doggy?"

"Tell me why. You have every reason to hate us. Me, especially."

Kalif nodded his head in agreement. "And I do hate you. I think. But I've done things now that not even your faults can surpass. I've come to hate myself more than I can ever hate you, and I'll never make it right. I just know I have to do what I can to make things better."

Hakoni knelt close to Kalif, grabbed his hair, and forced Kalif to look him in the eye. "What things?"

"Kid, you're not old enough. Not old enough to have done something you're ashamed of. Something you wish you could take back but know you can't. So you pray to your gods that the burning guilt will subside, except it doesn't. And you did it because you thought it was right. It all looked right, except it was all wrong. I guess now, I want to do one last thing. One last thing that is right. Even if it looks wrong to go against my people and help the Neroos. I'm tired of doing the wrong things for reasons I told myself were right. Tired of the stories and the lies and the anger. I'm just tired."

Hakoni sat back. Kalif could see the look in his eye. The shame. The burning guilt. *What could this kid have done?* Kalif wondered.

Kalif could see that Hakoni's mind whirled. But Kalif had no way to know that Hakoni couldn't get those eyes out of his head. Those bulging eyes and the feeling of a throat crushing beneath his leather sandal. "Yarlem." The name, whispered in the morning light, echoed in every cavity of Hakoni's conscious. What was wrong, though it looked right. Hakoni wondered if there would ever be a moment where he would have to do what was right, though it looked wrong, to make amends for what he had done. Hakoni wondered if this was that moment. It all played out on Hakoni's face plain enough, though the details were a great mystery to Kalif.

Kalif looked quizzically at this boy. No, no boy knew the things Hakoni knew. No boy knew the stench of charred flesh and the heartache of looking for loved ones, not knowing if they were maimed beyond recognition, if they had fled, or if they had been taken from him. No matter how old Hakoni was, he was not just a boy sitting in front of him. *And he has a secret,* Kalif recognized. *Something that I'm not seeing.*

"I need information," Hakoni said slowly. "And the prisoners in the quarry can't know you're passing me anything."

Realization dawned on Kalif. "So you have to maim me—"

"Just hurt you—"

"Sure, whatever. You're going to maim me so they don't get any ideas about where my loyalties lie."

Hakoni simply nodded.

"How many times do we get to have this little party?"

Hakoni shrugged.

Kalif grit his teeth. He felt his loose tooth move and he winced at the pain. "Perfect."

"Tell me everything you know about the prisoner rebellion," Hakoni said.

"How do you know I'm not going to lie?"

"I don't. But if the information doesn't help us, then we get to do this more until we get information that does."

Kalif cocked his head to one side as his eyebrows shot up for a moment. "Fair enough."

~~~~~

The guards dragged Kalif back to the quarry, lightly punching him in his right ribs again. Kalif screamed in pain and dropped to the ground.

"Get back to work!" They said and dropped a pickaxe next to him.

Zoram helped him into a sitting position. Breathing was extremely difficult.

"Did they ask about our little secret?" Zoram asked immediately.

Kalif shook his head as he sat against the rock, enduring the pain.

"What did they want, then?"

Kalif shook his head again. "They didn't…didn't ask me anything. They just wanted to hear me scream, I guess."

To Pay a Debt

"*Batarkres!*" Zoram swore through clinched teeth.

"Zoram," Kalif struggled through each word. "When are we getting out of here?"

Zoram looked around to make sure the guards weren't getting too picky about their conversation. Given Kalif's state, they were probably glad someone was making sure the prisoner was still alive.

"Soon," Zoram replied.

"Zoram, I need answers. I need to know when I can put this pickaxe through his head!"

Zoram nodded. Then he began to talk.

CHAPTER 18:
JUSTIFIED

Rierdan wasn't unconscious. Not entirely. He had once regretted his decision to use the drugs and hallucinogens. He had told himself that he was learning about his enemies and building immunity to their drugs, but a part of him wondered if that had been nothing more than an excuse. A way to escape his demons. Or worse—maybe it had been for pure gratification. But as he kept one eye open to get a bearing on his surroundings, Rierdan was grateful for the time he spent developing a resistance to certain drugs and plants. He told himself then that it could save his life one day. He hoped today was that day.

The outlook wasn't bright.

Though not entirely knocked out, Rierdan found it was hardly a difficult feat to feign unconsciousness. He could barely feel his arms and legs, and he would be in no position to fight, especially with his hands and feet bound. But at least he would be able to plan and try to gain an idea as to his surroundings. Knowledge, not strength, was Rierdan's greatest asset in virtually every tight situation.

Someone cut the ropes on his hands, and two men stood under each of his arms to carry him. Rierdan was vaguely aware of relief in his left shoulder, but his hands felt like someone had just placed a pile of hot coals right in his palm. It was impossible for him to hide a reaction to the pain. A slow moan began deep in his throat, though he kept a fairly passive face.

"He's a strong one, eh?"

"The Master didn't expect anything less. But not even he could entirely resist this stuff. I've seen much bigger men get knocked out cold from it. Come on, let's get him upstairs."

So. The Master. Rierdan began wracking his incredibly foggy brain. He had played all his cards right. Everything turned out perfectly. He played the Master and everyone else. He couldn't imagine the third member of the Triumvirate suspected that he was a spy. Sometimes even he had difficulty remembering that he wasn't, in fact, a Lima. Why had the Master brought him here like this?

No, that was the wrong question to ask. Whatever had happened, he couldn't undo it. Now his primary concern was survival. He had put too many chain reactions in motion and too many people in danger not to see this through. He had to survive. And he had to regain the Master's trust.

Rierdan felt himself lifted and each arm spread across the shoulder of a man much stronger than he. His feet dragged on the ground. Stone ground. Cobbled stone. Mixed with dirt. A threshold. One flight, two flights, three flights of stairs. The first flight was wood. Then second was plaster. The third was cut stone. The cold emanated through his soft boots as his toes dragged along the ground. The feeling had begun coming back to his limbs, and he was rapidly regaining his faculties once again.

The smell. What was that smell? It was familiar…like something being cooked, but his mind couldn't come to bear. Was it someone's dinner, or was it something else? It smelled like…like…like what?

The drugs were potent, and though Rierdan had resisted them valiantly, he had not fought off their effects completely.

He could not move his head at all without alerting the two mercenaries who dragged him along, and so he dared open his eyes just enough to look behind himself and at the floor. The floors were covered in stone. A yellow and orange marble. *The Master lives well,* Rierdan thought. *I wonder if he will die well, too.* But even Rierdan realized his bravado was like a conch shell on the beach—a tough exterior with a lot of noise when you put your ear to it, but ultimately full of absolutely nothing.

He was dropped unceremoniously in a chair, which then fell over backwards. Rierdan felt his head smack the floor. His shoulder and back had hit first as he fell out of the chair, so the impact was minimized. His mind still operated in a haze, and the pain still hadn't reached his brain. The two men picked him up and tied his hands together behind his back and behind the chair, his arms serving to hold his body up. Rierdan felt his lungs close off as his body slumped forward. In this position, he wouldn't last long before suffocating on his own weight.

"Wake him," came the soft voice of the Master.

Rierdan waited for a heavy hand to land on his head or face, but instead another pot was placed under his nose. Almost immediately upon breathing in the sharp odor, the fog dissipated from his mind and he sat up straight. A giant cough filled his lungs, and yet the man didn't remove the pot from his face. Once the mercenary was satisfied that Rierdan was fully possessed of his faculties, he stepped away and placed a lid on the concoction.

"What in the name of—" Rierdan was forced to pause and cough again for several moments. The pain in his head from its recent meeting with the stone floor raced to his temples, and a headache from the drugs set in with far too much haste. "What in the name of *porja* is all this about?"

"You, my dear assassin, think yourself far more important than you really are if you presume to continue breathing after speaking to me in so disrespectful a manner," the Master said. "Would you care to try again?"

"Well you don't have to have your mercenary here rearrange all my teeth for me to get the point, if that's what you mean," Rierdan said with his eyes shut tightly against the headache. "Sir," he added for good measure. There was that scent again. It was definitely not food. It smelled earthy, like rock or dirt or sand, but not like any of those that had been recently dug up. There was undoubtedly the smell of wood smoke mixed in with it.

"It has come to my attention, Mr. Rierdan, that your loyalties may not rest altogether with the Triumvirate and with the Lima way of life."

"Then kill me. It's what you do," Rierdan spat back.

"Undoubtedly. But in your case, I decided to give you a chance to…prove yourself," came the sibilant reply.

"You've been talking to Criton again, I see." Rierdan tried to look at the Master, but the pain coursed through his body as if his blood itself had turned against him. He was acutely aware of every vein in every finger and across every square inch of his hands. He'd almost rather be drugged again. "I am about to increase your holdings and your power beyond anything that your short-sighted counselors have ever been able to provide. I am expanding the reach of the marauders far beyond our borders and sending a message to both the Lima and the Neroos that we are a force that cannot be stopped and cannot be negotiated with. And you want to stop that? Fine. Fine. I won't be your lap dog, and I won't beg you for my life." Then, addressing one of the guards that brought him here, Rierdan craned his neck back and said, "Hey. *Merdapot.* Yes you, stupid. Put that knife across my throat or here below my left collarbone. Just sink it in wherever you please. I'm done with this masquerade."

The Master considered Rierdan carefully. The guard looked anxiously at the Master, not masking at all his eagerness to follow Rierdan's recommendation.

"I have simply come to the conclusion, assassin, that I have trusted you entirely, and that is simply unacceptable. I cannot allow another man to have that power over me. As they say, I won't put my eggs in one basket."

Don't grovel. Keep your confidence. He'll smell a rat if you just acquiesce. "Get to the point, old man," Rierdan said abruptly. "I've served you too well to dance around accusations like this."

The Master's lip curled and he nodded curtly to the guard. The guard punched Rierdan savagely in the stomach, sending the chair over backwards again. Rierdan landed on his tied hands and felt his arm strain against the impact. A pop in his shoulder warned Rierdan of something gone terribly wrong—worse, even, than his current situation. If he had broken a bone, then his chances of survival were completely eradicated. The same guard grabbed his left arm and lifted Rierdan's body and the chair, alerting Rierdan to the problem as soon as the guard first began to pull. Rierdan screamed out in pain as his now-dislocated shoulder felt the consequences. *Never thought I'd be happy about a dislocated shoulder. But at least it's not broken.*

"You aren't the first Neroos to serve me, Rierdan," the Master said simply and sharply, the sibilance almost gone as his tone hardened. "Yes, I know your heritage. But you have served me well, as have others. I suspected your true identity as a Neroos when I first saw your eyes. Your Lima accent is perfect, and your skin is dark enough. A Lima mother, perhaps? No matter. But your eyes were something different. There was something there that I've never been able to get out of my head. But between Criton's urgings that something was different about this attack you've been planning and your insistence to attack a better-defended city all brought me.... well, here."

Rierdan could barely speak. His hardened abdominal muscles had absorbed much of the blow, but he had no way to turn his body to deflect it. Nausea began to set in, threatening to seize what little control he had left. "I...want..." he began to whisper.

"A little louder, if you don't mind," the Master said as casually as if he were discussing the weather.

Rierdan spoke as loudly as he could, but the air did not come to him to speak beyond a whisper. "Power. I want power. That's why I came to you that day. I brought you deserters." Rierdan was beginning to catch his breath. "I brought you news that Kalif, the careless man who discovered your identity, was dead. I told you then, I wanted power that only the Triumvirate could provide."

"Kalif is alive."

Rierdan was too stunned to check the next words out of his mouth. "He came back?"

"No. But I have a source in Gidionhi who has recently informed me that he is alive and well. And though he's neutralized as a threat, one of the pillars of your admittance to my inner circle is now gone."

Rierdan paused only to cough and try to refrain from vomiting. His stomach ached where the burly guard had hit him. "So the *batarkre* survived. That doesn't change that Gideon is the better target."

"Because it will decimate our forces and leave you in charge?"

"Because you lack the vision to see the benefit!" Rierdan retorted. "Because you are becoming impotent as you carelessly throw your marauders after sheep and gold! You either must see the message you will be sending by attacking at Gideon, or you must get out of the way."

The Master placed his fingers together. "You said nothing of your heritage."

"You know nothing of my heritage. I won't reward your conjecturing by confirming or denying anything. It is beneath you to try to draw me out with those accusations. You and I both know that."

The Master raised his eyebrows and said casually, "If you're no Neroos, then you will have no problem with taking care of a certain issue for me."

He waved to another soldier standing at the door. The soldier opened it and motioned for someone to enter.

Rierdan watched a third guard yank on a chain, forcing a man wearing a collar attached to the chain fall to his knees and crawl as he was yanked and dragged into the room.

"This," the Master said of the man half walking, half crawling, "is a certain issue."

"*Corva*, old man. Looks like you've got plenty of swords around here to have taken care of this yourself."

"Kill him."

"I'm still tied to a chair, *merdapot*."

"Release him," the Master said to his guard.

Rierdan looked the guard in the eye and said, "I'll kill you." The guard only grinned back.

The guard knelt on one knee in front of Rierdan and began to saw at the ropes around his ankles with a knife until they fell to the ground. Just as he shifted his weight and began to stand up, Rierdan kicked up beneath the man's hand wielding the knife and drove it up into the guard's chin. The knife sank deep into his skull, and he fell over instantly.

Rierdan stood momentarily, brought his hands under himself, and then slipped his legs through his tied wrists. Rierdan smiled openly—had the guard he just killed not dislocated his shoulder, he never would have been able to bring his legs through his arms.

The other guards strode toward him with weapons in hand. Rierdan stooped to yank the knife out of the guard's skull, looked at the other guards and said, "Don't. Just…don't." They stopped, dumbfounded. Though Rierdan's hands were still tied, they didn't dare approach.

"Who is he?" Rierdan asked the Master as he sawed off the bindings on his own wrists.

"The enemy."

"Don't be simple. Who is the man?"

"Forgive me. I meant to say….a kinsman of yours."

"Killing him won't strengthen the Lima or the marauders."

"You're stalling."

"You're wasting my time! I'd kill you now if it weren't that you still served a purpose to me," Rierdan said plainly.

"Kill him, or this is all over. Your little game, your little life, it will all end. And whatever you were planning will blow away in the wind."

Rierdan stared at the Neroos, considering his options. The prisoner had been mute but he had worked his way to stand again and face the Master. Rierdan respected him. A man with this kind of fortitude didn't deserve to die. But Rierdan was so close. So close to toppling the Triumvirate. And he had put into motion a plan that would either wipe out the marauders' entire force, or it would jeopardize not just one city, but an entire region of the Neroos. And if the Master suspected Rierdan's loyalties were less than Rierdan had professed, then everything he had worked for would be for nothing. Was not this bigger than one man's life? Was not the whole plan greater than this brave, innocent soul standing to face a certain end?

And what was innocence? Rierdan had been so long in the shadows that he had begun to doubt the very existence of innocence. If he killed this man, Rierdan would be justified. No one could blame him for what he had done. The ends were too important. Everything looked right. So why this feeling in his heart that something was wrong?

Of course this was wrong. This was all wrong. This impossible situation was the result of years of evil. Evil that held onto power. Evil that forced its way in and damned good men, forcing them to make terrible decisions in order to dislodge the infection of evil. This man standing in front of Rierdan was already dead, whether he died by Rierdan's hand or not.

Damn him. Damn the Triumvirate. I'll make them pay. I'll send them to hell for this, Rierdan thought as he walked over to the man and, in a Neroos dialect, whispered in his ear, "You do this for your country." Then with a swift motion, he plunged the dagger that had been in the guard's head right into the Neroos man's heart. The man fell backwards from the momentum of Rierdan's strike, carrying the knife with his corpse to the ground.

Rierdan's shoulder ached. His body had been abused. Yet he had one more task to accomplish. He had to seal the plan. He could not be stopped. Rierdan stoically walked over to the Master, looked him in the eye, and bowed.

"We have begun something greater than the Triumvirate has ever tried before. Yes, the cost will be great. But the power will be unmatched! The Neroos fight their own civil war away to the north. Now is our time to strike Gideon and break the Neroos' spirit. It must be done now, and it must be led by the Triumvirate. Your power will be unmatched when you take Gideon, and the marauders will have a stronghold to stake further attacks, increase their holdings, and graduate from being a nuisance to being the most powerful political and military arm of Lima society. I implore you, Master, not to turn away now."

The Master considered him carefully. Rierdan knew he had played his last cards in the best light, though he loathed himself for what he had to sacrifice to get here. He didn't even know if it would be enough.

"Yes," the Master whispered. "Your allegiance, Rierdan, is true. A servant must sometimes endure a trial by fire before he can be made...pure. I will lead the marauders. And you will be by my side."

Rierdan couldn't say anything. He focused all his energy on not allowing his emotions to overcome him. The hate. The loathing. The passion. He had to stay in control.

Without another word, Rierdan stood and walked out the door with murder in his eyes for anyone who stood in his way. Even with his left arm hanging limply, the guards approached him cautiously.

"Let him go," he heard the Master say. "I have seen exactly what I need from him."

When the doors closed, the Master turned to his guard and said, "Rierdan is not wrong about the opportunity. But I'll not give him everything he asks for. Contact Criton. Find out how soon our soldiers will be ready to move on Borinihah. It's time to change the timeline."

But Rierdan heard none of it. He exited the room, the building, and then the compound. He immediately found himself in the bricking and plaster district with the fire kilns were close by. That was what he had been smelling. It was right outside of the Master's home. They were in the northeastern part of the city with easy access to the forest, which provided fuel for the brick ovens. Rierdan longed to grab a few embers and burn the Master's home to the ground. The fire that burned in his heart consumed his thoughts. But he had to leave. He had to keep going. There were Neroos out there that depended on him to stay strong and on the Triumvirate to stay alive...for now.

Rierdan exited the city with the guards at the gate gaping at the horrible wounds on his wrists and ankles. He walked into the forest until his ankles could endure no more, sank down to the ground, and wept bitterly.

He didn't know the Neroos man's name. But he prayed and asked for forgiveness, anyway, not knowing if anyone—God, man, or spirit—would listen to him after what he had done.

~~~~~

"How did it go?"

Hakoni stood in a small room with Garrick. A home, partially gutted by fire, had been converted to a makeshift command center, and like most homes in this area of Gidionhi, the entire house was only one room. It was a few houses down from where Rayanna used to live.

Hakoni barely heard Garrick's question. He held information critical to the safety of the village, but the thing he wanted most was to make his childhood friend, Rayanna, smile again. *If only I could make things right again. I just want them to be as they once were. I'm just a kid. How can I do this? How can I do any of this?* His eyes began to burn, and he had trouble breathing.

"Hakoni?" Garrick tried to get his attention again. Hakoni looked at him through blurred eyes.

"She lived three doors down," he said aloud, though he seemed to speak only to himself. "Rayanna. Her name was Rayanna. She might still be alive out there somewhere. She would always ask me how I could be so happy," Hakoni continued. "We'd been through so much already. I lost my mom the last time. Six years ago. They had cut her deeply. The wound completely opened up her side. I think her backbone is the only thing that stopped the blade. After I laid her in the mass grave, I knew that I'd miss her every day. And the hurting wouldn't stop. So I made people laugh. I made them happy so they'd never have to hurt like I hurt."

"Hakoni…" Garrick tried to start.

"Rayanna's brother is over in the children's barracks. He doesn't ask me when his mom is coming back. She slit her own throat, you know. Then the Lima beat her. He doesn't ask me when his sister is coming back, either. He knows they're gone. What kind of world is this where kids have to realize things like that?"

"You can make this right—" Garrick tried again.

"Nothing will make this right."

"—and you can help them fight through this."

Hakoni shook his head as the corners of his mouth plunged downward. He tried to stem the overflow of emotions, but they were finally overcoming him. "They aren't soldiers, Garrick. They are little kids. They aren't meant to fight anything right now."

"The world will make soldiers of us all, Hak," Garrick said, speaking as if he were deep in a thought and trying to find his way out. "It will push us, prod us, pull us, and kill the people we love. The world will fight you, and you have to decide whether to be a slave to it, or a soldier willing to stand up and fight back."

"What are we fighting for?" Hakoni asked hopelessly.

Garrick only shook his head. "You have to decide that. I could tell you, Hakoni, but then it would be my cause. You have to come to know truth for yourself. And when you do, you'll find it's worth the price. Any price."

"Well forgive me, but that's a load of *shosk*," Hakoni said with a quivering voice and eyes brimming with grief.

Garrick smiled sardonically. "You'll learn. But we have more... *immediate*...concerns," he said, choosing his words carefully. "What did you get from Kalif?"

Hakoni wiped his eyes and pulled a patch of cloth he had looped on his rope-belt to dry his nose. Straightening up and turning off the emotion that had so overcome him, he began his report. "He confirmed the rebellion. He doesn't know much at this point. He mainly serves as a decoy to let Zoram communicate with the other prisoners."

"A decoy? How?"

Garrick looked sheepish. "Because I have been watching him like a hawk—so much that I don't notice much else. But in all fairness, sir, the other guards also—"

"I know, Hak. It's fine. What else did he tell you?"

Clearing his throat and trying to regain composure, he continued, "There's supposed to be a signal. Zoram is the ring leader. He's supposed to give a signal, and then the prisoners are going to turn and attack the stakes that are holding them. Once they're free, they're supposed to swarm the lumber crew's guards and free the prisoners there. Once they have pickaxes, shovels, and saws, they will attack the building crew, who has the hammers. When they are all assembled, they'll make an assault on the garrison."

"Interesting. But how are they supposed to get out of the pit without the guards shooting them all?"

Hakoni shook his head. "Kalif says Zoram is very cautious about what information he relays. It looks like the prisoners know only enough to do their jobs while still depending on Zoram."

"Did he say how Zoram gets this information?"

Hakoni silently berated himself. "No. I, umm, didn't ask. I'll get it soon though."

"I'm sure you will. Time is short. Can you trust him?"

Hakoni hesitated a long time before responding. "I don't make a habit of trusting a Lima. But something about what he said...I can't see why he'd lie." But why Kalif told the truth was the enigma that puzzled Hakoni. He believed Kalif's confession; he knew too well the kind of shame Kalif had described. And though the raid on a peaceful people should have been enough to elicit the profoundest of regrets in any human being, Hakoni thought, there had to be something more. Something personal.

"Hakoni...how did he respond to the, ah, disguise?" Garrick asked, referring to the beating that Hakoni had delivered.

"He's a tough one." Hakoni's curt reply was supposed to curb any further inquiry. This was a path of questioning he wasn't entirely willing to go down with Garrick. No matter how much Hakoni wanted to hide some things from Garrick, there was actually very little that seemed to slip by those eyes. They saw everything. They saw the truth in a lie, and they saw the guilt in a liar. Hakoni knew he'd have to tread carefully.

"Can he take another round like what you dealt him this time?"

"Well...not every day, but..."

Garrick just sighed. "The Lima have to be kept in the dark. If they just think you're giving him a couple of black eyes, then we lose our mole. But if you kill him, Hakoni, I swear I'll put you on trial with a military tribunal. Do you understand?"

Hakoni nodded.

"I want to hear it."

"I understand, sir."

"Good. Now go get me more information. I need to know when this is going down, and I need to know where Zoram is getting his messages. I'm afraid we don't have much time left."

Hakoni turned and walked out. As he put his hand on the door to pull it open he heard Garrick call his name. Hakoni paused but didn't turn.

"Hakoni, the world has already made soldiers of us all. It is up to you to know what you're fighting for."

Hakoni didn't nod or give any indication of his thoughts on the matter. He just pulled on the door and walked out into the frigid winter air.

CHAPTER 19:
WHISPERS IN THE DARK

Amnesty.

Chism's eyes narrowed as he listened discreetly to the rumors. They were saying that anyone who signed up for this new mission would be granted amnesty. The weather was quickly warming here on the coast, and the marauders were expanding aggressively. Anyone who joined would be free from the charges against them. No more High Tide District. No more hiding at all. The furor it was stirring on the docks was palpable.

Chism moved slowly as he returned for another crate, listening for any details. Picking up a crate, he turned to continue about his work when Berrigen, a particularly large and often drunk dockworker called out to him.

"You better get in on this!" Berrigen shouted. "You aint just gonna walk away like that, are you?" Chism rolled his eyes at the burly man. He could never speak without sounding like he was issuing a challenge. It was probably the only way Berrigen survived in this place. It was also why Chism wouldn't feel too heartbroken if he had to stick a knife in Berrigen's gut. The man was a bully. And Chism hated bullies.

"Yeah, I am," Chism said without turning around. "But it sounds perfect for you, Berrigen."

"Perfect for me to get my hands on your pretty little Neroos girl, you mean."

Chism stopped and turned slowly. "You must be eager to die, Berrigen."

"How do you figure?"

Chism set his crate down and walked slowly back to the small circle of workers. "The marauders aren't expanding, you idiot. They're getting ready to lose a lot of guys. A *lot* of guys. You think you got what it takes to live through what they're up to? Go ahead. Me, I'm in the High Tide District to keep my head on my shoulders. You aren't getting any kind of amnesty. You're getting a shallow grave and an arrow through your eye socket." Chism stopped directly in front of Berrigen and looked up slightly to meet him eye to eye. "And if you talk about my friends again, I'll send you to a shallow grave before the marauders or the Neroos get a chance."

Berrigen sneered down at Chism. "Do it."

Chism nodded slowly. "I will."

"So what? You saying I should watch my back from now on?"

"No. I don't attack from behind. I'll kill you while staring you right in the eye."

Chism knew that Berrigen had been in a lot of fights. The man had probably been threatened in more bar rooms and alleys than Chism cared to count. But Chism could see the fear in Berrigen's eyes—the fear of a man who knew he was listening to someone speaking from experience. Chism knew his would-be opponent was a hard man to spook, but Chism knew exactly how to kill him in five different ways. And Berrigen knew that, too.

Berrigen swallowed a little harder than he meant to. But he was not about to be outdone. "Then maybe I'll have to get to you—or your Neroos girl—before you get to me."

Chism stepped back. If anything were to happen to Gala or to Rayanna...if Berrigen tried anything.... Chism shuddered. They weren't even supposed to know about Rayanna. But a girl can only stay in one small apartment so long, and she had begun venturing out more and more as her Lima dialect improved. Chism didn't like the idea of her being out, and he had expressly forbidden her to leave without him to accompany her. But obedience wasn't her style. People had come to notice the beauty with skin the golden color of a tree stripped of its bark. Berrigen wasn't the only lewd man in the High Tide District who had taken note of her.

Chism had come to admire Rayanna. She was more than a girl he was protecting. She was his anchor. His blood boiled even hotter at the thought of any harm coming to the child she carried. No threat—not even innuendo—could be allowed.

Berrigen turned and grinned at his posse, reveling in having made Chism take the first step back. Just as Berrigen turned his head, Chism took one long step forward with his left foot and brought his right knee up with incredible force into Berrigen's kidney. The man doubled forward as Chism stepped to the right, wound his arm back, and dealt a vicious right hook to Berrigen's left jaw. A sadistic smile played across Chism's face as he heard the bone separate and crack. Berrigen fell to the ground. Chism took one step over Berrigen's prone figure and swung a long, heavy kick right into the man's groin.

It was over in three seconds. Berrigen's cries of pain accented Chism's ferocity. He had barely exerted any energy, yet he breathed heavily as he stood over the downed giant. His adrenaline fed him like a drug, and he wanted more. Chism looked around at the four other men, wondering who was going to swing the sword or stab with the knife that he would use against them.

"The girl," Chism panted, "is mine."

The others nodded and quickly vacated the small alcove of boxes.

As he watched them leave, the feeling of triumph and victory were quickly replaced by guilt. He could have stopped Berrigen with less effort. He hadn't needed to break his jaw, and the gods only knew what he had done to the large man's groin. Chism had gone too far.

He hated to admit it, but he missed the excitement and the adrenaline that came with a fight. Part of him had come to love the violence, but he had no more stories to tell himself to justify it. He was an addict who had come to recognize the ripple effect of his addiction. The truth—the inescapable, inalterable truth—was that he had learned to cut the jugular veins of the Neroos. He had honed his muscles and his reflexes striking Neroos men where he was told to without question. He was paid to kill the Neroos without conscience. And the truth was that any one of the men he killed as a fringe soldier could have been Rayanna's brother. Rayanna's father.

Yes, every man he had captured or killed was armed. Each man had been a threat to Chism's life. But how many had he killed that he could have just as easily captured? How many had been armed for the sake of their own safety? How many men had been threats to his life only because he threatened theirs?

And here he stood over Berrigen—a bully. A lecher. But a Lima. A kinsman. Chism had hurt him to send a message. He had hurt him to protect Gala and Rayanna. But he had also done it for self-gratification. He had done it because he chose not to stop himself. The remorse began to weigh his shoulders down, and he went in search of a medicine man.

Stupid Berrigen, Chism thought to himself. *Stupid marauders for stirring things up again. Can I never be free of them? So long as I'm within these city walls, I will always be within their reach.*

Chism turned down an alley. He arrived at a door and knocked heavily. An elderly woman answered the door.

"A man's been injured," Chism said simply.

"Alive?" The woman asked. No details about the incident were necessary. She knew she didn't want the details—the less she knew, the less she could be implicated in case any soldiers got involved.

"Yes. Should be, anyway."

She looked at Chism with a pointed stare. "I was busy, you know," she said to show her irritation that the dockworkers couldn't keep their brawling to a minimum.

Chism didn't look into her eyes. He felt like a schoolboy as he stood on the doorstep. "You can leave him if you'd like."

She scoffed and wrapped a shawl tightly about her thin, strong shoulders. "I suppose it was an accident," she said, tired of hearing the same story.

"I never said that," Chism replied.

She turned sharply and looked at him with confusion written plainly in the wrinkles of her face. "What makes you so honest?" Then without waiting for a reply, she grabbed a burlap sack that lay just within the door, and marched out into the cold spring morning air. "Where is he?" She asked without turning or slowing.

"Docks."

Chism watched her back as she shuffled away. He knew he should follow her receding figure and continue his work, but he was so close to the apartment that he had to stop by and check on things. Berrigen's brazen attitude had him spooked.

As Chism came to the mouth of the alley, he heard the sound of horses. Two. A carriage. Or a wagon. No carriage would ever find itself in the High Tide District, but then again no one in the High Tide District could afford horses. Chism closed his eyes to listen for any other sounds.

Muffled sounds. A few thuds, like a solid object against wood. This was no wagon. This was an enclosed slave cart. Chism was amazed to see a slave cart here in the High Tide—the unspoken agreement was that if the government left the High Tide alone, then the High Tide would keep to itself. A slave cart was in direct violation of that agreement.

WHISPERS IN THE DARK

A quick, furtive movement across the street caught Chism's attention. A man popped his head around a corner to check for passersby. Chism flattened himself against the wall and peered around the corner of the alley. Two men then started dragging a third man between them to the cart hidden, Chism assumed, in the next alley. The man had a black hood over his head, and his head lolled forward. The two carrying the third man were dressed as regular High Tide urchins, but something in their gait bespoke a certain training. Military training. They passed right in front of Chism's alley, but they were too occupied with their burden to notice Chism in the shadows.

Chism waited for the sound of the horses leaving the alley, and he left the alley and headed in the opposite direction, following the tracks of dragged feet in dirty street. He had no intention of following them; indeed, the more they mirrored his own chosen path back to the apartment, the faster he moved to get there. The tracks were eventually lost in a tangle of footprints and mud, but he had a bad feeling about where he may find wet footprints.

Chism bounded up the stairs and then walked carefully down the hallway. Then Chism was stopped, frozen and unable to take another step. The grief washed over him, and his brow began to crease as a whisper escaped his lips. "No...please, no...not this. Not them."

The door to his apartment stood wide open.

~~~~~

It had only been three days since their last covert meeting. Hakoni had long since lost his passion for striking Kalif, but Kalif wouldn't allow him to relent.

"We have to make this believable. They know we aren't just going for a stroll, so I have to have something to show for these meetings."

"Kalif, I..."

"Do what you have to do!"

And with more pain in his eyes than Kalif felt in his body, Hakoni would swing again. Kalif had had to give up the pickaxe when he had tried to lift it above his head and felt stabbing pain wash over him. But he had to work. Even if the Neroos guards would allow him to rest and recuperate—and they wouldn't, he had no doubt—he had to be there next to Zoram to glean more information.

Kalif had picked up the shovel and maintained his post as a spy. A spy for the enemy, or so he would have once believed. Now, Kalif didn't know the difference between friends and enemies, justice and revenge.

Kalif knew he was gaining Zoram's trust by refusing to complain. Zoram hadn't called him *merdapot* since the first beating. Zoram saw Kalif as a victim and a symbol. The whispers that he passed throughout the quarry were to look to Kalif as evidence of brutality and injustice. *Yes, look to me*, thought Kalif. *I am proof that brutality and injustice is allowed to prowl the woods and strike with no warning and no provocation.* Kalif would have smiled at the irony. But he had no smile left for the life he had led.

Kalif's thoughts wound their way, as they always did, toward Gala. It had been a little over eight months since he last held her. Eight months since they were supposed to be married there on the same beach where they had set Loria's body adrift. *How different life would have been*, Kalif thought, *if I had just stayed and married her. We may have had a child on the way by now. I could have been a father.*

Gala had never allowed Kalif to stay the night with her; after the life he had led, he was accustomed to a certain lifestyle, and her abstinence had been frustrating. But he couldn't help but admire her determination that some things remain sacred. Kalif had always laughed at her and said that she was being stubborn, even though he had wanted to believe that there could be something pure in this world.

Kalif paused with a shovel full of dirt as he contemplated the life he left, and the life he had chosen instead. Even if he were to get out of here—even if she were to take him back—Kalif knew he could never ask her to give him her trust. Though she'd never know about the girl in the forest—how could she?—he would never forget what he had done. *But being here, stuck in a pit, chained like a devil in hell...this can't be how it ends.*

"Tools down!" A guard shouted into the quarry.

Kalif's shoulders sagged. He knew why they were here. He was to be summoned. *Maybe this* is *how it will end.* But Kalif was beginning to see meaning in life again, and for the first time since being made a slave, he felt fear. Fear for his life. Fear for what could be. For what could have been. And an ardent desire to regain the life he had lost. But that was going to come at a price.

He dropped his shovel and lined up. Hakoni grabbed his arms and forced them into cuffs behind his back. A guard pulled back his fist and landed a blow to the side of Kalif's head. Kalif coughed in the dirt as he inhaled quarry dust. Kalif heard Hakoni's sudden intake of breath at the blow. *Was he surprised?* Kalif wondered at Hakoni's reaction.

Kalif placed his hands and pushed himself to his hands and knees. A guard stepped to the side of Kalif and was about to kick him when a soldier—Garrick, if Kalif remembered correctly—held up a hand and stayed the kick. Kalif whispered thanks, but not so loud that anyone could hear. Hakoni reached down and helped him rise. Hakoni was hardly kind about the gesture. But whether it was for pretense or out of his well-placed angst, Kalif didn't know. Didn't care. The chain was removed from his foot, and a set of ankle chains were affixed once more.

"Kalif." One prisoner said.

"Silence!" A guard responded.

"Kalif." Three more said. "Kalif! Kalif! Kalif!" The rest of the prisoners chanted. The soldiers drew their weapons as two more rushed Kalif out of the quarry, half carrying him in their haste to avoid a riot. "Look to Kalif!" Zoram cried out just before Kalif disappeared from their sight. Even in the forest, they could hear the chanting in rhythm with their axes and shovels.

"Leave us," Garrick said when they arrived in the forest. Hakoni stayed as the other guards went out of earshot. Garrick turned to address Kalif. "Why are you helping us?"

Kalif rolled his eyes. No matter how much he was done fighting, he wasn't so sure he could ever have any love for these Neroos. And yet he owed them his life. He tried to keep his attitude in check as he said, "Questions already? Aren't you going to beat me first?"

Garrick raised an eyebrow at Hakoni, seeming to ask if Hakoni wished to take over. Hakoni only gestured back at Kalif. Kalif enjoyed playing with these soldiers who needed so much from their slave. But he knew he had to give up his information. It was the only way to make things right. As much as their accents got under his skin and their mannerisms seemed childish to him, he had lost the desire to hate them as a people. And he wasn't here to cause trouble. Not anymore.

"Let me start again," Kalif said as he tried to shift his legs to sit more comfortably with his arms chained around the circumference of a tree. "I assume the little doggy has given you all the information I gave him last time?"

"Yes," Garrick said, not flinching at the reference to Hakoni.

"Do you believe it?"

"I haven't decided."

Kalif nodded. He was beginning to have some respect for this Garrick. He was different. Somehow he was the quintessential Neroos, but Kalif actually liked him more for it. Something about Garrick was real. Genuine. And smart.

"I have a problem, Kalif, and I need your help. But I need to know why I should trust you."

Kalif shook his head as he pulled his mouth down in a frown of mock concentration. "*Corva cavesa*, Garrick. Sounds like you have more than one problem, then. Because I'm a slave—"

"A prisoner," Garrick corrected him.

"—and I told your little doggy last time why I was telling the truth. So you don't need to trust me. You just need to trust him."

Garrick stared at Kalif. Kalif could feel those eyes searching the innermost parts of him, but he didn't know what they would find. He didn't know what was in there himself.

"Should I trust you?"

"No," Kalif responded quickly.

"But are you telling the truth?"

Kalif smiled. "Yes."

"Then I'm listening."

"Zoram is the leader for the quarry. Ahaz is the leader for the wood crew, and Mossad is the leader for the builders. They are going to give a sign, at an appointed time, and we are to take out our guards—"

"I heard all of that," Garrick said impatiently. "When is he giving the sign?"

"Soon. He wouldn't say when. I don't think he knows. But there's an attack they're planning on a city to the east of Gidionhi. We're to take out as many soldiers as we can, and then disappear into the woods. There, we'll reconnoiter with troops and make another attack."

"Kalif, I need to know how Zoram is getting his information."

Kalif shook his head, honestly unsure. "He gets it from the latrine, that much I know. But I can't figure out how he gets the information. I go in before him, and I search everywhere—and I mean everywhere. I cannot find a single place where the note may be hiding. Then I leave, and the guard checks…" Kalif froze, then repeated softly, "Then the guard checks…"

"I don't have the same guard on latrine duty every day," Garrick said quickly.

"No, but Zoram doesn't get messages every day, either. In fact, I don't know when he gets the messages."

"How long between messages?"

Kalif was wracking his brain. What was the pattern? How could he have been so blind—he, the hunter, who noticed everything? There was something just on the fringe. Something he could almost touch, but couldn't quite see. "He stopped bringing the messages back months ago. He used to eat them to conceal the messages from the guards in the quarry, but then he started memorizing them and burying them in the latrine."

"What does the mole look like? Do you know *anything* that can help?"

"Lima," Kalif said. "He's a marauder that managed to blend in with the rest of you. I assume he's Neroos born or at least half Neroos. Don't you know the men in the village or in the barracks?"

"We got a new set of transfers a week before you attacked," Garrick said with closed eyes and gritted teeth. "I didn't get to know all of them."

Out of the corner of his eye, Kalif saw Hakoni break from his crossed-arm stance and lunge forward. Kalif had learned long ago never to close his eyes when he saw the attack. *Never, never give your enemy two advantages,* his father would tell him. *He's got you on the run with his attack already, so don't let him take you blind. Watch the attack. Spot the weakness. Use it against him. It's the only way to win.* But with his arms pulled behind him, there was no more advantage Hakoni could gain that he didn't already have. Besides, winning required fighting. And Kalif had little fight left. So he turned his head as he waited for the blow to fall.

But it wasn't a strike that Kalif felt next. It was a powerful hand, full of callouses from a life spent in the quarry that gripped Kalif's neck and choked off the air and the blood in a moment. "I swear to you," Hakoni said quietly with a voice full of passion, "I swear to you, I will crush your windpipe like I crushed Yarlem's if you're lying to me."

"Y...know...I...not," Kalif eked out.

Hakoni loosened his grip slightly. "Tell me why."

"No. I'll...take my....secret...to my grave," Kalif said bitterly.

"I'll send you there myself. And then you'll never fix whatever it is you're trying to make up for. So tell me what it is."

Kalif looked past Hakoni to see Garrick standing back. Listening carefully. Judging slowly. Garrick was the wild card. Kalif would have thought Garrick would stop too much violence, but Kalif had three cracked ribs and a throat with the life getting squeezed out of it that suggested otherwise. No, Garrick didn't enjoy the violence. Not like Hakoni, who used violence as an outlet for his grief. Garrick did what was necessary to get the results he needed. Kalif could provide the results he needed, and Garrick would condone whatever action necessary to get those results.

As he considered Garrick's urgent need and Hakoni's passionate distrust, he couldn't help but feel respect for them. Fellow soldiers. Different sides. *But whose side am I really on?* Kalif had to wonder. Respect aside, he still disdained them. They were, after all, Neroos. He didn't spy for them out of love for the Neroos nation. But he knew he had a debt to repay, and it could not go without a confession. Kalif tried to swallow pride and began to confess to these two who cared little for his repentance.

"They…they raped my sister. They raped her and tortured her and killed her. Then they left her to the dogs to hide their blade marks. But I've been around death long enough to know the proof when I see it. I wasn't on the guard that night. Otherwise I would have caught the Neroos who did it to her, and I would have…made them suffer," Kalif finished without going into the details he had dreamed of for so long. Hot tears welled to his bloodshot and pain ridden eyes as his throat tightened painfully against the abuse Hakoni had just left there moments ago. "And when I found a Neroos girl spying in the trees above me, I…I wanted revenge. And I took it," he said, though the words tasted like bile. "I could see my sister lying there on the forest floor, just like…like the girl that I left there, still alive but no less abused. That's when my brother came. I ran, or tried to run, and he shot me." Rivulets of quarry dust and sweat mingled with tears as the shame overwhelmed him. Kalif whispered, "I can see them both every time I close my eyes."

Kalif looked into Hakoni's eyes to see the horror and the rage Hakoni held for him. Kalif had seen that rage before. He had felt it himself and honed it with stories of the evils that the Neroos had committed. Stories and lies. Truths and half-truths. Kalif felt like he were floating in the middle of the ocean with no concept of direction anymore, much like he felt before he had found Gala.

Kalif blinked as his eyes burned with salty tears. "I wanted that arrow to find my heart. I wanted it to be the end. When you found me, I thought it was the end. I thought I would be free. The hate for so many years had burned me out. And the only thing to fill this charred shell are images of Loria, and of the girl laying there surrounded by gidionhi flowers." Hakoni took a sharp breath. "There's nothing left but guilt. I was supposed to get married to the only woman who could still have faith in me. We were supposed to have a life together. But it's gone. It's all gone."

"Hakoni, I need to speak with you," Garrick said quickly, and turned to walk away.

~~~~~

It could have been anyone, Hakoni told himself. *There had been a lot of terror that night. A lot of people were running. It could have been anyone there in the gidionhi flowers.* But Hakoni couldn't bring himself to believe his own explanation. There was something inextricably linked between Rayanna and those flowers. And in his heart of hearts, he knew it was her. That's where she had gone. The Lima had taken her. Imagining the horrors that she must have suffered before they killed her made Hakoni physically sick.

He felt like he was falling in the dark with no sense or bearing of when he would hit rock bottom. Because there was nothing to hang onto anymore. No amount of beating Kalif or of killing more

Lima would bring her back. She was gone. His ray of sunshine, as he once called her, was finally truly out of his reach.

"—platoon from Gideon to pass by here tonight, so we can shore up our…Hakoni, are you listening to me?" Garrick grabbed Hakoni's shoulder to get his attention.

Hakoni snapped his eyes back to Garrick, but he could still barely see his commanding officer. He could only see Rayanna's mother lying on the floor with her life flowing out of her neck and pooling on the ground. He could see a lone orphan boy in the barracks who knew long before Hakoni did that he would never see his sister again. He could see his own family mourning the loss of their mother, their brother, and so many other people they loved. Hakoni could see them all, but he could not see Garrick.

"Hakoni," Garrick said, trying to break his reverie. "I'm telling you we can end this. There's something huge about to happen, and we can stop the madness."

"You'll never stop the madness," Hakoni said quietly.

"Not if we stop fighting, we won't," Garrick reproved.

"The world will make soldiers of us all," Hakoni repeated sardonically from their previous conversation.

"What are you fighting for, Hak?"

Hakoni paused. "I don't know anymore. She's gone."

Garrick nodded. "We lose the people we love. But we fight because we believe in brighter days. Even when the light seems to have gone out of the sun itself."

The phrase stirred Hakoni back to reality. Yes. When the light seems to have gone out of the sun itself. Rayanna had seen dark days, and she got through it. She made the light shine for Hakoni. She was his sunshine. But he couldn't depend on her for all of his light, because one day—today, it would seem—her light would go out, and he would have to carry on.

"What's about to happen?"

"It's complicated, but the short version is that the marauders are attacking Borinihah. Our people have amassed an army there and are waiting to crush them. While the marauders are gone, they will have left Ombrar almost entirely defenseless. A smaller force of Neroos will take the city. They're coming here, tonight, to recruit some from our guard."

Hakoni's brow furrowed in anger. He felt that Garrick had betrayed him for withholding this opportunity. "Why haven't you told us about this?"

"Because we cannot spare a single man," Garrick replied. "And because we have a leak. If the Lima had even the smallest inkling that we had a counterattack planned, then it would all be for nothing. Now that they are coming, I can send word that we have a prisoner rebellion, and they can help us."

At that moment, a horn began to blow. It was coming from the quarry.

"What was that?" Hakoni said.

"That," Kalif responded from his place several feet away, "was the sign. It's beginning."

Chapter 20:
Headlong into the Dark

Hope. He had been filled with hope. It had been so long since he had any kind of hope in his life that the feeling had been strange and unfamiliar. He didn't even recognize it for what it was for months. But as Chism stared at his apartment door standing open with one lock broken, he knew only two things: hope looked a lot like family, and he would do anything to get it back.

He couldn't run after the carriage. The two men were long gone by now. He would have to find a way to identify them and then find them.

Chism stooped just outside the front door, trying to piece together exactly what had happened. He felt out of his element. He was far more accustomed to hunting in a forest, but he knew how to spot a hunter. The first thing he looked for were footprints. The wet leather prints of their feet had all but dried. One man was very large—six-foot three or four, he would guess from what was left of the damp spot just outside the doorframe. This large man must have stood in that spot for several moments, possibly listening at the door. Yes, he was the one to break the door in. The two men he spotted from the alley didn't quite fit that description, so there had to be others.

Inside, flour coated everything with a filmy residue. *Bless you, Gala,* Chism thought. He had taught her a long time ago to immediately throw sand, flour, sugar, anything she could find as soon as she was in a bad situation. She would always laugh at him and his silly precautions. She didn't know what kind of trouble Kalif would get into. Chism always worried for her safety, and apparently she hadn't laughed off quite everything he had told her. Then his thoughts turned sour. *If only she hadn't laughed off my warning to keep the door completely bolted.*

Chism carefully examined the sweeping motions in the flour. Two men came through the door. A blast pattern of flour appeared on the wall just to the left of the door—Gala must have thrown the flour just before they entered. The footprints skidded to a halt just inside the door. The flour confused them. They weren't ready. Chism continued to watch the dance play out. A few spots of blood, and they were covered by the marks of dragging feet. Someone bled first, then dragged a person out behind him. So where was the weapon?

Across the room toward the fireplace, the silhouette of Rayanna's heavily pregnant body still lay in her now-empty bed. She would have hardly been able move, much less react to a sudden entry. Gala had run to the small stash of food and grabbed the flour. And something else. A shallow pot that also served as a frying pan was missing. Chism looked to the other end of the room toward the bedroom. A chunk of cement had been taken out of the wall. There was the pot, and with it a few more splashes of blood. She had attacked the men immediately after throwing the flour. Striking one on the arm or the body wouldn't have drawn blood like that. She must have hit him where the bone was close to the surface of the skin—either the head or the hand. He would have to examine the pot in a moment.

The two footprints quickly diverged. One man had gone for Gala. He was smaller than the first—he imagined that this man was somewhere between five-foot six and five-foot nine. Fingers had skidded across the floor. Gala had been knocked to the ground and tried to catch herself. Blood mixed with a clear liquid on the ground. Saliva. He had hit her across the face, knocking her to the ground. He must have then picked her up and dragged her out.

In Rayanna's place, she had been allowed to stand. The large man had not treated her too forcefully. He had recognized and respected the pregnant woman. For all the Limas' faults, they at least understood the innocence of a child. Her footprints disappeared, indicating that the large man carried her. Chism breathed a sigh of relief. So long as she carried that baby, she would be safe. But they had to know by now that she was Neroos, meaning that her life lasted only as long as she continued to carry that baby. And between the incredible strain this attack must have taken and her very advanced pregnancy, Chism wondered if her body would go into labor very soon.

Chism crossed the room and examined the frying pan. The handle was coated in blood. Chism closed his eyes to imagine the encounter. The hand that grabbed the frying pan was bloody. So he raised his hand to block the frying pan? No, to draw blood, it would have had to strike his knuckles. Blood on the back of the hand with some on the fingers, but not coating the palm like that. So she had hit him in the head, he pushed her back, and then he grabbed the wound. Pull the hand away, find the palm full of blood. Catch the pan on the next swing, yank it from her hands, and throw it across the room. Strike Gala, then drag her out.

Chism was full of doubt that he had profiled any of it correctly. But he had nothing else to go on. Now he had to figure out what he already knew about the broader situation.

Two men had been dragging men out to the carriage. They had a militaristic bearing about them, but they weren't on military duty. Why would the military disrupt the delicate balance they had struck with the High Tide District?

Then it dawned on Chism. The military *wouldn't* disrupt the balance. But the marauders would, and they were planning a full-scale attack on the Neroos. They needed men for the front lines, so they were picking them out of the High Tide District where no one would notice or report their absence. They must have been combing the apartment block, listening for sounds within. The large man pressed his ear to the door, waiting long enough that his leather boot left a lingering footprint. He kicked in the door and found no men. Just two women. Did they take the women so as to leave no witnesses?

Chism had been around enough men long enough to know and hate their lust. They weren't concerned about witnesses. They were planning a large attack. Possibly a long attack. They needed cooks, nurses, and—Chism's heart grew cold at the thought—amusement.

But the marauders couldn't feed prisoners and conscripted soldiers for long. The attack had to be close. Very close. So where would they stage the army before setting off to march? Where could they hide an army big enough? No, they'd have the army separated into different parts of the city and forest with underground systems in place. Chism knew he'd never find them before the attack began.

Then don't try, Chism thought. *If they're going with the army, then so will I.*

Chism turned and darted out the door, knowing exactly where he must go.

~~~~~

Gala could hardly see straight. The pain in her left temple was making her eyes cross, and she had difficulty orienting herself.

Strong hands heaved her over a shoulder, and her worn wool dress did little to protect her from the cold winter wind.

Just as her vision began to clear, she was dropped unceremoniously in the back of a wagon with a dark canvas cover over tall arches. There were five men and two other women there, all sitting with their backs to the center with hands and feet tied to the rails. Muffled moans came from several of the wagon's occupants.

"Are you kidding me? You brought a pregnant woman?" An angry voice said in a shocked whispered.

"You said take everybody," came the voice from the larger man who had taken Rayanna.

"What are we going to do with her!" the angry voice tried desperately to keep his voice down and was failing miserably.

"We took everyone who was in that apartment. What is she supposed to do without her family with her? That baby would never make it," the larger man said quietly. Gala was astounded at the compassion he was showing. She, too, had grown up with the Lima customs—never take an innocent life. And though "innocent" was loosely defined, the people would never harm a child. But this was a level of compassion she had never known.

"Take her back!" the angry man demanded.

"If you keep bossing me around like this, I'll tie you up in the back of this wagon," the large man said evenly. The angry man scowled and stomped away as the larger man returned to his task of tying Gala and Rayanna.

Gala watched as the larger of the two men who entered her apartment gagged Rayanna, helped her into the wagon, and then tied her wrists and ankles. Gala could see Rayanna wincing periodically, though she knew they hadn't hurt her, nor would they.

As soon as they had Rayanna placed in the wagon, the man who had been carrying Gala roughly jammed a gag into her mouth and tied the rag behind her head. As he did it, he smeared his left hand across her cheek leaving a cold trail of blood from her jaw into her hairline. Despite the pain in her head and the gruesome smear on her face, Gala couldn't help but grin. She didn't go down without a fight, and this man's ear would not let him soon forget their encounter. Gala knew to expect a reprisal from him, but she would rather keep fighting than remain docile. Wise or foolish, she had always let the men in her life know that she demanded respect. And she always got it.

The man spat on Gala before yanking a canvas flap down and stomping over to his companion.

"What's taking them so long?" Gala heard one say. No audible response came from the other.

Her feet and hands were trussed with ropes tied too tightly. Gala knew that the pain was only beginning; when they finally pulled off those ropes—and she had no idea when that would be—the pain of the blood flowing back into her extremities would make her almost wish she were still tied. But she wasn't nearly as concerned for herself as she was for Rayanna. They had tied Gala and Rayanna to opposite sides of the wagon, so they had absolutely no means of communicating. She listened for Rayanna but had difficulty distinguishing her heavy breathing from the sounds of pain from everyone else.

What on earth are they doing? Gala wondered as the adrenaline left her system and she was left to finally consider the implications of her situation. *Why did they choose us? And how did they find us?* Had it been only Gala and Rayanna in the wagon, she might have thought that their game was up and that they had discovered Rayanna and Chism's identities. That could still be the case, but as far as she knew, no one stayed behind at the apartment to wait for Chism. *Why would they take us but leave him?*

The wagon shifted as both men climbed in at the front. The back flap shifted with the weight and opened slightly with a gust of wind. They were in an alley. No witnesses would come save them, she knew.

"*Shosk*, Ybarran. He's supposed to be alive enough to fight, you know that?" A rebuke came from the front of the wagon.

Someone yanked open the back flap and two new men set a third man up into the wagon. "He put up quite the fight. This *batarkre* gave me a broken rib." He looked over at the man Gala had hit and said, "Looks like one of them worked you over a bit, too, eh?"

The man resolutely refused to look at Gala. "Yeah, he was a fighter all right, but I still got him alive."

The larger man began to laugh. Gala's captor just looked away from the other men and said, "Well that makes ten, and I've got a few mugs to lift at the tavern. Let's get out of here."

From the way the new prisoner's head lolled, Gala wondered how badly he had been beaten. They leaned him up against Gala and slapped his face a few times to wake him up. When he began to moan a bit louder, one of the two said to the other, "He'll be fine. Tie him up with the rest and let's get this over with."

The man was gagged and trussed within a few seconds. He didn't struggle. He barely moved at all. When his hands and feet were tied to the wagon, his knees bent up at an awkward and uncomfortable angle like the rest of the wagon's occupants, they closed a gate and tied the canvas down. As they trundled away, Gala thought she saw someone staring back at the wagon.

Chism? Gala hoped. But when the wagon bounced again and gave her another chance to see, the figure was gone. She couldn't be sure she had seen anything in the first place.

After several minutes and biting pain in her wrists from the wagon's uneven ride, a voice spoke from the other side of the canvas, startlingly close to where Gala sat gagged. "Hold. We'll need to check the contents of your wagon before you exit the city."

The wagon shifted again as someone jumped down from the front. "I have a piece of paper here that says you don't."

A pause. Then in a quieter tone, "It takes more than paper, friend."

Several coins jingled.

"When are you leaving?"

"Tonight."

"Why'd they change plans?"

"Who knows? As long as I work for them, I have food in my stomach and money in my pocket. I go where and when they say. Why, you want out?"

"No," came a quick reply. "I just…"

"Sounds like you got something to hide, friend."

"No, I…here! Take it back! Just move on through. I'll be there, I swear."

"I know you will."

The voice standing just on the other side of the canvas from Gala called out, "All clear!" and the wagon trundled onward. The wagon bounced and moved over roots and rocks, and the ropes rubbed Gala's wrists raw. She could hardly imagine how difficult this was for Rayanna. More labored breathing came from the girl Gala had come to love.

Labored breathing. Then it dawned on Gala. Dread seemed to start like a cold spout of water and trickle all the way down her spine. *Please don't go into labor now! Please, just hold on!*

But from the emphatic moans with every bounce of the wagon, Gala feared the worst.

~~~~~

"It's time," Rierdan said as he stood in the hall of the judges at Borinihah.

"You told us it wouldn't be for two more weeks!" One judge shouted. The other fourteen joined in hurling abuses and declaring how they never should have trusted the man.

It was impossible to speak over them. Rierdan raised both his hands, imploring silence. "And did you think I promised that no good men would lose their lives? Did you think I promised that you could simply dig a pit and lure all the marauders into it? Tell me! What part of this did you think would be easy?"

"We never should have agreed to this," one silver-haired judge muttered.

"Shut up, Heloram," a woman to his right responded. "This was not our decision to make! The Lima are coming. They were always coming. This time is hardly different from any other time—"

"Their force is massive, Sereen!" A woman across the room countered. "Bigger than our walls have ever had to endure!"

"Then we stand to thank the man who brought us the warning and told us to build our walls higher!" Sereen replied with even more vigor as she came to her feet. "But that's not exactly what we did, is it? No, we quibbled over money—"

"We can't just spend the people's taxes like water!" Another replied.

"No, but I don't see you hurting for money yourself, Veral. How many of them will give their lives in this fight, and you would not give up so much as a few of your coins?" Sereen rejoined. Veral fell silent. "I've had enough of this in-fighting. So have the people. We have an army of marauders headed directly for us, and we have to stop them. If we don't, it's the rest of our lands that are at stake. So I suggest we cease the useless bickering and listen!" And with that, Sereen nodded to Rierdan and sat down.

Rierdan continued. "You have three days. The Lima begin their march today. It is thanks only to the coalitions we have formed in preparation for this day—this hour!—that we can possibly hope to withstand their onslaught. Send your couriers, your honors. The darkness is spreading from Ombrar, and they will try to beat down your gate in three days, if not less. Now is our chance to cripple them once and for all."

Rierdan fumed at them. The plan had not gone entirely as he anticipated, but they had had ample warning to build their fortifications and prepare their armies. But when he had come, the walls had only been fortified on the lower half of the front walls. The gate had no additional strength. Bare frames marked where further work was left unfinished, and the walls stood woefully unprepared for the onslaught from the marauders.

Rierdan began to wonder if any of it would work at all. He had sacrificed so much to save them, and yet they would not even follow simple instructions to save themselves. He was lucky enough to get out of Ombrar with his life. But he would be back. In three days, he would lead a counter army into the city while it stood defenseless, and there he would have his revenge. But for the first time in all his years, Rierdan wondered if he were saving a society that deserved to be saved.

"I will see you again in two days' time. I have more work to do."

Rierdan spun on his heel and walked out, leaving a stunned audience of judges to contemplate the terror they would face in a few days' time.

~~~~~

Chism picked his way carefully toward the barracks, obscuring his face as he went. After the stunt at the temple when he saved himself and Rayanna, the city guard was on the lookout for their former lieutenant. A severe scar and life in the High Tide District was enough to hide him, but this time he was leaving his sanctuary. He was walking right into the den of his enemies.

Chism still had some friends in the guard, and he needed information. The watch would change in less than half an hour, and guards would be coming and going. He hoped to find a sympathetic ear to hear his plight and a blind eye to ignore his passing.

Chism didn't have to wait long. A group of guards left the barracks, having reported in at the end of their shift, and were headed for the tavern or the docks, as was customary for off-duty guards. One man peeled away from the pack soldiers wrapped in coats against the humid cold. Chism recognized him—his name was Dahmen. Mossad, the man who died while helping him rescue

Gala and Rayanna, was his brother. *If anyone has a reason to give up the marauders' movements,* Chism thought, *it's Dahmen.*

Chism crossed the street and fell into step behind Dahmen. After two minutes of following closely behind, Chism noticed Dahmen's pace quickened. He allowed Dahmen to gain several yards on him, then watched him turn into an alley. Chism knew he would have to play this carefully. Dahmen was feeling hunted, and he had just set a trap for Chism. As soon as Chism stepped into that alley after him, Dahmen would be waiting. And Chism's wellbeing would not be the first thing on Dahmen's mind.

Chism stepped to the corner of the alley and said, "I'm going to turn this corner now, Dahmen, and I come unarmed. I'm not trying to hurt you."

Chism stepped back from the wall several feet and slowly came into view of the alley with his hands down at his side and his palms turned outward. Dahmen was leaning against the very corner where Chism had been, and he was playing with a long knife. The hood of his cloak was pulled over his head, so his eyes were somewhat obscured. "May I enter?" Chism asked. Dahmen shrugged and continued to twirl the knife.

"Dahmen, I need your help."

"I'm sure you do," came the wry reply. "That's quite the scar on your face. Looks a lot like the scar some guards down near High Tide once described ol' lieutenant Chism as sporting. He's a wanted man, you know."

"Good thing you're off duty, then," Chism said.

"Not off duty from finding out why my brother was found with an arrow in his throat," Dahmen said as he stopped playing with the knife and held it steady. Chism noted how much he looked like a viper coiling and preparing to strike.

"That's why I'm here, Dahmen. The marauders killed your brother. Now they've taken two people from me, and I have to get them back. You know how important it is to stop the marauders—"

"You think you're going to stop the marauders?" Dahmen scoffed. "I should kill you now just for talking to me."

"But you're not going to," Chism said.

"Why not?"

"Because you know I can go where you can't. You know I can get to the marauders and break a wagon wheel or put a blade in a captain's heart. And you know if I had anything to do with your brother's death, I'd stay a hundred miles away from you." Chism waited for the reaction. Dahmen was as cold as a stone. "They took my brother, too, Dahmen. Now they're planning something big, they've taken people I love, and I need to know where they are staging their soldiers before they march."

Dahmen stared at Chism. Chism felt like Dahmen was trying to discern the truth of his entire story from a single look. As much as Chism wanted to allay Dahmen's fears, he had little time. "Fine. I thought you could help. I know you don't trust me, but I thought you cared more about your brother." With that, Chism began walking away.

"You take another step, and I'll kill you," Dahmen said.

Chism rolled his eyes, then turned to look at Dahmen. "I'd like to see you try."

Dahmen's nostrils flared, and he lunged forward at Chism. Chism stepped to the side and reached out for Dahmen's wrist. But the man was quick, he had already halted his thrust, spun on his heel and was bringing the knife down toward Chism's collarbone. Chism knew Dahmen expected him to step back. So he stepped forward, breaking Dahmen's momentum and getting him tangled in his own feet. Chism snapped his hand up, grabbed Dahmen's wrist, and forced the arm down and toward Dahmen's chest. Dahmen stepped back quickly, and Chism pushed him to turn the step into a long movement into the opposite wall of the alley. Chism bent Dahmen's wrist back to break his grip, pulled the knife from his hand, and pressed the blade to Dahmen's heart as he stood locked against the opposite wall. Chism stood with his left arm pressed into Dahmen and the blade poised at his chest.

"Nice try," Chism said.

"Now what?" Dahmen asked.

"Now you tell me where to find the marauders."

"May as well kill me, Chism, because I'd rather die than help you."

Chism stepped back and casually threw the knife further down the alley. "I have no interest in killing you. If you're half the man your brother was, then you're a good man. There aren't enough men like you left in this world, and I have no interest in taking you out of it. I just want my family back." Then he turned again to go.

"Wait," Dahmen said. Chism paused, but Dahmen did not speak immediately. He took another step, and Dahmen said, "They're in the forest. They've been gathering there for some time. A wagon just passed at the end of my shift. They've paid off a few of my superiors, so they pass in wagons covered in dark canvas without checking the contents. But I've heard the coughing and the moaning. I know they are conscripting people. You could easily track them when you get outside the city."

"A little easier said than done," Chism replied with his back still turned.

Dahmen ran a hand through his hair and stared for a moment at the sky. Then with a heavy sigh he said, "I think I can take care of that. But look…how do I know I'm not aiding the enemy here?"

Chism turned and looked at Dahmen. The man was clearly pained to see Chism still breathing, much less actually receiving his help. But Chism couldn't help Dahmen's prejudices. "You are helping the enemy, Dahmen. Whether or not I'm *your* enemy is something you'll have to decide for yourself. But the marauders killed your brother, and I'm on my way to stop them. So I doubt you want to stop me right now."

"Actually, I think I want to arrest you."

"How? Your knife is over there."

"Yeah, I'll need that back. And I'll need you to let me tie you up."

Chism arched his eyebrow, waiting for further explanation.

"For the last month, we've been transferring all of our prisoners out of the city," Dahmen explained. "They've got some deal with the marauders. If you want to get outside the city to find out what the marauders are up to, I can just arrest you. They'll ship you out in a few hours, maybe less."

Chism weighed his options quickly. There would probably be several camps. The marauders couldn't all stay in one place. It would attract too much attention. Their operations all technically flew under the radar, and they operated in waves. It was the perfect reason to split everyone up and keep them on a short leash with specific orders. Chism had no idea in which camp Rayanna and Gala ended up, but he wasn't getting any closer to them while he was stuck inside these walls.

"How do I know you're not going to kill me?"

Dahmen grinned slightly, both at the question and at Chism's acquiescence. He jogged over to his knife, re-sheathed it, and started pulling a length of rope from his belt. "Because either you're telling the truth, and you want to get to the marauders' front line, or your not, and they'll stick you on the front line, anyway. One way or another, they'll kill you and I'll get the bounty."

Chism shook his head as Dahmen began tying his hands behind his back. "If I make it out of this, you and I are splitting that bounty."

Dahmen laughed slightly. "I almost hope we do."

CHAPTER 21:
RETRIBUTION AND ATONEMENT

He couldn't believe it. After years of learning, of planning, of suffering, Rierdan was watching everything fall apart mere hours before the end was within reach. He was supposed to be standing in front of troops right now as he led them to overtake Ombrar. But he had been refused. He had demanded to see the city's captain. He was again refused—or at least, the corporal tried to refuse him. But Rierdan had had enough. The corporal had stepped forward to take Rierdan's sword and knife, and Rierdan dropped him with a vicious blow squarely between the eyes.

Now he stood practically screaming in the council room where he had barged in. He had been berating them for fifteen minutes. Three people had tried to subdue him, and they lay unconscious at his feet.

"Now is the time! You will never have this opportunity again. I have sacrificed years of my life for this opportunity. You pledged your support for this mission. You were to be the task force that beheaded the Triumvirate once and for all! And now you're recanting on your pledge? You're pouring away the chance to be written down in history as the brave few who did what *no one else could do*! And like water in your hands you choose to let it run dry instead of drink in every drop!"

One man began to step forward and said, "Rierdan, I understand—"

"I swear, if you try to lay a hand on me—"

"No, I think three unconscious men is plenty for now."

"It will be thousands of dead men at Borinihah if you don't move your *urfors*," Rierdan swore.

"We simply cannot spare the forces right now. There's a war going on to the north, and we can't afford to empty the city, especially with the marauders out in such a force. Can you imagine if they turned toward our city instead of continuing toward Borinihah?"

Rierdan placed his hands on the table and lowered his head. The blood was pounding. *Someone* had to be willing to rise to the occasion. But all he could find were politicians filled with excuses and nothing else. No patriotism. No common sense. Not even self-preservation. Only self-interest and a false sense of security.

Rierdan continued to look at the table as he spoke from his heart. "There comes a time in men's lives when they must ask themselves if the system they live by deserves to continue to govern them. There comes a time when we must re-evaluate the authority we have given others and consider the freedoms we have handed over along with that authority." Rierdan looked up at the men in the room and stared each in the eye as he spoke. "I will go and accomplish the work that you would not. And if I succeed and still have the breath that God put in my body, I will use it to bring your system to its knees. And when you realize that your system is completely powerless, I will cut off its head. This will go no further."

Retribution and Atonement

Two men stared silently. Three others began to bluster and scoff. The chief captain spoke quickly and sharply, "How dare you threaten this great city! I should have you hanged for your threats!"

Rierdan stepped back from the table. "They are not threats. If you would like to send someone after me, that's up to you. But, ah," he gestured to the three men on the floor, "you may want to check for their pulse before you come after me."

Within ten minutes, Rierdan was outside the walls of the city, and not a single guard had seen him go.

Rierdan found himself in the forest breathing heavily. His head was spinning and his stomach knotted. Fear. He hated the feeling of fear. He had one last hope—Gidionhi. They were the last village before reaching Ombrar, and he had hoped to bolster their garrison as he passed through. He would have needed a stronger outpost at Gidionhi for his plans to work. But now he was fighting for a hope and dream that didn't exist anymore. Perhaps they never existed. And he feared that everything he had sacrificed would all have been for nothing.

But this he knew: he would not rest until the blood of the Triumvirate soaked his feet. He found his way to his horse, led it to the path, and began to ride southwest.

~~~~~

Forty-four prisoners had survived the last nine months. Forty-four prisoners and one guard disguised as a Neroos against thirty-two other guards who were sick of fighting and accustomed to a generally docile group of prisoners.

Hakoni didn't see the guards descend into the quarry. They didn't know that the sign would be the blowing horn that was supposed to alert the other guards to a revolt in their sector. They didn't know that when their attention was turned, the prisoners would attack. It was the perfect signal, because the Neroos themselves had initiated it. They never suspected their own tool would be used against them.

THE SOUND IN THE SILENCE

The prisoners from the quarry used their guards as shields from arrows above. Zoram himself came to find Kalif with Garrick and Hakoni standing over him. Hakoni heard Kalif cry out for Zoram to stop. Hakoni and Garrick had drawn their weapons, but they were completely surrounded. Two prisoners took their weapons, and Zoram stepped forward to cut them down with a pickaxe. Hakoni closed his eyes, waiting for the blow to land. But Kalif saved them. Said he wanted to do it. But after they unchained him, he came wavering to his feet. When he tried to heft the axe, he collapsed. Zoram picked up the axe and smashed the handle into Garrick's temple, then Hakoni's.

Twelve Neroos guards survived. Twenty-seven Lima prisoners now controlled Gidionhi.

Hakoni sat chained to the same wall where he had chained Kalif so many times. Garrick sat next to him with blood trickling out of his mouth and down the side of his head. Hakoni's head ached in a thousand different ways. But he had no more fear. Rayanna was gone. The Lima had won. The sound of pain echoed all around him. And he would be dead soon.

Hakoni was broken from his reverie with the creak of the wooden barn door and the clamor of keys. A rough voice barked, "That one!" and pointed at Hakoni.

As they unchained him, one man shoved his head to one side, and the other man backhanded Hakoni in the face. They stood him up and one man swung a knee into Hakoni's thigh. He cried out in pain and bent over, and the other man brought a fist down on his back, forcing Hakoni to the ground.

"*Buyao*," the Lima at the door said. *Not yet*, Hakoni translated to himself. "*Kalif yao ta de punibere para el-el verre.*" *Kalif wants to see my punishment himself*, Hakoni finished. He winced at the prospect.

Hakoni limped on the leg where they bruised his muscle. One of the guards scoffed. "*Ta tai febl. Kalif en kelke seggonds le tuera!*" The other guard laughed. *He's too weak*, they had said. *Kalif will kill him in a matter of seconds.* Hakoni could hear the bloodlust in that laugh. He had felt it before.

Two men stood waiting in the woods. Kalif and Zoram. Without a word between any of the Lima, one guard grabbed a rope and threw it over a branch. Then, tying a slipknot on either end, they tied each end to Hakoni's wrists with just enough room to hold his hands at waist height, but not to lower them completely.

"*Ni puut-itre bu connesse eyya Lima,*" Zoram began.

"Of course I understand Lima, you *merdapot,*" Hakoni spat back in Lima.

Zoram laughed a cold, mirthless laugh. "Yes, of course you do. Then perhaps you know the fighter's ring?" Hakoni did not respond. "Ah, yes. The fighter's ring is simple. We let you fight back—but you get to be tied to these ropes to make things interesting."

"That's because you're cowards," Hakoni was quick to respond.

Zoram immediately lost his sense of amusement. "We all know what you did to Kalif. In fact, we should probably thank you for it. You gave us the motivation to fight."

"Shut up and kill me already," Hakoni said with all the attitude of a teenage boy.

"Not until you bury our dead, and scatter your own in the woods for the vultures to rip apart," Zoram said. "Then we'll kill you. But you—you, little doggy, get to live for now. You tied Kalif to a tree like a coward. But we'll give you a fighting chance. Go ahead. Fight back. You'll learn pain."

"No weapons," Kalif said. "And try not to break any ribs. I want him to suffer. And to suffer, he has to be alive."

One of the guards that brought him from the prison stood in front of him and sneered. Hakoni crossed his arms. "I have nothing to lose."

The guard planted his back foot and turned his hips in an obvious right hook. Just as he began swinging, Hakoni threw his arms behind himself, propelling his body forward just as the guard twisted his hips and lunged forward. Hakoni smashed his forehead into the man's nose with a sickening crunch. He knew he'd pay for it. But he counted his life now in actions and statements, not days or even hours.

The other guard stepped in and punched Hakoni once on each side of the ribs and again in the stomach, forcing him to throw up on the guard who was just getting up from the ground with his bleeding and smashed nose held tightly in his hands. Hakoni spewed vomit on the man's head, but had no energy to derive satisfaction from it. The second guard gripped Hakoni by the ears and drove his head into Hakoni's face.

"That's enough!" Kalif called out.

The nausea swept over Hakoni, and he fell to his knees. When his knees wouldn't support him, he continued to fall forward until his arms swung backwards and suspended his body. The weight of his body was cutting off the airflow. Hakoni felt as if he were gasping for breath at the bottom of a pool of water. His throat parched in seconds, and his lungs were ablaze in pain and suffocation. Just as his face was turning from blue to purple, Kalif said, "Cut him down." Hakoni felt a hand grip his wrist and another hand begin to press a blade into it. "Cut the rope!" Kalif shouted. The tight pressure of a blade on his wrist immediately loosened, and his left hand felt loose. Hakoni dangled by his right hand until he fell a few more inches to the ground.

"Leave us," Kalif said.

"What for?" Zoram asked.

"We have unfinished business."

"Not anymore," Zoram said, his voice dripping with an appetite for Neroos blood.

"I'm not asking again," Kalif said quietly. "I'll call you when it's time to bring him back."

Zoram was silent for a minute. Then, without any cues that Hakoni could hear, three sets of feet began moving away. Hakoni felt a spout pressed to his lips and warm liquid running into his mouth.

"Sorry the water's warm," Kalif said quietly. "It's what you had on you from this morning."

Hakoni drank slowly. Kalif let him rest for several minutes as he cleaned blood from Hakoni's face. After a moment, Hakoni squinted at Kalif through one eye. The other was swelling shut from the head-butting.

"I had to do that," Kalif explained. "They trust me. I couldn't blow my cover."

"Yeah. We trusted you, too," Hakoni said with a garbled accent. His broken nose gave his speech the perpetually drowsy sound of someone with a cold.

"And so you still should."

"I told you already. Just kill me. You won. You've done what you came to do. Now leave me in peace."

"Peace?" Kalif said with some surprise. "The peace of death," he whispered. Hakoni felt like Kalif was no longer in these woods but somewhere far distant. "I once thought death held peace. But my sister is dead. So are my father and my mother. I have not had peace since. I longed for death, but I knew it would never satisfy my soul. I've been terrified of it all my life, even as I came so close to it so many times. I think I was dead for a long time. I was soulless. I had forsaken myself, so I never should have been surprised when I thought the gods had forsaken me. I see that now. If I were to have died nine months ago, I never would have known peace, because I never would have done anything in this world worth leaving behind." Kalif seemed to come to himself and looked Hakoni in the eye. "Have you done something worth leaving behind, my friend?"

Hakoni had no idea if his beaten face was capable of showing surprise, but he suspected surprise was written there nonetheless. "'Friend'? Am I your friend, Kalif?"

"You're more like me than I care to admit," Kalif said with a wry smile. "And for the first time in a long...long time, I may be ready to be my own friend. Don't settle for death, Hakoni. Death is cheap. Justice and peace must be found another way."

"What other way?"

Kalif didn't answer immediately. "You have to hang onto this." Kalif handed Hakoni a small, three-inch knife. "You'll need to use it to free the rest of your people tomorrow morning." Hakoni tucked it under his belt behind his back. The edge bit slightly into his skin.

"Free us?" Hakoni said. The surprise in his face was beginning to hurt.

"It's time for me to do something that always looked wrong, but something that feels right, anyway."

"I assume breaking my face has something to do with that?"

Kalif looked guilty. "Believe it or not, that was my way of saving you. They wanted to skin you alive. I convinced them that a beating similar to what you gave me would be sufficient for now, because you're strong enough to carry the dead bodies tomorrow. I had to maintain their trust."

"What are you going to do?"

Hakoni saw a grim determination cross his face. "What I do best," Kalif said simply. Then he turned and shouted to the guards, "Hey! Get your *geffes* over here! I told you to leave him well enough to talk, but the *punta* could barely say his own name. Now get this half-dead carcass back to the prisons!"

As Kalif tied Hakoni, Hakoni asked, "Who was the mole? What's his name?"

"They call him Fonga. That's his Lima name, I guess. But we knew him in the quarry as Erron."

Hakoni nodded. Erron. The one Hakoni tried to confide in about the prisoner revolt.

The men were drawing near. Kalif said hurriedly, "Tomorrow morning. Don't forget."

"Wait!" Hakoni hissed as the guards approached. "The girl. In the woods by the gidionhi flowers. Did she have red in her hair? Dark hair with just a hint of red?"

284

Kalif's lips became a tight line as his brow furrowed. "It was… dark. Too dark to tell." Then he turned his back on Hakoni just as the guards arrived.

"What was that all about?" Hakoni heard Zoram ask Kalif.

"We beat him, but we didn't break him," he heard Kalif respond. "You have to take his hope to break him, and then he won't fight. He'll just wait to die. I made sure he knew what we are doing to him and to his women and children. He's broken and powerless now."

Hakoni could barely walk as the two guards dragged him back to the stables. Everything he had believed about Kalif was coming undone. He wanted to hate him. But a small pinching from the knife now under his belt told Hakoni that for all of Kalif's sins and shortcomings, there was yet some good Kalif would do in this world.

The man to Hakoni's right moaned and turned his head slowly to face Hakoni. "Ha…Hak…," he said, and then began to cough. It came slowly at first, and then welled into a wracking cough and finished by the man vomiting. But his arms were chained to the wall as he sat against the wall, forcing the man to vomit all over himself. Hakoni watched in horror as the man's bruised face and torn clothing emphasized his depravity, magnified by the bile, which he was now forced to sit in. And vomit was not the only smell in the barn—the Lima did not allow the Neroos to be unchained for anything, including relieving themselves. The scent of urine and feces had induced vomiting from more men than just this one sitting beside Hakoni.

"Hak," the man whispered again and spat out vomit residue. Hakoni looked at him through his one good eye and felt his stomach sink. It was Garrick. He continued to speak, though every word was agony for the man. Hakoni wondered if they had broken every rib or even punctured a lung. "I don't care what you have to do. You kill that *batarkre* Kalif. Do you understand?"

"All is not as it seems, Garrick. You taught me that," Hakoni whispered, wanting to believe the words that came from his own mouth.

Garrick tried to reply, but he only managed to moan and gasp for breath.

"Help!" Hakoni tried to yell to the guards.

The guards shouted back, "*Arrestre shwoh-ne! Clappen hec jarg!*" No talking. Shut your mouth.

"This man is dying! He needs medical attention! Please, someone help him!"

The guards came back and said, "If you don't shut up, you'll be doing worse than him!"

Any worse than him, and I'd be dead, Hakoni thought. *And would that be so bad?* But Kalif's words rang in his ears. Death is hollow. You have to do something worth leaving behind. Friend. The truth of Kalif's words ran against everything Hakoni had seen. Had believed. Or wanted to see and believe. But Garrick was all Hakoni could see right now, and Hakoni was beginning to think that the greatest thing he could do in this world would be either to save Kalif, or take Kalif out of it.

~~~~~

A few hours later, Chism found himself in the back of the same kind of covered wagon he had seen back in the High Tide District. Beside him sat a man accused of being a deserter from the city guard, three accused thieves, and two men accused of murder. *Accusations and stories,* Chism said to himself. *They'll believe what they have to believe in order to justify their actions.* Three of the men looked scared. The others looked resigned to their fate. Chism had no idea anymore if it was guilt he saw in their eyes or innocence simply turned to terror. He didn't care anymore.

And yet, it wasn't fear that gripped Chism. He heard coins change hands at the gate and the predictably bumpy road of cobblestone and flagstones turn to the haphazard trundle of wagon wheels on uneven, natural ground. And he felt happy. Focused. Content.

It was a strange feeling to Chism, almost as unsettling as the constant anxiety and fear of death. Fear of losing his family. But his worst fear had been realized. His sister was dead, and he had killed his brother less than a week later. *What do you feel when your greatest fear becomes your living reality?* Chism often found himself wondering. One thing was certain—he lost his family and everything he had worked to gain, and yet he was still alive and well and capable of choosing. So he made the last choice he had left. He chose to be content.

What an ironic thing it is, Chism thought, *that this is how I ended up happy.* His brother lay in a mass grave, if not still in that forsaken forest where he had shot the last person on this earth he had cared about. He now cared for both the girl who unwillingly bore his brother's child, and Kalif's fiancée, who should have bore the child in the other girl's womb. He himself had been considered dead until just a few hours ago, and he had taken on an alias to live in the lowest part of society.

Chism suspected he owed his sanity in large part to that spunky girl several years his junior who nevertheless commanded respect and admiration. She had taught Chism to make a choice. To choose happiness, no matter his circumstances. Chism had lived so long in fear of the future and in longing for the past; he had allowed himself to be changed in too many ways by the society around him. Now he had learned to make a choice, thanks to Rayanna. And that made all the difference.

Still, there was a small corner of Chism's mind that had always felt anxious. Unsettled. He could hear a whisper that said such peace could not last. And now here he was, running headlong into the dark to save the last part of his family that still lived.

He knew that Rayanna would go back to her people once the baby was born. Whether she would take the baby with her, he did not know. But he did know that when she was gone, his world would be sorely lacking.

After several hours the wagon stopped, and a man yanked back the cover, looked over them, and yelled over his shoulder, "All right, let's get these *punta* outta here! We gotta get 'em to the front lines with the rest of the fugitives."

Fugitives? Chism thought. Then it hit him. The prisoners and criminals hadn't been sold to the marauders—not officially. There had been a jailbreak, and the prisoners were hiding outside the walls of the city. Chism and the rest of the city guard had always hated the marauders, but city guards love a big payoff more than they hate the marauders. Chism wondered how many *tregara* they had been offered to join the marauders on this one. *And if there are fugitives in the woods, how better to explain the absence—and loss—of a portion of the city guard?* Chism grinned at the elaborate plan. They would stop at nothing to get more power.

They untied his legs but left his hands together and his mouth gagged. As they walked around to the front of the wagon, he was met with the scene of a massive throng of people in a valley he had never seen. Considering the length of the cart ride and the position of the sun, Chism guessed he was only five to ten miles away from Gidionhi.

The horde of people must have been gathering here for about a week, given the state of the grass and the freshly cut trees. Fire pits stood cold. They must have only been using them at night when the smoke was not as easily detected, though it was much colder in this mountain pass than it was by the coast. Tents large enough to hold ten people each stood at regular intervals. The marauders kept warm during the day by sheer body heat. The odor as he passed through the place bespoke a place where heat and body odor were simultaneously captured. *All this for a few coins,* Chism thought in wonder. At the far edge of the camp, men swarmed tents and pack wagons as they occupied themselves with tearing down and packing up the massive tents.

Chism craned his head as he passed through the city of tents, looking for any sign of Gala and Rayanna. But the effort was useless. He was looking for a food area or a medical area. He prayed that he wouldn't find the women in any other place than that, but with five thousand men gathered, there was no doubt that women would be here for more than putting on bandages and serving soup. But not only did he not see either food wagons or a medic tent, he was struck by the conspicuous *lack* of either feature critical to a staging site like this.

"Line 'em up here!" A heavyset marauder called out. A soldier came by and began unraveling the bonds from their hands and pushed them to stand in front of the well-framed man whose two loves—food and booze—were readily apparent on his clothes and on his breath. But even though his gut stood out beyond his belt, his obvious biceps and broad shoulders were even more prominent. "Gentlemen, my name is Ahmek," the man growled. "And you have to prove to me that you deserve your freedom. You were caught performing some godforsaken atrocity, and this is your opportunity to be redeemed. You fight with us, and when you come back, you are free men. No jail. No lashes. We'll even put a few coins in your pocket. But you're going to earn *every minute of your freedom!*" He shouted each of the last words of his monologue. "We're going to attack the Neroos when they're weak and when their guard is down. The rest of the fugitives," he grinned at the word, "have been working all week to build our trebuchets and rams. Now you're going to help the beasts pull them to the front line. Now get in formation and get ready to move."

A younger marauder stepped in front of them. He unraveled a whip and lashed out at the man standing at the end of the line. He fell to the ground with a bloody lash across his chest. Then he started barking orders. No fires or you'll be killed. No fighting or you'll be killed. Form a line. March.

Chism's heart sank. They were heading out already, and he'd had no time to search. The wagons and medic tents were gone. Chism could only hope to find Gala and Rayanna by getting to the next drop point as soon as possible.

CHAPTER 22:
LIFE IN HIS HANDS

Rayanna had never been tired like this. She was fatigued and she ached, but it was more than the lengthy march and the subsequent wagon ride after she nearly fainted on the trail. There was something else, something beneath the surface that spoke of a deeper rest that she knew she needed. A rest she had waited so long to receive.

The pain in her stomach had subsided. It had been thirty-four weeks and three days since she was attacked. Rayanna had counted every day. Though Chism and Gala were kind to her—Gala, perhaps, in her own way—Rayanna knew that she was still a slave.

She didn't know much about childbirth. She was too young to remember Brego and Karrh's births, and few children had been born since the first attack on Gidionhi. When she was very young, she thought she'd have plenty of time to ask her mother all the questions she needed. After the attack, she didn't think about boys or children or the future at all. She just focused on what to eat for the next meal.

The thought of her mother brought the familiar sorrow to her heart. Her mother was stronger than she had ever known. Ever appreciated.

Rayanna had watched the girth of her belly slowly descend from close to her diaphragm to now be centered almost below her belly button. She didn't need a doctor to know that the child was coming. Early or late, she couldn't really say. But the strain of being kidnapped and then made to ride tied to the wagon for hours on a makeshift mountain road was taking an incredible toll on her body.

"No!" Gala shouted at three guards. "I don't care if Lima himself gave you orders. This woman is days away from having a child. Hours, maybe!" Rayanna could hear the familiar escalation in Gala's voice, and smiled. Gala was going to work on these men, and there was only one way it could end: with the men saying "yes, ma'am" and Gala smiling smugly to herself.

"Well who in *porja* sent a pregnant woman off to battle!" One of the soldiers cried out.

"Have you seen the workers in the kitchen? They weren't exactly picky when they grabbed the women, if you know what I mean," another man replied.

"Besides if we can get a few hours' work out of her, we can just leave her," the third said.

"If you stick her in a kitchen and force her to walk around and lift everything in sight, you're going to have a baby on your hands and more blood than you've ever seen on every scrap of food in here!"

The soldiers looked awkwardly at each other and grumbled. But Rayanna felt oddly safe. They wouldn't harm her so long as she carried a baby. An innocent life—or innocent insofar as it was Lima.

Rayanna's back was aching, and her stomach muscles were still sore from the contractions earlier in the day. She sat down on the grass and leaned back on her arms. She knew this show could go on for a while.

The guard in the middle looked to his left and right for help with the screaming woman that stood before them with her hands gesticulating wildly. With no help from his companions, he stammered in response, "Uh...where...I mean, what can...uh..."

"If you know what's good for you, you'll have her sit in the wagon and drink water!"

The guard on the left stepped in and said, "Look, you're not running this show. Everyone works! If she has a baby…" he paused as the reality of it descended on him, and he had no idea what to say next. "Then she'll deal with it!" he finished lamely.

"Oh yeah, that's great. That's prime leadership material, right here in the flesh," Gala said quietly, nodding her head vigorously. Then her feigned agreement turned to abject sneering, and she said, "Then you better put her where the bandages and hot water are, unless you want to clean up the mess with some bread."

The second guard inhaled and stuck his chest out as he started barking orders. "You! That woman can't be in the kitchen. Have her...organize...bandages in the medic tent. Take her there now!"

"Get up, you," the third said to Rayanna.

She looked up at him with the same arched eyebrow look she had learned from eight months of living with Gala. "I need help."

"I said get up!"

"Oh for the sake of the gods," Gala said angrily as she marched over to Rayanna. "Shouting at her isn't going to suddenly give her core muscles a boost, you moron."

Rayanna gratefully extended a hand as she and Gala worked together to bring Rayanna to her feet.

"Chism was better at this than I am," Gala said as they finally got Rayanna to her feet.

"You're doing fine," Rayanna said.

"What's your name?" Gala turned and asked the pompous one impatiently. "Or am I just supposed to say 'hey you' whenever I want your attention?"

"I'm 'sir' to you, or Sergeant Kauwen," the man replied.

"Well sir sergeant Kauwen, where's the medic tent?" Gala asked the three men.

"You're not going anywhere," Kauwen said to Gala. "There's work to be done here, and you're not—"

Gala's nostrils and temper both flared as she began to shout again. "If you think she's going there all alone when she can't even get off the ground herself—!"

"Oh, shut up! C'mon, just get them both out of here!" The guard who was supposed to guide them said. Rayanna wanted to laugh, but her body was so tired that she decided to simply log the event away and smile later. Gala wrapped Rayanna's arm around her shoulder and helped the young girl walk.

"Now...get these bandages...ready," the guard said as he left the two with a torch and quickly walked off.

"Yeah, we'll do that," Gala said when he was out of earshot. Rayanna moaned and sat against a wagon wheel. She leaned her head against the spokes, no longer caring how much mud or grime found its way into her hair. She ached, and nothing else mattered. Her eyes were closed as fatigue began to overcome her. But she knew she had a long, difficult road left to travel.

"Gala," she said, not opening her eyes to find her companion.

Gala stuck the torch in the ground near their wagon. In the fading light, she could see the lights of the approaching army several miles away. "What do you need?"

Rayanna felt flushed. Not just with the heat and difficulty of having walked and ridden for so long. This was something else. Something new. "Something's happening. I don't know what's going on, but it doesn't feel right."

Gala brought the torch closer. Rayanna opened her eyes in time to see Gala's face slacken with surprise. She blinked several times and then stated, "Rayanna...you're bleeding."

Rayanna couldn't see past her belly, so she reached down to touch her dress below her belly. "It's dry," she said.

"No, it's mostly in the back of your dress. Hang on, I'll get some bandages."

"*Papuana…Mamillera…*" Rayanna whispered for her father and mother as Gala hunted in various crates. "I need you." Tears came to her eyes as she thought of them. They felt so far away, and yet near enough to smell their skin as if she hugged them.

"Here are some bandages," Gala announced her return. "I also found some extra water skins. I don't think we're supposed to have them, but the way the bandages and supplies were thrown in there, they have no idea what's gone and what's not."

"Thank you," Rayanna said. "For everything. If I had been in that kitchen…"

"Oh, you think I did that for you?" Gala said with a smile. "I just didn't want to put up with all of them."

Rayanna smiled weakly in return. Gala was very different from her mother. She wondered if this raven-haired beauty might be what a sister would be like. Constantly fighting, yet always there beside her. Rayanna would never cease to be amazed at the peculiarity of their relationship and that a friendship between them could grow like a root—tough, ugly, and beneath the surface, but sturdy enough to withstand almost anything.

Gala helped Rayanna unravel her undergarment and wash the blood off of her legs. Rayanna didn't have the energy to feel embarrassed. As long as the baby was born healthy, she would endure whatever it took to bring him into the world. *I hope he's like you, Papuana,* she thought as Gala wrapped extra padding into the new undergarment barrier.

"What does it mean?" Rayanna asked.

Gala didn't answer immediately. She busied herself with scrubbing the blood off her hands. She said in a preoccupied tone as she held the soaked rags, "I can't just throw these into the trees. We've got enough wolves in this camp already." She nodded toward the soldiers, not distinguishing between one type of animal and another. "Though I gotta tell you, I might prefer the wolves that actually belong in this forest to the filthy men in this army, anyway."

"Who knows? Maybe there's one wolf out there looking for you." Rayanna said.

Gala's brow furrowed. "You mean Chism?"

Rayanna nodded.

"I hope so," Gala replied under her breath.

"If there's one thing I know about Chism, it's that he'll stop at nothing to save an innocent life. He's coming, Gala."

"I learned a long time ago to stop counting on people."

"Time to learn some faith."

Gala shook her head. "Are you ever going to give up on—"

Rayanna didn't hear the rest of Gala's sentence. She doubled over and cried out as her stomach seized up again for a full three minutes. Rayanna gasped for air as the pain slowly subsided. "Gala," she breathed. "If anything happens—"

"Nothing's going to—!"

"Name him Solay, if it's a boy. Please."

"What if it's a girl?"

"Then name her after me."

Rayanna felt hands around her face as Gala grabbed her to help her focus. "Listen to me. I need you to breathe slowly! I need you to relax. I can't deliver this baby right now!"

Rayanna nodded, but the pain was rising again. Gala was almost shouting as she said, "I'm going to find some medicine. We've got to slow this baby down. Just hang on!"

~~~~~

The sounds of men shifting in cots and beds filled the room. Zoram lay in the bed to his left. Three men lay in cots or sprawled on the floor with blankets. They had eaten their fill that night. Many had thrown up after binging. Their bodies simply were no longer capable of handling that much food. After incessant griping about the lack of ale and the interminable insults hurled at every Neroos down to the filthy *punta* who betrayed their first father, the Lima fell fast asleep.

He could have wanted anything at this moment—to hold Gala in his arms, to be working for her uncle in the fishing district, or to be able to look Chism in the eye and see a proud brother looking back. But all Kalif wanted was to shift around and get comfortable. Or just to sleep on the floor as he had been forced to do for so long. Anything but this bed. Kalif hadn't slept in one for months. Even before being captured, he slept on nothing softer than leaves and loam most nights of the week as he patrolled the perimeter of the city.

But there was something more than the feeling of cotton and clean blankets that disturbed him. With Kalif, there was always something more. Something beneath the surface, waiting for him to peel back the layers and find the truth hidden beneath the façade of the stories he told himself.

Kalif couldn't decide if he were restless or if he just felt guilty. Guilty for being in a Neroos bed while the beds' owners lay bloody, bruised, and beaten. Tomorrow they'd bury the dead. Then the Lima would kill them and drop them in the very graves they will have digged for their friends and families. *The Neroos know that will be their fate,* Kalif mused. *And they'll work just as hard as if the Lima had asked them nicely.*

No smile graced Kalif's lips at the thought. The same idea that would have spurred thoughts of Neroos simplicity now inspired thoughts of industry and feelings of begrudging admiration. *And all of it will be gone by the time the sun goes down tomorrow.* He couldn't let that happen.

Was it guilt, then, that kept him awake and begged him to shift—not just to shift so that his body could be comfortable, but to shift tonight's purpose so that he wouldn't have to face the reality of his actions? Was it guilt for stopping the Lima from committing more atrocities? Kalif felt the hilt of his long-lost dagger once again in his hands. With it, he would spill Lima blood. He had killed Lima before when he moonlighted as an assassin. But he had never felt this way.

The Neroos could have killed them, Kalif knew. He often wondered why they hadn't. He told himself it was only because they had work for the Lima to do, but Kalif couldn't hold onto that story any longer. No, there was something stopping the Neroos from killing the Lima, but there was nothing stopping the Lima from burning every man alive. *The Lima are the aggressors,* Kalif told himself as he stared at the ceiling. *It's their fault we're here. It's my fault we're here. And I have to set this right.*

Kalif looked at the men around him, snoring loudly and shifting uncomfortably in the Neroos cots. *They can't make a sound,* Kalif coached himself. *If one man cries out, then it's all over.* Then, after an hour of waiting, Kalif was certain that he could move. But he didn't. *What am I doing?* He asked himself. Then he heard his own answer, though it felt like more of an answer than he could provide himself. A thought came to him, and he could almost hear himself saying, *You're protecting those who can no longer protect themselves. But taking these men's lives won't bring back the men you killed. It won't unbreak the hearts you've broken. If what you're doing is right, it won't change yesterday. But it will change tomorrow.*

Kalif sat upright quickly. He knew that the canvas of the cot beneath him would creak and protest every move. Prolonged movement only equaled prolonged noise. It was best to move quickly so that any noise would be gone as quickly as it had come.

Kalif treaded softly across the floor. Though his muscles were no longer used to stalking prey in a forest, his legs had not forgotten years of practice. His shadow made more noise than he as he came to stand at the head of Zoram's cot.

Zoram drew in a deep breath.

Three, Kalif began to count.

Exhale. Deep inhale.

Two.

Exhale. Deep inhale.

One.

Exhale. At the edge of Zoram's breath, Kalif was ready.

~~~~~

The guard had long since slumped in his chair. Hakoni was almost ready to make his move when the guards slowly slid to his right. The blue glass bottle dropped a short distance to the stone floor, its contents sloshing over the cobblestone. Hakoni could almost count down to the moment the guard toppled out of his chair. The guard yelped in surprise.

Within less than a minute, two men turned the corner with bleary eyes and almost tripped over each other as they tried to unsheathe their blades with fumbling hands.

"What! What's wrong?" They shouted at the guard who had just picked himself up off the floor.

"What's wrong?" The drunken Lima responded.

"You shouted!" One of the two said, expecting that one fact to explain their appearance.

"You're shouting!" The guard repeated back with a blank look across his face.

Hakoni recognized one of the guard's voices, but it was difficult to recall who it was exactly. The guards were speaking Lima, but he had heard that voice speaking flawless Neroos at one point.

The two men stared at the first guard long and hard, and then they began looking around for alcohol. Hakoni would have laughed, but the situation demanded that he call as little attention to himself as possible.

One guard tapped the other's arm and nodded toward the blue glass bottle with a dark stain seeping into the corner of the floor and the wall. Both men sneered.

"You haven't even been free for twenty-four hours, and you're soaking drunk," the familiar voice said.

The drunk nodded and said, "It's...still fun. You should try it."

"I wouldn't touch a Neroos bottle to my lips to save my life. They don't know how to brew anything stronger than akava root with erlich leaves." His companion scoffed. "I don't know how you did it, Fonga."

Fonga! It's the mole, Erron, Hakoni realized.

The drunk man smiled vaguely. "But...this!...isn't Neroos." He held up an empty hand and finally noticed that it no longer held the bottle. His blithely serene face took on a look of confused concern and he started searching for the dearly departed booze.

Not Neroos? Where the devil did it come from, then? Hakoni thought with alarm at the idea of Neroos soldiers trading with Lima merchants. Hakoni considered the fact that the man was drunk out of his mind, and he could have been beyond reason. But the fact that he was drunk out of his mind was evidence enough that he was telling the truth: in Neroos culture, they typically didn't keep strong drinks long enough for them to addle the brains, and a drunk man is typically a very honest one. It must have been Fonga who posed as a guard. He was the one who brought the stuff into his society, Hakoni decided. Then, trying to quiet the unsettled feeling that everything was not as it seemed, he focused again on their conversation.

"Good grief, the man has no idea what he's talking about. If I catch you sleeping again, you're going to be locked up with the rest of them," Fonga said.

As he turned to leave, his companion said, "Is it a good idea to leave him alone?"

Fonga turned and squinted in the low torch light at the stables where the Neroos were tied and chained. "They don't have any fight left in them, anyway. And if someone does try something, then it's even more excuse to get rid of them."

"Too bad their women took off at the first blow of the horn," the second one lamented.

The Sound in the Silence

Hakoni had been relieved that the women and children had become so effective at evacuating. After the initial attack, many of those that had survived chose to leave, finding new homes with relatives in other cities or making new homes anywhere they could find. Those that remained did so out of defiance, unwilling to be moved from their homes. But staying meant constant preparation for the worst. They had seen the worst multiple times, and acceptance and preparation had replaced the fear of the unknown. When the horn blew, the families and children who were left had all but vacated the village in less than twenty minutes. Plenty of food and supplies had been left behind for the marauders, but no one would be caught unaware.

They are innocent, Hakoni wanted to scream. *They are innocent! Do what you will to me—to any of us here—but don't you dare touch them!* He felt anxious to be free and to push the little knife into their chests down to the hilt.

"Let me tell you—these Neroos women are worth the effort," Fonga bragged. "But I've got other work to do. You stay here."

"Something from the Master?"

Who's the Master? Hakoni wondered.

"There's a Lima who had worked in the quarry. He was supposed to die in the initial attack. The Master has asked me to finish the job," Fonga said as their voices trailed off. *Good,* Hakoni thought. *Do the work for us.* Hakoni hoped he was talking about Zoram.

Garrick wheezed beside him. Hakoni thought he heard a gurgling as Garrick breathed in, and he wondered if blood in the lungs sounded like what he was hearing now.

He quickly extracted the knife and began to saw at his ropes. The angle was difficult and the task arduous. As he worked, Hakoni began to wonder as he sawed when he had stopped counting himself among the innocent. He wondered when it had become so easy for him to desire retribution. To see killing as fitting justice. To see death as the only way to peace.

LIFE IN HIS HANDS

The drunken guard had fallen asleep and the torch on the wall had burned low long before Hakoni felt enough slack in his ropes to pull his hands free. As he pulled the ropes from his skin, he felt a sharp tearing where the blood had dried to the ropes. The wounds opened up when the ropes were separated from his hands.

Turning to Garrick, he lifted the man's head off his chest to help him breathe. Garrick began to cough and cry out. "No! No, leave us!"

Hakoni quickly clapped a hand over Garrick's mouth and whispered in his ear. "Garrick, it's me! I'm getting us out of here. You have to be silent!" Hakoni removed his hand before Garrick could show that he understood. He had no idea if Garrick could breathe at all through his nose.

Hakoni gently leaned Garrick forward and made quick work of the ropes holding him. They had tied him up after beating him and left him just as they had with Hakoni. Hakoni freed three more, and then ran into issues with the metal cuffs. The other four men who had been in ropes could not move without significant pain. Anyone who was at least marginally healthy was in metal cuffs.

Hakoni tried to pick the lock on one of the men with his knife. As he worked on the cuff holding Hamas, his fellow guard at the quarry, Hamas stifled a scream as Hakoni jostled his arm. Hamas sat chained to the wall with a broken arm barely splinted. "Hak," he said louder than he should have. Everyone froze and turned an eye to the guard who sat slumped in his chair. He didn't move. "Hak, we need the key."

"Where is it?" Hakoni replied.

"The guard had it last. I don't think he hung it anywhere," Hamas said.

"How do I search him without waking him?"

"You kill him."

Hakoni looked away from Hamas and stared at the drunk. Kalif's words still rang in his ears. *You have to do what's right, even when it looks wrong. But what is right? This man and his people have killed so many of us!* Hakoni simply nodded to Hamas in the dark.

Hakoni couldn't open the wrought iron gate to walk out there. He knew that even if the screeching of the metal hinges didn't wake the drunk, then it would certainly alert the other guards outside. Hakoni just hoped that Fonga was still away hunting Zoram or another Lima from the quarry. He placed his palms on the five-foot wooden fence that separated the stables from the center walkway where the guard sat. With great effort and considerable pain in his ribs and shoulders, he hoisted his body up and over, and then lowered himself quietly on the other side. The drunk snored on.

Hakoni walked slowly toward him. The grey light of the morning was piercing the sky. Time was short. A sword lay on the ground to the man's right where he had carelessly dropped it.

Hakoni knelt next to the man and carefully lifted his arm to search for the keys at his belt. Nothing on the right-hand side. Hakoni placed the arm back on the man's lap and stepped around him to the left. He could just barely make out the keys in the dim light of the torch. The Lima's left arm hung limply at his side, blocking Hakoni's access to the keys.

"Hak!" Hamas hissed. "Do it! Just kill him! If he wakes up, then we're all dead."

Just then, the man snored loudly and lifted his head. Hakoni froze. He opened his eyes for a moment and looked at Hakoni without seeing him. Then realization dawned in his eyes. Hakoni stood up to punch the man, but his legs were so stiff that he fell over backward. The man yelped and dove for his sword. The man fell off his chair as Hakoni struggled to stand. The Lima came up with sword in hand swinging wildly.

~~~~~

Kalif heard the door open on the far end of the room. *Corva cavesa!* He swore to himself as he wiped his blade on the bedding

302

of the man he had just killed and stepped into the shadows. He had worked slower than he anticipated. He had to take long pauses as he endured pain in his ribs and risked waking the others up as he continued his work of death. He had killed fourteen men in total silence. Five were left in this room. The rest of the men stood as guards for the night around the compound. One, apparently, had come back.

Kalif watched as he stooped closely to Zoram's cot. Kalif had drawn blankets up to each man's neck to hide the hole he had put in each man's heart. Kalif knew that the dark stains on the blankets were easily discernible, but he had hoped that if anyone were to wake up or walk in the dark, they wouldn't look too closely. But this man was looking closely. He looked at the cot where Kalif had slept and saw it empty, then placed his hand on Zoram's neck. Kalif could see he was checking for a pulse.

The man stood up suddenly, rushed to the door, and closed it. The room went virtually pitch black with the gray morning light coming faintly through the windows. But Kalif was accustomed to the dark and could use his sight. This man was probably working by hearing alone.

Kalif stepped quietly toward him. The man stood attentively, listening for the smallest sound. Kalif recognized the position. Were Kalif able to see him clearly, he knew he'd see the man's fingers twitching ever so slightly, ready to react, to attack, to kill as soon as danger touched the smallest nerve.

"I know you're here, Kalif," the man said quietly. Kalif froze. "The Master is impressed that you lived so long. You were not supposed to make it through the first attack alive. Then you were supposed to be killed during the revolt. You won't escape me now."

"Who are you?" Kalif whispered, then quickly stepped back fifteen feet. The man turned his head at the sound and walked closer, passing in front of a window as he approached. Fonga, Kalif saw.

"I am death, Kalif," he whispered back. "And you won't escape me a third time."

Kalif worked his way over to the last bunk and quietly woke the man by placing a hand over the man's mouth. He woke up suddenly.

Kalif whispered quietly in his ear, "There's a Neroos in here! He's killed so many of us! Please, help me stop him!" The man nodded with wide eyes, quietly slipped out of bed, and grabbed his sword.

"You've been wanting to kill me ever since guarding me at the quarry," Kalif whispered a little louder. Fonga's feet shifted in response. Kalif's newfound companion moved to cut off Fonga's route.

"Yes. I have wanted to kill you for a long time. And when the marauders get here tomorrow, I'll report back to the Master that I cleaned up your little mess. That kind of devotion goes a long way, Kalif."

"What marauders?" Kalif asked anxiously. Too anxiously. Fonga turned his attention to the very spot where Kalif stood. He would have taken the risk of meeting Fonga head-on to get more information. But Kalif's newfound companion was quicker.

Kalif's companion raised his sword above his head and quickly took a breath. Fonga heard it, and turned in time for the sword to come crashing down on the dirt floor. Fonga swung a backhanded attack and caught the man in the small of the back. The other four men stirred awake as their companion screamed in agony and arched his back. Fonga's sword was stuck in the vertebrae and he kicked the other man over and yanked the sword out just as the other four converged on him.

Kalif slipped out into the early morning and made his way as quickly as possible to the stables. He could only hope that Hakoni had gotten them free in time.

Just as he got there, he saw three men moving slowly into the stable from the other end. They weren't just walking; they were stalking something. Kalif closed his eyes and prayed the Neroos men had already made it out. But he knew that if they were, the Lima wouldn't be moving as if they were hunting. He moved as quickly as he could to cut the soldiers off.

~~~~~

The pathway was narrow, and the man was screaming. Hakoni did the only thing he could think to do—he threw the little knife as hard as he could.

The blade bit the man's eyebrow and cheekbone, and the Lima stumbled backward and tripped over his chair. Hakoni had no idea why no one had come to find out what was happening, but he didn't want to let this man's screams last any longer. He had flung his sword in his wild swinging when Hakoni hit him with the knife. Neither blade was in sight as Hakoni limped over to the downed, screaming man.

Hakoni raised his right leg and brought his heel down squarely on the man's throat. The screaming stopped immediately. The man gasped slightly and painfully. Hakoni yanked the torch off the wall and went looking for a blade. It took him over a minute to find the sword, and the man's gasping rang in his ears the entire time. Hakoni wondered if he would ever be able to forget those horrible sounds. He walked back with the sword in hand and said, "I'm so sorry." Then he plunged the tip of the sword into the man's heart. He stopped moving instantly.

Hakoni dropped the sword, stooped slowly to get the keys, and walked back to the stables, throwing the gate open as he entered. He began unlocking men as fast as he could. Hamas was the first out.

Hamas cradled his arm as he stepped out into the hallway and grabbed the sword on the ground. He also found the small knife that Hakoni had dropped, but no more weapons were to be found in the stables. He came back in and gave the knife to Hakoni to keep cutting ties.

"You idiot," Hamas berated him. "We could have them pouring in here at any minute! You're a gutless child."

"Save it, Hamas," Hakoni said. "You're getting out of here because of me."

"We could die in here because of you."

"Then at least I don't have to listen to you whine for long, do I?" Hakoni said as he unlocked the others.

A voice tinged with a Lima accent spoke from the far doorway to the stables. "No, you don't."

CHAPTER 23:
ALL WAS BLACK

Chism estimated that they had come almost twenty miles through the dark and rugged terrain in only six hours. He had heard the whipping steadily increase with every passing mile, and he could smell the lather on the horses just in front of him. He and his fellow fugitives had been called more than once to help a horse heave its load up a steep incline or pull a wagon over numerous obstacles as they blazed a trail through the mountains. Chism had been pushing behind a wagon so hard that when the horse pulling it finally reached the top and outpaced them, he slipped forward and landed squarely in the mud. In two hours, the mud didn't dry as the sweat continually soaked it and kept it from drying and pulling at his skin.

His group was among the first to arrive, and they headed straight for the food.

"*Arrestre*, you bunch of *batarkres*," Ahmek called out, cracking the whip at several men who meandered through a clearing to find the food station. "You fugitives have to wait for the rest of the army to eat. Then you can have what's left."

Punch him in the throat to silence him. Grab the whip. Tie his hands with it. Cradle his neck in the crook of the elbow, and squeeze. Chism couldn't help but play out how he would silence and knock out the man with the whip, though his better judgment told him to stay behind the scenes. He had work to do, and the less attention he called to himself, the better.

As the man with the whip barked orders about clearing ground space for a few hours' rest before the army took up its march again, Chism slipped noiselessly into the forest. He was covered in grime and mud, and sweat made rivulets down his face and arms. Chism grinned slightly, feeling a small pull at the corners of his mouth where some mud had dried, pleased that he had an added disguise. He glided across the forest floor. He felt a renewed energy now that he was back in his element. No one with a whip or a sword or a bow could touch him in here.

The food tent came first. He stayed well outside of the firelight, but he didn't need a close view. None of the women had a preponderous belly. And wherever Rayanna was, Gala would not be far behind. Chism grinned as he thought of the transformation in Gala. It had been so difficult to accept someone from the life she had always shunned and feared. But then Rayanna had turned everything upside down for the two, and Chism wondered if upside down were actually right side up.

He moved swiftly past the kitchen and found a lone torch by a set of five wagons. Rayanna lay with her back against a wagon wheel and her legs sprawled out on the ground in front of her. Bloody rags lay cast aside on the ground. Her head hung slightly to one side, and her face was passive with eyes closed. Chism held his breath, not willing to breathe until he saw her chest rise and fall. Nothing.

Chism wanted to run to her, but he had not yet seen Gala. If there were a guard around or someone who had intentionally hurt the women, he had to find the danger before he could make himself known. He at least knew where to find Rayanna—*or Rayanna's body, anyway,* he thought bitterly, though he willed her to still be alive. *Gala, where are you?*

Chism was on the hunt. He had to suspend emotion and accomplish the task at hand. He circled the wagons, staying out of the light cast by the single torch.

Chism heard footsteps. Several pair. Then a voice shouted, "I told you to organize these wagons!"

"Kauwen, she's going into labor!" Gala's voice responded with her characteristic fire. "I could barely find the right herbs to help stop her contractions as it is. Your supplies will get organized, no thanks to your men. You're going to have soldiers bleeding to death while someone hunts for the needles with these wagons like this."

Chism came around to keep Rayanna in view. She stirred slightly at all the noise, and Chism breathed a heavy sigh of relief. But she was heavily sedated. Or exhausted. Or both.

Gala came into view between the wagons with two other guards. "Sleeping!" Kauwen yelled upon seeing Rayanna. He approached her and raised his hand to beat Rayanna for not working.

"No!" Gala yelled and tried to grab his hand. Kauwen threw her off his arm and shouted, "I'll deal with you after her. I've had enough of you and this stinking Neroos!"

Chism had seen enough. As he stepped out into the light of the torch, he said, "That's why you'll hand them over to me, soldier. And I expect you to report to my tent in three hours about your disorderly conduct toward this woman," he said gesturing to Gala as she stood herself up.

"And who do you think you are?" Kauwen asked as he placed his hand on his sword hilt at his hip.

"Someone more powerful than you," Chism answered.

Kauwen blinked several times at Chism's unexpected reply. He had been prepared to argue about rank, but Chism's outright declaration of power made him stop. Then seeing the fire in

Chism's eye and the scar across his eye, nose, and chin coupled with his mud-coated brawn made Chism a complete mystery—a very imposing, potentially violent mystery.

"I think you have a kitchen to attend to," Chism said as he stared directly in the man's eye. Kauwen didn't argue. Grumbling to himself and his companion, he turned around to leave, paused, half turned back, and then finally ordered his companion to accompany him back toward the kitchen tent.

"Gala, thank *el-nuajs* you're all right," Chism said as he wrapped her into a tight embrace. "What's wrong with Rayanna?"

Gala didn't back away from Chism's arms as she quietly relayed to him everything that had happened since the previous morning. "She's bleeding a lot. More than she should. I think it's internal."

"Is the child in danger?"

"I don't know. But I think she is. I know we need to escape, but I swear if we try to run for it in the woods, she'll have the baby right in the open."

"Well she can't have the baby in the middle of a battle!"

"I know, but..." Gala lowered her voice even more to a whisper. "Chism, I don't know how to make the bleeding stop."

Chism bit his lip. He knew more about battle wounds than women's health, but he knew two things: that it was early for the baby to come, and constantly bleeding only has one end. The strain Rayanna had endured was likely the catalyst for an early delivery, and Chism began to feel the weight of culpability settle on his shoulders. *Keep this family...I'm sorry, Pahpon. Every move I made to keep them safe only made them slip out of this life a little faster.*

Chism bent down to talk to Rayanna and give her some more water. "Rayanna, how are you feeling?"

Rayanna could barely open her eyes. "Chism...I knew...I knew it...."

"*Corva*," Chism muttered to himself. She needed rest more than anything, and when she woke up, she would need to have a baby. And they were marching off to war.

"I need you to stay with her, and for the love of *el-nuajs*, do what you can to get her into a wagon on the next leg of the journey," Chism said.

Gala nodded. "How do you think we got away from the food tents in the first place?"

Chism grinned at her, and she smiled back.

"Hey!" a burly voice cried out. Chism knew the voice very well. He froze in place.

"There they are! Do you know that man?" said the same guard that Chism had chased off before.

"Yes. Yes, I do," Ahmek's burly voice replied.

"Oh *fecanne*," Chism uttered. A whip cracked above his head, and Chism slowly raised his arms then stood and turned to face them.

~~~~~

Rierdan crept up on the village. He had ridden all night and was exhausted. But Gidionhi was quiet. No smoke plumes announced morning meals. No trees shook as prisoners cut lumber, and no sound of pickaxes and shovels emanated from the quarry. This wasn't just silence, Rierdan remarked. This was death. The death of an entire village. The husk of a village stood with buildings and roofs and tools scattered about. But the soul of the village was entirely absent. As he picked his way through the woods, he found Neroos and Lima bodies alike gathered in small pockets.

Rierdan shook his head in unbelief. He wondered if the death of the Triumvirate would truly avert such bloodshed, or if the Triumvirate were themselves only pawns in a greater game where all were victims and none were innocent.

There would be no rest. There would be no peace. Not until after he had finished what he started. Rierdan knew this scene well. When he started this quest, he had walked out of a burned and broken husk of a village that the Lima had left entirely desolate. His wife. His brothers. His three sisters and their families. It all started with the same scene that lay at his feet now. It was fitting, really. Thus it began, and thus it would end.

He walked back to his horse, and rode away.

~~~~~

Kalif knew the look of danger, of attentive ears and hands with swords ready to strike. The Lima walking carefully toward the stables were ready to attack, and that could only mean one thing: Hakoni and Garrick hadn't gotten out yet. Kalif took off at a sprint, though his lungs were on fire with every step. He still hadn't recovered from the vicious beating he had received from Hakoni, and his body was not ready to respond. Still he sprinted.

He stopped just outside the stables and outside of their line of sight. He took a deep breath and held it. Exhale slowly. Deep breath. Exhale slowly. He was still breathing heavily through his nose, but he could at least maintain general silence. The Lima were just reaching the door of the stables, and Kalif was ready.

Using hand gestures that the Ombrar guard would use when silence was necessary, one man asked one of his companions, *Asleep?*

The man responded with one shake of his head. *So,* Kalif thought, *they've killed the guard. That's probably what drew the guards in the first place.*

One Lima stepped in first, listening for anything to give away a sign of others still in the stables. All their attention was focused on the inside of the stables. Kalif smiled. "Focus straight ahead, and from behind you're dead," he said, quoting yet another one of Chism's aphorisms.

Once the guards had entered the stables, Kalif knew they'd never look behind them again. He grabbed his knife and flipped it around so that the hilt pointed up and the blade was ready to be brought down on an unsuspecting victim. Chains were rattling inside the stables where the Neroos were kept.

"You idiot," a voice said derisively as Kalif stepped up behind the last Lima. All three of them turned their attention to the voice that came from inside the stable where the prisoners were kept. "We could have them pouring in here any minute!" the voice spoke again. Kalif eyed the spot right in the middle of the neck. He could feel the point on his own neck tingle. He brought the knife down swiftly, killing the man before he had a chance to breathe out his surprise. "You're a gutless child," the voice spoke again.

Kalif laid the man down hastily as he moved on to the next one.

"Save it, Hamas," Hakoni spoke. Time was of the essence now. Kalif dropped the second Lima quickly. As he laid his victim down, he spotted a small knife on the floor. He scooped it up and rushed the last man.

"We could die in here because of you."

The last soldier turned to grin at his companions and saw their corpses lying with that of the guard. He eyes went wide as he saw Kalif standing there with a blood stained knife already drawn back to his ear, ready to fly. The guard instinctively raised his left arm to block his face, and Kalif shifted his aim away from the man's neck and down to his armpit. He sank the knife into the man's armpit and cut a deep hole in his lung. Blood started filling the lung, but it didn't make a difference. The blade had found his heart. Kalif was grateful that the man would not have to suffer drowning in his last moments. He withdrew his knife and wiped the blade on the dead man's shirt.

"Then at least I don't have to listen to you whine for long, do I?" Hakoni retorted.

"No, you don't," Kalif said as he stepped forward into the view of the prisoners.

Everyone froze. "You," said the Neroos who had been berating Hakoni. He stepped forward, and five other Neroos fell in behind him. No one took his eyes off of Kalif.

"Hakoni," Kalif said imploringly. Then men circled Kalif as he stood still. "Please, I'm here to help you. Look," he moved slowly to throw his knife back the way he had come.

"Not wise, you filthy dog," the same Neroos said.

"Help us?" said another. Kalif could see that none of them cared that he was armed and they weren't. If it was with their own dying breath, they would choke the life out of him before this day was over if they could help it.

Hakoni spoke up and said, "Hamas, stop this! He's the only reason I got untied. Kalif is the reason we are free right now!"

"No!" Hamas shouted. "He's the reason my wife burned alive in our home as she held our youngest child!" His voice broke, and his eyes spoke volumes of anguish that Kalif could not even begin to imagine.

Kalif spoke in as nonthreatening a manner as he possibly could, "I'm also the reason three Lima are dead on the floor. I'm also the reason fourteen Lima are dead in the mess hall. I'm here to help you leave this place. I'm here to get you out before the marauders come to rescue what they think will be fifty Lima prisoners."

"He brought the marauders back on us!" one man declared.

"He wants us to lead him to our families!"

"He's lying!"

"He doesn't deserve to keep breathing!" Others from the stables came out and began to converge on him.

"Wait!" Hakoni shouted. "Wait, you don't know what you're doing!"

Kalif simply bowed his head as the men began to grab his hands and roughly tie them. Hakoni began pushing men aside, shouting at them not to hurt Kalif. They couldn't find enough rope quickly enough, so the Neroos held him. Hakoni brought his full strength to bear and punched one man in the nose. It was the man who had been holding Kalif's left arm, and Kalif felt his arm suddenly come free. The men started pulling at Hakoni as he struggled with them as well.

"Give me a knife," Hamas said to his companions, as he looked Hakoni in the eye. Someone grabbed a short sword from a Lima body and handed it to Hamas. "I'm going to enjoy this," he said, and walked toward Kalif.

"NO!" Hakoni broke free of the two men holding him and ran at Hamas, shoving him to the ground. The men temporarily forgot about Kalif as they tried to break up the fight between Hamas and Hakoni. "Run, Kalif!" Run!"

Kalif turned and ran, scooping up his knife as he went. Four men pursued him. Then they stopped suddenly, turning back at an anguished cry. "Hamas!" Hakoni shouted loud enough for Kalif to hear. The sobs in his voice echoed through the stables and gripped Kalif's heart. "Hamas, no! No, I didn't mean to. I didn't mean to! I'm so sorry!"

Kalif wanted to go back. To save him. To sacrifice himself for Hakoni. But he knew that he would simply be killed alongside Hakoni. *Would they make me watch them kill Hakoni first? Or would Hakoni watch my throat bleed out before they killed him, too?* Unwilling to undo Hakoni's sacrifice, Kalif turned and blindly crashed through the woods.

No one was following him. No Neroos man could be spared for such a trivial pursuit. And yet he ran as if death itself were at his heels. When his lungs were completely spent, he fell to his knees and sobbed as the purging agony of guilt and remorse washed over him.

"I'm sorry!" he sobbed. "Hakoni, I'm so sorry! It's my fault! It's all my fault!" *If I had died nine months ago, I never would have known peace, because I never would have done anything in this world worth leaving behind,* Kalif had said to Hakoni. *Have you done something worth leaving behind, my friend?* "I'm what you left behind," Kalif whispered. "You were capable of so much more than this. You had more to offer this world than to save someone like me!"

Kalif felt himself falling, falling, falling with nothing—no hope, no faith, no friends—to stop him. Then all was black.

~~~~~

"Fight them!" Gala had cried out. "Don't let them do this!"

"No!" Chism had replied quickly as two guards grabbed her roughly and raised fists to silence her. "No, just leave her be. The women didn't ask me to come. The punishment belongs only to me." He took off his shirt and stood silently.

Shoving her to the ground, the two guards then moved to Chism and tied his hands in front of him and forced him to the ground in front of the wagon wheel. He knelt calmly and resolutely as they tied him in place. Each guard shoved Chism's head to one side or the other, seeking retaliation from Chism to signal justification for what they were doing. But Chism wouldn't give it to them. Then Ahmek cracked his whip against Chism's back.

One.

Two.

Three.

The flesh danced and the blood coursed down Chism's back as Gala and Rayanna were forced to look on. Rayanna sobbed and Gala had silent tears running through her closed eyes, her face twitching with every snap of the whip. Chism couldn't hear anything. He grunted and growled with each whip, but he would not cry out. He forced his mind to another place as they dealt his punishment with his shirt torn off and his hands tied to the wagon wheel.

Eight.

Nine.

Ten.

Chism could hardly keep his mind separated from the pain anymore. He continued to groan now in between lashes. The whip snaked around his side, leaving lacerations crawling around his torso like the legs of a spider. He had seen whippings before. Deserters were tied to posts at the temple and beaten with whips interlaced with bone and metal. After ten strikes, the victims were usually unconscious. After twenty, their flesh was gone. Chism knew that this bullwhip would certainly scar, but he told himself that he wasn't in danger of bleeding out his life. It was becoming more difficult to believe with every lash.

"Hey!" Kauwen called out. Ahmek paused as his attention was diverted.

"Are the captains here yet?" a new voice said, panting heavily.

"I'm the one in charge!" Ahmek said with a loud voice, as if volume could dispel doubt. Chism didn't need to see Kauwen's face to know the doubtful look that was there. The silence that followed Ahmek's loud declaration was pregnant with incredulity. Ahmek was many things, but a leader was obviously not one of them. After a brief silence, Ahmek growled with less confidence, "Until the rest of the captains arrive, I'm in charge. I lead the advance group, so if there's something important, you better spit it out."

"It's Borinihah," the runner started.

"You've only just figured that out?" Ahmek said.

"No, it's that they've figured it out, you *merdapot*," the runner replied. "They've got oil boiling, and their war machines are moving into place. They've got a slew of men trenching the outer wall as we speak!"

"Who're ya calling *merdapot*!" Ahmek bellowed and brought his whip cutting through the air. Chism waited for the crack of the whip to cut through the air, but he heard nothing more than the sound of a sword or knife coming out of a sheath. "Hey!" Ahmek cried out a second later, and Chism felt two pieces of the whip land on his back and fall to the ground.

"It's just the whip this time, but I swear to you I'll cut your heart out if you ever try something like that again," the runner said. "Now is anyone with any kind of authority in the camp?"

Ahmek was silent. Kauwen spoke up for the first time and said, "They're still two miles out. You can wait here if—"

The runner had disappeared as soon as he heard "two miles." Chism knew how far he must have come, but for a runner, two miles was a casual distance. He would carry the message himself.

Kauwen turned to Ahmek and asked, "What do I do about the kitchen and these medic wagons?"

"What do I care?" Ahmek replied. "I gotta get me some food before we're all ordered out of here on the double." He started to walk off, then turned back. "Send that pile of ground meat back when you get a minute," he said referring to Chism. "Leave the wenches out of this. Especially the pregnant one."

"But she's Neroos," Kauwen explained.

"She is. But if that baby's Lima, then it's your head. Maybe I'll even make me a new whip and try it out on you if you kill an innocent Lima child." Then he continued toward the food tent.

Kauwen turned to one of his companions and said, "Go find out what's going on. Get back to me as soon as you know something."

Chism groaned, feeling the blood seeping through his pants and running down his legs. Gala stepped forward silently and began to grab bandages.

"What are you—?" Kauwen began to say.

"You need every good soldier you can get," Gala said calmly. "He came to make sure..." Chism could hear the wheels turning in her head, but he had no idea what was going to happen next. The only thing he cared about was getting the treatment over with—it would likely sting as badly as getting another lashing.

"Speak up, woman!"

"He came to make sure his child hadn't been born yet!" Gala finished. "And you'd better hope he dies on the front lines if you do anything to this woman or the baby. Because he'll hunt you and kill you. He's very good at it."

"You have five minutes to clean him up before we take him back to his regiment," Kauwen said as he cut Chism loose.

Gala soaked rags in water and oils and pressed them into Chism's back. A wave of nausea overcame him as the sting of the oils sank into his flesh. Leaning against the wagon wheel, he vomited while Gala continued her work. She did her best to dry off the rest of the blood and staunch the open wounds. Chism wanted to cry out when he raised his hands over his head to put his shirt back on. But he held his tongue. There was yet work to do, and he had to push through.

When he reached the regiment of fugitives, they were already lining up.

"Time to go?" Chism asked one man. The man nodded. "Any food?" The man shook his head.

A horn blew, signaling time to get into marching formation. Chism's shirt was stuck to his back, and he knew it would be the devil to pay when that shirt came off and reopened all of the wounds. But he didn't care. The only thought he had was for Rayanna, Gala, and the child, and how their odds at survival were rapidly diminishing.

"AND MARCH!" Ahmek bellowed.

In the grey morning light, Chism could see Gala rushing to Rayanna's side as he marched passed. There was nothing he could do to help them.

~~~~~

The first thing Kalif felt was a tug on his shoulder sheath as someone removed his knife. A shadow passed over his face, blocking the sun that streamed through the trees.

"*Nimen pensarre shenme ne?*" *What do you think?* Someone asked. The accent was Lima.

"*Lima-ren,*" came the response. *He's a Lima.*

Kalif sat up slowly. Deliberately. They held his blade, and probably others. They weren't from Gidionhi; any Lima would have recognized him. But Kalif had run due east from Gidionhi. These men were out too far.

"What is a Lima scouting party doing this far away into Neroos territory?" Kalif asked as he looked around. Twenty men were fanned out in the woods immediately surrounding him, and eighty more stood ready to march. Judging from their lack of equipment, Kalif could tell they were ready to move quickly.

"What is your name?" came the response.

"Kalif."

"What happened at Gidionhi, Kalif?"

Kalif's eyes narrowed at the man's tone. *If only he hadn't taken the knife,* Kalif thought. "Can't remember much," Kalif said with as much attitude as he could muster. "Maybe your own name would help jog my memory."

"You can call me 'sir,'" he replied coolly.

"Your mother didn't have much of an imagination," Kalif said quickly without even thinking about the words as they came out. He stood up and looked around, taking his time to reply. He could see his knife tucked loosely into the man's belt standing in front of him. "I was with the marauders that attacked almost nine months ago. Two days ago, we revolted. Some idiot didn't lock 'em all up, and they killed most of us in our sleep. I was on watch on the other side of the village. I barely got out."

"If you were on watch, how did you know they killed the others in their sleep?"

Kalif refused to let his face betray him. As he tried to frame his next reply, another soldier approached. "Jebor, sir. The rest of the army has received orders to double their march. Borinihah has discovered us, and they're already preparing for the siege."

"Jebor, eh?" Kalif mocked. "I'd stick with 'sir' if I were you, too. I guess I was wrong. Your mother had *quite* the imagination..."

Jebor grabbed Kalif by the throat. "How did you know they killed the others?"

"I'm no deserter. They told me as we fought to the last man. I was the only one to get out."

Jebor released his grip. "Kalif, you're coming with us."

"Where might that be?"

"To get justice for what they've done."

Kalif crossed his arms. "And what of the rest of the Neroos you found back in Gidionhi?"

Jebor stepped up closer so that Kalif could smell his breath as he spoke. "Every Neroos we take out of this world brings more peace into it. So you're coming with us, soldier. We have work to do."

Kalif reached up slowly as he slid his knife into his shoulder sheath. Jebor looked stunned and placed his hand on his belt where the knife had been. "Sorry, Jebor sir. I've had enough of war."

"You don't have that option." Jebor turned to the men surrounding him and Kalif. "I want him where I can see him! Let's go."

CHAPTER 24:
DREAMS AND NIGHTMARES

"Are you scared?" Gala asked as she walked alongside the wagon.

The wagon bounced and wobbled, so Gala often disappeared from Rayanna's view. Rayanna sat in the back of the wagon with her back against one rail and her feet stretched out and resting on the other. Gala and the two soldiers driving the wagon had had to find a way to rope her in so that the jostling motion wouldn't send her flying out. She ended up with a makeshift net with too few ropes keeping her braced inside. They had been traveling since the grey morning light, and now the late afternoon sun was turning the cloudy sky a bright orange.

As Gala put her hand up on the wagon rail yet again for support, Rayanna could see the fatigue written across her brow. Rayanna's stomach ached, and she felt like a waterskin with only a little liquid left in the bottom: she was still here, but somehow she felt empty. She knew her body had reached its peak. Gala kept a constant check on her bandages, and they were always soaked with blood after a few hours. Rayanna could feel her inner will begging her body to be strong. And her body simply replied, "No."

"No," Rayanna said aloud as she transitioned back into reality. Her thoughts seemed to overwhelm her like a blanket, and she was losing track of the here and now. *Gala needs me to stay awake. Stay awake!* Forcing herself to talk, she continued, "But I feel funny. Happy. Yet tired. It's like there's something waiting for me on the horizon, and I don't know what it is."

"Happy?" Gala rolled her eyes at Rayanna's perpetual optimism. "Whatever you say, sunshine. There's definitely something waiting for you on the horizon, but it's not a gift, I can tell you that."

Rayanna snapped fully back into the present as Gala's comment struck her. "What did you just say?"

Gala looked at Rayanna very concerned. "Do you know where you are right now, Rayanna? We're headed into a battle—"

"Yes, of course. But you called me 'sunshine.' Why did you say that?"

"No one in their right mind would be happy about this situation," Gala said. "No one. So if you're feeling so optimistic, then you must be...I don't know...a little ray of sunshine."

Rayanna opened her mouth and closed it again, thinking of Hakoni and how he always teased her for being so glum. "Maybe," Rayanna said with her voice trailing off.

"Maybe what?"

"Maybe..." Rayanna paused again, thinking about the road that had brought her here. About her time in Ombrar, among the people she had feared more than anything. *Maybe I'm happy to just be out of there,* Rayanna wondered. But as she thought of Chism and Rayanna and making *falhanna* in that small room with a pitiful fire, she couldn't help but smile. "Nothing," she said louder, though she closed her eyes again and turned her head away from Gala. "I'm just...not thinking straight."

"No, you're not. How are your bandages doing?"

"Fine," Rayanna replied automatically without even looking back at Gala. "*Corva cavesa,* I wish they could have picked a better time of year to do this," Rayanna said absent-mindedly as she tried to change the subject. The truth was that she could feel the blood gathering, and the pain was incredible. She had sobbed for an hour and passed out for three hours because of the pain. She had since learned to tune out the intense contractions. They had been infrequent after Gala gave her that horrible medicine, but over the past several hours, they were becoming more regular and much closer together. She turned her head away from Gala each time the tightening began.

"I imagine they did it because sun sets sooner and lets them travel longer—and attack sooner," Gala said. "And I imagine you've been having contractions again. What, about every five minutes or so? What, are you just going to have this baby on your own and leave me out of it?"

Rayanna turned back to look at Gala as her eyes welled up. "I'm so sorry, Gala," she choked out. "You've done so much already, and you're so tired. I couldn't...as..ask...ah!"

Gala tried to climb up into the wagon and finally landed on the other side of the ropes, all while the wagon bounced and jostled. With complete disregard to Rayanna's modesty, she flipped up the wool dress she had on and saw the blood had soaked through the bandages and pooled right where Rayanna sat.

Gala could barely speak as she barely breathed out, "Rayanna...!"

Then the wagon stopped as a command was repeated down the line of soldiers. Gala looked around for someone to tell her what was going on, but quickly returned her attention to the task at hand.

Rayanna could see the wheels spinning in Gala's head. Rayanna had already gone through the list in her own mind that Gala must have been thinking about all day. No hot water. A few oils on hand, but not the kind she thought Gala would prefer. No bedding. Not even a good sharp knife to cut the cord. But one thing above all was missing, and Rayanna could not bear the thought of going without it: she asked, "Gala, where's Chism?"

Gala's dirt-streaked face was framed by wisps of dark hair that had fallen out of the makeshift tie she had pulled her hair back into. Gala blinked several times as thoughts raced across her eyes, completely oblivious to what Rayanna had just said.

"Gala!"

She snapped her head around to face Rayanna. "What?"

"Chism! Where is he?"

Gala shook her head and turned her face down, not willing to deal this one last blow to her friend who had endured so much. "They sent his platoon on ahead of us. They're at the front." Gala paused, clearly struggling with what she had to say next. "Rayanna, he's…going to attack first. And they…they usually don't make it."

Tears came down her face as she nodded slowly. Her mouth twitched and her brow furrowed as she endured another contraction. *Not much longer. Please be strong!* She thought to herself.

"I think it's time," Rayanna said once the tightening in her abdomen had passed. "It will be here tonight."

"Yes, it's time," Gala replied.

A high-pitched horn sounded in the distance. Rayanna knew that horn. It was the third time in her life she had heard it, and terror threatened to creep through her body at the sound. But it didn't. Somehow, Rayanna knew she could not be frightened by it anymore.

"Still feeling like a little ray of sunshine?" Gala said wryly.

Rayanna couldn't help but smile ever so slightly at the comment. "Actually, I do."

~~~~~

Chism had been in these woods for the better part of three hours. The sun was setting, and he was receiving his second allotment of water. They had stopped within a half-mile of the city, and more troops joined the ranks every few minutes. The caravan of food, tent, and medic wagons had stopped five miles back. The army had given up all pretenses of a surprise attack once they learned that the Neroos were expecting them. The goal had become to attack as quickly as possible before they had all their war machines in place.

Chism reached back and slowly poured his water over the wounds on his back. He could feel the itching and the pain, and he knew that to survive, he'd need a full range of motion. The water cooled his back and softened the dried blood.

Blood. There would be plenty of blood tonight. Chism just hoped that some of it would be Ahmek's. They hadn't given him his sword yet. He wondered if Ahmek waited to hand out weapons because he was afraid of Chism. *If he's not afraid, then he should be.* Yes, he would keep his family safe. And Ahmek stood between him and the people—and child—he loved. So long as Ahmek kept him from them, Chism's enemy tonight would not be on the other side of a city wall.

"Ahmek!"

Chism and several other soldiers turned their heads to see seven lightly equipped soldiers march into the midst of the fugitives and other soldiers relegated to the front line. Chism recognized their garb. They were a raiding party, meant to travel far, strike fast, and leave as quickly as they had come.

Ahmek appeared from view with leaves stuck to his back from where he had apparently been trying to sleep. "Who's the devil who…?!" Upon seeing the leader who called his name—a man somewhat shorter than Ahmek but who had the look of a hunter in his eyes—Ahmek immediately changed tone and replied in a softer voice, "Yessir?"

"I've brought you…reinforcements," the man told him.

Ahmek looked at the entourage accompanying this hunter and couldn't suppress the incredulity in his voice. "Only six men, sir?"

"No. Just one."

"Umm...tha...thank you. Sir." From Chism's vantage point only a few feet away, Chism could see the utter perplexity on Ahmek's face. He would have smiled if he weren't waiting for this hunter to kill Ahmek, even if just out of sheer boredom.

"He's the only surviving marauder left from Gidionhi. I think you could use some of his luck on the front line, don't you?" The hunter explained as he motioned to the other five to unshackle the man they had brought with them. Chism saw that short stubble covered the prisoner's head and face. A burn mark crept around the man's neck, and Chism had to blink several times. He couldn't truly be seeing what he was seeing. Yet there he was.

"He's got some fight, so don't give him a sword until you have to."

"What's his name?" Ahmek asked.

"My name," said a loud, clear voice that Chism had heard all his life, "is Kalif."

Ahmek grabbed the front of Kalif's tunic and stuck his nose into Kalif's face. "You think so, eh? You show some respect or I'll give you a sword straight in your gut now."

Kalif didn't back away. "Do it now, then. Because this is the only chance you'll get."

"See what I mean? He's got some fight," the hunter said, clearly enjoying Ahmek's inability to intimidate Kalif.

"Get over there. You're going right at the front. There's another one like you who doesn't like authority, either." Ahmek waved behind him at no one in particular. No one rose to his command. "Hey!" He bellowed at an unsuspected soldier. "Get over here and pay attention!" The man stumbled to his feet and came over to Ahmek and Kalif. "You take this *punta* and put him over there by that one." Ahmek pointed at Chism.

Chism turned his back as Kalif and the other soldier approached. In the months since the attack on Gidionhi, Chism had never even considered a moment like this.

The guard swatted Chism's shoulder, and Chism breathed in sharply at the touch. "Ahmek says that you're going to show this guy where to line up."

Chism didn't respond. He just stared at the ground.

"Hey!" the guard said loudly and reached out to grab Chism's shoulder to get his attention.

Chism shot his hand up and grabbed the soldier by the wrist. Standing slowly, Chism turned to face Kalif. With the guard's wrist tightly in his grip, Chism looked Kalif in the eye and said, "I'll make sure he knows where to go."

Chism let go of the man's wrist and let the soldier back away. He stared at Kalif. His breathing didn't quicken. His eyes didn't dilate. And his tongue wouldn't move. Chism was only surprised to see the cocky attitude so typical of his brother entirely absent in this man standing before him.

"I don't deserve to be here—" Kalif started.

"Yes, you do. This is no place of honor, I can tell you that," Chism quickly responded.

"I mean *here*, alive, taking this breath. Too many..." Kalif blinked quickly and swallowed. "Too many good people are gone because of me. Too many good men have laid down their lives..." he paused again. Then through clenched teeth he finished, "and I have walked on their graves to be able to be here. So no, Chism, I don't deserve to be here."

Chism stared at the man who once was his brother. Kalif didn't return his gaze any longer. But he didn't move, either. "The last time I saw you, I shot your cowardly, fleeing back."

Kalif raised his eyebrows and nodded slowly. "I suppose I was given another chance—"

"The mother of your child is dying. Where's her second chance?"

Kalif looked up, dumbfounded. "I...have a...child?"

"What did you think!" Chism yelled as his emotions began to appear as if from behind a curtain. "You thought what you always did. That your actions had no consequences! That you were hurting nameless faceless animals. Well these aren't animals, Kalif! You need to wake up!"

"I have woken up," Kalif said quietly. "And I cannot bear the reality that I have opened my eyes to. I'm not running, Chism. I'm right here. I have to make this…." Chism could see Kalif wanted to say, "make this right," but the word wouldn't come. Instead, Kalif said, "I'll never make it right, Chism. But I can't leave this world without leaving something good in it."

Chism nodded slowly. "We have work to do. If I can trust you, that is." The high-pitched horn sounded, and men leapt up and began to fall into formation. Chism raised an eyebrow at Kalif and said, "Follow me."

In ten minutes, three hundred men were formed into a column five men wide and sixty men back. Chism and Kalif formed on the outer edge of the formation where guards patrolled on horseback, looking for deserters. Chism told Kalif the essentials of where Rayanna and Gala were and where they needed to go from there.

"The medic wagons? Those are miles behind the front line, Chism," Kalif warned him as they marched with swords and small shields in hand.

"I know it. We've got to get past Ahmek to get there, too."

"And an entire column of soldiers who don't handle deserters too kindly," Kalif warned.

"I know the danger," Chism replied.

"So what's the plan?"

"Short of falling out of line and fighting every guard from here to the medic wagon, there's really only one way to get there quickly," Chism said cautiously.

Kalif realized what his brother was saying. "So not only do we have to survive the front line, but have to get ourselves almost killed so that we're transported back?"

"Yup," Chism said simply.

"Chism, they don't send the front lines back. They just let us bleed out and take more arrows."

"Yup," Chism said again.

Kalif was beginning to get frustrated with his brother. "You're telling me we have to take out Ahmek and one of his guards, grab their marauders' cloaks, *get ourselves injured,* and then get back to the medic wagon?"

Chism smiled out of sheer insanity. "That's the gist."

"I'd almost rather just fight the guards all the way back..."

"Cheer up. We're almost there."

Kalif looked sideways at his brother as they marched. "You're sure this is going work?"

"No," Chism said with a small laugh. "No, I'm not."

"Perfect."

~~~~~

Rierdan had always enjoyed the smell of the brickyard. The kilns burned brightly and reminded him of better days. Before the marauders took his wife and killed his children. Before his brother burned alive with his wife and son in their home. Before he took the name "Rierdan" and embarked on this quest. The smell of burning wood and cooling bricks reminded him of his purpose and his humanity.

"'This is your trial by fire,'" Rierdan repeated the words of the Master from their last encounter as he held up a red-hot brand he had set in one of the fires. Trial. Rierdan considered the dual meaning of the word. Trials make you stronger. Trials by judges and juries bring justice. He stood inside the walls of the senator's compound, considering the curtains and lush carpets the senator enjoyed so much in his private chambers. "Well, dear senator. The evidence is stacked against you. The judge has weighed the events. And you are found guilty. It's time to burn."

He broke the expensive glass separating him from the curtains and touched the brand to the cloth. It flamed instantly, and he moved on casually to the next window. And the next. Finally, he took aim and launched the brand through the air to land right where he anticipated the Master's bed to be.

Now it was time to wait.

Rierdan ran out of the compound, blending into the fray of workers searching for water and buckets. Picking up the bow and quiver of arrows he had hidden on the side of the building, he waited for the senator. In less than five minutes, the main building of the compound was engulfed in smoke and flames. Half an hour later, a horse tied to a carriage came barreling down the street. Leaving off all decorum, the Master came spilling out of his carriage only ten yards away from Rierdan. The Master stood transfixed in the street as he watched the building flame and the plaster crumble.

"Senator!"

The senator whipped around to see Rierdan with an arrow tip pointed right at him.

"You can't stop us, assassin!" The senator called out. "We are an idea! A disease! Nothing you do will ever stop our work!"

Rierdan ignored his ranting as bodyguards ran toward him. Recalling their last conversation when the senator had threatened him and forced him to kill a Neroos, Reridan said, "This is your trial by fire, senator. And I am the judge."

Rierdan released the arrow, and almost immediately disappeared into a cloud of smoke. The bodyguards had no idea where to run to pursue him.

Rierdan didn't need to stay to know that the arrow pierced the Master's chest. He knew what had happened. He had heard the gurgling before. He had seen the head wounds from the victims' falls. Sometimes the head wound killed before the arrow did. Rierdan had not even tried to shoot the man in the heart or in the eye. He wanted the senator to live. He wanted him to feel the hope that he would survive and then have one last moment of utter despair when he realized his hopes were in vain. Then he would die. *One down*, he counted. *One council chamber to go.*

~~~~~

Rierdan turned his confident gait into a measured, slow pace. He stooped his shoulders carefully so as to hide their definition and appear more aged. More stately. More like the Master.

He stepped over the messenger he had just knocked out and turned the corner. He had read the courier's message. The battle had commenced earlier than anticipated. The Neroos had discovered their army, but the number of soldiers present at Gidionhi was twice what their estimates had been. Expect severe losses. Rierdan couldn't even smile about the news; he knew that the Triumvirate had not only anticipated heavy losses, but they wanted it. When all the soldiers from the city guard and even all the men they could round up from High Tide were thrown in a ditch in Borinihah, the marauders would be the only force left. They would control the city. He was here to make sure that didn't happen.

"Welcome, Master," the Teacher said. "We heard the news. What caused the fire?"

Reirdan paused behind the Teacher in between his counselors as he rested a hand on the man's back. He said in a sibilant tone, "Negligence."

"Was the perpetrator punished?"

"Fully," Rierdan responded. Then he continued around the table and stopped behind the Judge as her counselors stepped aside. "Greetings, Judge."

The pause in the Judge's hands alerted the room of something out of the ordinary. "Greetings," she signed slowly. "Are you well, Master?"

"Quite," Rierdan said, resting his hand carefully on the back of her neck.

DREAMS AND NIGHTMARES

The Teacher slumped forward onto the table and his counselors rushed to his side. "Sir! Are you all right?" One of his counselors asked. The Teacher moaned and tried to raise his hand, but he was completely powerless. "Get water!" The senior counselor barked to his counterpart who immediately brought water from his hip flask to the Teacher's lips.

The room was focused on the Teacher as Rierdan slipped his hands into the folds of his cloak and came to the counselors who stood behind the Master's seat. He reached out and grabbed Criton by the neck and pulled Criton's ear down to his mouth. He whispered in his own voice, "Goodbye, Criton," and pushed a blade straight into the man's heart.

He dropped Criton's body at the same time that the Judge slumped forward in her seat. The counselors' attention quickly shifted to the cloaked form of the Master just as he quickly cut the second counselor's throat. Rierdan dispatched of the Judge's counselors as one of the Teacher's counselors stepped over the two dead men and forced Rierdan to fight on two sides. Before the second reached him, the first jabbed at Rierdan, who reached out and grabbed the man's wrist and forced him to trip over the bodies of the Judge's counselors. Then he turned, parried several blows, and cut a deep gash down to the bone of the man who attacked from behind.

The first man to attack was staring at a small pinprick on his wrist where Rierdan had grabbed him. He looked quizzically at Rierdan, who threw his hood back. Realization dawned on the man just as the paralysis set in, and he slumped to the floor.

Rierdan finished off both men, then carefully removed the ring with the impossibly thin needle and cast it aside. Grabbing the Judge's shoulders, he forced her to sit up in her chair. If the substance he had pricked them with worked—and so far it was doing a marvelous job—they should be able to hear everything perfectly.

"Your battle is going poorly," Rierdan spoke very close to her ear. "Your money now sits in Neroos pockets. Your protégés are soaking the floor with their blood. And you are powerless. You like that irony? When I found this substance to paralyze you and render you literally powerless, I knew I had found the perfect method. You have to know that you have nothing. In one day, I have taken everything from you. Your kingdom is toppled. You will never hurt a Neroos again. Because this Neroos has come to end you."

A sword to the heart of the Judge and the Teacher, and it was over. Rierdan walked out of the room and closed the door, noting the rivulet of blood that seeped out from under the door. He removed the robe and wiped the blood from his boots as best he could. When he left, there could be no further trace.

He wobbled down the hall as he considered what he had just done. It was over. Leaning against the stone wall with a torch flickering faintly a few feet away, he sank to the floor. *She's not coming back. Nor is my brother. His children. His wife. They aren't coming back.*

He wanted nothing more than to be with them as tears rolled quietly down his face. He stared at the blade in his hand, covered with streaks of blood still wet with revenge. He considered placing the hilt against the ground and leaning his chest against the tip pointed straight into his heart. *Would the bite of the blade be excruciating or relieving? Is there really peace in death?* As he contemplated taking one more life—one last life—he remembered a conversation he had with the only Lima he could call a good man.

"Is this to protect your brother, or to kill Lima?" Rierdan had asked Chism.

"Perhaps it doesn't matter. We'll be dead by dawn one way or another," Chism had said wryly. *"Dead and at peace."*

"Peace. If peace were in death, we would not be so afraid of it."

"How can you be sure?"

"Because you haven't fallen on your own sword yet, my Lima companion. And if killing our enemies filled the void, then we—a Neroos and a Lima— would have killed each other by now."

Dreams and Nightmares

"That's a nice sentiment coming from Ombrar's most famous assassin. Then how do you fill the void? How do you find peace?"

"Justice," Rierdan remembered having replied.

"Well, assassin," Rierdan spoke to himself as he sat in that hallway, "here's your justice. Now where is your peace?"

But tears and a void in his heart were the only answers he had. He bowed his head, lost in thoughts of his family, and wept.

"You can't stop us assassin!" The Master's words echoed in his ears. *"We are an idea! A disease!"*

A disease. A disease he had seen spread to the Neroos. They were full of the same symptoms. He was supposed to have taken the capitol and killed or captured the rest of the senators. He was supposed to have purged Ombrar. Instead he was sitting in the bowels of the city, and he had only the Neroos to thank for his failure.

Now there was more work to do. He had made a promise to the Neroos to visit the success or failure of tonight's battle on their heads. And he would keep his promise.

CHAPTER 25:
A BRIGHTER DAY

The sun sat low on the horizon behind them, sinking into the dark blue evening with every passing minute. The front lines had been positioned in two rows of fifty broad shields, eight feet across and eight feet high, with three men assigned to each. The shields consisted of nothing more than a broad board to stand behind and weather the volleys of arrows before turning around and firing back. Chism and Kalif arrived at a shield on the second row near the tree line. The shield already had two men in it.

"Out," Chism barked at both.

"Find your own!" One of the men shouted at him. Kalif stepped forward and punched him square in the nose, knocking him out from behind the bunker. As he scrambled to his feet and ran to the next bunker, a series of arrows thudded into the ground where he lay and flew over his shoulder. Just as he passed behind the next bunker, an arrow struck him in the leg.

"What was that for?" The remaining man shouted back with a red face.

Chism opened and closed his mouth and turned to glare at Kalif. Kalif grumbled, "He's not dead, and that arrow may actually get him out of here sooner than later."

"Well you're mad if you think I've got your back tonight!" their companion shouted vehemently. "There's your gear, you *puntas*. Grab a bow and start killing some Neroos already."

Chism couldn't draw a bow. The pain in his back was excruciating. As he sat hunched behind a makeshift wooden barrier with Kalif and one other man, the front lines were firing arrows at the soldiers on the city wall. The air rained arrows from the wall above and both armies moved trebuchets into position.

"Your aim is horrible!" Their companion said to Kalif.

Kalif just shrugged. "I've never been any good with a bow." Then he turned and winked at Chism.

"Yeah, well quit wasting shots! And you—raw meat," the man said, addressing Chism. "Get us more arrows, would ya?"

Chism nodded and rushed out to the tree line as no fewer than five arrows chased him back into the forest. He bent over and picked one up.

"Come on, where are you?" he said nervously, scanning the inner tree line. Any man caught deserting would be thrown back into the front line without any weapons, and that meant several guards patrolled the woods while the war machines were in place. Chism faked a limp and hobbled through the woods in the dim evening light and hid the arrow as best he could in his belt, crashing through the undergrowth toward the supply wagons. After only a few feet, a man on a horse appeared.

"What are you doing this far out?" the mounted guard demanded.

"I have to go and..." Chism's voice trailed off as he breathed heavily.

"What?" The guard said, nudging the horse closer.

"We need some of the…" he said as he rested his hands on his knees and panted.

The guard bent down at an odd angle from his horse and grabbed Chism by the shirtfront. "Speak up!"

As Chism straightened up, he brought the arrow with him and rammed it into the man's neck. "Ah!" Chism cried out as he simultaneously yanked the man from the horse and reopened the dried wounds on his back. The man gasped on the ground, and Chism placed his foot on the arrow and forced the arrow in deeper. Another horseman came riding up after hearing Chism cry out.

"What happened here?"

"I was on the front line, and I was coming back for some arrows. This soldier came closer, and the Neroos got him, sir! Look at the arrow! I tried to keep him on his horse and lead him back, but he fell!"

The man jumped off his horse and knelt next to the soldier. Chism grimaced as he raised the sword, his skin pulling against the shirt dried to his open wounds, and brought the blade down on the man's head. Chism grabbed their cloaks, rushed back to the tree line, and shouted for his brother.

Kalif slung his leather shield over his back and came running. Two arrows thudded into the hard leather protecting Kalif's back.

"Hey!" Their companion cried out. "Hey, stop!"

"He just needs a hand! I'll be right back!" Kalif shouted from behind a tree.

"Get back here now, or I'll report you!" The man shouted.

But they didn't have time to stay and argue. Chism handed Kalif a cloak and they ran toward the horses.

"Seriously?" Kalif said with an eyebrow raised at their luck.

"It's too dark, and we'll make too much noise with the horses," Chism said. "But we can grab some water and the weapons. Besides, if anyone sees us on horses and knows that we don't belong, then we're dead."

A Brighter Day

The moon shone through the trees as they began to move, making fallen branches appear small and small rocks appear enormous. Navigating the terrain would have been difficult for anyone else. But everything important in Chism and Kalif's lives had happened in the woods. This was home. The brothers glided through the undergrowth with only the occasional snap of a branch.

"Getting rusty?" Chism whispered at the sound of a small snap.

"Better rusty than fat, old man," Kalif chided. "Quit your huffing and puffing over there."

"I'd like to see you get whipped like I did and then see how well you move."

"I bet you would," Kalif responded with a hint of the old humor in his voice.

Chism had no humor when he responded simply, "Actually, yes, I would."

Chism couldn't see it with his eyes, but he knew his brother had set his jaw and nodded to himself. Chism had seen that face enough times, knew every line and every muscle. The memories of what life used to be like with his brother gathered in that moment and found a small chink in Chism's anger, and he allowed himself a private smile for the past. But the smile quickly faded as the reality of the entire situation settled in.

"I guess I deserved that," Kalif said quietly as they continued to move through the woods.

"Oh, you deserve much more than that," Chism retorted, then wished he had checked his tongue. He waited for the insipid threat that was as sure to come as the set jaw and nod of the head when his brother had been bested.

Instead, Kalif responded grimly, "That's why I'm here."

Chism snapped his head around to look at his brother, hoping to detect something there that he had hoped all his life to see. But the night concealed any evidence that Chism hoped to see. Out of the corner of his eye, he saw the tree right in his path and dodged aside at the last minute, scraping his shoulder and opening more lacerations. He waited for his brother to snort and chuckle at his blunder. Again, he was disappointed. *What happened to you in Gidionhi?* Chism wondered.

The two continued on in silence, preferring to pass hand signals and whistles to communicate only when absolutely necessary.

Finally, they reached the tree line where the wagons and tents had been erected. Chism had drained his water skin, and he was breathing heavily. He knew he had lost more blood. His body and mind were begging him to shut down. He slowly and gingerly stooped to sit on the ground against a tree. He tried to raise his arms over his head to expand his lungs, but the pain in his back forced him to keep his arms at his side.

"Here," Chism heard Kalif say. Opening his eyes, he saw Kalif presenting him with his own water. "Come on, don't be a hero. Take the water."

The skin was heavy. Chism wondered if Kalif had taken a drink at all. Eying his brother and wondering yet again what had happened in Gidionhi, he put the spout to his lips.

"That battle sounds a lot closer," Chism remarked. "They're not just staying in the city walls."

Kalif nodded and began describing the scene before them as Chism tried to regain some strength. "It looks like the medic tents and wagons are sitting behind the kitchen. There are horses tied along the tree line, but they are draft horses. They aren't built for speed."

"The child could be born any minute," Chism said. "It may already be here. I don't know how else to move Rayanna if not by a cart, but a horse will have to do. It's not ideal, but we have to move her and Gala immediately."

"Rayanna?" Kalif asked with emotion in his voice. "Did you say her name is Rayanna?"

"Yes," Chism said stoically.

"And her hair...it has...a tinge of red in it? Like the gidionhi flower?"

"Yes." Chism said. Kalif breathed out heavily and rested his hands on his knees with his head bowed.

"How did she ever come to be with you?" Kalif asked.

Chism arched an eyebrow. "When I shot you in Gidionhi, I knew what you had done. And I've been trying to repair the damage ever since."

"*Expianore...*" Kalif whispered the word for "atonement."

Kalif sniffed and wiped his hand against both eyes. His cheeks were stained with tears as he looked earnestly towards the medic tents as if trying to catch a glimpse of her.

"Kalif, I...what..." Chism was lost for words. "I hope we get a chance to talk after this is all over," he finished.

Kalif barked out a short laugh through his tears. "Is this ever going to be over, Chism? Not even death can stop the events I have put into motion. The pain I have caused will live long after I will. Death is in the silence, Chism, but peace is not. It is not."

Chism groaned against the pain as he came to his feet. "No. There is a sound in the silence of death. But it doesn't have to be the sound of suffering. It can be greater than that. You can't make it right, *freramo*," Chism said, using the Lima word for fraternity and brotherhood. "You can't turn back the clock. But you can make it better."

"I don't know if that's true," Kalif said bitterly.

"Let's go find out."

Kalif nodded, and the two men donned their marauder capes and walked into the camp.

~~~~~

"Gala!" Rayanna said weakly.

Gala busied herself with pans of hot and cold water, lots of bandages, a sewing kit, and blankets. She didn't know where Chism was, and she couldn't carry Rayanna out of here herself. Gala didn't know if Chism was alive. But Rayanna couldn't last much longer.

"OK, Rayanna. Push!"

Gala looked at Rayanna's face as the young woman bore down. But there wasn't enough pain written there. *She should be feeling more than this,* Gala thought. "Rayanna, you've got to push harder!"

Rayanna nodded weakly, propped herself up on her elbows and began to heave.

"Good! That's good. You can do it. Just a little more!" Gala shouted as if trying to infuse energy into the room and into Rayanna.

Gala put oil on her fingers and lubricated the opening, searching for the sign of a head. Nothing showed itself. "OK, Rayanna, that's fine. The next time you feel a contraction, push with everything you have."

"I don't have…any…more," Rayanna said.

"You have to!" Gala said, her voice breaking. "Rayanna, you have to be strong. Now push!"

"Ah! AAH!" Rayanna belted out.

"That's wonderful!" Gala said as she stretched out the opening again and looked for the head. Still nothing. Clenching her teeth and steeling herself for what she'd find, she pushed her hand through the opening to feel the child. Between her first two fingers and her thumb, she felt two small feet and tiny toes. *Breech,* Gala thought with a groan. *The child is breech.*

"Why are you groaning?" Rayanna asked with the same worry in her voice that Gala felt in her heart.

"Rayanna, the baby is turned," Gala explained.

"Do…what…you have to," Rayanna said as another contraction hit.

A single tear rolled down Gala's face, but she nodded. Grabbing a few more herbs, Gala pounded them together with oil to make a paste. Then she spread the paste on Rayanna's abdomen right where the baby bulged. Rayanna grabbed a rolled piece of leather four inches in length and put it between Rayanna's teeth.

"I've put something on to numb you," Gala said. "But this will probably still hurt."

Rayanna nodded. She took the leather out of her mouth for a moment and said, "Gala. Thank you. For everything."

Gala nodded through her tears, steeling herself for what she had to do. Then she grabbed an obsidian knife with a fine blade, placed it against Rayanna's stomach, and carefully pushed.

~~~~~

Chism and Kalif approached the row of medical tents, peering quickly into each that had a candle lit.

"Chism," Kalif said as his stomach threatened to completely empty itself. "I don't know if I can go in there. I don't think I can face them." *Hakoni, I wish you were here.*

Chism nodded but kept moving. "I understand that it's going to be difficult. But I can't get these women out of here without you. I can barely move myself."

"I know," Kalif said with his eyes focused on the ground. "But I can't face them."

Kalif felt his brother's hand on his shoulder. "We have to do this. Now!"

Kalif nodded and kept moving down the row of tents. Chism peered into a tent, and Kalif heard a sweet, familiar voice declare softly, "Chism!"

Chism disappeared into the tent and Kalif heard nothing. But he thought of the embrace they shared and knew he didn't deserve such a welcome. He didn't deserve such a woman. *How can I face her?*

"Gala, we have to get out of here," Chism said quickly.

"I know, but there's someone you have to meet."

Kalif stood outside the door with his eyes tightly shut, imagining the scene within. Chism gasped. "He's perfect. He's beautiful!"

A boy. I'm a...no. I'm not a father. This isn't what a father is. But he is my son. He's my son.

"How is she?"

"She's weak. Incredibly weak. The baby was breech, and I couldn't turn it. I sewed her up the best I could, but..." Gala's voice cracked as the words halted in her throat.

"Chism," a small voice croaked from a bed. "You came."

"I did," Chism replied, addressing Rayanna. Then, looking Gala in the eye, he said, "There's someone here to help us."

"Is it safe to trust anyone else?" Gala asked.

Silence reigned inside the tent. Kalif could feel their gazes piercing the open doorway. Almost against his own will, Kalif stepped out into view with his eyes cast down.

"Kalif..." Gala breathed out.

"I'm here to repair what I have broken," Kalif said quietly. He looked up briefly enough to see Gala nod. For a moment, he thought he saw in her eyes the same faith she had had in him so long ago. The same faith that had taught him to love once more.

Kalif stepped slowly over to the bed where Rayanna lay on her side. He had never imagined how beautiful she was. Even now, her body ravaged and swollen and pale, Rayanna seemed to Kalif somehow perfect.

"Are you...?" Rayanna began to ask.

Kalif knelt to the ground and placed his hands on the side of her bed. Unable to raise his eyes to meet hers, he whispered, "I am so sorry. Please. Please forgive me."

Rayanna's eyes widened and her breathing quickened slightly at seeing Kalif again. She shook her head slightly, gasping out neither forgiveness nor condemnation, but a single request. "S...s...." Rayanna tried. "Solay. Save....Solay."

Kalif nodded as he stayed on his knees in front of Rayanna.

"We have to move," Chism said. "Once the men start pouring into these tents, they'll have no concern for a Neroos woman now that she no longer carries the boy."

Kalif stood and walked over to Chism who held the boy. The infant had a shock of black hair and bright red skin that looked to Kalif to be softer than the morning light.

Kalif looked back at Rayanna and said, "I'll carry her. Chism is too weak, and we can't get away on any horses right now. I'll carry her as far as I have to."

"You'll carry her to her grave," said a voice at the door of the tent. Kalif spun around to see four guards standing at the door.

~~~~~

Chism softly handed the baby off to Gala and drew his sword.

"Put that away, or the Neroos isn't the only one who's going to die in here," Kauwen said.

"Kauwen," Chism said as he gripped his sword tightly, "I've had enough of you, you gutless worm. Anyone who treats women like you do has to answer to the gods and the devils for what he's done." Chism swung his sword lightly in front of him. "And since I ain't one of the gods, you can consider me one of the devils."

Before Chism could take another step, Kalif attacked from the side. Swinging down hard at the base of Kauwen's blade, he snapped the man's sword and brought his own blade swinging up to force Kauwen to step backward. As he did, he pushed one of his men out of the tent, leaving only two to stand against Chism and Kalif. The man closest to Kalif lunged with his sword. Kalif knocked it wide, grabbed the man's wrist, and yanked him off balance. The man took a big step forward to save his balance, and Kalif brought the sword pommel smashing down on the man's head, knocking him out cold. Chism parried back and forth with the other man, obviously fighting through great pain in his back.

Kalif stepped back to the doorway as Kauwen finally stood, found a sword, and began to enter the tent again. Kalif blocked him, forcing his last companion to stay out. Kauwen swung his blade from low to high, trying to catch Kalif in the leg or torso. Kalif stepped quickly to the side and brought his blade down again on Kauwen's wrist, almost severing the hand. Just as Kauwen opened his mouth to scream in horror, Kalif punched him viciously in the teeth, knocking him out of the tent.

Kalif saw the fourth guard run away. *He's not trying to save himself,* he realized. *He's getting more guards!*

He turned to see Chism parry to the side and finally deal an upper cut to the man's jaw and then knock him out with the hilt of his sword.

"Sorry about that," Chism panted.

"We've got bigger problems now," Kalif warned.

He ran over to Rayanna and, kneeling again, said, "We have to leave. Now. Will you let me carry you?"

She nodded weakly, and Kalif scooped her up into his arms.

They didn't take time to look for the safest way out. The shortest way to the woods was their safest route, no matter who saw them or what stood in their way. As soon as they were out of the tent, they were moving as quickly as possible. Shouts began to arise in the camp, and the small company went crashing into the woods.

"Where do we go?" Kalif said, panting.

"The only way to save Rayanna is to get her to Borinihah," Chism said.

Kalif knew that Borinihah meant imprisonment—maybe even torture. But he didn't ask any questions. He just started running. Chism and Gala quickly caught up to him as he moved. The sounds of Lima soldiers drew nearer. Kalif knew he was leaving a trail wide enough for anyone with any skill in tracking to follow like a beacon fire. But the night was both an advantage and a hindrance. The woods were dark and he had to move much slower as he carried Rayanna. Casting a glance behind his shoulder, he saw their pursuers carrying torches.

They'll never see more than ten feet in front of them, Kalif told himself. *The shadows that the torches cast might even hide our tracks.*

After two miles, Kalif said, "Chism. It's too far to the city, and the marauders are too close. We need to buy more time."

Chism shook his head in bewilderment, and Kalif saw the moonlight glint off his arms as he spread them wide. "Kalif, there's nowhere else to go."

"I know. You have to carry her. I'm going to stop them."

"Kalif, there are ten of them!"

Kalif ignored his brother. "You're not going to make the city anytime soon. Go a mile out, wait for the battle to slow, then find your way in through the north or the east gate."

Chism shook his head vigorously. "I'm not leaving you—"

"I'll be right behind you!" Kalif hissed as the sounds of their pursuers drew nearer. "But you have to go! Now!"

Chism nodded and accepted Rayanna from Kalif's arms. Kalif heard him take a sharp breath through his nose as the wounds on his back opened under the strain of Rayanna's weight. But he held her gently.

"Kalif...come back to us," Chism said.

Kalif nodded. "I already have, Chism. I just hope it was soon enough."

Chism turned and started walking up a hill immediately to the north. Gala kept herself distant, wanting to go to him but not able to move her feet. "I believed in you, Kalif," she said. There was more to say—so much more—but she didn't know how. She turned and walked away.

"I still love you," Kalif whispered to her departing figure as tears rolled down his face.

Wiping the tears from his eyes, Kalif hid behind a tree and waited for the men to come. The light from their torches came nearer. Two torches. He would focus on eliminating the torches, plunging the men into darkness. Then he would have a fighting chance.

"Please forgive me," Kalif whispered as he waited for the torches to pass. He knew Rayanna would never hear him ask it again. Nor would Gala. Or Chism. The countless people he had hurt would never hear his plea for absolution. But Kalif felt for a fleeting moment that this sacrifice right now could have a profound impact on the future. A glimmer of hope began to glow in his chest as he thought of the child he had sired and would never know. But if he could save that child now, then maybe this sacrifice would mean something.

Maybe.

A soldier with the torch passed right next to Kalif's tree. It was time.

~~~~~

Rayanna began coughing weakly just as the sound of men screaming in pain and surprise erupted from behind them. Chism looked down at her to see in the moonlight a dark stain at her midsection. He realized that his arms were sticky with warm blood, and it wasn't his own.

"Gala!" Chism whispered. "Gala, she's still bleeding. What do we do?"

The sound of battle echoed on the other side of the hill. Swords clanged together, and Chism heard Kalif's voice crescendo with each stroke. Suddenly, Kalif's battle cry turned a cry of pain. Then it was cut short, midbreath. A cheer went up among a few men. Had Chism counted, he might have guessed that only three or four men at most had raised their voices. But he couldn't concentrate. Tears began to flow unabated as he thought of his brother bleeding out the last bit of his life. The last part of his sacrifice.

Gala held the infant Solay in one arm as she used the other to pull back Rayanna's skirt to check the stitching. She froze, her face a mask of serenity as she tried to quell the grief that welled up at the sound of Kalif's death in the distance. *Was it enough? Is there redemption for people like us?* She asked, never expecting to receive an answer.

A Brighter Day

Gala struggled to speak as she addressed Rayanna's own bleeding. "The stitches are pulling a bit, but that's not the problem. She's still bleeding internally. Chism, there's nothing I can do!"

Chism began breathing faster. It wasn't because of physical exertion. "Rayanna," he sobbed, choking out the words from the depth of his soul. "I'm sorry. I'm so sorry!"

She shook her head faintly. In a voice barely above a whisper, she said, "I am leaving behind...something...greater than myself. You are the great...the greatest...man..." Chism eagerly leaned closer as the sounds of trebuchets and death screamed out from over the hill and came closer. "Teach Solay..."

Gala knelt beside them with the infant in her arms, weeping for what might have been.

"Teach him what?" Chism said as he softly patted her cheek. "Rayanna, please! Teach him what?"

Rayanna's eyes closed. He could feel a weak pulse, and then it too faded. Chism scooped her body and hugged her close, rocking her and stroking her hair as he screamed out his anguish. Soldiers swarmed over the hill and ran past them, with a few circling them.

"What's this?" A Neroos soldier asked. Gala looked at him with the wish in her eyes that the world could understand the incredible loss it endured only minutes before, yet knowing that it never would.

Chism held Rayanna more tightly. "If you dare touch her...!" His Lima accent was evident.

"Don't kill them," the Neroos said to his comrades who had circled the scene as the battle continued further on. "But bring them in."

Chism felt arms pulling at him, trying to prise him away from Rayanna's body. But he would not let go. He tried to stand, and felt the world fall out from beneath him. His back bled profusely, and he had difficulty breathing. Someone caught him. He didn't know who. But as the black closed around him, his only thought was, *Thank you, Rayanna. Thank you for teaching me what is worth fighting for.*

Then all was dark.

CHAPTER 26:
REDEEMED

Three horizontal cuts. One down the middle. The mark of an exile.

"NO!" Hakoni broke free of the two men holding him and ran at Hamas, shoving him to the ground. The men temporarily forgot about Kalif as they tried to break up the fight between Hamas and Hakoni. "Run, Kalif!" Run!"

Looking down, Hakoni saw two pools of blood—one gathering beneath Hamas's head, and the other blossoming at his chest where Hakoni's knife sank up to the hilt. Horror gripped Hakoni as he realized what he had done. "Hamas!" Hakoni shouted. The sobs in his voice echoed through the stables. "Hamas, no! No, I didn't mean to. I didn't mean to! I'm so sorry!"

"You will die for this!" One of the men shouted as they grabbed at Hakoni. "You killed one of *us* to save one of *them*?!"

The sound of wretched coughing stopped everyone as they looked to see Garrick leaning heavily against the gate. "No," he said

350

with what little force he could muster in his voice. "No, don't kill him."

"But look at what he has done!"

Hakoni felt as if the blood on his hands were scorching his flesh. He wanted nothing more than to be rid of it, but he knew he never would.

"Yes," Garrick wheezed. "He has taken a life. For this, he must be exiled. Never to return to Neroos society. But please—no more blood. Can you not see the pain that even an ounce of blood can cause an entire nation?" He paused as coughing wracked his body, and he sank to the floor.

The men nodded. Two men grabbed Hakoni's left forearm and forced him to hold it out. Hakoni did not resist. They carved the mark of an exile onto the top of his forearm where he could not possibly hide it. As blood coursed down his arm, Garrick said, "Bring me a bandage." Then turning to Hakoni he said weakly, "Hakoni, come here."

Hakoni was dragged and forced down to the ground in front of Garrick. Garrick motioned for Hakoni to lean closer. Hakoni knew that his leader, mentor, and friend did not have long to live. "Punishment is only revenge if not administered with the intent to teach. Go find yourself. Find out who you are and what you are fighting for. I hope that you will become the man I've always seen in you."

It had been only a few hours ago. But they were the final hours of an old life—a life as a Neroos. Now his life as an exile had begun. As Hakoni sat on the ledge overlooking the smoldering city of Gidionhi, he pondered Garrick's words and wondered what the future had in store.

EPILOGUE

Three months had passed, and mass graves pockmarked the forests around Borinihah. The north end of Borinihah had been scorched when marauders circled around to that part of the city to force the Neroos to fight on two fronts and divide their forces. The west gate had been all but destroyed, and the wall's poor reinforcements had easily given way to the marauders' constant barrage of trebuchets. All captured Lima—including Chism—were forced to repair the damages.

Gala had seen Chism in passing only a handful of times as she walked to the market to pick up supplies. She was given more freedom than the other prisoners, because her parentage was Neroos. She longed to talk to Chism, to thank him, to tell him everything would turn out all right in the end.

"All right in the end." She had no idea what that was even supposed to mean. But she hoped for it, anyway.

Because Gala had been with Rayanna when she passed, Captain Malek made a special exception to allow her to care for Solay in his first months. Gala encouraged the infant to breastfeed on her instead of giving him a bottle. Gala's own milk came in slowly and painfully, but it came. She knew she only had until the child was six months old to care for him before the maids in the captain's *fangzi*, or house, took him back. He would forget her quickly, and she would be relegated back to the prisoners' quarters and reassigned to manual labor.

Gala reached under her pillow in her meager servant's quarters to find a few oddly shaped pieces of parchment. They had obviously been the only material around on which Chism could write. A few soldiers took pity on him after having read the letter and chose to deliver them to Gala as she was in the market.

Extracting the letter one more time from her pillow, she read again the words that Chism had penned. Inkblots and sudden changes in line spacing indicated that Chism had painstakingly written the letter a little bit at a time when circumstances allowed it. She wondered what effort it must have taken for Chism to write this. Had they allowed him to write it, or was it done quickly, surreptitiously by the light of the stars, and delivered by a kindhearted guard? She smiled at the thought of his tenacity. She remembered one of his favorite quips: *Everything must be done right. It would never be perfect. But it would be right,* he'd say. Looking down at the creased words and carefully penned message, she began to read again the words she had practically memorized:

Solay,

My name was Chism. You probably have little memory of me, if any at all. As I write this, I don't know if I will live another hour or another year, so I have no idea when or if you will read this letter.

I cared for your mother and protected you like a father. And maybe that means I was your father. But I spent my life trying to unravel the web of stories that had become my reality, so I want to leave something behind for you that is absolutely true. No matter where you go or what you become, I hope you can trust that there is absolute truth in this world, even if it takes your entire life to find it.

The woman who gave birth to you was named Rayanna. She was of Neroos descent. The man who sired you was named Kalif. He was of Lima descent. He was also my brother. That is absolutely true, to the best of my knowledge.

Everything else in this letter is another story. I just hope I can tell it as truthfully as it deserves to be told…"

About the Author

I'm one of those guys who can't *not* write. I started my career in marketing and have been published in dozens of publications—online and print—as a writer and ghostwriter for various companies and clients.

But I wanted more than articles, advertisements, whitepapers, and web copy. I needed more. And so I began to write something different. Something that I could pass down to my children. Something that mattered.

You are holding in your hands the genesis of a passion that keeps me up until all hours of the night and morning. Now that I've started, there's really no stopping. And I'm honored to have you along for the ride.

I reside with my wife and family in a valley in the Western United States. But I live in the words you're holding in your hands.

- Jared Heath